Andrea Badenoch lives in Newcastle. She lectures part-time and co-edits *Writing Women*, an annual anthology of new voices. *Mortal* is her first novel. Her new novel, *Driven*, is also available in hardback from Macmillan.

Andrea Badenoch

Mortal

PAN BOOKS

First published 1998 by Macmillan

This edition published 1999 by Pan Books
an imprint of Macmillan Publishers Ltd
25 Eccleston Place, London SW1W 9NF
Basingstoke and Oxford
Associated companies throughout the world
www.macmillan.co.uk

ISBN 0 330 36925 3

1 3 5 7 9 8 6 4 2

A CIP catalogue record for this book is available from
the British Library.

Phototypeset by Intype London Ltd
Printed and bound in Great Britain by
Mackays of Chatham plc, Chatham, Kent

To my parents

Acknowledgements

Many friends have given advice and encouragement. Without their help this book would never have been written. Amongst these, I am particularly indebted to Margaret Wilkinson. I would also like to thank Julia Darling, Kitty Fitzgerald, Matthew Green, Maggie Hannan, Valerie Laws, Steve Manchee, Paul Miller, Peter Mortimer, Sean O'Brien, Penny Smith, Barry Stone and Debbie Taylor. In addition, Northern Arts gave me financial assistance which made a big difference when both funds and morale were very low.

Prologue

It was 10.30 when I got home. My clothes felt wet and uncomfortable so I threw them off and turned on the shower. I washed away the London grime with strong carbolic soap then wrapped myself in a dressing gown. I towelled my hair and combed it back. Food seemed impossible but I opened a can of cider. I turned the heating on to maximum and the boiler roared. The living room was a mess but I cleared an armchair and sat down. After a while I played the video I'd taken from Camilla's room.

It was what I expected – a series of TV commercials she'd made two years before. She always called them the Stinkers because they were designed to sell deodorant. In one, she was shown walking around the Barbican in a smart suit, holding a briefcase. In another, she was arriving at the opera, unaccompanied, in a low-cut evening dress. The message was supposed to be about an independent, successful woman managing without men. The men were there, of course, looking at her longingly, from the edges of the frames.

I watched the video, over and over again. Seeing Camilla gave me pleasure, as well as pain. I looked at her long hair and legs, the way she shrugged her shoulders, her wonderful relaxed walk. I remembered she told me she'd copied it from a black model at the agency. She leaned backwards and walked slowly, from the hips. She was never coy. Her look was either direct and challenging, or supercilious. The bones of her face seemed carved from marble. She'd been well cast in these commercials because she wasn't acting. She'd commanded this kind of attention just going into Sainsbury's.

I drank steadily, working my way through all the cans of cider and then a bottle of wine. Of course this didn't help. It didn't make me feel any better. I felt the same, only more so. It deepened my misery and moved its boundaries. I wanted to crawl under a blanket and stay there for ever. I wanted to run through the streets, screaming. Instead, I cried a little, talked to myself, watched a documentary about haute couture and then a blur of a late-night film with Tom Cruise. I kept seeing women who reminded me of her.

Camilla was my best friend and the amazing thing about her was that she didn't care. This was her great attraction. She wasn't like anyone else, because she didn't give a damn. In this respect, she was out of her time. She didn't care about houses, cars, status or authority. She wasn't interested in New Labour or personal growth. She wasn't bothered about marriage or equality or meaningful sex. She didn't let her job interfere with her life. She adored money but spent it wildly. She had no loyalty, except perhaps to me. Or so I thought.

Her carelessness had always lured me. It kept me with her. It was like a drug. I watched her charm traffic wardens and abuse restaurateurs, with the same smile and shrug. I saw her borrow things and then lose them. I noticed that she hardly ever opened her mail. She was always late but made everyone feel early. She did exactly as she pleased. 'Never explain,' she advised me, 'never apologize.'

I wanted to be the same. My version was to be street-wise and unconcerned. Turning up the collar of my jacket, I set my mouth in a hard line. I was tall and sometimes felt attractive enough to gain respect, even admiration, but I never could achieve her confidence, her upper-class manners, her easy at-home-anywhere slouch. Even when we went out together and got blitzed, I was the one who couldn't let go.

I thought about the time we'd met up in a pub in the West End. Camilla said to come after work. It was about six o'clock and very hot. Glancing around, she said she liked the pub. It was a meeting place for gay men. She said it was nice not to be leered at.

Peter arrived, then Josh and Pip. Josh ordered a tired-looking baguette. As he bit into it he swore. Something fell from his mouth and rolled under a bar stool. Pip picked it up and showed it to us. It was a crown. Josh felt the gap to the left of his front teeth. 'Shit,' he said. 'That cost me three days' work on *Prime Suspect*.' He put on a cockney accent. 'What a bleedin' waste.'

Camilla picked at some lettuce from the abandoned sandwich. 'D'you know something? I haven't eaten since Wednesday.'

Afterwards, Peter left to go to a reception and Camilla promised we'd come on later. We went to the River Café and then a wine bar. Eventually we ended up in a big drawing room above Hyde Park. Camilla waved her invitation at the doorman and we all trooped in. There was a string quartet. We discovered Peter talking privately to the Duchess of Kent in a kind of side room. I wasn't hungry but we ate tiny sandwiches and drank wine.

The hot afternoon had changed into a hot night. Camilla was wearing a sleeveless, baggy top that slipped down to show her bony chest and her bra. I had on a blue denim shirt, half open over a skimpy T-shirt. Josh and Pip were in jeans. No one seemed to mind. We were very drunk but polite. Josh adopted a French accent and waved his hands. Pip talked to the waiters. I leaned against a pillar and gazed at the frescos and the gold leaf. The wine was delicious and the music swirled around my head. I remember thinking that I'd never been so happy.

Much later, in the street, Camilla demanded a party. 'I'm not going home,' she told Peter, 'not yet. I'll see you later.'

Peter got into a car with an elderly man. There were chauffeurs waiting and minicabs. In the end, a small gang of us was left behind, leaning on the railings and stepping on and off the pavement. We were quite rowdy. Some people were in evening dress. One woman was encased in silver-grey silk like a steel pen. Another flounced in chiffon. They were both expensive and pretty but neither of them looked as good as me, or Camilla. I glanced up at the floodlit house. I saw the pale face of a maid and someone behind her, hoovering. It was 2 a.m. There was a half moon over the park and it was warm. The treetops rustled against a purple sky. London seemed peaceful. In the distance a dog barked and there was a flurry of ducks. One of the men walked away and was quietly sick behind a bush. Josh and Pip disappeared saying they were going to look for the waiters.

A very young Japanese man stood next to Camilla. He'd been near her for hours. 'If you like, you will come to my home,' he offered. He bowed formally. I remember thinking how clean his hair was.

'A party?' she answered, too loudly. 'Where?'

'Yes, please,' he said, grinning.

'A party, everyone,' she called out, laughing. She pulled a stolen champagne bottle from her big model's bag and waved it in the air. Someone spoke on a portable phone and in seconds four taxis appeared. I looked at the Japanese man but I couldn't tell what he was thinking. I was sure he hadn't meant to invite all of us. He was only interested in Camilla.

The flat was very small and everyone made a lot of noise. The Japanese man looked bewildered. There were too many people for the size of the room. I felt dizzy. Someone found lager in the fridge and the radio was turned up loud. Our host produced some tiny glasses and a long-necked decanter containing sake. He poured and offered this with beautiful manners. People didn't like it and laughed. A group of men were shouting and singing and someone fell against a bookcase. A short, elderly man with a cigarette holder in his mouth put his hand on my bottom and invited me to a houseboat. I was embarrassed and pushed my way to a corner, where a woman was lighting a joint.

Camilla draped herself over the arm of a sofa, her top dipping low, her eyes smudged and black. She gathered the Japanese man in her thin arms and held him there, briefly, stroking his trousers. After a very short time, everyone decided to leave. Our host stood at the door, bowing and handing out gifts. These were tiny wooden painted dolls. I realized this was some polite custom of his own. I took one. 'Thank you very much,' I said, but most people ignored him and jostled past.

It was still hot outside. Everyone disappeared into the night. I felt ashamed. We'd abused his hospitality. 'That was awful,' I said to Camilla as we staggered down the street.

'It was crap,' she answered, in her usual guilt-free way. 'Let me get my bearings.' She stopped and looked about. She held on to the roof of a car. 'We're in bloody Kensington.' She rummaged in her bag. 'Have you got any money?'

We set off walking, hoping to see a cab. It was very quiet and Camilla started singing. She sang all the verses of the 'Internationale' and then started again. The houses were shuttered and prim. I joined in and our voices soared into the night. Camilla stopped, breathless. She opened her bag and produced the decanter of sake. We drank some and sang again. Camilla took off her top and waved it slowly above her head like a flag. Then she swung the empty decanter against a parking meter and it shattered.

'Come on,' I said.

She tipped her bag upside down and then crouched on the pavement amongst the broken glass and dirty tissues, make-up and other paraphernalia. 'I've got some ciggies somewhere.'

At that moment a police car glided up. I sat on the wall. Two policemen got out and leaned against the car looking serious. Camilla stood up, pulling her top on over her head, smoothing it down over her lean body, like an athlete after a race. She smiled. 'I'm so glad you've come,' she said.

'A bit noisy, you are,' said one of them. He had a scowl and a thin moustache. 'Drunk?'

Camilla walked towards them. 'D'you know, officer, I think we're lost.' She sounded sober, like Princess Anne.

My hands were clenched into tight fists and I was sweating. I rubbed my forehead with the bottom of my shirt. Looking at the serious faces of the policemen, I could tell they weren't amused. They stared at the mess on the pavement.

'It would be terribly wonderful if you could help us out,' she cooed.

I looked at the ground.

'Could you drive us home?'

I sat in the back of the police car, disbelieving. I half thought we'd been arrested, but as good as their word, they crossed the river. They took their caps off and grinned. Camilla chatted amiably and borrowed a cigarette. In the end, we were all good friends.

Chapter One

I'd arranged to meet Camilla in a pub on Blackfriars Road. She'd been doing a photo shoot all day, in a warehouse on the river.

I stood in the doorway, glancing around. It was 7.30. I saw her in an alcove. Her pale sweater was the same colour as her hair. She slowly crossed her legs and her tight skirt rose up her thighs. She was slim, long, girlish and I paused, watching her bend over a cigarette lighter. Her hair fell forwards like a satin curtain and her nylons glinted in the light from the fire.

The door swung closed behind me. She puffed twice then stubbed out the cigarette. I walked over and felt for change in my pockets. 'The usual?' I asked, gruffly. I noticed her fingers and her frosted nails.

She looked up, smiled and nodded.

Thinking back, I remember her face, particularly at that moment. It was heavily powdered, and a tension around her mouth and eyes gave away her age. She was born the same year as me. We were both thirty-five.

Unlike me, Camilla came from a wealthy family. She was a model and had been hugely successful, years before, with lots of magazine work. She'd peaked briefly as a hostess on a TV game show. Now assignments were getting hard to come by. She'd done a few commercials, but during the last year her agent had hardly ever rung. She complained that someone in the business was bad-mouthing her. She talked about a vendetta, blacklists. Sometimes she worried that her eyes were unfashionable or her shoulders narrow. I thought it likely that under studio lights she was simply too old. Of course, in the real world, she was still exquisite. She breathed in admiration like the rest of us breathed air.

I turned and went over to the bar where the staff, neat in white shirts and bow ties, huddled together, waiting for the evening rush. Glancing in the mirror I saw myself stand head and shoulders above them. I was six foot three and taller than everyone in the pub. I was taller than everyone I knew.

I wasn't bothered any more, about my height, like I'd been when I was younger. At thirteen I was five foot nine, the same as my dad. The boys in my class called me 'Lofty'. At sixteen I was still growing and doctors gave me pills which didn't work. I was miserable and walked with a slouch for a few years, but I got over my negative feelings. Once I realized my size could work to my advantage I tried to make the most of it. Nobody messed with me. I was self-conscious about other things, but my height had ceased to be a problem.

The landlord knew me. He knew Camilla. I looked down on his bald head as he grinned and fitted a new bottle to the optic.

I'd spent my lunch hour, that Friday, at the hair-dressers'. I nervously examined my new short haircut and decided that it was OK. I twisted my head and looked at it from different positions. It was parted at the side and cut into a sleek geometric shape. It was dyed deep black and a glossy triangle slipped over one eye. My face was

9

very white. A silver stud, in the side of my nose, caught the light. 'And a pint of Director's,' I called out loudly, as the landlord measured Camilla's gin.

As I counted coins and paid him, I stared at a pen hanging from a chain around his neck. It was shaped like a headless naked female. It made me think of the murders. The Walworth Whistler had killed five women in recent months and they'd all died within spitting distance of this pub. 'Nice pen,' I said.

He handed me change, made a thumbs-up sign and muttered something to a barman.

It was happy hour and the place was half full. Christmas decorations hung from the fake beams and coloured lights were strung along the pretend-Victorian cornice above the bar. Glancing in the mirror again, I turned up the collar of my silk jacket and pushed my T-shirt tight under the belt of my jeans. I carried away our drinks, past men who crouched over the little iron tables, raising their heads to stare at me. The windows behind them had the word 'Courage' etched, back to front, in the glass. All around, like fairy rings, the carpet was pitted with burns.

Camilla sat apart, visible only in the light from the fire. She seemed to glow as I approached; her pale face, the pearls in her ears, the chains at her throat, the glint from her belt. I looked for the silver line that I knew would be painted around her eyes. At that moment the jukebox started up. It played 'No More "I Love Yous" ' by Annie Lennox. I placed the drinks on the table and Camilla smoothed her hands over a thigh, then opened and repositioned a suspender. She pursed her lips like a glossy kiss. 'I'm premenstrual,' she said. 'Don't look at my spots.'

I felt too big for the stool and my legs wouldn't fit under the table. I sat next to the fire. The flames were gas, and gave only the illusion of warmth. Camilla sipped her gin. There was an awkward silence. 'Cheers,' I said lamely. I looked at her delicate thumbs, cradling her wineglass next to my big hand around the pint. I knew she'd had a reason for ringing me. She'd said on the phone there was something she wanted me to do. I sat in silence, my mind flashing back over sixteen years. Despite the differences in our backgrounds, we'd always been the best of friends.

She flicked her hair. 'I've spent forty-five pounds on moisturizer,' she confided, opening her big white model's bag, showing me a box. 'I can't believe I did it.' She picked up another cigarette from the ashtray and sucked without inhaling.

'Smoking's bad for the skin,' My voice was rough, Northern. 'So's gin, I expect.' I sounded graceless. I was uneasy and needed to relax. I bit my lip.

She seemed not to hear. She rummaged in her bag again. She handed me a fashion magazine. 'I've looked at this,' she said. 'You can have it.'

I glanced at the cover. It was a glossy. Camilla was addicted to reading beauty tips and the latest trends in clothes. She was concerned about accessories, hemlines, the whims of designers. I rolled it up and put it in my pocket. 'Thanks,' I muttered.

'Your hair's very short. You look . . . what's the word?' She paused. 'Contemporary.' She smiled, pleased with this definition, considering the sharp, clipped angles around my ears. I looked into my glass.

The song on the jukebox ended. 'Listen,' she said, 'I've got a problem. It's a double booking. I've made a mistake.

11

Will you take Peter off my hands? We're supposed to be going to a party in Vauxhall.'

'Who, me?' I felt shocked. It was a crazy suggestion. 'He's hardly going to want to go with me, is he?'

Peter was Camilla's boyfriend. He was mad about her. He was a baronet and so upper class he was off the map. I'd spent plenty of time with him, but only when Camilla was there. I didn't know him well. I'd never been alone in his company. The idea of him taking me to a party was ridiculous.

I leaned back in my chair and took a pull on my beer. My recent resolution was to cut down on alcohol. I put the thought to one side.

'It's Penny's party, later on,' she said, 'but I'm not going. I've got to stay here and meet someone.'

'Do me a favour,' I smiled. 'Peter won't want to go anywhere without you.' I realized as I said this that the same was true for me.

Much later, Camilla played darts. She was drunk by then, but this seemed to improve her aim. Each time she threw a good dart she laughed, wildly. Everyone stared. Her opponent was the double booking, the second man she'd arranged to meet. He was fair, and wore a leather flying jacket. He had gold signet rings on his fingers, a bracelet and tattoos. He wasn't one of her usual crowd, but I had a feeling I knew him from somewhere. He looked like a criminal, or maybe a footballer.

Camilla had always been attracted to working-class men. She said they did 'real' things like build cars or mend motorways. She insisted this made them better lovers. She flirted with them in an obvious way. She was unaware of their circumstances, bitterness or bluster. She didn't understand their different set of rules from the ones by which she played.

I sometimes wondered if she liked me for similar reasons. I'd left Newcastle at eighteen, to go to university, despite the expectation of my family that I stay at home, work in a factory and get married. I'd been in London for twelve years, feeling displaced but not wanting to go back to the life I'd left behind. Camilla knew that my background and my job in an Advice Centre meant that I was in touch with ordinary life. Unlike me, the rest of her friends were buoyed high up on money or ambition.

As she increased her lead with every throw, the man pretended to strangle her. His bracelet got caught in her hair. She freed it, but didn't push him away. He had a cockney accent and next to him Camilla sounded posh, but despite this, they somehow seemed the same. They were both lithe and blond. They had the same kind of confidence. They both knew they looked good, as if this was all that mattered. As they laughed and touched each other, there was nothing else to watch. They were the centre of attention. I wanted to leave the margins and stand at their side and chalk up their scores. Inhibition held me back.

The pub was a regular watering hole for me. It was over the road from my office. I'd introduced Camilla to the place and she decided she liked it. Recently, it had become popular with all of her crowd. I knew their loyalty wouldn't last. They moved restlessly around South London, looking for novelty.

Josh, her flatmate, was at the bar. He was watching the darts, with a little smile on his mouth. He wore a cummerbund and baggy silk patterned trousers tucked into heavy boots. He stood at the end, next to an artificial Christmas tree. Josh was a television actor. His face had that eerie, nameless familiarity that meant he was waiting for a big break. He liked acting parts, even in real life. Tonight he was an Arabian prince. I watched his narrow, patrician face, his supercilious smile, his deliberate isolation. When he raised his hand to scratch a cheek, I saw a big jewelled bangle. He waved to me and pointed at his glass. I nodded. He bought me a drink and the barmaid carried it down. I didn't go and join him. He seemed to want to be on his own.

Peter, Camilla's boyfriend, stood near him, as if they were strangers. They didn't exchange a word. I knew Peter had come straight from a business meeting because he was in his pinstripes. An emerald glinted in the folds of his tie. Unhappy, he watched Camilla, as she teased and posed, self-consciously.

As well as being an aristocrat, Peter was a publisher. He worked in Bloomsbury. This was when he wasn't playing cricket or sailing off the south coast. It occurred to me that both Peter and Josh wore pained expressions, as if they were slumming. Camilla's flirtation was affecting us all. Without her at the centre, we couldn't form a group.

After a while I bought more drinks and asked Peter if he wanted one. I remembered I was supposed to distract him. He shook his head and raised one hand, politely. 'Are you going to Penny's party?' I said, trying to be friendly.

'I'm the chauffeur,' he replied. 'I go where she tells me.'

I felt awkward around him, without Camilla. I was aware of my accent and my manners. I realized my voice was a little slurred. I hesitated. I didn't dare suggest we go to the party together. It seemed impossible. I smiled, unable to think of anything else to say.

Peter continued to watch Camilla. He looked more and more unhappy. He turned to me for an instant, but his eyes were blank. He ran his fingers around the inside of his collar. For a crazy moment I thought he'd forgotten who I was.

I watched him stare at Camilla. She tossed her hair back, preparing to throw. As his emerald caught the light I remembered that his eyes were green. 'You poor bastard,' I thought. All he wanted was to get Camilla out of the pub. He wanted to drive her straight home in his new Saab convertible.

I followed Camilla into the Ladies. I took a deep breath. 'Peter's getting really pissed off.'

She stood at the mirror, putting on mascara.

'Who's the darts player?' I felt dizzy. I'd drunk several pints and I hadn't eaten all day. 'He's gorgeous.'

She brushed her hair. 'That's my plasterer. You know, we've talked about him. His name's Sean.' She put her brush down and carefully disarranged her hair with her fingers. 'You *do* know. You introduced me to him. He was one of your clients.'

I paused for a second. 'I thought that was all over?'

'Christ. It's only a game of darts.'

'I'll have him,' I said boldly, 'if you've finished with him. He's the best-looking thing I've seen in a while.'

'I asked you to take Peter off my hands.'

I shrugged.

'You always let me down.'

I swallowed. She often said this, but tonight it seemed unjust. Peter had no interest in me. I stood next to her and studied us both. The fluorescent glare, reflected back on us, wasn't flattering. Camilla was five foot ten, but was small next to me. We were both drunk. My shoulders seemed broader than ever in my man's jacket and my large breasts strained against my T-shirt. I looked enormous. She was too thin, painted and a little haggard. I stared at her, then back at my curved hips, my over-sculpted, fashion-victim hair, my colourless face. My eyes were bleary. I remembered my decision to drink less. It would have to wait until another day.

'It's happened again,' said Camilla. 'I was supposed to be working two more days on this shoot. They've dropped me.'

'Why?'

'Someone's spreading rumours about me.'

I felt uneasy. I was always uncomfortable when she said this. It seemed like an excuse for her declining popularity, her age. There was an awkward silence.

'That's a great jacket,' she changed the subject. 'I'd never wear it myself, but it's a truly great jacket. You look so dangerous . . . ' She opened her handbag and took out a paper bag. It contained a squashed chocolate eclair. She shoved it in her mouth, chewed, then wiped the cream off her chin. She reapplied her lip gloss. 'I'm out of control,' she said.

I followed her from the Ladies, but she didn't go back to the darts. She went along a shabby corridor, hung with silver reindeer and Santas, and returned to the lounge, where we'd spent the early part of the evening, alone. She positioned herself in the same dark alcove, where we'd sat together before, next to the pretend fire. Here we were hidden behind a group of women in shellsuits. She said she'd had enough of Sean and all the others. I bought some more drinks and sat down. 'Why don't you go to the party with Peter, and I'll look after the darts player?' I spoke as if I was joking, but it didn't sound like a bad idea.

Camilla shrugged and settled back in her seat. 'Sod them,' she muttered.

I tried again. 'I thought you were going to try and make a go of it with Peter? You could do a lot worse.' I thought about how Camilla had often done a lot worse.

She frowned and drank the gin. I looked at her closely, trying to imagine her married to Peter. I saw how impossible this would be. She was too wayward to be a baronet's wife. She didn't care about rules. She was too used to doing as she liked. All she really wanted was to stay in his beautiful house when it suited her and ring up and order clothes on his Selfridges account.

'D'you know what he did today?' She leaned over and helped herself to a cigarette from a neighbouring woman's packet. 'He sacked his cleaner. He's so mean. Just because she went home early. He thinks he's God. He phoned the agency and sacked her. I mean the woman was good. She did all my ironing. Good cleaners are like gold dust in Dulwich.'

'She probably needed the money,' I agreed.

'I hate him.'

'Is he taking us to this party? Are we going?'

'Oh, God. He'll only go on and on about Sean. He's so jealous. It's such a bore. Anyway, it'll just be lecherous producers and BBC hacks.'

I imagined laughter, chinking wineglasses and TV personalities. I quite fancied going. I wondered if Peter had left. He'd probably gone home. 'Has Sean got a car?' I asked.

The landlord announced the start of a quiz. Camilla volunteered us both in a team with four of the women in shellsuits. They were lady footballers from Salford. They'd been playing in the women's league. I chatted to one of them about the Premiership. I told her I supported Newcastle. She said she'd always followed Man. U. We traded opinions on sponsorship deals.

I saw Peter come into the lounge. He looked for Camilla, failed to spot her and then left. Then Josh stuck his head round the door. I wondered why he wasn't with his lover, Pip. After a moment, he disappeared.

'There go our lifts,' I said. I went to the bar and bought another round.

Camilla answered questions on films, TV and pop music. The others were good on sport, although I got two points on a really obscure scoreline from the first round of the World Cup. Camilla was laughing, excitedly. She held the arm of one her team-mates. In the end, we were the runners up. Camilla leaned towards me and said too loudly, 'I wonder what it's like, doing it with a woman.'

Reluctantly, the football players left. Some of them had work the next day. They gave us each a scarf and we waved in the doorway. They sang rowdy carols as they walked towards their minibus.

Back inside, we bought more drinks. We sat down and stayed in the pub until the landlord, still wearing his pen on a chain, started putting the chairs upside down on tables.

I went to the Ladies again, then looked in the public bar to see if the darts player was still around. He wasn't. The place was empty. 'You know that Sean,' I asked as I rejoined Camilla. 'Didn't you say he was bothering you? Wasn't he coming round to the flat and banging on your door in the night?'

She shrugged. 'It's all over. He rings me now. I look out of the window and see him in a callbox on the Green staring up at my window. He's always doing it. When I answer, he hassles me. Then he rings again.'

I thought about his back and his arms, strong from manual work. 'He looks like someone off *Gladiators*,' I said, 'aren't you scared?'

'Scared?' She swallowed the last of her gin and shrugged.

As we left Camilla gave a barman her phone number. She hung on him briefly before announcing he was a creep. It was way past closing time. We staggered out with our arms around each other. We were both wearing our scarves. She tried to light a cigarette, giggling, as I cupped my hands around the lighter. 'We're mortal,' I snorted. It was a Geordie expression. 'We're mortal drunk.'

The flame illuminated her face and her mouth made a little wet noise as she sucked in smoke.

We walked past the turning to my office and down towards the Elephant and Castle. Camilla needed a bus to Camberwell. I decided to get the last Tube to the Oval. The street seemed curiously bare without traffic. The buildings were blank and unlit and we could hear our footsteps. I wanted to hurry, remembering the murders. Camilla decided to tap-dance. She shrugged her fur coat on and off her shoulders. She was singing 'It ain't what you do, it's the way that you do it'.

'You know Al,' I said, 'at the Centre? She's got a mobile

phone. She goes around with it wedged under her chin, after dark. Says it stops her getting attacked.'

Camilla laughed. 'That Al's a wimp.'

'This is the Whistler's patch. The South London press is on about a curfew.'

Camilla stopped and looked at me. All at once her face was serious. 'Someone I know is trying to scare me.'

I started to laugh. 'Someone you know? You only know rich pissheads. TV stars, models, lords—'

'Someone's threatening me,' she interrupted. 'He wants to hurt me. Someone I know.'

I swallowed. I didn't know what to say. I didn't believe her. I thought she was making a joke which I was unable to understand.

She tap-danced ahead again, her singing was tuneless. She broke off the song. Her voice was lighter, unconcerned. 'Don't worry. I know who it is.'

The homeless men at St George's Circus had left for the night. The pavement was littered with bottles. Suddenly, across the road, the doors of a pub opened with a crash. Two bouncers in dinner suits burst out. From the space between them, a body pitched forwards through the air. There was a crack as his head hit the pavement. The doors banged shut. The place once again looked uninhabited and closed. I walked towards him.

Camilla grabbed my arm. 'Come on,' she said, suddenly in a hurry.

I was too drunk to argue. I looked over my shoulder as we walked away. The man was in evening dress, but rumpled. He moved a little, groaning.

A car pulled up on the opposite side of the road. A

woman emerged from a dark alley. I watched her, surprised. She was wearing fishnet tights and hot pants. She stepped over the half conscious man, walked to the kerb and bent down to speak to the driver. She climbed in beside him. He drove away with a screech of tyres.

I suddenly felt tired. I leant against a wall. The cold air had made me more dizzy. I wanted to lie on the pavement. I thought about how I walked up and down this street all the time, during the day. A woman I'd never seen before was selling sex, very close to my office. I wondered if she did it in daylight hours. I considered what it must be like as a job. I took a deep breath and tried to steady myself. It was a long time since I'd had sex with anyone. It was more than a year.

'Come on,' Camilla called. 'Give up and you're finished.'

At the Elephant a few people stood at the bus stops, in huddles, their backs turned against the draught which swept through the tower blocks and underpasses. 'This is the most dangerous part of London,' I announced. This sounded important, so I said it again. The wind made me feel even more unstable. I was cold in my thin silk jacket. I shivered. 'D'you know,' I said, 'I avoid the tunnels even during the day.'

Camilla laughed and linked my arm.

'It's so easy to get lost and come up on the wrong side.'

'Or not come up at all. Every weirdo in London turns up here at night. D'you think he's down there? The Walworth bloody Whistler?' She started whistling loudly. She whistled a few bars of 'Jerusalem', then 'O Lord My Help In Ages Past'.

I covered my hands with my ears. 'It's not funny. We should've got a taxi. Every other woman in South London's spending a fortune on taxis.'

She whistled a snatch of another hymn. 'I'm not worried. Go and get your Tube.'

'Will you be all right?'

She swayed and stumbled a little. 'I'm fine.' She smiled, releasing my arm. I think she said, 'I went to boarding school.'

I turned to face her.

'Remember?' She was laughing. 'Maniacs. Religious sadists. I survived them for years. Survive that, you're not afraid of anything.'

I hesitated. 'I don't want to leave you.' She gave me a drunken, lopsided smile. 'You think you lead a charmed life.'

'Go home,' she insisted. 'You'll miss the last train.'

As I walked away she stood waiting for her bus, her back against a concrete wall. I thought she'd be all right, above ground, with other people around. She was standing next to a group of skinheads. They were passing around a plastic bag. A man was walking to and fro, flapping his coat. As I strode off towards the station, a poorly dressed, unattractive couple, with lots of shopping bags, seemed to be arguing. A young woman, enormously fat with bare feet, clutched a bottle of cider. Cars and lorries roared past. Their beams shone in my eyes before they veered away on the fast bends. The crazy wind blew, lifting sheets of newspaper in the air and grazing my face with grit. Buses swayed through the roundabouts without stopping. The yellow glow of their platforms were like refuges, moving out of reach. I thought I saw Josh, in his car. I raised both my arms and shouted but he was quickly gone. It might have been anyone.

I reached the entrance of the Tube and I didn't look back. It seemed normal and safe inside the station. I wished I'd turned round and looked at her. I wished I'd waved.

Chapter Two

On Saturday morning I was hung-over. I wanted to be sick and my head felt like it was inside a tight metal ring. I tried to drink black coffee but I ended up pouring it down the sink. I couldn't find my watch so I turned on the TV. The news was ending and it sounded like the Walworth Whistler had killed another woman. The bulletin finished and a rap band came on. My headache felt worse so I flicked channels. I watched some children's television and cartoons then switched off. I tried to eat some dry toast then swallowed aspirin and paracetemol washed down with Resolve. After a while I still felt bad but forced myself to get dressed. I went out to get a paper.

I lived in Stockwell. My street was old and dirty, with broken pavements. A few of the houses were unmodernized. These were owned by bitter Londoners whose sons and daughters were on the dole. The rest were in flats. From these, single youngish people emerged. People like me. We didn't speak to each other.

The flats were cowboy conversions. The drains blocked up because of too much plumbing in each building. My flat was divided by partitions. I had a neighbour above me and a panic button fitted to my alarm.

Apart from an unsuccessful relationship with a

Lambeth councillor, I'd lived alone in London. He'd hurt me badly when he dumped me. Since then I'd had a few one-night stands. There'd been several social workers, two trades union officials and the odd acquaintance of Camilla. They'd all turned out to be married.

If I thought about it, I didn't much care for London. Camilla's crowd were my only regular friends. I spent a lot of time drinking by myself. I battled to and from work on the Tube. On Saturdays I watched football, usually on TV. I pushed a trolley round Sainsbury's buying lager and microwave dinners for one. London was hard and bleak but I rarely thought about it. It seemed normal. There was no where else I wanted to go.

'They've found another body,' said the newsagent behind the counter, looking up at me.

I leaned over, scanning the headlines.

'It's not in the papers yet. It was on the radio.'

'Walworth?'

'The Elephant. It was in the underpass. A contract cleaner found her on his way to work.'

I turned away without speaking. I don't know how I knew, but I did, straight away. The woman called me back because I'd left my paper but I didn't turn around. I thought I might throw up. The metal ring around my head was tightening. I got home and phoned the police. They said they'd been trying to trace me. I gave my address.

'You were with Camilla Harding,' he kept asking, 'last night?'

'Is she dead?'

'We have reason to believe . . .'

I slammed down the phone.

*

Two policemen came to my flat. I was numb and deaf with aspirin. I went to the station and made a statement. It took a long time and I sat in a draught from an open window. Outside, a group of people paraded up and down with a discordant tape recorder, playing Christmas carols. They were collecting for charity.

A sergeant stood at my side. He had a phone in his shirt pocket, a belly, keys and a cosh hanging from his belt. He kept calling me 'mate'. He told me Camilla was dead. She'd been killed the night before at the Elephant and Castle. I waited in the cold room, where the furniture was fastened to the floor. I drank bitter tea. In the end, I signed the document and left.

Camilla was murdered at twelve forty-five, not that long after we'd parted. Her body was found at 5 a.m., below ground, some distance from where I'd left her at the bus stop. I wondered what she'd been doing. It occurred to me that she might have waited a while, decided she'd missed the last bus then tried for an all-night bus, down the Old Kent Road. This would have meant crossing the roundabouts by using the underpasses.

After I got home, the murder was reported on the television. It was announced that Camilla was hit on the head, but died as a result of strangulation. She'd been strangled with the football scarf. Her clothes and hair were soaked with expensive perfume, probably her own. Her big white model's bag was missing. The killer had taken it.

Because of her old job as a game-show hostess she was treated in a different way from the other victims. The tone was more sensational. The newsreader seemed to suggest she was one of their own – a minor TV celebrity.

They showed clips from the programme that were at least ten years old. I had the bizarre thought that if she'd been alive to see it, she would have laughed.

Later, the news bulletin was repeated, with words flashing up on the screen – 'Walworth Whistler, The Latest Victim'. The reporter was excited and cheerful. He said the pattern seemed to conform with that of the five other murders of young women, in the area, during the last few months. There was one difference. No one had heard him whistling this time. The TV company had a policy of interviewing all locals who'd heard whistling in the vicinity of a murder. No one had come forward. 'It's too noisy, at the Elephant and Castle, even at night.' The reporter repeated this detail several times.

In my mind, there was still doubt that the news was really about Camilla. I wished I'd asked to see the body. There was no other way I could be absolutely sure. I started crying, but after a while I stopped. I rang the police and asked if I could see her in the morgue. They said something about the coroner's court and an autopsy and that it was impossible. I started crying again, and shouting at them. 'But she was my friend,' I sobbed into the phone. 'Camilla was my best friend!'

I rang her number, half expecting her to answer the phone. When Josh spoke, I hung up. Later, I rang again. 'Josh, I can't believe this.'

'Who is it? Imogen?'

'Tell me she's really there.'

'No, she's not here. It's terrible.' His voice sounded hoarse. 'Get someone to come and stay with you. I've just rung Pip. He's coming back from Dymchurch.'

I wished that I had a lover who would come round

and hold me close. I couldn't think of anyone I wanted to see, except Camilla.

I took some Temazepam and went to bed. I half slept, with phantoms of Camilla floating through my mind, listening to car alarms and the noise of police vans taking prisoners to Brixton on remand.

Chapter Three

The next day I got up late. After putting all the lights on,
I turned them off again. I tried to eat some Weetabix, but
couldn't swallow. I turned the heating on high and tuned
my radio, listening for news about the murder. It just
kept repeating bald facts and then played pop music.
Lying on the settee, I tried to cry, but couldn't. It was
impossible to relax. I wandered around the flat, reluctant
to tidy up or clear away dirty glasses or even make my
bed. I decided to get dressed and go out.

I ironed a pair of grey Levi's and unfolded a black
roll-neck, smoothing it with my hands before putting it
on. I changed the studs in my ears for rings and found a
silver crescent for my nose. I eased on my suede jacket.
When I looked in the mirror my haircut seemed greasy
and lank so I took off my jacket and sweater and washed
it, using a mug to rinse it over the sink. Drying it in even
triangles, like I'd been shown, I managed to pull it straight
and smooth. I was still dissatisfied. I wanted to go out
looking like someone bereaved. After rummaging in my
bathroom cabinet I stroked powder across my cheeks.
Outlining my lips in pencil, I filled them in with lipstick
until they were purple. I put my sweater and jacket back
on. Finally, I put on my Ray-Bans.

My local was a bit off the beaten track, but the bar

staff knew me. I was considered a regular. As I walked in there was something on the TV about Camilla's murder. An MP was being interviewed and she was advising women to stay indoors and not go out unaccompanied after dark. I remembered giving Camilla the same advice.

'The usual?' George, the landlord put aside his newspaper. He looked up at me, then glanced at my breasts. 'A bad business,' he said, shaking his head.

I thought for a second he meant Camilla, but she'd never been to this pub. He wasn't watching the screen. He handed me a glass and I swallowed some lager. It was cold. It immediately filled my stomach with gas. I had a mental flash of the poster in the health centre which showed recommended numbers of units. I'd read it more than once. It seemed like a joke. I raised the glass to my lips and drank some more. 'I'm drowning my sorrows,' I said.

'A bad business,' George repeated. I realized he was talking about Newcastle United's result the previous day. We'd lost three-nil at Liverpool. 'Shearer's injured and who else is there? He didn't have to fill the team with veterans. Clapped out has-beens.' George was a Tottenham supporter. He'd lived in Newcastle in the seventies and been a frequent visitor to St James' Park.

I shrugged, placed some coins on the bar and turned away.

'What's Dalglish playing at?'

My reflection appeared in the cigarette machine and I touched my hair.

George continued. He was still examining the league tables. 'He's got rid of the best soddin' players! Ginola. Ferdinand. They've come down here. And Beardsley! I mean, Beardsley! Is he mental, or what? That Dalglish. Is he real?'

On the screen, a TV reporter was interviewing the head of the murder investigation. He'd been on television many times in recent months. He looked both tired and shifty. He said he was sure that the Whistler had murdered Camilla, but that there were no real new lines of enquiry.

George looked up at the screen and then over at me as I sat down. 'I've told the missus to stay in,' he informed me. 'It's a jungle out there. My girls get cabs all the time. Think I'm made of bleedin' money.'

The pub was empty. I read the darts fixtures and the beer mats. I picked up the *Sunday Sport*. There was a coloured picture of a fat woman on the front. She was naked but her folds of stomach concealed her pubic hair. She was smiling. 'Big Appetite!' the headline read. 'Four at a Time, Three Times a Night!'

George's wife appeared. She ran a dishcloth listlessly over the Formica tables. She was a large woman, like me, but untoned, running to fat. I studied her, wondering if I'd end up like her in middle age, shapeless and short of breath. I decided she wasn't nearly as big as the newspaper's main news item. 'I got followed last night,' she said, indicating the television. 'Followed off the bus.'

I drained my glass and swallowed a burp.

'It gets them excited, rapists and suchlike.'

'What does?' I took off my Ray-Bans.

'The bus. Especially on the top deck. It's the vibrations. Gets them going.'

'What happened?'

'Just a kid. He kept gaining on me and dropping back.

31

Then he overtook me. I could see him ahead, hiding in a garden.'

I stood up to go back to the bar.

'It was only six o'clock. I went up to him. I said, "Sod off, you little scumbag." I won't tell you what he called me.'

'Did you tell the police?'

She looked at me, her eyebrows raised and started wiping the ashtrays. I ordered another pint, drank it quickly, then left.

It was cold outside, and dreary. The day had never really got light. I couldn't think of anywhere I wanted to go. I put my sunglasses on because my pockets weren't deep enough to hold them. Wind rustled the litter under the railway bridge. A few Christmas trees glimmered inside windows, making the empty street even more desolate. I started hurrying because I needed the toilet. When I got to the main road I waited to cross. Coloured lights were strung overhead and they swayed in the wind, creaking. The smiling snowmen looked sad and pointless. I heard angry shouting coming from the Tube station. Over the crossing, I almost stepped on a drunk, whose cap seemed empty of coins. Hot tears filled my eyes again. I blinked them away. There was a hoot, and a car pulled up alongside me.

It was Pip. He was driving Josh's Scirocco. 'Get in, Imogen,' he said, leaning over and opening the door. 'It's not safe to be out.'

I slid awkwardly into the front seat and pushed the chair right back to make room for my legs. I slammed the door, thankfully.

Pip was an actor like Josh, but not nearly as successful. Sometimes he signed on, or he worked evenings in an Italian restaurant. He and Josh had been together as a couple for several years. He seemed tiny next to me, like a child. He peered over the steering wheel. 'I'll take you back,' he said.

Despite his leisurely drama-school vowels, Pip's life had been hard. He once told me he'd been fostered out as a baby when his mother died. He'd gone back to live with his dad when he was twelve. His dad lived in a caravan in Dymchurch. Pip made people laugh with stories of his fold-down bed and one-pot Camping Gaz cookery. There was sadness underneath. His dad was an unemployed brickie and an alcoholic. He'd had no tolerance of his son's camp manners and desire to go on the stage. Pip was always sad and edgy. He had low self-esteem. He sometimes hinted that he'd suffered a lot at home.

I tried to smile at him. I eased the seat belt across the bulk of my chest. Suddenly I felt less lonely.

He took a Nicorette from a packet on the dashboard and popped it into his mouth. He was wearing a navy-blue peaked cap and his little wire-framed glasses caught the light from a passing bus. 'I'm shaking like a leaf,' he said. 'It's just dreadful.' He paused, then repeated, 'Dreadful.' He started the car.

'How's Josh?' I asked.

'Oh, the poor love's taking it really hard. He's blaming himself. He went to Penny's party in Vauxhall. Camilla was meant to be going. She must've had another tiff with Peter, but Josh says he could have taken her. He could have given her a lift.'

33

'She'd decided not to go to the party. She was on her way home.'

He looked at me quizzically.

'I was there.' I blew my nose. 'I was with her.'

He turned to me briefly, pursing his lips. 'Christ,' he muttered. 'Where did you leave her?'

'At the bus stop. The Elephant and Castle.' We drove in silence for a while. He handled the controls as if he was afraid of them. We proceeded very slowly.

I noticed that Pip had an engraved silver ring on his right hand which exactly matched one worn by Josh. In his lapel he wore an Aids ribbon. 'It's the next street on the left,' I said.

He turned the corner and stopped.

'What're you going to do now?' I knew he hated his bedsit. 'Are you going to move in with Josh?'

'It's so spooky in that flat. I can't bear it. I can still smell her perfume. Her hair's in the shower plug. We're eating her food.' He paused and looked down at his knees. 'I never really liked her, you know.'

I was just about to climb out, but I sat back in my seat.

'I mean I'm sorry she's dead, I'm deeply shocked and everything, but I never liked her. I always thought she was laughing at me.'

I felt the need to defend Camilla. 'Oh, that was just her way. She took the piss out of everybody.'

'Yes, I know, but it was more than that with me. She sneered at me. As if I was a piece of shit.'

I was used to Pip's poor self-image. 'You're being over-sensitive,' I said. 'She didn't laugh at you.' I knew he thought that all models were overpaid. He hated it when Camilla got commercials. He said she wasn't trained.

'She wasn't a nice person,' he said. 'She resented the fact she couldn't manipulate me. Not sexually, like she could most people. She had to get the better of me. She humiliated me instead. All the fucking time.'

My breath caught in my throat. I felt a surge of anger. 'She's not even . . . '

'I know, I'm sorry, Imogen. I know you idolized her, but she wasn't kind. She wasn't kind at all. She despised me for being poor. For being working class.'

I opened the door. I knew he was right, Camilla hadn't liked him. I also knew he'd got hold of the wrong reasons. She'd disliked him because he was weak.

'She was working less and less,' I said. Awkwardly, I climbed out of the car. As I said these words, I wondered who I was excusing. 'She was worried about her age.'

'She had friends,' he called out.

I was in the street. I turned back, took off my Ray-Bans and bent down level with the window, meeting his gaze. 'Maybe so.' My voice was cold. 'But she's still dead.'

After Pip dropped me, I went in and changed into my dressing gown. It was pink and outsize and stained down the front with food. I pulled off my loafers and nuzzled my feet in my fluffy slippers. I washed the make-up off my face and opened a bottle of wine.

Inside my flat, it always felt like a refuge from London. It was messy, unstylish and needed decorating but no one ever visited me, except Camilla. I had a lumpy old sofa which I liked lying on, and a huge TV with a remote control. The garish, patterned carpet, inherited from the previous owner, the nylon curtains and plastic tablecloth all reminded me of my family's home in New-castle.

I tried hard to settle, in my usual way. I switched on the television. The football highlights started, but I decided I couldn't bear to see the Lads lose to Liverpool. I was nervous and upset and I wasn't feeling strong enough. I switched off the TV and listened to an old Johnny Cash tape. It made me cry. I buried my face in my soft unwashed sleeve and stretched out on the settee. When I stopped, I thought again about Pip's words.

It was true that Camilla had disliked him, but not because he was working class. This was way off the mark. She'd always romanticized ordinary people. She thought they were honest and simple. She liked what she saw as their lack of ambition. I told her that this was crap. She persisted. The truth was, Camilla had probably been impressed by Pip's working-class credentials. What she couldn't stand was lack of verve. She hated caution.

I thought about the time the three of us had gone down to Bristol. Josh was filming a comedy series. He'd invited us to see him, for the weekend. I'd gone along because Camilla asked me, and because I'd hoped to get a ticket for the City game.

Camilla borrowed Peter's car. She shared the driving with Pip. She'd nagged him, all the way down the M4. She said he was too scared to move out of the inside lane. I remember we were listening to *The Archers*. The ponderous radio accents and Pip's slow driving together were almost unbearable. We were doing thirty miles an hour. He was tense. He was gripping the steering wheel like a learner.

'For Christ's sake!' Camilla shouted when we got stuck behind a convoy of army vehicles.

Pip pulled over onto the hard shoulder and got out of the car. Camilla slid over into the driver's seat. As he was getting back on the passenger side, she accelerated hard. He half fell in, dragging his door shut.

Things got worse. Pip had forgotten Josh's letter, with the map. He said he knew the way but once in Bristol we kept going round the Downs. We came out, time after time, at the top of Whiteladies Road. Camilla slammed the car into a car park. She hailed a taxi. Pip and I climbed into the back seat. We were silent in the face of her temper.

That night, in Bristol, we went to a pub. It was crowded and loud. We were with the cast from the TV show. I perched high on a stool at the edge of the circle. My back ached and I kept leaning sideways as men pushed past me to get to the Gents. An electronic games machine bleeped in my ear. It had yellow and red flashing aliens and a message which read 'Welcome to Clifton'.

The actors were talking shop and they were noisy. They drank wine, but I'd ordered lager. My stomach was frozen and bloated. My jeans ached. I hadn't eaten for ten hours. I shook some peanuts into my hand.

Josh's colleagues competed around the table. He was still in role and spoke with a local accent. Josh often took on the persona of the character he was playing. He grinned in a new, wide way. I looked inside his mouth. 'Crowns,' I said aloud. I realized I was drunk. Several of the actors looked at me suspiciously. 'Who's she?' one of them mouthed.

Then Camilla started saying that Pip was her son. 'Get the boy a Coke,' she kept insisting.

The talk turned to the director. 'Bo!' Camilla shouted. 'What kind of a name is that?'

I remember Josh looking over his shoulder nervously. He didn't want to offend anyone, particularly the man in charge. In the car, Camilla said he'd admitted to sleeping with more than one person to get the part. Pip insisted Josh was speaking metaphorically. I wasn't sure.

He was reassured by the director's absence. However, when he joined in, he was full of praise for the show. People smiled and looked at each other. Josh wasn't playing the game. I suddenly understood his ambition. His feet were firmly on the ladder and he was going upwards. I looked at Camilla. She glanced at Josh and raised her eyebrows.

Someone reached out and touched her arm. 'Bo's short for bogey.' There was giggling and Camilla pretended to blow her nose on the corner of Pip's shirt.

'Oh, come on, darlings,' Pip interrupted. He was looking at Josh, anxiously. 'Bo's a comedy genius . . . '

'And you're a baby,' said Camilla sharply. I saw her sway slightly, spilling her wine. 'It's past your bedtime, little Pippo. You're a babybo.'

My ears and my throat were numb with chilled beer. I was so lightheaded, I thought I might faint. Camilla crossed her legs and I saw her thighs. I looked away and noticed two men staring at her. They both had wide noses and hair like wigs.

I felt sick. I stood up and fought my way outside. The staring men turned to me and one tried to grab my arm. 'French and Saunders,' he said, drunkenly.

In the car park the night was lit by a big moon. Triangles of floodlight beamed up at a bridge from the valley floor. Its ironwork was silver. Red and orange lights winked as cars crossed its span and it hung delicately, from cobweb girders.

MORTAL

I breathed deeply. The air was cold and sweet. My head swam as I leaned over the dizzy balcony where rhododendrons cloaked the drop. There was a glint from the river. I wished I hadn't come.

Chapter Four

I didn't go to work on Monday. I phoned in sick and spent most of the day listening to old Queen CDs and watching television with the sound turned off. I drank a six-pack of lager. When I finally got round to opening the curtains, it was already completely dark.

I decided to go and see Josh. I wanted to go to the flat because Camilla would normally be there, late afternoon, watching her backlogged videotapes of *The X Files*. Her absence was the one thing that would make her death seem real. I tried to work out how many hours she'd been dead, but I kept getting different numbers.

I sifted through a pile of unsealed Christmas cards and found the one I'd written for Josh. Opening it, I was confronted with cartoon angels tipsy on whisky. I decided not to give it to him. I put the whole lot in the bin. Slowly, I got dressed. I put on a pair of denim jeans and my black Levi's jacket.

The flat Josh had shared with Camilla was in Camberwell Green. It was a tenement, built in Victorian times to house the poor. Camilla called it the Workhouse. It was convenient, next to the shops and buses. Most of the flats belonged to a housing association but Josh's was private. He'd always been rather cagey about how he'd acquired it. Camilla had been sharing with him for about two years.

I knew Josh had mixed feelings about his flat. I'd sometimes heard him refer to it as 'near Camberwell Grove', which implied a grace and a price tag that were entirely misleading. Once, oddly, he'd talked about 'going down to the country' as if Camberwell was just a weekday necessity.

On other occasions, with different people, he talked about 'The Green'. Then he took on the street credibility of a risky South London neighbourhood. Whenever he did this, he raised his collar, sneered a little and sounded tough. He changed according to his company. He was out to impress. His real views on London were unknown to me.

I got off the bus and looked up at the second floor. There was a light on. The vicious little wind carried a smatter of rain.

An old man held out his arm to stop me. He was tiny and crooked. 'Excuse me, sonny,' he said, courteously, looking up at me. 'Can you put me straight? Is it Saturday or Sunday?'

I thought for a second. I felt confused. 'I'm sorry. I don't know.'

I crossed the cobbled courtyard, picturing the interior of the flat. It was pale and modern, with venetian blinds and abstract paintings. There was very little furniture, but the floor was covered in thick white carpet. I climbed the steps and knocked on the door. In the few seconds I stood waiting, I realized I had only ever come here with Camilla, or to visit Camilla. I looked down at my jeans. They were clean and recently ironed. I ran my fingers through my hair, rearranging its sharp angles. I wondered how friendly Josh would be.

I needn't have worried. He threw open the door and

clasped me in an embrace. He was shorter than me and I felt awkward. His chest felt hard and solid. He smelled of Fahrenheit scent and there was a faint trace of garlic on his breath. He released me but held my arms. He was wearing a white T-shirt and white trousers.

Josh was trying, with his agent, to land a part in *Coronation Street*. This seemed ironic. In real life he was effeminate. He had an Oxbridge accent and his camp voice was both dramatic and amusing. The first time I saw him on telly playing a straight macho type, I was amazed. 'He can be anyone,' I said to Camilla. 'He can pretend to be anyone he likes.'

'Of course he can,' she agreed. 'That's his bloody job.'

I followed him in. 'We're all just devastated.' He gestured towards the only chair. 'Utterly gobsmacked. I mean, Camilla! She was indestructible! And her things are still here. Her laundry's in the drier. I keep expecting her to walk in through the door.' He raised both his hands to the sides of his face.

I sat down.

'Drink?'

I nodded.

He raised himself onto his toes and did a half-pirouette. 'I've been totally hung over all day.'

I watched him move gracefully within the tiny kitchen. He was big, but light on his feet, like a dancer. I remembered Camilla once opening the door of his room and showing me his weights.

I heard a blade slice and a bottle top unscrew. I looked at the white-and-chrome units, the glinting gadgets. It was odd sitting there without Camilla. I studied the walls and the floor as if they might somehow still contain her.

I realized I was breathing the same air that she had recently breathed.

Josh returned and handed me a glass. It rang with ice pieces shaped like stars. There was a smear of salt and a wedge of lime. 'Get that down you, hinnie,' he whispered, mimicking my accent. His eyes met mine. I couldn't judge his expression. I noticed his scent again, mixed with the sharp odour of my drink. He sank down on the floor, then spread out on the carpet, balancing his glass on his chest and stretching his hands behind his head. I could see only the bottom of his face.

I realized my hands were shaking. Camilla's absence was like an uninvited stranger. I circled the glass with eight fingers and held my knees together. Josh always made me feel gruff and graceless. The crotch of my jeans was too tight and I wondered if I needed to pee. I stared at the place where his T-shirt gaped from the waistband of his trousers. He had sparse hairs on his stomach and a tiny silver ring above his navel.

'Darling, I'm just numb,' he said. 'I'm at a loss for words.'

I licked the salt from the rim of my glass.

Suddenly I wanted to cry. I wanted to put my head in my hands and howl like a baby. I sat up straight, my back rigid, and tried to swallow. The salt was making my tongue swell. My lips were dry.

'What can I say?' he asked. He lifted an arm. His hand moved in little curves, one finger extended. His nails were long and painted in white pearl. He studied his hand, smiling. It was the one with the ring that matched Pip's. 'I'm devastated.'

There was a silence. Rain spattered the window.

Down below, raucous singing rose from the bus shelters and someone screamed, 'Davey! Davey!'

I swallowed the tequila. It grazed my food-free stomach like a blunt knife. 'She's not here,' I spoke at last. I felt as if I had a trapped bird in my chest. My words sounded like somebody else.

Josh seized his drink and sat up. His trained body moved smoothly, without effort. 'I'd like to read,' he said, 'at the funeral.'

I looked at him, shocked. I knew what he meant. He saw it as a career opportunity. 'I thought you were at a loss for words.' My voice was lime-sour. I might have said, 'You're always thinking of yourself.' The alcohol moved through my limbs making them light and my head was weightless on my shoulders. This was one drink too many.

His face shifted, but he seemed not to hear. 'I'd like to read a psalm.' A diamond shone from within his ear. He seemed covered in discreet jewellery. 'They'll invite those cousins to the funeral. I never did get to meet them, and I want to. Camilla's got cousins who were friends of Princess Diana. Went to the funeral and everything. Hang out with Patrick Cox, Kate Moss.' He paused. 'And Kenneth Brannagh. Listen to this, Imogen. I want to read it to them. It's great.'

He pulled a piece of paper out of the pocket of his trousers. I lay back in my chair, feeling dizzy and emotional. I looked hard at a row of Christmas cards on the mantelpiece. They were the only coloured things in the room. The table lamp shone broken beams on the ceiling. I remembered the last time I'd been here. I'd wondered aloud what the patterns were. 'Tadpoles,' I'd asked Camilla, 'or sperm?'

'Comets,' she'd insisted, laughing.

'In my distress,' Josh read, 'I cried unto the Lord.' He spoke the words as if they were round. His voice rose from deep in his chest. 'Deliver my soul from lying lips.'

I felt the room move slowly in a circle. I wondered if at last I was drunk. Somewhere a washing machine shifted to spin. I closed my eyes. Behind my eyelids, in my imagination, Camilla leaned in the doorway.

Josh raised his voice. 'And from a deceitful tongue.'

The floor vibrated. With my eyes still closed, I drained my glass. I knew Josh's choice of psalm was crazily inappropriate, but he was more concerned with the sound of his own voice than anything else.

Somewhere in the building, music started playing. I couldn't remember the song. Camilla had liked it, but I knew it wasn't coming from her room. It was too indistinct. I listened, desperate to identify the music. I blanked out Josh's sonorous tones. The lyrics came in, eventually. It was a dance remake of 'Eight Miles High'.

Josh was finishing. 'I am for peace,' he declared. 'But when I speak, they are for war.' He paused, expectantly.

The muffled pop song and the tremor of the washing machine filled the room. I opened my eyes. Josh was staring at his invisible audience. 'That's some drink,' I said. I tipped it to my lips and sucked on the ice. I rubbed the cold glass on my forehead.

He gave a little smile. 'They're old stock, the Hardings. They might even be sort of related to the Spencers. Her uncles are judges, fucking bishops.' He pursed his lips. 'Stinking rich.'

I thought about Camilla's family and imagined only a paddock and an Aga, overhung with bunches of dried herbs. I couldn't bring to mind faces or names. She'd never mentioned cousins. Not for the first time, I understood that Josh was a snob. He collected people, and measured them by their status. Again I felt lumpish and ordinary. I tried to smooth imaginary creases in my jacket.

He looked at me suspiciously. 'That Peter was here earlier. He's a silly tart. Poking about. Wouldn't even stay for a drink.'

'What did he want?'

'He was in her room. There was something belonging to him. I don't know. The police were here, and her brother too, this morning. He had a rummage.'

'Already?'

'I know. She's barely cold.' Carefully, Josh rotated his little finger inside his ear, before examining the tip. 'Pity he hasn't got her bone structure, poor darling. The brother. He's terribly dreary.'

This was Josh's other main yardstick. He had little time for unattractive men.

'What does he do?'

'A researcher? A lecturer? Something boring in a university.' He shrugged, polishing his nails on his chest. 'Works in your neck of the woods. Newcastle.' He met my eye. 'Camilla was screwing his boss.'

I knew Camilla had never been to Tyneside. She'd thought York was practically in Scotland. I tried to smile. 'First I've heard of it.'

Josh jumped to his feet. He took a swallow of his drink. I noticed that the eerie music and the washing machine appeared to have stopped. I stood up, next to him. Looking down at his face, I felt more in control.

'You thought you knew her,' Josh said, 'but none of us did. She wasn't what she seemed.'

46

I didn't understand what he meant. I shook my head.

We stood side by side. He appeared uncertain what to do next. He was uneasy. He glanced up at me. 'D'you want another drink?'

I shook my head.

'She was a dark horse,' he said eventually, sounding very camp. 'Did you know about the workman? She picked him up off a building site.' He ran his hand over his scalp. His hair was so close cropped, I heard it rasp. 'He was there, you know, playing darts, the other night.'

I moved towards the door. I felt irritated. 'Sean? No, I introduced them in the pub. One night after work. He was one of our clients.'

'Well, he was a funny parcel of fish. He came to dinner once. He stubbed his cigarettes out on his plate. And his accent! Glorious! And then there was that other one. I've forgotten his name. A Geordie. Claimed he was a painter. House painter, I should think. Pip always said she liked a bit of rough.'

'Like me, you mean,' I said, under my breath.

Josh seemed to be talking for the sake of it. He appeared unwilling to let me go, as if there was more expected of him. It was the first time I'd been in Josh's company without Camilla. I wondered if his flippancy ever got on her nerves.

'Is there anything you want?' he asked, as I reached for the door.

I paused. 'What, here?'

'Well, you know. A memento?'

I thought about her clothes. They were beautiful, but too feminine and too small for me. 'I'll see.'

I went into Camilla's bedroom. Josh waited in the hall. The place was a mess. After the stark minimalism of the lounge it looked like a whirlwind had passed through. Camilla had always treated it like a hotel, and there had never been many of her belongings on display. Now all the contents of her drawers and cupboards were strewn across the floor. I picked up the clothes and folded them on the bed. This didn't seem to make much difference. I felt helpless. Absently I opened the bedside cabinet. I picked up a videotape and put it inside my jacket. 'There's nothing here,' I called out. I was close to tears again.

'I can't stand to go in there,' Josh said from outside the door.

Suddenly, I wanted to be somewhere else.

'Pip is probably moving in.' Josh opened the front door and reached up to kiss me on the cheek. 'I think we've decided to commit.' He paused. 'Come round for a drink,' he murmured, 'soon.'

He seemed older in the yellow light from the stairwell. I could see little creases and furrows on his face.

Chapter Five

As I went down the stairs I remembered another visit, when I'd climbed them slowly, feeling nervous.

Soon after Camilla moved in with Josh they'd had a dinner party. Peter was invited, and Pip, of course, and Penny, Camilla's friend from the BBC. I think I was asked to balance the numbers although Camilla seemed keen for me to go. 'Josh is cooking,' she told me, 'he cooks like an angel.'

I wore a tuxedo from the Oxfam shop and a man's white linen shirt, new from Paul Smith. It cost more than a week's wages. I fastened a wide ribbon round my collar, like a casual bow tie, and pressed some narrow black trousers.

I was nervous. When I arrived I was sat at the table and handed a drink. I faced Pip and Camilla over a low bank of lilies. We were dimly lit by candles in brackets on the walls. Opera played in the kitchen and there was a smell of browning onions.

We waited a long time for Peter, and finished several gins. Eventually he phoned to say he was dining with Viscount Linley and would arrive late for coffee. Josh told us this in a low voice. He seemed thrilled rather than offended.

'He might have rung us earlier,' said Camilla. 'The selfish bastard.'

'I didn't know Peter knew David Linley,' said Pip.

'They were at school together,' replied Camilla. 'They're doing a book.'

'Who'd be a publisher,' laughed Penny, as if we should feel sorry for him.

I wasn't used to dinner parties. Neither Camilla nor I could cook. Whenever I'd visited her in the past we'd got a takeaway. I was embarrassed. I studied the rows of cutlery. I looked at the different sized glasses. There was a bowl of impenetrable shellfish. They were as ordinary to everyone else as breathing. I watched carefully. 'Don't get drunk,' I told myself, pointlessly.

The room was full of shadows and golden light. The table shone and there were glints of rings and bracelets. Camilla's shoulders were bare and her hair was fastened in a high, loose knot. Penny, her friend, was beautiful too, with silver combs and glossy lips. They laughed and told stories. Pip was witty about a disastrous production of *The Tempest*, where the front stalls had been deluged with water. Penny said she'd bought a house in Normandy. Camilla mentioned a reflexologist in Camden Town. Lots of famous names were tossed to and fro. I knew Josh was enjoying himself. He served each course with a flourish. He was like an excited restaurateur. With each bottle of wine he became louder and more expansive, his arms waving like windmills. 'Don't worry, Imogen,' he said at one point, seeing me hesitate. 'Just copy Pip.'

I decided to ignore this. I wanted to join in, but I wasn't sure what to talk about. As usual, Camilla came to my aid. 'Imogen's a real hot-shot solicitor,' she said, warmly. 'Go on, Imogen, tell everybody about your job.'

'I'm not exactly a lawyer,' I said, modestly, 'I'm an advice worker.' I talked about work. My Newcastle accent sounded stronger than usual and I told them about some of the oddballs who'd recently come in for help. After a while, I realized I was using real people's problems to raise a cheap laugh, so I stopped.

It was the nicest food I'd ever tasted. Once the wine had relaxed me, I took seconds, then thirds. I wanted to eat and eat. 'This is lovely, Josh,' I said, appreciatively, as a tender sliver of meat dissolved in my mouth.

'Why aye, pet,' he said, sounding more Geordie than I ever could, 'it's canny scran, this.' He laughed and refilled my glass. I tried to smile.

I stared at Camilla. I felt privileged to know her. She caught my eye and winked. She pretended to zip her lips closed, in a sad way. She was dieting. She'd eaten next to nothing. She pushed the food aside, smiling at me. She lit a cigarette.

Later, as the candles flickered in their holders and the remains of three different puddings were picked over, Josh started talking about Oxford. He leaned back in his chair with his hands behind his head. He mentioned weddings and cafés, winters with real fires, summer parties. He seemed to know the children of cabinet ministers and several poets. He talked about cricket and bicycles and hiring a suit. I tried to imagine him, younger, in a college scarf.

'Where are you from, Josh?' asked Penny. 'Where were you brought up? You're such a mystery.'

Josh tipped further back in his chair, his eyes on the

ceiling. 'Mater and pater live in Surrey,' he said, camply. 'Near Bagshot Heath.'

'Oh,' said Penny, 'you must know—'

The doorbell rang. 'It's Peter,' said Josh, interrupting. He jumped to his feet. 'God, I can't wait to hear about his evening.'

I left Josh's courtyard and waited for a bus. Camilla is dead, I reminded myself again. There was a loose coin in the pocket of my jacket. 'Camilla is dead,' I repeated several times. I squeezed the coin on the word 'dead' so that my hand hurt.

A group of drunken men harassed a teenage girl. She hurried down a side street. A man stood in a doorway, eating fish and chips and muttering to himself. At his side a torn poster flapped. It showed a black woman, provocative and naked, except for a handkerchief, advertising dry cleaning. The air was damp with drizzle. My Levi's jacket was too thin and I was cold. I held my hands under my armpits and hugged myself, Camilla's video pressed against my chest. After a while, I decided to walk home. I hurried up Camberwell Grove and the bright lights from the pub looked inviting and warm.

I was surprised to see people I knew inside. My colleague Al was sitting near the bar. Her matted blond dreadlocks were spread out over a holey black sweater. Her fingers, covered in rings, were wrapped round a bottle of White Diamond. Her mobile phone was on the table.

She was sitting with two older women, a lesbian couple, who worked in a women's health project nearby. I knew them slightly. They were serious, old-fashioned feminists, with unkempt grey hair and massive bosoms. They were talking animatedly to Al. She was less than half their age and for once was looking bewildered, her normal serene confidence slightly ruffled. She pulled at the ends of her pigtails and examined her black-varnished nails. She smiled with relief when she saw me.

I bought a pint and went over to join them.

'I'm sorry, Imogen,' said Al, as I approached, 'about Camilla.'

Before I could dodge away, she stood up on tiptoe, and tried to kiss me. She'd never done this before. She smelled of Body Shop ananya.

I stepped back, out of her embrace, and looked around for a stool.

She introduced me, unnecessarily. 'This is Beryl and Cheryl,' she said. She turned to them and reminded them that I was the best friend of the woman who had just been killed. They both shook their heads and one brushed away an invisible tear. They tut-tutted compassionately.

I sat down, grim-faced, my back against the bar.

Al seemed to regain her composure. She started talking easily about one time she'd been with Camilla and how Camilla's period had started and how she'd asked her to swap a box of Tampax for a pack of Marlboros. The story seemed to go on and on. She explained how she'd only had Lil-lets, not Tampax, but Camilla had said they would do. After a while I was only half listening and lost her drift. I didn't feel like talking.

Al finished her story with a tinkle of laughter. She'd expertly made four roll-ups and started passing them around.

'You know I don't smoke,' I muttered, pocketing mine.

Not for the first time, I wondered how she could talk so effortlessly, and for so long, about nothing.

'Have you got enough tobacco?' asked Cheryl, pointing to the empty tin.

'It's all right,' Al answered lightly, 'I'm only a part-time smoker.'

I realized I was exhausted. I leaned back, uncomfortable. The rain had wet my jacket and my hair was damp. I watched the Christmas tree lights flash on and off then read some quiz questions on my beer mat. 'Who or what were a) The Young Pretender, b) the Great Pretender, c) The Mock Turtle.'

Beryl started explaining how the recent murders had increased her fear of men. She said she would always cross the road if a group of men were approaching. She told us that she always sat next to a woman on the bus. 'I get anxious with men,' she offered. 'I hate it if one asks me directions in the street.' She shrugged and looked at Cheryl. They began discussing male curfews and women-only taxi services. 'We're radical, not separatist, of course,' Beryl explained to Al, 'in the wider context of the struggle.'

Al looked blank, but she was anxious not to be left out of the conversation. 'Women can choose to be victims,' she said. I thought she sounded uncertain, but she smiled engagingly. 'Sometimes they can. I saw it on Oprah Winfrey. A big fat woman from Miami, or somewhere, said she chose the victim mode.' She paused and frowned. 'I think it must have been a sex thing.'

Beryl and Cheryl ignored her. They continued their debate. After a while, Beryl told us she'd been by the river, the previous week, looking at a new building. It was late afternoon, getting dark, and the builders had gone home. She heard footsteps and a man came up to her.

Al looked interested. 'Was he nice?"

'I ran,' Beryl replied, 'only I was in a dead end. He came up to me again.'

Cheryl gasped.

'I was going to give him this.' Beryl produced an aerosol from her bag and held it up. Al reached over. She took it and examined the label.

Beryl raised her voice. 'Give him it in the face. But then d'you know what he did?' She paused.

'Go on,' said Cheryl.

'He took some papers out of his briefcase and spread them on the wall. He was the architect. He wanted to talk about public access. The riverside walk.'

'You weren't to know,' said Cheryl quickly.

'I felt a little ashamed.'

Cheryl sighed, deeply. 'All men are potential rapists.' I swallowed several mouthfuls of cold lager.

Al leaned forwards, glancing at me. 'A boy tried to rape me once,' she said, 'at a party.' She deliberately altered her face into shocked disapproval. 'But I managed to get away.'

I felt worse than tired. I finished my drink and turned to Beryl and Cheryl. 'Camilla wasn't afraid,' I said. 'She told me fear just makes you vulnerable.' I suddenly remembered her breezy laughter when I left her for the last time, at that bus stop. I leaned back again, even more awkwardly, against the bar. I wondered what point I was trying to make. My mind was cloudy as I drained my glass and stood up. I stumbled slightly.

'Maybe that was the trouble,' Beryl said. 'She wasn't careful with herself. She put herself too much at risk.'

Outside, I set off home. I kept looking over my shoulder. The rain had stopped and away from the main road, the streets were quiet and deserted. I thought I heard whistling, but there was no one around. I passed some high green doors under a streetlight and read a sign which said KEEP OUT, DANGER OF DEATH. I started walking faster. My feet felt disconnected and wayward. I wanted to look big and confident, but I had trouble keeping to a straight line.

I kicked a bruised Coke can and it rattled loudly. For an instant I thought I could smell cigar smoke. Pausing, I pulled my jacket as close as possible, at the neck. My clothes were damp and my hands numb with cold. I heard more whistling, but then it stopped. I decided I was imagining things. There was an empty packet of Silk Cut on the ground and for the first time in a year I wanted a cigarette. I took the roll-up out of my pocket, but I had no matches. I sucked it, the taste of tobacco familiar on my tongue. I thought about becoming a part-time smoker, like Al, but straightaway dismissed it as a ridiculous idea.

I rewound Camilla's video when I got back to my flat and discovered it was the series of adverts she'd made, a few years before, for a body spray deodorant. She filled the screen, beautiful, confident and strong. Tossing her head at shadowy men, she seemed to insist on their irrelevance. I watched it lots of times.

I didn't want to go to bed. I drank several cans of cider and then some wine. The alcohol, in the end, made me tearful. I tried to imagine someone going up to

Camilla in the poor light of an underpass and hitting her over the head. A man they called the Whistler had followed her, perhaps followed both of us, all the way from the pub, then crept up behind her. He'd beaten her over the head, strangled her with her scarf and soaked her with her own perfume. He'd taken her bag then left her body below ground.

I tried to imagine this. I could see him, in a dim way, but not her. I just couldn't place her in that situation. I sat upright, then leaned forwards staring at the screen. This version of events just didn't hang together.

I made myself some strong, black coffee and ate some stale biscuits. The video ended and an early-hours American chat show came on. Later, I rewound the tape and tried to put my thoughts in order.

Playing and replaying the video, I became absolutely certain that Camilla hadn't been attacked by a stranger – even one as crazy as the Walworth Whistler. She was too stately, she was too arrogant. She was untouchable. No one in the world would have dared. The thought filled my head and wouldn't go away.

I went to bed. I tried to read the copy of *Elle* that Camilla had given me. It was her last gift. The words and pictures danced before my eyes. I rubbed it against my face before dropping it on the floor and turning off the light.

A neighbour's burglar alarm was ringing and ringing. Despite the fact that I'd been drinking nearly all day, I couldn't sleep. I thought about the last night I'd sat with Camilla in the pub. I ran through our conversations in my mind. I tossed and turned. Suddenly, my heart lurched. I held the covers to my face, in the dark. Camilla had said she'd been scared by someone. She'd said a person she knew was threatening her, wanting to hurt her. She'd said this as we were walking down Blackfriars Road. I tried to remember her exact words.

I wished I'd asked her what she meant. I recalled she'd been interrupted by bouncers, chucking a drunk from a doorway. Her words had been left hanging, unanswered. She'd been on the verge of telling me something important; probably the name of her killer.

I knew then, at that moment, that it wasn't the Walworth Whistler who'd murdered Camilla. She wasn't killed by a stranger. It had been someone known to her, someone with a grudge. The police were wasting time, on the wrong scent chasing entirely the wrong suspect. The real trail was going cold by the hour.

Chapter Six

The next morning I stood in a queue at the reception desk, behind a woman who said her son was missing. 'It's Tuesday,' she kept saying. He should have been back for his overalls.'

The duty policeman spelled her name wrong. He seemed uncertain what to do. She turned to me. 'This one's new,' she whispered.

I was directed to a waiting room with faded, dirty cream walls and stained seats. A small artificial Christmas tree stood in a corner.

I read a few posters asking for information about accidents and missing persons. There was nothing concerning the Whistler. I put some money in a drinks machine, but it didn't work. I read a leaflet about Aids. There were other people waiting, but no one spoke. An old man sighed and coughed. A skinhead twiddled his thumbs, trying to appear unconcerned.

Eventually, a man in plain clothes showed me upstairs. 'We'll go to the incident room,' he said. I decided he looked like Kevin Keegan, only younger. He was about six inches shorter than me, with curly hair.

We went into a big open-plan office. Policemen rushed about and telephones rang. Christmas cards were stuck to the walls. I had a headache but found a packet of

Solpadeine capsules in the pocket of my leather jacket. Thankfully, I swallowed two.

We sat down. 'Well, what can we do you for?' He was chirpy, but bored.

I wished I'd put on some make-up. I felt big and hung-over. I wasn't at my best and could tell he wasn't interested in me. I gave him the video and outlined my theory. 'I want this back, mind,' I said, 'you can't keep it.'

'I'll put it in the property cupboard,' he told me.

This didn't sound too hopeful. 'You are going to watch it?'

'You've been here before, haven't you, Miss Webb?' He looked at me, as if I was a timewaster. 'It is *miss*, isn't it?' His tone suggested I'd been rejected by every man in London. He took a half-smoked Camel from a pack and lit it.

'Camilla Harding was my best friend.'

He opened his notebook.

'I was probably the last person to see her alive.' I met his eyes. They were turquoise blue. I knew I had his attention. 'I'm a key witness.' He looked me up and down. I took a deep breath and told him my opinion in more detail. 'It wasn't the Whistler,' I repeated. 'The Whistler didn't do it.'

'We don't call him that here,' he sighed. 'The press. The TV. They've cranked that one up.'

'I thought people heard him whistling hymns?'

'One or two did. Told the TV. Now every bastard's hearing him. Southwark's just heaving with whistling bloody Christians.'

'And he sprays the victims with perfume? Takes their bags?'

He gave me a hard look.

'It wasn't him this time. *He* didn't get Camilla.'

He leaned back in his chair, squinting through his own tobacco smoke. He scratched his ankle. Like most men of his type, he thought he was sexy. 'Why are you so sure, I wonder?'

I didn't look at his body and tried not to breathe his smoke. I stared at his notes. 'She was going home. She wouldn't have wandered away from the bus stop, where it was safe. She must have met someone she knew.'

'I'm sorry,' he paused, 'Imogen.' He smiled. His use of my first name was too intimate. 'But you've just told me she wasn't afraid of anything. Maybe she did just that. Maybe she didn't heed the police warnings and decided to walk home. Or maybe she set off for Vauxhall. She was expected at a party in Vauxhall.' His voice was quiet.

'She'd decided not to go.'

He was listening. There was a long silence. I felt his eyes on me. Then a guffaw of laughter filled the room. A policewoman came over and handed him a cup of tea. As she turned, he leaned forward to tap her bottom, but missed. He swung round in his swivel chair, muttering something to a man sitting behind a monitor. They both sniggered. I knew I'd lost him. He turned back to me. 'We've just got these things,' he said, grinning again. 'New hardware. New damned software. Nobody knows what the hell's going on.'

I didn't meet his eye. 'That's very reassuring.'

He smiled again, widely. He lit one cigarette from another.

I fished in my pocket for more Solpadeine. 'What makes you so sure it was the Whistler?'

He drank some tea. 'We know.' There was a pause. He raised his hand and clicked his fingers at a woman in a far corner. 'Believe me. It was him.' He turned away, dismissively. 'Now I've made a note of your remarks, Miss Webb, is there anything else?'

'Thanks for nothing,' I muttered.

It was only ten thirty and my head was pounding, but I needed a drink. I went into a big tarty pub on the Borough Road. My hands shook as I counted out change for a pint. I was suddenly hungry and the barmaid brought me a cheese roll.

I remembered an article I'd read in the hairdressers' a few months before. It said that most crimes against women are carried out by men who are known to them and that they are most at risk at home. The journalist was trying to reassure her readers. She was suggesting that fears of dark alleys and strangers are irrational. She implied that rape and murder are almost always a domestic business and quoted statistics, showing that cases are usually solved within a month. If Camilla's murderer had been someone known to her, every day wasted by the police made his detection less likely.

I thought about the crazy misogynist stalking the streets of Walworth. I imagined Camilla in the video. Once more, I tried very hard to picture the two of them together. I went over it again and again, but I still couldn't believe she'd been his victim. The conclusion remained the same. She was killed by someone she knew. The police were looking for the wrong man. She'd said someone was trying to scare her. I was sure this person was the real killer. The chances were, I probably knew him too. This thought made my heart beat fast.

A person dressed as a teddy bear came round rattling

a bucket of money. He had tinsel around his neck and a Santa hat. I shook my head and sipped my pint. It tasted sour. A man sat down opposite me. 'Cheer up, love,' he said, looking at my breasts. 'It might never happen.'

'Fuck off,' I replied. I stood up and put the cheese roll in the teddy bear's bucket. I left the pub without finishing my beer.

I worked in an Advice Centre. It was one of the few in London to survive the Tory cuts and it was a small agency, near the Thames, in a truncated terrace of old houses. Most of the surrounding property had been pulled down, or bombed, then rebuilt. The view of the river disappeared in the seventies. We were hemmed in on all sides by modern office blocks.

'I'm sorry, Imogen,' said Al, for the second time, as I pushed open the door to the office. 'I'm really sorry.' She sounded uncomfortable and somewhat subdued. 'How are you? You looked terrible last night. We were worried.'

I walked over to my desk, shuffling the post.

'D'you want a cup of . . . something? There's herbal or . . . ' She approached me, one arm raised, as if about to hug me.

I turned my back. I didn't want to be touched. 'Coffee,' I said gruffly. 'Not decaff. Instant and strong.'

I stood by the in-tray and started opening the post. Automatically, I sifted letters into a pile for myself, a handful of less important ones for Al and some others that could wait. As usual, there was far too much to do.

'Coffee,' she said, slopping the overfilled mug over the letters at my side. She pulled her raggy sleeve down over one hand, and mopped, ineffectually.

I sighed. I could sense her hesitation. My bad moods always made her silent. She preferred to prattle and giggle, but if this wasn't possible she moved about the office inside a wall of omniscient calm. 'Why don't you go home?' she said eventually. 'I can manage here.'

I looked down at her girlish heart-shaped face. I frowned.

'Hey, I'm sorry,' she said, shrugging. 'I was only thinking of you.' She glided away, unperturbed.

My job at the centre was to advise people about their rights and offer debt counselling. I wasn't a qualified lawyer, but I knew a lot about social policy, benefits, housing and employment law. I did battle, on behalf of clients, with big bureaucracies like the DSS and the council Housing Department. Camilla always said she didn't know how I stuck it. She said I must be a saint. I spent a lot of time on the phone. For some reason the telephone made me clever and insistent. I got wheels turning fast, with clerks and officers paying up or backing down. I was good on the phone, saying what I meant, patient or stroppy, but without getting tongue-tied. I liked my job. At work, I talked in a bullying, persuasive, articulate kind of way that I could never manage in my life outside.

I went over to my desk, sat down and picked up my drink. The mug was chipped and old. It said FREE NELSON MANDELA. The coffee was scalding and horrible. My hands were shaking. I wondered if this was shock, or alcohol poisoning.

For some reason, I thought about Camilla laughing in the pub with the women footballers and the way she'd sat at their table, leaning on one elbow. I glanced over at Al. She had a case file on her lap and was using it to balance tobacco and papers as she rolled a cigarette. I noticed her leopardskin leggings, ripped at both knees. She was wearing headphones and whistled tunelessly. She was in a world of her own.

Al was in her first job and thought she knew it all. Really, she was hopeless. She was supposed to be my assistant but she got on my nerves because she gave up too easily on the phone. She used a lot of useless charm but in the end the bureaucrats gave her the runaround. She couldn't bully them and didn't back them into exitless corners, like I did. She was only nineteen. Her letters were well typed, but written with terrible grammar. She couldn't spell.

I sipped my coffee and watched her tapping at her keyboard. I had to admit that my computer skills were practically nonexistent, whilst hers were faultless. She could retrieve facts on law and public policy that were far more detailed and up to date than the knowledge I had in my head. She pulled out information, effortlessly. The trouble was, she couldn't apply it to real life. She couldn't deal with clients in the right way. People with problems disturbed her.

She understood their lack of money, their desperation or their resignation. She also had all the facts at her disposal, on the background reasons for their plights. Nevertheless she seemed unable to balance the two sides of the equation. I saw this the first time she tried to persuade the DSS to buy a family a washing machine.

'They haven't got any food,' I said. 'They're in massive debt to a moneylender. They're about to be evicted. Their children might be taken into care.'

'A washing machine would help,' she'd said, innocently. 'Everybody has to have a washing machine.'

Al had led a sheltered life, although she was good at pretending otherwise.

'How've you coped this morning?' I asked.

'Fine,' she said, flicking her lighter and blowing smoke upwards, from the corner of her mouth. 'I had to leave the answering machine on, but everyone was seen. Don't worry. I didn't screw up. I wrote it all down.'

Al was my own fault. At her interview, I'd insisted that she have the job. She was from the north-east and I thought we'd be friends. As it turned out, her provincial posh accent and private-school manners clashed with her raggy, unwashed clothes. She was brattish and naive. Her hair looked dirty and she never polished her boots. In the pub, she drank Hooch or Pepsi or sweet cider. She made me feel old.

I opened the cabinet to get my case files. There was a new poster on the wall, about battery hens. Underneath there was a petition and a tray of stick-on fluffy chickens with paper beaks.

This was typical of Al. She had no politics but she was into issues. She'd never used her vote. Half the time she didn't turn up at work because she was out with the eco-warriors, opposing bypasses or sitting in endangered oak trees or lying down in front of lorryloads of calves.

I heard her lift up the phone and begin to dial. 'Al!' I shouted.

'Just a minute,' she said, calmly, 'I've got to phone my bank.'

I opened the filing cabinet, then banged it closed. I heard her talking about opening a new kind of high-yield account. She was careful with her money. I felt my headache worsening. I groped in my pocket for the pills.

When I turned around Al was leaning against my desk. She smelled of patchouli. She opened her eyes wide and quizzical, like a little girl, knowing that this had disarmed me in the past.

'I thought we'd agreed about this animal rights shit?' She didn't reply.

'It's not relevant here.' I spoke slowly and distinctly. 'It's – not – what – we – do.' My voice was harsh. 'Our funds aren't secure. I've said all this. I said it at the management committee. The funders could cut us any time. It went to a vote.' She often drove me crazy, but this time I'd lost my temper.

She wrinkled her nose. I noticed she was wearing a badge which said VIRTUAL ENERGY. 'What funders?' she replied, looking up at me. Her voice was innocent.

My headache pounded like a drum. Al knew nothing about structures, organizations, procedure. She fell asleep at management meetings.

I sounded loud. 'I worked bloody hard to secure the funding for your job.' I wanted to add, 'And you're overpaid,' but I choked it back. 'Where's your priorities? Fucking chickens? We're not here to help furry fucking animals.' I paused. 'Jesus wept!'

I leaned against the wall. Not for the first time I had a sense of my mind racing, with images of Camilla jostling for attention. I wanted to meet her somewhere, have a drink and tell her about these stupid chickens. Only Camilla could share my outrage then turn it into humour. For a second, I wondered who else I could talk to. She'd been my only real friend. I steadied myself against a chair and took a deep breath. The coffee had given me heartburn. 'Al, what the hell's all this?' I picked up the stick-ons then dropped them.

She stared at me. She was like a motionless model in a shop window. I suddenly remembered she was a Buddhist, or a vegan or maybe even a born-again Christian. I swallowed hard. Her steady gaze unnerved me. I felt my cheeks redden. I lowered my voice. 'You shouldn't be doing this in work time.'

Al's gaze moved to the ceiling. She sighed and eased on her headphones. She started whistling again.

My headache was like a hammer and I wanted to cry. Pushing past her, I took a deep breath. I sat at my desk and washed down more Solpadeine with the cooling coffee. My hands were shaking and tears filled my eyes. Listening to the tinny murmur of Al's Walkman, I pretended to be reading a case file. I heard her fill the kettle again, turn off her tape, then play back the messages on the answering machine. She made a couple of phone calls about a family's eviction order and sent a fax. After a while she said tentatively, 'It's terrible that women can't walk the streets in safety.' She was quoting Cheryl and Beryl, from the night before. I knew she was blaming my outburst on Camilla's death and she was searching for appropriate words. I could almost hear her thought processes. 'Women have rights,' she offered, lamely.

I didn't answer.

She fell back on secure ground. 'My parents knew somebody who knew somebody who was murdered in Mozambique. Or was it Marrakesh? They were backpacking. Anyway, my mum told me—'

I interrupted. 'Don't start going on about your bloody parents. Please. Not now. I don't want to hear about them.' I suddenly wanted some fresh air. I stood up, overturning my chair. Walking out, I banged the door behind me. From the corridor I could see two elderly women in the waiting room, sitting next to the Calor gas heater. I punched the air with my fist and flung open the door to the street. 'Why Camilla?' I asked. 'Why did it have to happen to her?' I glanced round. The clients looked over at me briefly, then turned back to the heater, waiting patiently for their names to be called.

Chapter Seven

I went to the place on Blackfriars Road where I'd got drunk with Camilla on Friday night. I realized this was the second pub I'd been in, and it was still before midday. I ordered a large whisky and a bar meal, expecting to be recognized and questioned, but no one said anything. I sat in the same alcove. I ran my hand over the seat where she'd been.

After a few minutes I went back to the bar and bought another whisky. The barman was the same one that Camilla had drunkenly embraced. I wanted to talk to him, but I stopped myself. I sat down again and tried to find one of her long blond hairs on the seat or carpet.

When my meal arrived, I still wasn't hungry. I ate the chips, then pushed the plate to one side. The pub filled up with men wearing unpleasant ties and young women in badly cut jackets. The men ate greasy dinners and the women picked at sad-looking rolls. I studied their bad complexions and their glasses of imported, over-priced beer. I felt enraged. My grief had turned to anger. I wanted to overturn tables, stamp on glasses, push the innocent lunch-eaters off their stools. I wanted to run my arms across the shelves behind the bar, breaking bottles, scattering cigars. Most of all I wanted to smash the windows. I hated the way they said 'Courage', back to front, like some kind of deranged slogan. I didn't need to be reminded about the need for courage in London. It was as necessary as money.

The barman cleared away my uneaten food. I went over and ordered another drink. I looked in the same mirror that had faced me on Friday night. I was paler than ever and dishevelled. My new haircut was untidy. I wondered if I'd lost any weight. My jeans felt a bit loose. I thought about my liver and decided, as soon as I got home, to take some vitamins.

I remembered once advising Camilla to take vitamins. She'd not been eating and she was drinking too much. It was when she came back from Madrid. She'd been on a winter fashion shoot for *Vogue*. She gave me the key to her flat. It was before she moved in with Josh. She lived in Brixton. She was worried about break-ins.

'D'you remember that time someone forced a window?' she asked.

'Wasn't it some kind of pervert?'

'He did things to my underwear. It was draped all around the furniture. I think he'd been trying it on. I had to throw it all away.'

She said she was worried about her lilac suede suit. 'I don't want some wanker squeezing his fat butt into that,' she said, 'it costs a fortune to clean.'

'I'll call in,' I promised.

'Turn a few lights on and off,' she advised. 'You know. Curtains. That kind of thing.'

I opened the door, the first night, and the hall smelled of hairspray. I went from room to room. In the kitchen I switched on the radio. Someone said that Gianni Versace had died for gay rights. I moved the dial to pop music. Opening the fridge, I poured myself some orange juice. It tasted odd, as if it had been there for a long time. Looking around, I decided the kitchen was dirty.

I went into the bedroom, clicked the bedside lamp and drew the curtains. The room was bathed in a pink glow. The silk counterpane gleamed. One of the walls was hung with lace. Behind this was a rail of clothes, crammed haphazardly into an alcove. Underneath was a heap of shoes. My shadow was crooked and strange on the wall.

I lifted an armful of dresses. The hangers rattled as I raised them to my face. There was the smell of her scent and tobacco and something musty. I stood for a while, then released them. I tried on a pair of her shoes. They had high heels and were much too small.

I walked unsteadily over to the dressing table and sat down. I felt almost too heavy for the flimsy stool. I smelt inside a jar of face cream and rubbed some into my cheeks. It smelled of coconuts. I looked at my feet and then at the greasy smears on my face. I picked up her brush and pulled it through my hair. I'd never been closer to her. I hesitated, then opened all the drawers. Slowly, carefully, I pulled out the thin nightdresses, the stockings, the camisoles, the pants and bras. I draped them over my knees. The silk was soft and the lace was hard. I stroked them and turned them over in my hands.

The night she got back she came in wearing a beige cashmere suit and a cloche hat. She flung down her case and her bags. 'Fix me a drink,' she called from the bathroom. 'There's something in that airport carrier. It's vile. You'll have to mix it.'

I stood at the window. The living room was tidy but not very clean. There were mouldy coffee cups on a table and an ashtray overflowed. Outside, it was dark. Rain smeared the glass. The lights from the traffic distorted into bright blooms. I cleared away the cups, emptied the ashtray, made the drinks. I wanted to go out for a meal. I glanced in the mirror, licking a smear of lipstick from the front of my teeth.

After a long time, Camilla appeared in her kimono. Her hair was loose and her face cleansed of make-up. She looked tired. She turned on the gas fire and sat down. We swallowed gin mixed with the stale orange juice. She produced a long golden box wrapped in cellophane.

'Good trip?' I asked.

'Bloody hell,' she replied. She opened the box and took out a pack of cigarettes. She lit one and sighed. I noticed how bony her wrists were. The gas fire hissed and the windows steamed up. I turned on the television. For some reason, we watched the end of *Casualty*.

'Is there anything in the fridge?' she asked.

I tried to smile. 'More orange juice. A yogurt past its date. Some coffee beans.'

She said nothing.

I realized she wanted to stay in. 'D'you want me to get a takeaway?' I glanced over and saw that she was crying. I put down my glass, went over and knelt at the side of her chair.

'They didn't use me,' she whispered. Her face was wet but she was trying to hold back her sobs. 'They said I looked terrible.' On this she buried her face in her hands and cried hard.

I felt awkward. I turned the sound off the television. This had never happened before. I put my arm stiffly around her shoulders.

She looked at me. 'Promise you won't tell anyone.' She gulped. 'Shit, everyone knows anyway.' She stopped crying. 'The bastards.'

I felt at a loss. 'What was it?'

She grimaced. There was a long pause. 'I was bingeing on chocolate cake all the time and being sick. They wouldn't use me. They said I looked ill. They said if they'd wanted a waif they'd have hired a teenager. They said I'm too old to be abusing myself.'

I took her hand and squeezed it. 'I'm sorry,' I said. I tried not to stare. I suddenly saw her collarbones jutting and the way the skin on her arms and neck was slack and dry. Only her face wasn't thin. Crying had made it puffy and swollen.

'Maybe you need vitamins,' I said.

I went out and bought a curry. When I got back, Camilla tried to swallow some rice. Her eating problem was worse. I'd never seen her this bad. I could tell she wanted to talk about it.

She lit another cigarette. 'I can't remember when it started. I've had problems with food for so long. After my mother left, nobody bothered. There was always food in the house, but the only people who ever cooked were caterers. Now and again. Dinner parties. I lived on Frosties. Tinned pears. Toast.'

I was hungry. I chewed the chicken tikka and sag aloo. I spilled some oily sauce on my jeans. Camilla drank more gin.

'Eating was a ritual in my house,' I said. I'd always known what to expect, according to the day of the week. 'Dinner was the same time every day. Half-past twelve. We came home from school.'

'You ate at lunchtime?'

'That was dinner. At five o'clock we had tea. At nine o'clock we had supper. Every Monday was cold cuts. That was Sunday's leftovers. Tuesday was mince and dumplings. Wednesday was plate pie . . . '

'I don't believe you!'

'It's true. Meat and two veg every day. How d'you think I grew so big? Fish on Fridays. I never even saw an aubergine until I was twenty-four.' I scooped the last of the curry from its aluminium container onto my plate. 'We all sat round the kitchen table. My dad was given the most. Then my brother. We had suet puddings. Rhubarb and custard. Cups of tea. We had to clean our plates. Mop the gravy with old bread until they shone.'

Camilla was smiling.

'It's not funny,' I said, 'all that red meat. All that cholesterol.'

'Its wonderful,' she murmured. She seemed happier.

'Black pudding for breakfast,' I continued, 'tripe and onions.'

She started to giggle. 'I don't believe that last bit.'

She was relaxing. I was relieved. I smiled. 'Pigs' trotters,' I continued.

She laughed.

'Tea was tongue sandwiches.' I thought hard. 'Oh, yes, kippers. Finnan haddie.' I started laughing myself. 'Stovies!' I gasped. 'Stotties!'

An advert came on the television. It was for a chocolate bar and showed a rail-thin girl twirling across St

Mark's Square. Camilla's eyes rested on the screen and as instantly as she'd brightened, she was sad again. My laughter sounded hollow and died away. We looked at each other. I knew she wanted help, but I couldn't think of anything else to say. I felt useless and no words of sympathy would come to me. I sensed her disappointment.

Later, she fished a cardboard tube out of her big white bag. 'Look at this,' she said. She unrolled a print and held it up. 'I saw the real one in the Prado.'

At the top was a heavenly paradise, floating in an eerie way.

'I think it's the Last Judgement,' she said.

I looked at it more closely. 'It's horrible,' I commented.

It was a scene of hell. Scrawny people were being tortured in bizarre ways.

'It's going on the wall,' she said.

I swished ice cubes around in my glass.

She spread the print on the floor. 'In Madrid,' she said, 'it reminded me of home.' She sniffed. 'It's the scene from the top of the number twelve bus.' As she sat down again, several packets tumbled from the golden box. I turned the television over for the football.

She picked up the cigarettes. 'I'll be dead,' she said, 'before I've finished all of these.'

I went back to the office. I decided to try to look calm. As I entered, the telephone rang and Al switched on the answering machine. I flicked impatiently through the in-tray. She hadn't dealt with a medical appeal tribunal which was coming up soon. 'Christ,' I snapped, 'what about this independent medical evidence?'

She didn't answer. She went to unlock the outside door. There was a queue of people in the street. 'You deal with this lot,' I called out, as they streamed into the waiting room. 'I'll start on the backlog.'

I worked without a break. I banged out letters about unpaid unemployment benefit and families trapped in bed-and-breakfast accommodation. Every so often, I picked up a phone and argued with an official. At four o'clock there was hardly room to move. Al asked for some help.

I sat next to a homeless man whose only overcoat had been stolen. I opened a new case file. NFA, I wrote under his name. That meant no fixed abode. He had a bag of books.

'What have you got there?' I asked.

'Library books,' he said. 'They were throwing them out. I found them in a skip.'

I gave him a note for the WRVS. 'They'll give you a new coat, if you show them this.'

Next there was a family, with two babies, recently off a train from Scotland, with nowhere to go. I got on the phone to the Housing Department, argued that they had a local connection and got them fixed up with an interview. 'Thanks,' said the father, 'here.' He handed me a small badge. 'That's for you.' I looked at the gift as they manoeuvred their pushchair out the door. It was a lapel pin. It had a wheel in the centre which formed the middle of a thistle. Around the edges it said THE SCOTTISH AREA. NAT. UNION OF MINEWORKERS.

Finally, I talked to a sad-looking couple whose electricity had been cut off. They weren't from our area. Al had tried to refer them to the Citizen's Advice Bureau in Camberwell, but they were refusing to leave. They looked depressed. 'They're going to sit this out,' whispered Al.

The man was overweight and his jumper was old and too small. He had thin greasy hair, combed sideways to hide a bald patch. The woman was wearing a pair of disintegrating trainers without tights and her face was puffy and red. 'We've got candles but no heating,' she said. She held the sides of her chair, in a determined way. 'We've been everywhere,' she added. 'We've seen everyone.' She coughed into her sleeve. 'We eat cold beans. Pies and chips. We've got no hot water.'

They seemed familiar. I wondered where I'd seen them before. They reminded me of the couple I'd noticed at the Elephant and Castle, the night I'd left Camilla at the bus stop. I looked at their faces and decided this was ridiculous. I could have come across them, as well as lots of others like them, anywhere in South London.

I phoned the electricity company and gave their name and account number. I was surprised to see they were living in the same block as Josh. Camilla had been their neighbour.

I put my hand over the mouthpiece. 'Are you with the housing association?'

The woman shook her head.

I spoke to someone in the accounts department. I turned to the woman again. 'They say you've already been given time to pay. What happened to your instalment plan?'

She looked at me blankly.

'They say you've tampered with the meter.' I put the phone down. It didn't look too hopeful. 'Have you any children or disabled people living with you?'

The woman frowned and shrugged.

'Are either of you under the doctor?'

She started to describe her angina.

'Go down that route,' I said to Al. 'They're not in our area, but they're here. Get a doctor's letter. Make a fuss about the heart condition with the electricity people and the DSS. Don't bother with social services. They won't be interested.'

She picked up the phone.

I turned back to the couple. 'Did you know Camilla Harding?' My voice sounded strange.

They looked at me, at each other, then stared at the floor.

Camilla always said that my work was soul destroying but I never let it get me down. Most cases were resolved in the end. I stuck at them in a determined way. Al said we should empower people. She said we should get them to deal with the bureaucracies on their own. I didn't think this was realistic. By the time they got to us, our clients had given up the fight. They were lost and disorientated. They wanted somebody to get angry on their behalf.

At six o'clock, Al left to go to a Fuming Mad meeting. 'Car emissions and stuff,' she said, cheerfully. This was one of the issues that preoccupied her.

I felt better. A lot of work was finished. Many people had been helped. I had a sense of creating order where there had been none.

I leaned back in my chair. It seemed very quiet in the office, but outside I could hear an alarm, a siren and the rhythmic beat of the police helicopter, swooping low. The man who killed Camilla might be sitting at a table eating a meal, or walking down a street, his face in shadow. He might be on the Tube or watching television. The more I considered it, the more I thought he wasn't some random madman. It was someone she'd known, someone she'd trusted.

I remembered Pip's unkind words and how he'd disliked her. She'd had enemies as well as friends. Perhaps Pip had hated her enough to kill her.

I looked at my pile of notes, my memos and my folders. At that moment I decided to take Camilla's case on board. I vowed to sort it out, like I did the problems of my clients at work. It seemed all I had to do was find someone with a reason, someone with a motive to do her harm. Someone she knew had been threatening her. It couldn't be that difficult to find him. Not if I checked everything out, made a few waves and refused to give up.

Chapter Eight

I switched off the lights and the Calor gas heater. A sleety wind blew hard as I locked the outer door. Despite this, I felt better. I'd chosen a course of action and this made me less helpless. There was no one in the street. I raised my collar, squared my shoulders into the cold and walked to Blackfriars Road. The bus shelter was deserted. The traffic had quietened down, and there was just the occasional car. I hesitated under the railway bridge and looked at my watch. It was nearly eight o'clock. I could smell kebabs from a nearby takeaway, and I was suddenly hungry. I waited for a while. There were no buses in sight. I plugged in my Walkman and listened to Country Joe and the Fish sing 'Feel Like I'm Fixin' to Die'. After ten minutes I decided to walk to the Elephant and Castle.

I followed the same route Camilla and I had taken on Friday night, passing the pub we'd been in. I stopped at St George's Circus to change the tape in my Walkman. I struggled, because my hands were cold and lifeless. I stamped my feet, trying to warm them. Looking over my shoulder, I saw there was no one around. Lights shone in the Salvation Army hostel but the office blocks were in darkness. At the pub where the well-dressed drunk had been thrown in the street everything seemed closed. Not only that, it looked boarded up, as if it had been abandoned for years. The shuttered doors and windows were covered in torn fly-posters, and graffiti. There was an accumulation of litter in the doorway. This was strange. I couldn't understand it. I remembered Camilla telling me, exactly at this spot, that someone had been threatening her. I'd been very disorientated, at the time. I wished I'd questioned her, asked her more about what was going on.

The sleet turned to heavy, driving rain. Water ran down my face, and inside my collar. My jeans stuck to my legs. A taxi stopped, about fifty yards away but its for hire sign was switched off. I could hear the chug of its diesel engine. A man and a woman got out. He was black and tall and wore a leather coat. The woman seemed almost naked in a sleeveless minidress. They were arguing. As I drew closer I wondered if her exaggerated make-up and patent stilettos meant she was a prostitute. I remembered the woman in hotpants I'd seen getting into a car, nearby, on Friday night. As I approached, the couple got back into the taxi and slammed the door.

Someone was standing to the side of a post which supported an advertising hoarding. I paused, taking in the vast advert for Nike trainers, the dull orange of the stormy sky, the glittering pavement. Lines of rain bounced in the gutter. The loiterer was well back, half hidden amongst rubble and weeds. He looked like he was lying in wait. Nervously, I switched off my Walkman and put it in my pocket. With a shock, I heard him whistling. He was whistling 'O Worship the King'. I crossed over the road, away from him.

In the distance, my bus approached. It was like a big red ship, churning up waves on the road. The man emerged from the darkness. Under the street light I saw he was holding a bottle by its neck. I couldn't see his face but I had the impression that he was thin, middle-aged and balding. He was wearing an anorak.

I started hurrying towards the distant bus stop. I passed a phone box. I noticed that its light was out and its phone was hanging from its cord. I was sure the man was following me. It crossed my mind that he was probably smaller than me and I might be able to overpower him. I was too scared to take a chance.

I ran but I could hear his footsteps behind me. The roar of the bus drew nearer. There was a clatter as my Walkman fell from my pocket and hit the pavement. Its lead tangled for a second around my leg. I dragged it, but then it fell away. I was running as fast as I could. I glanced behind and could see him following. I had the impression that the gap was narrowing.

The bus approached. Frantically, I signalled with one arm, my breath coming in sharp gasps. The bus passed me, but slowed. The stop was just ahead. With a last effort, I ran and grabbed the rail. For a second I was plunged forwards and dragged in the road. I scrambled onto the platform at the rear. The conductor was at the front. He nodded to me, rang the bell and the bus picked up speed.

I leaned against the back window, completely breathless. I rested my hot cheek on the chrome rail. My heart was beating hard. The glass was too dirty to see clearly. We were at the Elephant. The bus swept round the wide curve of the roundabout, its lights reflected a thousand times in the towering office blocks. I lurched inside and sat down, fishing in my pockets for change. The conductor chuckled at my heavy breathing. I paid him,

wiping sweat from my brow with the cuff of my sleeve.
I lay back on the seat.

'Lovely night for ducks,' said a woman opposite,
opening a paper bag and taking out a meat pie.

Chapter Nine

Camilla's body was released and the funeral arranged, much quicker than I expected. I rang the police and they told me she was to be buried on Thursday, less than a week after her death. I asked if I could see her body. They said she was already at the undertaker's and added something about me being a witness at a future inquest, as the first one had been adjourned.

I looked up the undertaker's in the phone book. When I rang them, they told me to contact the next of kin. The funeral was due to take place the following day.

Camilla's father was abrupt when he answered the phone. He said he didn't have any idea who I was.

I explained that I wanted to say goodbye. 'She was my best friend.'

'My daughter is dead,' he said, harshly. 'Forgive me, but there have been enough prying eyes.'

'Mr Harding, I'm sorry but I really want to—'

'Goodbye,' he said. He sounded very upset. He hung up.

I left the office and took a taxi over to Clapham. The undertakers had a plate-glass window draped in purple silk. Inside it was dark and the room was filled with flowers. A man in a formal suit appeared and started carrying out the wreaths. He laid them on top of a coffin in a hearse parked in the road.

The sweet smell of the flowers made my head swim. I asked him about Camilla's funeral and he said it was in Berkshire. 'Ask at the desk,' he told me.

I waited and wondered about the little I knew of Camilla's background. She rarely talked of her family. She came from a house with an orchard and she'd had a pony when she was a child.

The man in the suit reappeared. He was still carrying flowers. I asked him if any of the wreaths were Camilla's. He shook his head. 'I told you. It's in Berkshire. Tomorrow.'

I carried on waiting at the desk but no one appeared. There was a black-edged card propped against the phone. Someone had written, incongruously, 'Merry Christmas to all our customers'. I kept pressing an old-fashioned brass bell. On the bottom of the card was printed *Discreet, Dependable, Est. 1873.*

I gave up and went through to a back room. I was nervous in case there were bodies. Instead, I found an office with computers, a fax and a photocopier. A young man tapped on a keyboard. He looked like a travel agent.

'Excuse me,' I said.

He glanced up, irritated. There was a cartoon on the wall above his head which said YOU DON'T HAVE TO BE MAD TO WORK HERE, BUT IT HELPS.

'I'm enquiring about Camilla Harding.'

Wordlessly, he fished in a tray and handed me a piece of paper. It said 'A Commemoration'. At the bottom there was the address of a church. I wondered why nobody had sent me one.

'Cheers,' I said. 'Is she here? Can I see her?' My voice

sounded odd, as if Camilla might be relaxing somewhere, in an adjacent office, sipping decaff.

He shook his head.

'Is she in Berkshire?'

He shrugged his shoulders, without taking his eyes off the screen.

Later, back at the office, Al suggested we go for a drink after work. I hesitated then agreed. I was sick of my own company. At five thirty we went to the same pub where I'd been at lunchtime the day before, and where I'd met Camilla on Friday night.

Walking ahead of me, Al crossed the lounge and went to the alcove with the fire and the same seat that Camilla had chosen the night she died. I followed her, but then stopped in my tracks. As she sat down, raised her head and then smiled at me, I was suddenly shocked by the blondness of her hair, her thin shoulders, her long fingers lighting a cigarette. She looked just like Camilla.

Swallowing hard, trying not to tremble, I turned away and went to the bar. I bought her a bottle of Hooch and a pint of lager for myself. Carrying them over, I took a deep breath, then blinked a few times. The ghost of Camilla gradually faded and was replaced by Al's ragged sweater, the lustreless tangle of her dreadlocks, the tightness of her roll-up, now wedged in the corner of her mouth.

'I don't want to sit here,' I said gruffly.

She smiled her fake little girl's smile, picked up her tobacco, her Rizlas and her carrier bags and moved to the centre of the room. I watched her find a stool. Unflustered, she organized her belongings. She hitched up her baggy sweater in a lazy gesture. Underneath was a see-through summer minidress, grazing thick black leggings. Her clothes were deliberately mismatched and torn. Her heavy boots were purple, with CND symbols painted on the toecaps.

I sat down. Carefully, I dusted the lapels of my suede jacket with my palms. Camilla had thought my street style was aggressive, but next to Al, I looked prosperous, even staid.

'How are you feeling now?' she said. She sounded nervous.

'Lousy,' I replied.

There was a silence. I looked around. Grinning paper snowmen and Santas, suspended on strings, continued to whirl every time someone opened the door. The landlord was wearing his offensive pen, on a chain. The jukebox played 'Rudolph the Rednosed Reindeer'. I wished I hadn't come.

'Look,' she said hesitantly, 'd'you want me to come and stay? A few days? A night? I don't mind.'

'No,' I replied. In an instant, I pictured her in my living room, amongst my scatter cushions, my garish curtains, my Country and Western music. 'No,' I repeated. I swallowed some beer. Nobody ever came to my flat, and I wanted Al there less than most. I drained my pint. 'She was in this pub on Friday night,' I added, changing the subject. 'Camilla was doing a fashion shoot, near Tooley Street. We met in here.'

'I know.' She stood up and rummaged in a leather pouch attached to her belt.

'Same again,' I said.

'I could have been a model,' she offered.

I laughed.

She looked at me. I realized she was serious. 'I've worked with Camilla. I had a contract with Élite when I was fifteen.'

I glanced down at her slim calves, her adolescent knees.

She turned towards the bar. 'But I hate all that shit.'

She joined a crowd waiting to be served. Surreptitiously, I opened her carrier bags. Inside one was a packet of organic flour, a *Beano*, a freezer pack of icepops and a new Lancôme nail polish, still in its box. The other contained her charity-shop jacket, neatly folded, her mobile phone and a bunch of flowers. I picked up her tin of tobacco from the table. I fingered her lighter. I didn't understand anything about her. I wondered if she was still dating the young Malaysian student we'd employed as a volunteer in the centre a few months before. He'd been handsome and politically earnest. He was studying agricultural economics. Al had never appeared to listen to a word he said.

'Are you still going out with whatsisname?' I asked as she sat down again. 'Mao Tse-tung?'

She smiled. 'No,' she answered.

'What happened to him?' I wanted to get the conversation onto neutral subjects.

'He's working as a barman in a TV club near Leicester Square.'

I tried to imagine this, but failed.

'Did you know he was a transvestite?'

I shook my head. Sipping my pint, I realized she'd bought me cider.

'He used to come round and wear my dresses. He'd put on bras, panties, everything. He was really into it.

He had a wig. He had high heels, specially made.' She laughed. 'Red ones.'

I struggled to transform the intense, opinionated Oriental of my memory into a kind of chorus girl.

'He loved cocktail frocks. He'd dress up and pretend to be Cher, miming with the music on. He was wild. Then he'd partially strip off and shag me in the window with the curtains open.'

I was shocked. I swallowed hard. 'Are you winding me up?'

She opened her eyes wide. 'It was you he fancied. He said you're much more butch than me.'

I felt myself blushing. The lager made me want to burp. I raised a hand to my face, hiding my confusion. 'Sounds like he had a few problems,' I said lamely.

She tossed her matted hair back over one shoulder. 'Oh, no. He was totally sussed.' Her tinkling voice became adamant. 'I've never met anyone in my life more clear about his sexual needs. He was really worked out.'

I didn't want to talk about this. With an effort, I pushed from my mind the disturbing image of Al and the transformed student, copulating in a lighted window. I finished my drink. 'Another?' I asked.

We sat in the pub for a long time. Talk eddied around the safer subject of work. She said she was thinking of studying for a law degree, at evening class. She asked for my opinion. She said she wanted to get qualified.

I told her how to progress a few cases she was busy on. I had the impression of my words settling briefly on the surface of her consciousness, then blowing away. Her conversational style was dreamy, yet opaque. 'We could go to Nicaragua together,' she said at one point. 'We could help save all those Amazonian rainforests and tigers and all that stuff, over there.'

As time was called, I stood up to leave. I felt drunk, but more cheerful than I'd expected. 'It's been nice,' I managed to say.

Al bent forward and rummaged in a carrier bag. She straightened up and handed me the bunch of flowers. 'I care about you, Imogen,' she said.

Awkwardly, I took them.

'Can I come home with you?' She added, 'I could cheer you up.' She smiled, hopefully.

My mouth went suddenly dry. I suspected she wanted to sleep with me. 'No,' I spluttered, 'another time, I mean, I don't think . . . '

'It's OK,' she smiled serenely, 'either way.'

I turned and made for the door, without looking round. I hurried out. As I approached the bus stop, I dumped the flowers in a waste bin. I glanced over my shoulder, but to my relief she wasn't following me.

Chapter Ten

I wondered what to wear for the funeral. I found an old black dress in my wardrobe, but immediately decided against it. It hadn't seen the light of day for a long time. I hadn't worn anything but trousers or jeans for about six years. In the end, I chose black chinos, a grey denim shirt under a black heavy-knit sweater and my leather jacket. I washed my hair and styled it. My expertise was growing but I decided hair as short as this was surprisingly difficult to manage. I outlined my eyes with kohl pencil and found a bright-red lipstick, which I applied liberally. I'd already replaced my nose pin with a tiny hammer and sickle. It glinted, subversively.

On the Tube to Paddington, I remembered the studs on the back of my jacket said 'Grateful Dead'. This wasn't really appropriate for the occasion but it was too late to go back and change.

I dozed on the train thinking about the time we went with Pip, to visit Josh on location in Bristol. Camilla and I slept in the same bed. Josh had booked us into a B&B, although he'd taken Pip to the Dragonara Hotel for what he called their second honeymoon.

We got back very late to the lodgings. We were both

drunk. Camilla was noisy, giggling and falling over on the stairs. I tried to hurry her because I knew the landlady had a small child asleep on the ground floor. I pushed her up and across the landing and closed the door behind us. There was a double bed. Camilla collapsed onto it and then leant over and rummaged in her big white bag. She pulled out a bar of chocolate, a packet of Fig Rolls and some Pringles. She started eating these, quickly, stuffing them all into her mouth together. 'Aren't you hungry?' she asked.

I was used to her binges. I'd been starving earlier, but I'd got beyond the point where it was possible to eat. 'It's two o'clock.' I opened my rucksack then disappeared into the bathroom to take out my contact lenses and brush my teeth. I had a long thick nightie with sleeves, because the nights had been chilly. Before I put this on, I sprayed some deodorant under my arms.

Suddenly, she burst into the bathroom. She was naked. She knelt in front of the toilet, put her fingers in her mouth and was sick. This seemed to go on and on, even after she'd brought everything up. She was crying. 'I'm sorry,' she said, standing up, then pushing me aside.

I stood by, helplessly. She rinsed her face with cold water, dried herself and went back to the bedroom.

I flushed the toilet and wiped the seat. I gathered together my clothes. Camilla was spread across the bed, uncovered and unconscious. Her things were thrown on the floor and the light was still on. I picked up her dress and hung it on a hanger. I covered her with the duvet.

I tried to sleep on the edge of the bed. Her breathing was heavy and regular. I lay in the dark, listening to it. I was aware of her warmth, the sourness of her breath, and the faint animal smell coming from her unwashed skin.

I arrived at the funeral on time, but the church was already full. I stood at the back, trying to see who I knew. Josh and Pip were there, and some models from the agency. Josh was standing very erect, glancing around. He had a little smile on his face, as if he thought people were looking at him. He was wearing a black suit. Pip looked the same as usual.

The police inspector bowed his head. I recognized him from the TV news. The young officer who'd taken the video from me, at the station, was at his side. I wondered if they were looking for the murderer in the congregation, like on television.

Peter was at the front with the family. He seemed nervous and kept looking at his watch. The organ started playing in a sombre way. The coffin was below the altar, half hidden by candles and tiers of purple and red flowers. All around the walls were plaques and inscriptions. The name Harding was mentioned more than once.

The vicar started to speak. I couldn't concentrate on his words. I felt too hot in my sweater and jacket and my head swam. I heard the door creak. Someone joined me at the back and I turned to look. It was the man who'd played darts with Camilla on that last night. He stood very near me, leaning on the back pew. His eyes were fixed on the coffin.

I peered at him again. Sean was handsome, a little smaller than me, and stocky, with broad shoulders. His hair was long, with bleached highlights. He was wearing jeans, a nylon bomber jacket and lots of gold rings. His body and his hair reminded me of Darren Peacock. I tried to picture him in the black-and-white football strip, and thought about how I'd introduced him to Camilla, months before. I recalled him coming into the Advice Centre and nonchalantly sitting in my chair.

The vicar started praying. I forced myself to listen to the singsong righteous tones. Nothing he said, nothing in the church seemed to have anything to do with Camilla. After about fifteen minutes, I decided to wait outside. I didn't like the religion and the smell of Sean's aftershave was making me feel faint.

It was a dull, cloudy day, not quite cold. The wind released a shower of dead leaves from the trees in the churchyard. The drunken gravestones were covered in moss. In a corner there was some green baize flapping over newly turned earth, beside a dark hole in the ground.

A group of undertakers stood under a tree. They were sharing a cigarette. I went up to them. I pulled myself to my full height and stood, hands on hips. 'Did any of you see her?' I asked.

There was a silence. They shuffled and looked at their feet.

Anger flared up. 'I wanted to see her. What did she look like?'

One of them whistled under his breath. I stared at their tall hats which were in a row on top of a car. 'She was peaceful, miss,' said the oldest of them. His face was creased in permanent sadness. 'She was beautiful.'

'I wanted to see her,' I repeated. I sounded gruff and aggressive. I went and stood away from them, half hidden in a corner beside the wall, kicking a stone in my path.

After a while everyone came out and stood in huddles

around the grave. No one seemed to notice me. I kept apart from the crowd.

The long-haired latecomer also stood alone, by the wall. I went over to join him. 'Hello, Sean.'

He was startled. He took a step backwards but then tried to reassume a confident slouch.

'Remember me?'

We looked at each other but he didn't reply.

'I bet you weren't invited.'

Abruptly, he turned and walked towards the road.

'Neither was I,' I called.

He had a taxi waiting. In a few seconds he'd disappeared.

A new thought came into my mind. I wondered if he'd killed Camilla. She told me she'd thrown him over. She said he'd kept ringing her and banging on her door in the middle of the night.

I went back to my corner and watched the coffin being lowered into the hole. People were crying. I tried to imagine Camilla inside the box, with her eyes shut. I thought about her underneath the earth. A fleeting image of her dead body passed through my mind but I couldn't hold it. Nothing seemed real. I felt like an extra in a film.

When it was over some mourners left and walked in the direction of the village. I didn't speak to anyone. I held back. Camilla's friends from London didn't notice me and got into their own cars and drove away. Josh and Pip left together. I saw Penny depart with a tall man who might have been a TV newsreader. The policemen talked to the vicar. Peter ushered those remaining into funeral cars. These were the guests going back with the family. They weren't people from London. I got into a black Bentley with two middle-aged women and a child. I felt it was important to go to the house, find out what it was like, look for clues. I stared out of the window. On the short journey one of the women talked about Camilla and loose living up in London.

Camilla had told me she'd been brought up in the country. I expected a tumbledown old cottage with roses around the door. I was ready for chintz curtains, a real fire, a field out the back, with cows.

The line of cars swept down a wide avenue and pulled up in a swirl of gravel. I looked up at the house and was reminded of places I'd visited as a child, with my parents, where we'd paid to get in. It was huge. Rows of leaded windows glittered in the disappearing light. Two lions stood to attention on either side of the steps. On the door was a wreath, but it wasn't a Christmas one with holly and suchlike. It was made of white, waxy lilies and black ribbons.

Inside, maids from a catering firm handed us glasses. I stood by myself. With the exception of Peter, there was no one I knew. I seemed to be amongst relatives and county gentry who were friends of the family. I knocked back several sherries.

The room was like a library, lined with books on three walls. The fourth was oak panelled and hung with oil paintings. There was a smell of wax polish and wood-smoke. A grand piano stood in one corner. I tried to imagine Camilla sitting at the piano, or in a window seat, reading one of the leather-bound books. I studied some photographs arranged on a small table. One was a four-teen-year-old Camilla, with a boy who was probably her brother. I spotted him leaning against the mantelpiece. I remembered Josh's comment. St John Harding was not even half as good looking as his sister. He was balding and overweight and there was a shaving rash on his neck.

'Hallo, Imogen,' said Peter, 'I don't think you were expected.' He didn't smile. He looked elegant and expensive.

I felt bulky in my inappropriate clothes, like a tourist. 'You could have told me,' I said coldly, 'about the service.'

There was a movement into an adjoining room. An oval table was piled with food. Everyone started eating sandwiches and chicken legs and grabbing wine off passing trays. There was a certain amount of hearty laughter from older men. Women twittered and rattled their jewellery.

I drank more wine. I didn't want to eat. Feeling a little lightheaded, I went up to Camilla's brother and a waitress handed me another glass. 'She ought to be here,' I said to him. 'She'd have loved this.'

'What?' he asked, surprised. He took a step backwards, as if I was dangerous. He looked up at me, warily. He was surprisingly short, with small eyes and a disappointed mouth.

'I was just thinking about her,' I said, 'sitting at the piano.'

'Oh, she didn't play,' he replied, flustered. He was looking at my leather jacket. I noticed that his teeth were good, like hers. 'We both had lessons, of course, but she never got the hang of it.' He eyed me suspiciously. 'I'm sorry, do I know you?'

I took yet another glass of wine and swallowed it down. 'No,' I said, 'I'm a gatecrasher.'

He didn't smile. He looked offended. He clearly lacked Camilla's sense of irony, as well as her looks.

'We were very good friends,' I added, trying to sound friendly.

'It sounds like you're from Tyneside.' His eyes became focused on the tiny silver hammer and sickle in the side of my nose. 'I work up there. For my sins.'

The waitress refilled my glass.

He was looking over my shoulder, wanting to get away. 'I have a house in London, of course. Finsbury Park.'

I smiled.

'D'you know Gosforth? I've a *pied-à-terre* near The Grove. Do you know . . . ?'

'Nah, not me,' I interrupted, broadening my accent. I deliberately prodded inside my nostril with my little finger. 'I'm from Walker. The other side of the tracks.'

I sat down for a while on a tiny hard chair, listening to different conversations. Nobody mentioned Camilla.

'You've not had anything to eat.' A silver-haired woman in a tight black dress offered me a plate of food.

'I've got no appetite,' I told her.

'You must be Imogen,' she said. 'Camilla's lawyer friend.'

I was surprised. 'Sort of,' I replied.

'Peter just told me. I believe you telephoned.'

I guessed this was Camilla's stepmother. 'You're Mrs Harding?'

She smiled, thinly.

'Did Camilla ever mention me?'

'No.'

I stood up. My arm jogged a tiny table and a bowl of

peanuts cascaded onto the floor. One of the hired maids came over and started picking them up.

'I'm sorry,' I muttered. I felt big and clumsy. Camilla's stepmother reminded me of an ageing former ballerina I'd seen interviewed on television. She was graceful, with delicate hands.

'I'm Camilla's best friend.' My voice sounded very Northern but also distant, as if it was coming from a long way off. I'd had nothing to eat and I felt drunk. I wondered if I was going to be sick. Mrs Harding and I looked at one another in silence. Her hair was starting to escape from its bun and her face looked lopsided. She swayed slightly. She was drunk, too.

'I'm going to the lav,' I said, and made for the door. It was cold in the hall. I leaned my head against the banister. After a few deep breaths I felt better. Pine needles were scattered on the polished floor. There had been a Christmas tree, but it had been taken down. I remembered why I had come. I climbed the wide curving stairs two at a time.

There was a corridor at the top, and rooms with closed doors. It seemed smaller than it had looked from the outside, but I still imagined red cords strung between posts, keeping visitors off the furniture. I walked along until I came to another, narrower staircase.

On the top floor, I realized I was in Camilla's part of the house. There was a huge attic bedroom with a four-poster bed draped in lace. I went inside. I wanted to look for clues. I wanted to find out more about her life.

Dresses were tossed on the bed, and underwear. The sun came out and a dormer window filled the space with light. Under it, and around, plants grew up the walls. I looked out at a garden and beyond were misty woods and hills.

I sat down at her writing desk and stared at a toy rabbit propped in one corner. The polished floor had a threadbare Oriental rug. Her dressing table was strewn with bottles and open jars and used tissues. In the corner was a rocking horse. A pile of wrapped Christmas presents lay in a heap. I knew she came back here regularly. There'd obviously been a recent visit.

I noticed a photograph at the side of the bed and crossed the room to have a look. It was some elderly people, probably grandparents, who I hadn't seen downstairs. They were leaning, with a picnic hamper, against an old black car.

I lay down on the bed placing my head in the hollow of the pillow and held one of her dresses to my face. It smelled of her perfume. I thought again of the night in Bristol, when we'd slept in the same bed. I rolled over and buried my head in the sheets. They weren't clean. They had a sour, sweaty odour. I rubbed my face on the bedclothes, hoping that the smell of Camilla's body would stay with me.

I think I slept for a while. When I opened my eyes I thought about how I could no longer ring her, or meet her in the pub, or call round to Josh's with a bottle of wine. I sat up. There was more of Camilla here than there was in her room in London. I wondered why.

I noticed an old briefcase at the side of the bed. Its handle was broken, but she had fixed a belt to it, making a shoulder strap. I started stuffing things into it. These weren't clues, or even mementoes, but I wanted to squeeze something, anything that was Camilla into the bag, and take it away with me.

I picked things up at random: papers, books, clothes. I filled the case and forced it shut. I really wanted everything – the furniture, the wallpaper, the view from the window. I wanted Camilla back.

'What the hell are you doing?'

I jumped with fright and turned to the door.

It was Peter. 'You've absolutely no right to be here.' His voice was icy.

I tried to smile. I eased the strap of the case over my shoulder. 'She was my best friend,' I said again.

He came into the room and took my arm. I was surprised. His fingers were tight and painful. He tried to pull me towards the door. He was smaller than me, and slender. I didn't like him touching me. I grabbed his wrist and wrenched him off. I pushed him away, roughly.

He staggered slightly, his balance lost.

'Are you the bouncer?' I demanded. I walked past him. I felt like hitting him. Shouldering the briefcase more firmly, I went out and along towards the stairs.

He called after me, 'Camilla had no time for women.'

I turned round. For a crazy moment I wondered if I could flatten him. 'Really? Is that so? She certainly didn't have much time for you.'

I went downstairs. In the hall, Camilla's father and stepmother were standing, staring, their arms linked. Their backs were against a grandfather clock. No one spoke. I went outside and the lobby door banged behind me.

The funeral cars had gone. There was no one about. I went round the side of the house and into a cobbled courtyard where lines of washing were strung. There was a potting shed and a row of outbuildings. Inside, I could see stalls and an iron manger. No horse appeared to have been stabled for a long time. I tried to imagine a young Camilla, astride a pony. She once told me that she'd loved her pony more than anyone else at home.

In the corner of the stables, I noticed a bicycle. It was a lady's model, old and a little rusty. I went in and tested the tyres. Surprisingly, they weren't flat. I wheeled it out and slung the briefcase around my neck. I rode the bicycle out onto the drive.

As I pedalled down the avenue, I gathered speed. I leant back in the saddle, reckless, my face turned upwards. There was a thin strip of light between the flashing branches. I called to Camilla and heard my voice rise up through the trees.

Chapter Eleven

I caught a train back to London. I put the bike in the guard's van, alongside some greyhounds in baskets on their way to Catford Stadium. When I got to Paddington I cycled, a little unsteadily, to the office. I propped up the bike in the waiting room.

'Where d'you get that thing?' asked Al, leaning in the doorway. 'It's crap.'

'I liberated it.'

'You mean you pinched it?'

'That's right.'

I avoided her eye. I decided to ignore the embarrassing turn of events of the previous evening.

The centre had just closed for the day and the work was piled up. I didn't care. I went over to the stationery cupboard and pulled out a new case file. On the front and on the spine I wrote Camilla Harding. Underneath, instead of Housing, or Employment or Benefit Claim, I wrote Murder. Inside, I filled in Camilla's name and address and a brief synopsis of the situation. I paused when I got to the typed subheading Action.

'Al?' I turned round.

There was a strong smell of varnish. She was painting her nails black.

'D'you remember a guy coming in earlier in the year?

Sean somebody. Tall, big shoulders, fair. Looks like Darren Peacock. He's a plasterer or something?'

She glanced over, then blew on her nails. Her desk was empty, apart from her make-up bag. She was preparing to leave. 'Who's Darren Peacock?' She walked over and switched on the PC, shoving in the disk that was used to store closed file names.

'You must remember him. Was it an Irish name? O'Neill? O'Connor?'

She kept the key pressed down, running a few names over the screen. 'Docherty,' she said finally, yawning.

I noticed a fake tattoo on her forearm as she shook her hands to dry her nails. It was a swastika.

'Sean Docherty,' she said. She glanced through the information on the screen. 'Employment case. You started it, then I took over when we realized it wasn't going to Tribunal. They settled. He did quite nicely out of it. Last February.' She ran a print-off then switched off the machine.

I looked at his reference number.

'What are you doing? Is that a new case?'

'Yes, it is.'

'Are you coming to the pub?' She'd forgotten I'd been to the funeral.

'No, I've got work to do. I'll lock up.'

She pulled on an old woollen poncho. As she left, I called her back.

'What?' she asked.

'That tattoo's not funny.'

'What d'you mean?'

'That tattoo on your arm. It's sick. It's not funny, right?'

*

I found Sean's folder in the filing cabinet. He'd been sacked by a building company and had claimed unfair dismissal. I'd started proceedings, but he'd agreed to accept £2,000 compensation and withdrew. At that time he'd been living in a hostel on Tower Bridge Road but Al had made some effort to get him a 'hard to let' council flat. I looked at my watch. It was five fifteen. I telephoned the local authority Housing Department and spoke to the clerk who was afraid of my telephone manner. 'I want his address,' I insisted.

There was some coughing and the tapping of keys. 'OK, Ms Webb,' she said. She seemed relieved that I wasn't harassing her about something difficult. She read out Sean's address, phone number and date of birth. He was two years younger than me. This meant he'd been two years younger than Camilla – thirty-three. I tried to picture his big hands around her neck. I remembered him, that final night, pretending to strangle her when they were playing darts. I wrote down all the information about him in the case file.

Sean lived on an unmodernized low-rise estate in Peckham. After work the next day I set off on the bike, down the Old Kent Road. I was steadier now, but with no lights I kept well into the side. It was raining and the cars were crawling along, churning up water. I was grateful for my leather jacket. I wished I had a hat. After a while the traffic stopped altogether, and drivers hooted angrily. I slipped by them, overtaking the vehicles and the even less fortunate people on the pavements, their heads bent against the drizzle and the fumes.

As I gained confidence in my cycling, pedalling rhythmically, I thought about being followed and frightened at the Elephant and Castle. The bicycle was the safest way to get around. I entered the estate, looping round the blocks like a professional. Most of the flats seemed boarded up. The council had erected some high, bright floodlighting in the courtyards and children were playing football. I parked the bike and tried to find Sean's number.

'Fifty pence to look after that,' called a little boy, running over. The ball followed him. I heeled it in then tapped it around his feet. Surprised, he tried to get it off me but I turned and dribbled it away. He ran up hard behind. I saw the goal, chalked on the pramsheds and was just about to take a shot but he was on me, suddenly, tackling hard, his leg between mine. In a second he'd lobbed the ball away and it was back among his cheering playmates. I bent over, winded. 'OK,' I said. 'Fifty pence. Where's number eighteen?'

Sean's door was on the ground floor and I rang the bell. A young woman appeared. She was wearing a thin blouse and she held the neck together as if she was cold. In her other hand was a cigarette. I noticed a wedding ring. I was still breathless. 'Hi,' I said, 'is Sean in?' I held out an Advice Centre card.

She beckoned me towards the hall. 'Close the door,' she said. She had an Irish accent. 'Have you come about the windows?'

I realized I was very wet and rubbed my face with my hand. I tried to smooth my hair back out of my eyes. My shoes squelched on the carpet.

The woman was pretty and pale and she dabbed at her red nose with a tissue. I saw that we were surrounded by plastic toys, a pushchair and a clothes horse draped in sheets. I could hear a baby shouting and the sound of children's TV.

'I'm from the Advice Centre. I'm glad you got rehoused.'

She looked at me, surprised. 'We're on the transfer list.' She pointed to a damp patch on the wall. 'I've got the flu. It's this place. Running it is. Soaking.'

I took in her straggly blond hair, her cheap, fashionable clothes, her bare legs, her tired eyes in a young face. 'Is your husband in, Mrs Docherty?'

'I'm Mary O'Dwyer.'

'Can I speak to Sean?'

'He's away to his work.'

'Where does he work now?'

She narrowed her eyes and puffed on her cigarette. 'Are you from the council or aren't you?'

'I'm from the Advice Centre. We helped him get his compensation.'

I saw the disappointment in her face. She told me the address of a construction site on the Isle of Dogs.

I handed her the Advice Centre card. 'Come in about your housing transfer. We're open on Monday.' I turned to let myself out. I heard the baby screaming and a toddler ran into the hall, grabbing her legs. He started crying too. I closed the door on the noise.

Outside, the footballers had gone, except for the boy guarding my bike. I gave him fifty pence. 'Are you a Palace fan?' I asked.

He nodded, spat on the coin and rubbed it on his sleeve. 'You effing social worker,' he said, 'you've got mud on your face.'

*

I cycled to the Tower and took the bike onto the Light Railway. It felt like Disneyland, high above the ground with no driver. We kept stopping for ages between stations. A uniformed woman got on board, shook her head and muttered into a portable phone. We stood motionless for fifteen minutes under Canary Wharf. 'Is this so I can admire the architecture?' I had to ask. There was a weight in my stomach. It was somehow connected with finding Mary in Sean's flat.

She shook her head. 'Bikes aren't allowed,' she told me. She handed me a tissue. 'You've got mud on your face.'

When I got off, I rode around amongst half-finished buildings. The tall cranes had flashing Christmas reindeer on the top, in lights. Even the council houses were being done up. I finally found the site where Sean was working and cycled towards some Portakabins. I saw him through the glass of a closed door, playing cards and drinking a mug of tea. His feet were on a table.

I propped up the bike. 'Hello, Sean,' I said, stepping inside.

Three men stared at me. I gazed back, biting the inside of my cheek. One of them sniggered and looked me up and down. 'You're a big girl,' he said. Another put aside his cards. There was a silence. Sean's mouth quivered with what might have been a smile. His two workmates stood up. 'We'll leave you to it, then,' one said, laughing. They went out, their boots clomping on the metal steps.

Sean was wearing a dusty white cap pushed back on his head. I tried not to look at the place where the buttons of his overalls were undone, showing his jeans underneath. He shuffled the pack of cards, lazily, then put them down again. He grinned. He had gold rings on five of his fingers and real tattoos on his wrists. He wasn't wearing the bracelet I remembered from the pub. Behind his head there were pin-ups on the wall.

'Do you remember me from yesterday?' My voice was a whisper from my tight throat. 'I was at the funeral.'

He pushed a chair towards me. 'You're wet,' he said. I rubbed my face. I hoped all the mud had gone. The heat from the Calor gas stove was making me steam. I sat down. 'I'm from the Advice Centre.'

'Mary phoned.' He pronounced it Marie. He pointed to a phone on the wall. 'She said she'd had a visit.' He smiled again, showing perfect teeth. 'Do all your punters get the personal touch?' He was looking me straight in the face. For a moment, I thought of my interview at the police station. Sean, like the policeman, had that direct gaze used by men who know they're attractive to women. A picture of him playing darts with Camilla formed in my mind. I remembered how, on that last night, they'd radiated the same blond glamour.

I swallowed. 'I haven't come about . . . '

'You've seen the flat.' He slapped his hand lightly on the table. 'We need rehousing.'

I raised my voice above a mutter. 'I've come about Camilla.'

His teasing smile vanished. He sat up in his chair. There was a pause. 'You didn't mention that to Mary?'

I shook my head. There was a longer silence. 'You were at the funeral,' I said. 'I saw you there.'

'Just paying my respects,' he replied. 'Nothing wrong with that.' He looked down, then his eyes flashed back up, suspicious.

I couldn't get rid of the image of him standing with

Camilla, in front of the darts board, his lithe body matching hers. Everyone had watched them flirt, that night, fascinated by their sex appeal. I took a deep breath. 'She gave you the big E, didn't she?'

He looked at the door, whistling under his breath. His assurance had vanished.

'She did, didn't she? She finished it.'

'Yeah, well, she had bigger fish to fry.'

'Have you talked to the police?'

He stood up. 'What is this?'

I felt threatened and stood up too. He stepped back, surprised. He was over six foot tall and clearly unused to feeling short.

'I don't buy this Whistler shit.' My voice was low. 'Someone else killed Camilla. I'm investigating her murder.'

His mouth dropped open, giving him a stupid look.

'You saw her the night she was killed. You were playing darts.' In my mind, I replayed the heavy swing of her hair, as she tossed it back, her narrow waist, and his arm raised to throw. Their identical smiles were only for each other.

He pulled a pack of Gauloises from the breast pocket of his overalls and offered me one. I shook my head. His hand was trembling as he clicked his lighter. 'It was no big deal,' he said, trying to regain his composure. 'It was just a bunk-up.' He paused. 'It wasn't even that. She went off somewhere Friday night and left me in the pub, on my own.' He coughed, embarrassed. 'Before that I hadn't seen her for weeks.' He thrust a thumb in a side pocket.

I remembered watching him with Camilla, as if they'd been actors on a stage. I'd wanted to be in their play. 'A bunk-up? Is that what you call it? What did Camilla call it?' I swallowed. 'What would Mary call it?'

He took a deep breath, then exhaled smoke. 'If you even think about bothering Mary . . . ' His voice was raised. 'She's had enough trouble—'

'I don't give a toss about Mary,' I interrupted. 'It's Camilla I'm concerned about. Did you kill her?'

He stared at me, looked up at the ceiling, then slumped down heavily in his chair. My words hung in the air.

'Don't be fucking stupid,' he said. He wiped his face with the back of his hand.

My heart was beating fast. 'I want to know who killed her.'

Outside, there was the sound of a fire engine in the distance and a cement mixer started turning. Sean produced a handkerchief and blew his nose.

'Where did you go after the pub?'

There was a silence. 'I was nothing to her. I hadn't been with her for weeks. I came up here afterwards.' He paused. 'This job's shifts. A three thirty start, like today, or ten thirty. She wasn't interested that night so I came on here, for overtime.'

'Have you spoken to the police?'

A faint tremor appeared in his cheek. 'No. No police. Keep the police out of this. We played darts. I came here. That's it.'

'You used to bother her.'

'Bother her? What d'you mean, bother her? What d'you want me to say? Some bastard's done her in. Whenever I gave her a bell, I was nowhere. She didn't want to see me. I just got that poofy bloke saying she was out.'

Suddenly I realized what it must have been like for

him. Camilla had toyed with him, then given him a hard time. She'd always been heartless with her cast-offs. I felt sorry for him and leaned forward to touch his arm. 'OK, Sean, I apologize.' My hand stayed on his sleeve. 'OK?'

He examined the contents of his handkerchief, then put it away. He grinned again. 'How about a drink?'

I could sense his relief. He swung his legs up onto the table again. I realized he was the kind of man who used his charm on women like a reflex. It was instinctive but it was also a weapon. His smile was irresistible.

'When?'

He deliberately ran his eyes over me. His look was approving and suggested desire. Camilla's ghost lingered at his side. 'Monday lunchtime,' he said. 'The same pub?'

I remembered again what she'd told me about him coming round and pestering her late at night. I knew I shouldn't agree to go out with him. I decided to stand him up. It would serve him right. 'Aren't slim blonds more your type?' I asked, moving towards the door.

He winked. 'I owe you one.' He buttoned up the flies of his overalls.

Chapter Twelve

I'd planned to do my Christmas shopping at the weekend but my heart wasn't in it. I woke up on Saturday morning, switched off the alarm and stayed in bed.

I thought about Sean and pictured his wide shoulders and the little scar I'd noticed, below his left eye. I tried to imagine him making love to Camilla in her room in Josh's flat. In my mind, they were alike, both blond, long-limbed and graceful. Their proportions were the modern ideal. Thinking about them, naked, was like a scene from a film.

I looked under the covers at my own body. I had an unfashionable hourglass figure, like a pneumatic fifties starlet, only bigger. My breasts were heavy, my hips wide. I stroked my flat stomach. My waist was small. Below, my pubic hair was black and unruly and my thighs were round and smooth.

I thought again of Camilla's lean frame, her delicacy. Sean couldn't possibly fancy me, I decided. I pictured them sharing a cigarette. Then I remembered that in terms of background they were as distant as the moon from the sun. Camilla might have looked more like his wife, Mary, I told myself, but I had the same kind of manners.

I let loose my imagination. I fantasized an image of

holding him, in a dark doorway, putting my arm round his waist. Soon, I felt his hard back, then his rough cheek against mine. In my mind, I pulled his body towards me and slipped my hand between his thighs. Aroused, he began kissing my neck and then my face, his arms wrapped around me. Then, as my lips lingered on his, it was all at once Camilla's mouth I tasted and Camilla's breath I breathed. She was embracing me, in his place. She felt warm. Startled by this sensation, my body became tense.

Only a day before, I reminded myself, Sean had seemed dangerous. I clenched my fists. I'd suspected him of being my friend's murderer and now she'd driven him from my thoughts. Camilla wasn't warm, or close to me, any more. She was dead. I turned over onto my stomach and buried my head in the pillow. I tried to force myself to cry but I couldn't manage it. My head was too full of strange, conflicting thoughts.

Later, I felt I had to progress Camilla's case, even though I wasn't at work. I wished I'd brought her case notes home. I decided to examine the things I'd taken from her parents' house. Before I opened the briefcase I got a pen and paper, intending to itemize everything inside.

First I pulled out a small toilet bag full of cosmetics. These were Leichner stage make-up and professional samples. More interesting was a well-thumbed address book. I quickly flicked through it. It wasn't Camilla's writing and there were no names I knew. They had been entered in red ink, with a fountain pen, and they were in small, cramped capital letters, totally unlike Camilla's flowing italic script. There were no addresses, only telephone numbers, and they were mainly London codes. Some were work numbers with extensions. It seemed likely that the book belonged to someone else in the family. I wondered if I should return it. This seemed tricky. I considered giving it to the police, but then I decided that they would just put it in the property cupboard with the video.

There was a silk camisole stuffed down a side pocket. It was cream and trimmed with lace and still had a trace of her scent. Wrapped inside was a pair of briefs slightly spotted with dried blood. There was also a chiffon scarf she'd probably used to tie up her hair in the shower. I held these in my hands for a while and thought how strange it was that the scent and the blood should still be there, even though Camilla was gone. I folded them and put them under my pillow. Methodically, I mentioned everything in my notes.

I pulled out a photograph album. I opened it in the middle and saw four childhood pictures of Camilla, two at school, the others with her family. The colours had started to fade to blue. I put the album to one side with the intention of studying it another time.

At the bottom of the case, screwed up small, was a dress. I shook it out. It was silk, very light and filmy, pale pinkish-grey with pearl buttons down the front. I slipped it over my clothes like a coat but couldn't fasten the buttons. It was much too small.

I found a Barclaycard statement from November, on which she'd scribbled *paid*. I was surprised to see that she'd owed more than four thousand. I ran my finger down the sheet. It was nearly all clothes. The amounts were large and they were from shops like Browns and

Issey Miyake. She'd bought underwear that had cost five hundred and fifty pounds.

I wrote *Visa?* on my list. Camilla had been more or less unemployed for months. She'd only worked for a few odd days. She'd scrapped her Fiat after it failed its MOT and she'd only eaten in restaurants recently if somebody else was paying. Despite her background and her wealthy parents, Camilla had been hard up all year. She'd asked me how to sign on the dole, although she'd never done it. This reckless shopping didn't make sense.

I thought about her clothes. She was always beautifully dressed, in a careful Sloaney way, although sometimes she wore things too many times without washing them. Camilla wasn't interested in street fashion. She said she liked my clothes, but that they weren't for her. I looked at the statement again. Her outfits had cost a fortune. I wondered where she'd got the four thousand pounds. I wrote *Peter*, and then a row of question marks.

The briefcase also contained a letter from her grandfather about the weather and her granny's arthritis. There was a list of reminders. It said *phone florist, book manicure, Apex ticket* and *B'card tomorrow*. There was a number for her brother, in Newcastle, and the words *direct line*. There were also two addresses. One was for a cleaning agency in Dulwich and another, headed *Gerard*, was in the East End.

There were two postcards. The palm tree and deserted white beach was from Peter in the Seychelles. I remembered him going last spring. He'd written 'My Precious, you really should have come. Weather etc. lovely, but I'm missing you and counting the days. Meet me at Heathrow? Car keys in usual place. All my love, P.'

Camilla had been on holiday with Peter in the past

but on this occasion she'd refused to go. She told me that two weeks listening to him going on about work, without a break, was unbearable. She said she didn't like the beach, with the sand and people frying like sausages, because it was bad for her skin. She spent most of the two weeks shut up in her room in Camberwell, with another man. That's what she told me afterwards. I wondered if it had been Sean.

The other was a birthday card from me. It was a painting. I turned it over and read *Seurat - Bathing at Asnières*. It had holes in the corners which meant she had once pinned it on the wall. Inside I had written: *To Desdemona, love from Imogen*. These names had been a joke when we were students. Imogen wasn't my real name but it had stuck. Camilla had described Imogen as 'gloriously inappropriate'. Despite this, I'd been known as this in London, for the last twelve years.

I finished making notes. Camilla had been dead eight days. I remembered reading that most murderers are caught within a month, before the trail turns cold.

I took the birthday card into the kitchen and pinned it on my noticeboard. I leaned against the wall for a while looking at it, remembering the old days when we'd found ourselves next door to each other in university hall. The very first time we met, Camilla said, 'Listen to you. You're a proper Northerner. Does your mother wear a pinny and curlers in the street?'

'Clogs and a shawl,' I told her, 'what about yours?'

'Designer sportswear,' she said, 'probably. I don't know. She pissed off with her tennis coach when I was tiny.'

'I'm sorry,' I said, taken aback.

She yawned and stretched her long, pale arms. We

were friends from that moment. We were impressed by each other. We made each other laugh.

I picked up the stage cosmetics again and took them over to a mirror. My face looked white and pinched. Camilla had introduced me to people at university. I was awkward about my accent and my manners and, in those days, my height. She'd eased the way for me through college. She did the same in London. I didn't have much of a social life, but what I had, I owed to her.

I opened a tube of greasepaint and stroked deep-beige stripes across my forehead and cheeks. I coloured my lips pale pink and drew blue lines under my eyelids. I twirled round in Camilla's too-small silk dress and ran my fingers through my dirty hair until it stuck up like a clowns. Taking off the dress, I draped it across the back of the settee. I stood in front of my poster of Warren Barton. He grinned at me, amused. 'Life is shit,' I told him.

I decided Camilla's spending habits might have a bearing on the case. I read the Barclaycard statement several times. I looked up Peter's number in the directory and phoned him.

'It's Imogen,' I said, 'don't hang up. I'm coming over. There's something I want to ask you.'

'Ask me now.'

'No, I'm coming over, OK?'

Chapter Thirteen

Peter lived in a part of South London that had always been expensive. The houses were old with long gardens, shaded by trees. His was one of the smaller ones, tucked away in a little cul-de-sac. I'd been before. Camilla used to invite me after the pub, and there'd been parties. Once I'd been there when Peter was in New York. Camilla made herself at home. We watched Robert de Niro videos and she kept opening bottles of vintage wine from the cupboard under the stairs.

As I wheeled the bike up the front path, security lights came on. I noticed a camera above the front door. I rang the bell and Peter appeared. 'I didn't know you had a bike,' he said. He helped me lift it into the hall.

Peter was slim, dark and elegant. His suits and shirts looked handmade. His face was handsome, pale, a little gaunt and his hair frequently fell forwards in a boyish way. Until the scene at the Hardings, after the funeral, I had only ever seen his perfect manners, his self-control. I knew he never laughed.

I followed him upstairs and we went into the big room that ran across the front of the house. It had floor-to-ceiling windows and a marble fireplace. There was no fire. I wondered why he'd brought me in here. I knew he rarely used this room and I could hear his CD player downstairs. I felt goose pimples on my arms as he pulled the velvet drapes, shutting out the dismal night. I buttoned up my jacket.

'Can I get you a drink? Or tea? Are you allowed to drink and ride a bicycle?' He seemed embarrassed.

'I'll have a beer.'

'Hang on, there's one in the fridge.' He disappeared.

The kitchen was two floors down in the basement. I looked around the room. The polished surfaces were uncluttered apart from a few pieces of porcelain. There was a large painting above the fireplace and an ornate gold clock. I walked over to a mirror. With a shock, I saw that I still had two stripes of Camilla's stage make-up across my cheeks. I looked like a Red Indian. I tried to rub them off with the back of my hand.

I noticed a row of invitations on the mantelpiece. They were all old and were obviously there as keepsakes. One was from the Duke of Northumberland and another was from Elton John.

The phone rang downstairs. I went out onto the landing and heard Peter say, 'Yes, we've had the funeral.' He paused. 'Right, if you hang on I'll go and get it.'

I listened in case he was coming back up, and decided he wasn't. I crossed the landing, opened the door of his study and went inside. Turning on the light, I saw a framed photograph of Camilla on his desk. There was a smaller snapshot propped against his Apple Mac. On the wall was a large oil portrait of a younger Peter with a gun and a Labrador.

I turned over some papers with his firm's letterhead. They were about publishing contracts. There was no time to have a proper look around, but I pocketed the smaller photo. It was of the two of them sitting on a lawn, in deckchairs, drinking wine. They were both squinting at the sun. It was probably Oxford. In those days, when Peter was a student, Camilla was still at school. She told me they'd always been friends.

I went back into the drawing room, and seconds later heard his feet on the stairs. 'You're in luck,' he said, handing me a Carlsberg.

'Is that a print?' I pointed to a small painting near the door.

He looked nervous and wary. He didn't ask me to sit down.

'The Canaletto? Actually it's a fake, but it's a good fake, don't you think? The one above the fireplace is genuine.' He paused. His voice sounded even more clipped than usual. 'It's a Matisse.'

He opened a cabinet and poured himself a whisky. Then he crossed the room and stood with his back to the empty fire, as if warming himself. His hair was combed back and was unusually greasy. He was paler than ever and there were bruiselike shadows under his eyes. He was wearing a soft rosy sweater and jeans. His slippers had a hole in one toe.

'To Camilla,' I said, raising my can. Tears sprang to my eyes and I saw him notice them. I blinked them away. My free hand was a fist and my nails cut into the palm. I looked at a chair but didn't feel I could sit, uninvited. My legs felt tired from cycling.

He straightened up, standing stiffly, his legs apart, one hand behind his back, the other holding up his drink. He looked up at me, then fixed his gaze on my left shoulder. There was a silence. He stood like his father would have done and his grandfather. He was cold and cut off and I thought of Prince Charles.

'I haven't come for an apology.' My words seemed to echo in a vulgar, Northern way around the grand, uncomfortable room. My accent sounded very pronounced.

He raised his eyebrows. His lips narrowed to a soundless O.

I swallowed some beer and tried to soften my voice. 'Does she drink, Camilla's stepmother?'

He drew in his breath. 'Really,' he whispered. Then he added, 'We all drink too much. Don't we, Imogen?'

I fingered the stolen photo in my pocket. 'How are you coping?'

He ran his fingers through his hair. It was a question for which he would have no answer.

He sipped his whisky. 'What do you want?'

'I've been feeling really untogether,' I said, trying to appear open. 'I'm disorientated. Crazy. I've decided to investigate the case.' My words hung in the cold air, sounding naive.

He moved his eyes to my face but seemed impassive. 'The case?'

'Camilla's case. Her murder.'

'You mean professionally?'

I nodded.

'Whatever for? Do the police know?'

I took a deep breath. 'Yes. They do. Can I ask you some questions?'

He shrugged and glanced at his watch.

'When did Camilla last stay here?'

He sighed and sipped more of his drink. 'Wednesday night. We'd been to see *The Full Monty*.' His mouth narrowed for an instant. 'She'd already seen it, but she wanted to go again.'

123

'Did the police tell you what he did to her?'

He winced but answered unemotionally. 'She was knocked down with a heavy blow, then strangled.' He went back to the drinks cabinet. His hand shook slightly as he poured another whisky. 'He strangled her with his scarf. It was a football scarf.'

My legs were suddenly too weak to hold me. I could feel my heart beating. I swallowed some beer and sat on the arm of a chair. 'I don't think the Whistler did it.'

He stared at me and frowned. 'Of course he did it. The police are in no doubt. There's a pattern. He took that big white bag. The one with all her model's gear in. Apparently, he always takes their bags. He also does this bizarre thing with perfume.' He sipped more whisky. There was a break in his voice. 'God, I hope they get him soon. If only I'd taken her to the party. I should have kept her with me . . . '

'She was playing darts.'

His eyes met mine. 'Yes, of course. I'd forgotten. You were there.'

'You were angry with her. Did you have a row on Wednesday night?'

He was startled and I thought he blushed slightly. He took a deep breath. 'I know Camilla may have told you things,' he said, 'but you know how she used to exaggerate. We were engaged. Our mothers are old friends. Everything was fine between us.' He put his glass on the mantelpiece.

'But you had a row?'

He looked down and then decided to stop pretending. 'Yes, as a matter of fact we did. It makes it even more painful.'

'You rowed about Sean.'

He glanced at me. 'About lots of silly things. I think she invited him along that night to pay me back.' Suddenly I could sense his pain. 'God, Imogen, can you imagine how I feel?' For the first time, I felt he was talking to me, rather than using rehearsed phrases. He picked up his glass, finished his second drink, then replaced it. He fished in his sleeve for a handkerchief.

'When were you planning to get married?'

'Soon. Very soon.' He held the handkerchief, folded, to his nose.

There was a silence. I knew that Camilla had never intended marrying Peter. We had talked about it many times and even on that final evening it was clear she was keeping him dangling. I looked at Peter's sad, guarded face and I suddenly felt sorry for him. I wondered if he'd been able to cry when he was on his own. 'Look, Peter,' I said, 'I hope you don't mind me asking you this, but did you give Camilla money?'

'Money? She had her own money.'

'She was mostly unemployed.'

'Her father gave her an allowance. What is this Imogen? It can't be relevant . . . ' He paused. 'Did she owe you money? Is that the problem? Is that why you're here?'

'Did you pay off her Barclaycard?'

'No, I did not. She didn't need . . .'

'She seemed to be spending a lot recently.'

'What d'you mean?'

'On clothes and things.'

He thought about this, then gave a short laugh. He rubbed both hands back across his hair. 'Clothes!' I felt him relax. 'She was always one for clothes.'

'More than usual. I mean really spending.'

125

He composed his face into a thoughtful expression but I felt that he was humouring me. 'Well, now you mention it, I did pay for a few things. She used my Selfridges account.'

'No, I don't mean that. I'm talking about Bond Street. Paris designers.'

'What are you suggesting?' He smiled. 'She needed to look good, you know. It was her job to look good.'

I realized that for someone as rich as Peter, discussing money was a pointless exercise. As far as he was concerned, if you wanted something you bought it, and if you had a problem, money was the answer. 'You never talked about money? With Camilla?'

'No. I don't think we ever did.'

'Never?'

'It just wasn't an issue.'

'Did you pay off her Barclaycard recently? Four thousand pounds?'

'No, I don't think so. I've already told you . . .'

I walked over to the fake painting and pretended to examine it.

'What exactly are you getting at, Imogen?' He sounded baffled.

'I've told you. I'm looking into this case. It wasn't the Whistler. Somebody was copying him, that's all.' I turned to face him. 'I think I better get going.' I drained my can and handed it to him. 'Thanks for the drink.'

He was relieved. He led the way downstairs and unlocked the door. I bumped the bike down the steps. I turned to face him. Back-lit in the doorway he seemed vulnerable and alone.

'I miss her,' I said.

'I loved her,' he replied.

I climbed on the bike and freewheeled down the path and out into the road. The gassy lager regurgitated into my mouth. I heard his door slam closed.

A burglar alarm was sounding on the corner and a police car screeched up, almost dismounting me. A group of teenagers swore and jostled each other, moving away as the police approached them. A woman ran from a driveway, sobbing, clutching a small child and jumped into the back of the car. It wasn't clear what was going on, but I didn't care.

I pedalled away, thinking about Peter's grief and bottled-up emotions. I'd gone to see him wondering if he'd killed Camilla in a jealous rage about Sean. This didn't seem likely. He was so self-contained he was like a waxwork. Then I remembered his loving postcard, his looks of longing for Camilla that last night in the pub. I couldn't rule him out of my enquiries. He was a rich, powerful, protected man. He was used to having his own way. She'd probably been the only person in the world who'd ever dared to mess him around.

I cycled quickly through the dark streets. A slight drizzle began falling, making the road greasy. I heard the purr of a car behind me and moved closer to the side. The edge of the gutter was rutted and broken. The car roared and accelerated, but instead of giving me a wide berth, it veered towards the pavement. I felt my wheel hit the kerb as the side of the car brushed my leg. Losing control, I tumbled, almost slowly, over the handlebars and landed heavily on a grass verge. I lay on my back for a second, winded, staring at the orange light pollution in the clouds. I groaned and stood up, hoping there was no dog shit on my clothes. The car was in the distance. I could see its red tail spots and the flash of an indicator. As it turned left it was illuminated by the window of a takeaway. It was a silver-blue convertible. I wondered if it was Peter's Saab.

Chapter Fourteen

I lay in bed on Sunday morning, trying to read the papers. It was only seven o'clock, but I'd woken early and couldn't doze. I kept returning to a feature on the Walworth murders with photographs of all the victims. There were also three pictures of women from Manchester who'd been killed four years earlier. The Met claimed to be 'cooperating and liaising' with their Northern colleagues because of 'similarities' in the psychological profiling of the killer.

Of the nine women in the pictures, six were described as prostitutes. The other victims, including Camilla, were placed separately on the page and described as 'innocent' and 'ordinary' women. Camilla possessed neither of these qualities. I wondered about the value judgements of journalists. She'd never played by the rules. If they knew her true nature, her recklessness and her glamour, they might put her with the whores – deserving of her fate.

I tossed the paper on the floor. For a while, I stared at the ceiling. Upstairs, my neighbour was noisily making love. I thought about Sean again and tried to imagine him as the Whistler, his head full of hate, stalking women. This brought to mind the shadowy figure who'd chased me at the Elephant and Castle. I decided he was probably a copycat; a sad case who'd decided to jump on the band-wagon. London was full of nutters, I reminded myself.

Judging by the photographs in the paper, the real serial killer on the loose in Walworth hated blonds, especially young, frail-looking blonds. He wasn't interested in tall, broad-shouldered women with leather jackets and jeans.

I thought again about my belief that the Whistler hadn't killed Camilla. Physically, she was like the other victims, but I was still sure he wasn't her murderer. It was instinct, based on my understanding of her invulner-ability. It was also mixed up with guilt.

I'd wished a hundred times that I'd followed up Cam-illa's comment that somebody was frightening her. She'd said this very clearly on that last Friday. Her anxiety echoed in my mind. She'd said, 'Someone I know is trying to scare me,' and then, 'Someone's threatening me. He wants to hurt me. Someone I know.' I struggled to recall the exact words. She'd said, 'Don't worry. I know who it is.'

I wondered if this had been a cry for help. I should have asked her, been more supportive. I wished I'd ques-tioned her. I might have been told the killer's identity. Instead, it was a chance remark, blown away in the city wind.

When I got up, I decided to paint my living room. I thought it would fill the time. The paint was called Carib-bean Mango and I chose it because I liked the name. It had sat with a paintbrush and some sandpaper in a carrier bag in the kitchen for almost three months.

My experience of decorating was limited. Full of

energy, I moved the furniture and rolled back the carpet.
I started slapping paint over the sprigged, flowery wallpaper. It was Laura Ashley nostalgia and I'd disliked it
since moving in. I turned up my cassette player really
loud. I listened to the Cranberries a few times and the
Pogues and something really old and depressing by Roy
Harper. After two hours my right arm was aching so
much it was almost numb and I was exhausted.

The phone rang. It was Josh. Pleased, the thought
passed through my mind that despite Camilla's death I
might still have friends in London.

He said he'd finally heard he'd got the part in *Coronation Street*. His agent had rung him at six in the morning.
He'd already heard his audition and screen tests had been
a success, but the final decision had been taken in a
Manchester nightclub in the early hours. He said the
casting director was worried about the fact that he was
gay. He'd promised to keep it quiet. 'I'm going to be a real
telly star! It's the perfect Christmas present.' He sounded
excited and happy.

'I saw you at the funeral,' I said.

There was a silence. Josh coughed. 'We didn't see you
there. Pip and I were surprised. We wondered about
you.'

'I was right at the back.' I felt uncomfortable. I hadn't
talked to them at the service, and now I was failing to
sound pleased enough about the TV role. 'I'm very happy
for you,' I said. I sounded awkward. I remembered the
uncomfortable visit I'd paid him recently. 'I thought you
were going to read, at the ceremony.'

He was suddenly huffy. 'I wasn't asked!' He sniffed.
'I offered, of course.' He addressed someone else in the
room. 'We were wrong, Imogen was at the funeral.'

'Who's there with you? Pip?'

'Yes.'

'I went back to the Hardings' house.'

There was a long pause. 'Did you? Imogen, did you really?'

As I expected, he was impressed. His voice became muffled again. 'Guess what? She went back to the Hardings' house!'

'I sort of barged in.'

'What was it like? Fabulous, I expect.'

'Peter practically threw me out.'

'Georgian, isn't it? It was on the box.'

'I went to look for clues.'

'Clues?' There was another silence. 'What for?'

'I don't think the Whistler did it.'

His voice was muffled. 'She doesn't think the Whistler did it.' He came back on the phone. 'What exactly d'you mean, Imogen?'

'I told you. I don't think the Whistler did it. The police have got it all wrong.'

'You're potty, darling,' he said, sounding very camp. 'I've got to go.'

'Congratulations about the—' There was a click as he hung up.

Later there was a bulletin about the Whistler on TV. They showed a photofit compiled by witnesses who'd come forward to say they'd noticed whistling men, near the Elephant, around the day of Camilla's death. I realized the police must be desperate. They had no real leads. I studied the featureless face. He looked like a million people you see in the street every day of your life.

132

Photos of the nine women appeared. There was a shot of the Hardings' house, taken from the gates. I saw a back view of someone hurrying inside and then the door closed. All the curtains at the windows were drawn.

I drank a bottle of wine then forced myself to finish the decorating. The paint smell was making me feel sick. I decided not to bother with the gloss or the ceiling. Painting was only interesting for about twenty minutes. After that it was boring and a chore.

Later, unable to settle, I stripped down the bike in the hallway, cleaned and oiled it in appropriate looking places and repaired two slow punctures, using a kit I'd bought at Halfords. This proved to be easier than I expected, and I was pleased with myself. I knew the machine was old, but I was glad to have it. It had been Camilla's, and now it was mine.

Al phoned and asked if I wanted to meet for a drink, but I still didn't feel like going out. I kept thinking about the copycat creep who'd chased me down Blackfriars Road. It was safer in the flat.

I cleared the paint pots to the side of the room with the stepladders and dustsheets. I didn't tidy up, but took a long time to arrange my Newcastle United memorabilia on the mantelpiece and on the sideboard. When the walls were dry, I put my Peter Beardsley poster back up and rehung a canvas painted by my brother. I heated up a frozen pizza and took it to bed. It was still early.

I left my answering machine on, hoping that Sean might ring, but this was stupid because he didn't have my number. I wanted to go back to work, to progress Camilla's case. I needed to be in my office to feel in a professional frame of mind.

I had a portable TV in my bedroom. I was watching football highlights on Sky, in the dark, working my way through another bottle of wine, when there was a noise outside. I pressed the remote, extinguishing the sound. Someone was trying to force down the sash window of the bedroom. I slipped out of bed and pulled on my dressing gown. The squeak of the sash was unmistakable. There was a scrabbling noise and a thump of what sounded like a hand on the glass. The window wasn't giving. There were special locks screwed into the wood on either side.

I felt myself shaking. My mouth was dry. I stood behind the open wardrobe door, afraid to move or speak. There was a silence and then a terrible smash and splinter of breaking glass. My curtains blew inwards and the carpet was covered in shards.

My heart was jumping in my chest like an animal. I stood frozen to the spot, waiting for someone to appear through the curtains. There was no more noise except a couple of cars driving past in the street. The curtains continued to stir in the draught.

After a few minutes I crept over to the window. Trembling, I moved one curtain aside. There was no one there. The hole in the glass was quite small. I saw a stone on the floor and realized this had caused the damage.

I went into the kitchen and then the living room and peered outside. No one seemed to be lurking near the building. I swallowed half a glass of gin, neat, and swept up the glass in the bedroom. I stood in the bathroom for a while and allowed myself to cry. I took three Temazepam.

Half awake, I lay with my arms wrapped around my chest. Just before dawn, I drifted into sleep. I dreamed I was at a Christmas party, held on a small ship. Suddenly it listed, sank a little and went dark. People were screaming and cold water lapped my ankles as I struggled to find an open porthole or a door.

Chapter Fifteen

I woke late on Monday, with another bad headache. My chest burned with acid. I stood in the bathroom, resting my forehead on the cool tiles, wondering if I was going to be sick. My contact lenses were a struggle. I mixed two Resolves, using them to wash down aspirin. I swallowed an anti-depressant which I'd been saving for emergencies. My face, in the bathroom cabinet, looked bleary and old.

I inspected the damage to my bedroom window. In the light of day it seemed trivial. I stuck some cardboard over the hole and examined the locks. They were still secure. Thinking about the last few days, I decided I'd just been unlucky. I'd been followed by a drunk between bus stops, then knocked off my bike by a selfish bastard. Damage to my windows had happened twice before. Stockwell was full of vandals and opportunists. Drinking black instant coffee that tasted of burnt rubber, I wondered why I'd ever decided to come to London. The city seemed teeming with disaffected and antisocial misfits who made the quality of life, for everyone else, lower than low. I picked up the phone and used my Visa card to book a train ticket out of town for Christmas. Whatever happened, I needed a break.

There was a message on my answering machine. My stomach fluttered for an instant, thinking it might be

Sean, but it was Al. She said that she'd checked the Advice Centre constitution, phoned the chair of the management committee and they'd decided to give me compassionate leave. Annoyed, I slammed down the phone. I got dressed quickly and left without putting on any make-up. I cycled to Blackfriars Road, sweeping around the bends at the Elephant as if I'd been on two wheels all my life. When I arrived at the office, Al was pretending to tidy the leaflets.

'You don't get rid of me that easily.' I was surprised by the anger in my voice.

'I was only trying to be caring,' she replied.

I put the clues I'd gathered in Camilla's file. These were the address book with the unknown writing, the Barclaycard statement, the list and the snapshot I'd stolen from Peter's study. I took three sheets marked CASE NOTES and headed each with the names PIP, PETER and SEAN. I was just about to start writing when Al said, 'There's someone to see you. It's that Sean Docherty. He says it's personal.'

I sat for a moment, dismayed. I'd forgotten I'd agreed to meet him in the pub. Opening my drawer, I took out a small handmirror and looked at my blotchy, hung-over face. My hair was a mess. 'Al!' I shouted.

She lounged at the far end of the office, sucking a lollipop.

'Tell him I'm on the phone.' As she moved towards the waiting room, I called out, 'Al! Let me borrow your make-up.'

Her foundation wasn't pale enough but I smeared some on. I outlined my lips and eyes. I rubbed dollops of gel into the sides of my hair and combed them flat. The effect wasn't wonderful, but it was an improvement.

'What's the big deal?' asked Al as I left the office. She sounded huffy.

'Housing transfer,' I replied.

Sean half lay in a chair in a corner, surrounded by four old-age pensioners who were waiting for the afternoon advice session. He was wearing his white overalls and plasterer's cap and his boots were stained with powder. He was reading a newspaper which was folded in a narrow strip. When he saw me in the doorway, he stood, stepped over the pensioners' shopping bags, reached up and kissed me on the mouth. His lips were soft and a little damp. His breath smelled of chewing gum. 'We had a date,' he said.

I led him into the hallway where I'd parked my bike. I couldn't think of anything to say. It was too late to go to the pub. My lunch break was over and I didn't want Al thinking I was taking 'compassionate leave'.

'Where were you?

'I forgot. Sorry. How about later on?' I gestured towards the waiting room. 'I'm busy right now.'

'I've just come off shift. I'll go home and get my head down for a couple of hours. Four o'clock?'

'OK. I'll see you.' I watched him go and I realized I was excited. I could feel it, low down in my body, like an ache.

I spent the afternoon interviewing clients. The advice session was too busy to get back to Camilla's file. The couple without electricity came in, sitting doggedly in a corner. I made a few phone calls on their behalf and extracted some promises from clerks and officers. Reluctantly, they shuffled out, promising to return soon.

'I'm going to talk to Sean Docherty in the pub,' I said to Al, after the last clients had left. 'He needs help with a housing transfer.'

She smiled. 'Really?' she asked, her voice heavy with irony.

I felt myself blush.

'You can't fool me,' she continued, teasingly.

I gave her an angry glance and drew in breath, ready to defend myself.

'It's about Camilla,' she said, surprisingly. She tapped lightly on her keyboard and her printer started whirring. She stared at me, knowingly.

I turned my back and walked towards the door. 'I won't be long,' I muttered.

Sean was in the pub before me. He ordered me a lemonade shandy without asking me what I wanted. I stood at his elbow, slouching a little so we were nearer the same height. 'I'm not drinking that piss,' I said. 'Get me a pint of bitter.'

I sat down and slipped off my denim jacket. I eased a sculptured point of sticky hair down over one eye. I was wearing a tight grey boy's V-necked sweater which showed off my body. I tightened my belt a notch and smoothed the knees of my trousers. They were black drainpipes from a man's boutique in the King's Road. I'd thrown them on without thinking that morning, but it had been a fortunate choice. I knew that belted firmly they fitted me well.

Several people appeared at the bar, dressed as Santa Claus. They ordered whiskies and drank them through their fake beards. I watched Sean walk towards me holding our glasses. He had on a brown suede jacket with fringes, and jeans tucked into high boots. His hair was short and combed back at the front, but long at the back. He looked old-fashioned in a seventies kind of way, but he was so self-assured it didn't matter. Everything about his appearance suggested he really meant it. He was so handsome it was breathtaking.

'Dressed to kill,' I said, stupidly as he placed the drinks on the table. I felt myself blushing again.

A tableful of young women turned round and stared. They weren't giggling or passing comments. They were impressed. I realized I was out on a proper date.

'Well, here's to us,' he said. 'Cheers.'

I was never normally pursued by men. I was good-looking, when I made an effort, but I didn't fit any female stereotype. Long ago, I'd decided to stop buying women's clothes. They were overpriced, not warm enough and badly made. They didn't fit me. I wore men's shirts and sweaters, denim and leather, Levi's and chinos. I was curvy but not girlish. I was busty and big hipped without being fat but inches taller than everyone. My pale face had strong features – big nose, big eyes, big mouth, but with or without make-up it didn't normally invite sexual attention. As far as men were concerned, I seemed to give off the wrong signals. More often than not I saw them weigh up the shapeliness of my body against my towering height and my clothes and decide to leave me alone.

I had trouble fitting in. Most middle-class men found me gauche and blunt. Working-class men were intimidated by my education. In the past I'd dated left-wing has-beens who fancied me because of my accent and my job. Occasionally Camilla fixed me up with a photographer or a production assistant. Recently, I just hadn't met anyone. I was lonely and frustrated, much of the time.

Sean's interest was surprising. I couldn't think of a thing to talk about, but I remembered the blank sheet of paper in Camilla's file. 'Is this the pub where I introduced you to Camilla,' I asked, 'when we came to celebrate your compensation?'

'Yeah, that's right. And I never thanked you. About the compensation, I mean.' He winked.

I was fiddling with a beer mat and he put his fingers on mine. I looked down. The back of his hand was covered in wiry hairs and gold rings. His wedding finger sported a signet ring with a diamond. 'No, I'm not married,' he said.

I thought uneasily about Mary, back at his flat, and the children.

The Santas at the bar finished their drinks, shouldered their sacks and left. As they went out, one of them turned, saluted everyone in the room and called out, 'Ho, ho, ho!'

I drank my beer. 'You played darts with her, that last night. You were what my mam calls a handsome couple.'

He lit a cigarette.

'How many months had it been going on?'

He inhaled deeply, as if irritated. 'I told you. We were finished. Look, what d'you want me to say? What's done is done. Don't keep raking it up.'

For some reason, I suddenly didn't want to get sidetracked. I wanted some information to get me started on my case. I'd begun by asking about Camilla, and I felt I couldn't stop. I wanted some real notes inside the file. 'Where did you go, the two of you? Her room in Camberwell? Your place wouldn't have been too convenient with Mary and the kids around, would it?'

He stood up and went back to the bar.

'It's my round,' I called out, but he ignored this.

He returned with more beer. 'Drop it, will you?' he said again.

I changed tack. 'I'm sorry,' I said, 'it's just that I can't get it out of my mind. I'm upset.'

He picked up his drink, swallowed half of it and suppressed a burp.

'She was my best friend.' Saying this made me want to cry again, as if the words acted as a kind of trigger.

He took another drag on his cigarette. 'I wouldn't have thought that you had much in common.' His cockney accent suddenly disappeared.

I drank more beer and considered the ebb and flow of his London drawl. I wondered what his history was, whether or not he came from Ireland. He could be like me, I thought, away from home, unsure of his identity. Or he might be exaggerating his accent to try to impress me. I decided that he couldn't quite place me. He knew I wasn't upper class like Camilla, but I was professional in his eyes, and college educated. He wasn't sure if he should play up being a workman, or play it down. He didn't know if I'd go for the working-class-hero image, which had appealed to Camilla.

'We were students together,' I said.

'Where?'

'At university.' I tried not to sound smug.

There was a pause. 'I went to the LSE.'

I couldn't hide my shock. I spilled some of my beer. 'Oh,' I stuttered, 'when? I mean what . . .'

'International relations,' he said. He got up and put some money in a fruit machine.

I leaned back, trying to picture him in a tutorial, discussing the Austro-Hungarian Empire, or the Cold War. I struggled to imagine him in Senate House library, surrounded by piles of books. It was impossible. He was working on a building site. I'd assumed he had no education at all.

When he came back and sat down, I remembered that he was a suspect. I took a deep breath. I decided to test his reactions, look for signs of guilt. I told him what I knew about the Walworth Whistler. I described Camilla's death in the same words that Peter had used. 'She was knocked down with a heavy blow, then strangled. He took her model's bag. He does this bizarre thing with perfume.' I felt I was being a real detective. I watched him carefully, trying to judge if he was disconcerted, hearing my words.

He said, 'Women ought not to go out on their own.'

'Camilla went out on her own a lot,' I said. 'She always did.'

'She should have stuck to taxis. What did she think she was doing, that night?'

'She was a free spirit.'

'Well, look where it got her.'

I decided to try to lever his mask up further. 'He's probably somewhere near here right now,' I said, 'the Whistler. This is his patch. Whatever makes him do it, it'll be building up in him again right now. He's addicted to killing. It's like drink or crack, or sex. He likes the high. He has to do it again.' I stood up. Before Sean could stop me, I bought the next round.

He leaned back in his seat. 'You told me you thought the Whistler didn't do Camilla.'

I ignored this. 'They leave their marks,' I said, 'psychopaths. Each one has their trademark. The police never release those details.'

He stared at me, but his face was unreadable.

'Who did it?' I whispered.

'I wish I knew who did it.' He turned to me. 'I certainly didn't want her dead.' His voice was slightly slurred. 'We had a lot of unfinished business.'

I realized I'd sunk too much beer without eating any lunch and I was drunk. This made anything possible. I moved closer and put my arm around his shoulders. He hunched up, over his glass.

'She was beautiful,' I said. I hugged him towards me. 'Like an angel.'

We sat close for a while. I thought again about him having a degree. This made me value him in a different way and I wondered what it would be like to lie naked under him and let him inside me, in the same way he'd been inside her. The skin under his ear was soft, like a child's. He smelled of Obsession. I licked his neck and tried to imagine her tongue doing the same.

Suddenly he turned around and kissed me on the mouth. He forced his tongue between my lips. I remembered he might have killed Camilla. I jumped back, pushing him away.

I left abruptly and went back to the Centre. I felt dazed and cursed myself for drinking so much beer on an empty stomach. Once again, I told myself that I'd have to cut down on alcohol. I had work to do, and I wasn't properly in control.

Al had disappeared. She'd left an illegible note which said something about the Green Network. I pictured her lying down on a half-built bypass while her scruffy friends swung about in trees, like monkeys.

I left the answerphone on record and sat at my desk. Sipping scalding coffee, I prayed for my head to clear. I think I slept for a while. In the end I opened Camilla's file and tried to think logically. I wondered how the police were going about the investigation. They certainly weren't getting drunk on duty and almost getting into bed with their main suspect. They might not be making progress, but they would surely have a more professional approach. I decided to be more determined and more rational. I was always on top of things in the office but I seemed to fall apart outside. I promised myself I'd try harder.

I made notes about people's motives. On the page headed SEAN I wrote: *Infatuated and jilted. Feelings for Camilla possibly turned into anger and obsession. Bothered her late at night by banging on door and phoning. Working-class pride – wouldn't like a woman messing with him. Unfaithful to live-in partner, Mary. Jealous? Physically strong.* I thought for a moment and then added, *Well educated.* This still seemed inconceivable, and I wondered if he'd been lying. I continued writing: *Where did he go after the pub? Work? Need to check alibi.*

Under PIP I wrote: *Hated Camilla because she humiliated him. Long-standing grudge. Physically small and ineffectual. Says he was visiting father at time of murder? Check. Doesn't seem a violent type.*

I made out a page for JOSH, but realized there was nothing to say about him. My last real suspect so far was Peter. On his sheet I scribbled: *Wanted to marry Camilla but she was wary of total commitment. Possibly a jealous rage over Sean on final night. Used to getting his own way. Killed through temporary loss of self control? Unlikely but possible. Was he at party at time of murder?*

I picked up the phone and dialled Sean's number. I was pretty sure he'd be asleep but I wanted to talk to Mary. It rang for a long time but she eventually answered. I could hear her baby crying and the noise of the television.

I used my telephone skill, putting on my poshest accent. 'I'm Annabel Snow,' I gushed, 'from the *News of the World*.' I told her I had reason to believe that her partner was drinking with the latest Whistler victim on the night of her death. I said I was writing an article on Camilla's last hours.

There was a silence. I could hear her breathing. 'My husband's not been in no pub,' she said quietly. Her voice was hard, with a smoker's rasp. 'He's been nowhere outside Parkhurst for the last six months.'

'I do apologize,' I murmured, 'it's Mr Docherty I'm enquiring . . .'

'Sean's my brother.'

I let this sink in. I felt a warm wave of relief. I told her I was wondering about Sean's movements that night in the pub after he had played darts.

'Why don't you ask him? I'll wake him up.'

'No, no, don't do that. It's a minor point. It's just that I've a deadline to meet. Was he late home that night?'

'Look,' she said, getting irritated, 'whatever your name

is, it's nothing to do with Sean. He works hard. He does nights. When he's not at work he's sleeping.'

'You're sure he was at work on the night of Friday the ninth . . .'

'I told you. He works hard.' She sounded angry. 'I'm going to go and get him and . . .'

I hung up. I smiled broadly. I felt very happy that Mary wasn't his girlfriend. I wrote everything down in the file.

Pip had said he was at his father's caravan on the night of Camilla's death. I phoned Directory Enquiries and asked for a Mr Baxendale on a caravan site in Dymchurch. It seemed a long shot. To my surprise there was an electronic buzz and a voice said, 'The number you require . . .'

I didn't disguise my voice. I said I was from the Playhouse Theatre in Newcastle. Mr Baxendale sounded frail and nervous; not like the ogre in Pip's stories.

'Can I speak to Pip Baxendale?' I asked. I was told he was in London. 'I'm writing a report for the Arts Council,' I said brusquely, 'I need to know if Pip was understudying here two Fridays ago. Do you know if he was in Newcastle on the ninth of December?'

Pip's father became more firm and definite. 'He was in Dymchurch,' he said, 'I know that. He was here Thursday, Friday and on Saturday until eleven. He doesn't come very often and . . .'

I put the phone down. Pip seemed to be in the clear too. He had a good alibi, Sean had a weak one, I hadn't discovered one for Peter. I scratched my head, but Josh's page remained blank. I finished making notes and put the file on top of my in-tray.

Chapter Sixteen

As the dull afternoon slid into darkness I cycled over to
Vauxhall. I fastened the bike to some railings outside an
imposing Victorian terrace. I tried to imagine the neighbourhood when it was as impressive as the buildings.
Now the dirt and traffic were unrelenting. There were no
trees and no gardens. Trains rattled overhead and the
pavements were stacked with bulging bin liners and cardboard boxes full of refuse.

I gazed up at the house where the party had been
held, the night of the murder. I rang the bell and took a
deep breath. I didn't know Penny that well, and I'd never
been to her house before. I'd got her address out of the
phone book.

On the corner, two men were watching me, silently
passing a bottle. One was old, with long white hair and a
stuffed overcoat tied together with string. The other was
young with a pinched face and hair in a ponytail. He
wasn't wearing a coat and his mismatched plimsolls were
wet and stained. A blast of wind hit us from the river and
he turned up the collar of his shirt and stepped further
into the doorway. I knew he'd probably got off the train
at Euston a few weeks earlier, thinking he'd find work.
It's not easy without an address.

There was a crackle by my shoulder. I turned and

said my name into the intercom. The lock buzzed open. I pushed the heavy door.

The hallway was like Aladdin's cave. I was relieved by the warmth. The floor was covered in bright ceramics, probably original, and the stairs were glowing with Oriental carpet. All the walls were hung with batik, lit by hidden spotlights. Classical music was wafting up from the basement alongside the scent of chicken and spices.

I climbed the stairs until I came to an open door. Two teenage boys were lounging in front of a television. They were watching Children's BBC. One of them turned to me. 'It's the Big Friendly Giant,' he said.

'Ma's upstairs,' said the other one, without removing his eyes from the screen.

I hesitated, taking in the size of the room. It was enormous, thickly carpeted, and shutters were thrown back from tall rectangular windows. The sky outside was darkening over the tops of the warehouses. In a corner stood a Christmas tree. It was covered in baubles and tinsel. They were all silver, without any colours, and the lights were white orbs. It was dazzling.

I climbed another flight of stairs to the attic. 'Come in,' called a woman's voice. From the doorway I saw a tall dormer window and through it was the wide sweep of the Thames, the speeding river pilot and the lights of Westminster. 'I didn't know you had this view,' I said, entering the room. 'You'd never know from the street.'

Penny was invisible behind a computer. 'Hi, Imogen, I got your message.'

I crossed the room but her back was towards me.

She continued talking. 'We bought the house for the view. It's only this room, unfortunately. But of course, it's fantastically central.' She swivelled round and faced me. 'Haven't seen you for ages.' She was bright, but her smile lacked pleasure. 'I love the hair!'

I sat on a big cushion, dirty with cat fur. I looked around. The room was her study, lined with shelves piled up with box files and videotapes.

Penny stretched her arms and yawned. Her bosom lifted and fell. I noticed the bulge of muscle in her calves and upper arms and I remembered she was a keep-fit fanatic. The room was overheated and she was wearing a pink T-shirt with Japanese writing and cycling shorts. I felt hot in my street clothes. The room was small and I felt I was taking up a lot of room.

My eyes strayed to a full bottle of wine on top of her monitor. She poured herself a glass but didn't offer me any. 'Just a minute, sweetie.' She turned back to her keyboard. 'I must just get this down before it goes out of my head.' She recommenced her typing.

Penny worked for London Weekend as a producer. She'd previously been at the BBC. I'd met her a few times but we weren't friends; she was one of Camilla's cronies. They used to meet for lunch, or in the pub, early evening, for what they called a chinwag. This consisted of gossip and discussion about diets and gynaecologists. Camilla said she always changed the subject when Penny got onto the menopause, because it was depressing and made her queasy, especially after a few gins.

'Hang on,' Penny said. There was a pause in her tapping. 'How d'you spell cunnilingus? Is it like Aer Lingus? D'you know, Imogen?'

I leaned back uncomfortably, staring at the bottle of wine. The cat fur was making my eyes and nose prickle. I remembered the time Penny had been to see me at work about a programme she was making on the collapse of the welfare state. She had wanted me to put her in touch with claimants, people in bed and breakfasts and patients who had been on hospital waiting lists for years. She needed to interview them at home and had been very friendly and persuasive. She was surprised when I said I'd have to ask people before handing out their names and addresses. 'But everybody wants to be on the telly!' she'd argued.

I'd once said to Camilla that her friend wasn't above exploiting people. She laughed. 'Don't be stupid,' she said, 'what else would she do?'

Penny turned back to me, swallowing her drink in one gulp. She poured herself another. 'Well, what can I do for you, darling?' Her eyes narrowed suspiciously. 'I presume this isn't just a social call?'

I sneezed. 'It's about Camilla.'

Penny sighed and leaned back, looking at the ceiling. I thought she sounded irritated. 'I've talked about little else recently. Well, go on, then, shoot.'

'I'm sorry to bother you, but I've really got to know.'

'Know what?' She sipped her wine.

'Who was here that night.' I sneezed again.

She sat forwards again and looked me up and down. 'Have you got a cold? Don't give it to me.' She seemed tired, as if she had told the story many times. 'The party got going around nine, but most people turned up later, around eleven. She'd rung earlier in the day to say she was coming and that Peter was coming separately. You know? The aristocratic boyfriend?'

I nodded.

'Of course you know him. Well, he came sure enough, and waited. He was a real drag, staring out of the window all evening.' She drained her glass again. 'He was doing his lost-puppy act. Camilla never turned up. None of us were really worried, except him. He just kept sipping Perrier and looking at his watch. We just thought it was typical. She was pretty unreliable.'

'How long was he here?'

'I've no idea.'

'Try to remember. It's important.'

'Why?'

'I want to know.' I knew Camilla had been killed some time after midnight.

'He was here just before eleven. About a quarter to. He left before twelve. I don't know. I was pissed by then.'

'Who else was here?'

'God knows. Fifty or so, plus hangers on. Telly people. Josh was here, with some guy from Granada and his agent. The agent was pretty well legless. He fell over and broke a vase.' She sniffed, disapproving. 'He was smoking cannabis.'

'Was Pip here?' I'd been told he was at his father's caravan, but I wanted to be sure.

'Who?'

'He's an actor. Friend of Josh. You've met him.'

'Oh, yes. He wasn't here. I thought you were coming. Camilla wanted you to come. She mentioned it on the phone.'

For a moment I thought she was offended we hadn't taken up the invitation. 'I was tired. Camilla had a lot to drink. We were in the pub in the early evening. Anyway, I think she was avoiding Peter.'

'You mean she never intended coming?' She leaned towards me, suddenly interested.

'No. She was going home. I left her at the Elephant.'

152

'The police must have interviewed you.'

'How about you?'

'Two of them, twice. They're just like that pair in *Morse*.'

'They think it was the Whistler. I don't think he did it.'

Penny stood up and started rummaging in a drawer. 'Have you got a fag?'

I shook my head. I found a dirty tissue in my pocket and blew my nose. A cat wandered in, gave me a cold stare and went out again. I sneezed even more violently.

'I'm supposed to have given up. I've got some somewhere.' She tipped the drawer out, found a crumpled packet and lit one. She inhaled deeply then sighed. 'What d'you mean? Of course it was the Whistler.'

'Think about it, Penny,' I said. I paused for a moment. 'Can you imagine a stranger attacking Camilla? Think about the way she walked. She was confident. Tall. Frightening. She looked everyone straight in the eye. She was never a victim.'

She stared at me, then glanced at the floor. I followed her gaze. My feet looked enormous.

'I know you're a lawyer, Imogen . . . '

'I'm not a lawyer.'

'But the police must know what they're doing. They must be able to tell it's the same man.'

'Since when have you had total confidence in the police? They might look like something out of *Inspector Morse*, but that's pure television. Real ones lack his brains. And his scripts.'

'You're not telling me there's two nutcases running around on the loose?'

'I think it was someone she knew. She was worried about someone. Nervous. Someone had a motive.

Someone close to her. Did you know that someone was bothering her? Somebody was threatening her.'

She sucked on her cigarette again.

'Did you know Sean?'

She seemed pale and her hand shook slightly. It could have been the nicotine, but I wondered if the mention of Sean had scared her. She coughed. 'This is mad, darling. Whatever are you on about? Camilla seemed fine to me. What d'you mean, bothering her?' She turned halfway back to her keyboard.

I could tell I was losing her. For whatever reason, she was clamming up. I tried another approach. 'I'm grieving.' I blew my nose again. 'Trying to understand the events leading up to a death is good therapy. It's part of the grieving process.'

She turned back towards me and gave me a hard look. 'Of course we're all devastated. Don't get me wrong. Numb, that's the only word. She had such talent, such *joie de vivre*. I mean, where will anyone be without Camilla and her jokes?'

I jumped in again. 'Was Sean here?'

She didn't hesitate. 'No, of course he wasn't. I wouldn't have a person like that in my house.' She swatted an invisible fly in front of her face and poured herself some more wine. I realized she was becoming slightly drunk.

'You knew him, though.'

'Oh, yes. Camilla was sleeping with him for a while. God knows why, he was uncouth. Ignorant. A lout. She did bring him here once. He was a workman! I told her what I thought of that.'

'When was that?'

'When it was all going on. When Peter was on holiday,

or just after. I never knew what she saw in those types. Good in the sack, I suppose. Honestly, Imogen! She was asking for trouble.'

'That's what I mean,' I said, 'trouble. Was there more than one like him? Recently? Another . . .' I hesitated. 'Workman?' I suddenly remembered Josh had said the same thing. He'd mentioned another labourer.

'She liked rough diamonds. Actually, I think there were a few. There was definitely a Geordie.'

I laughed.

'Not like you. Don't be silly. This was a painter. A decorator. Tall, with huge shoulders. Attractive, mind. He had a broken nose.'

There was a pause. Penny scratched her head and then raked her fingers through her hair. It was dyed red but it was grey at the roots. She seemed to be choosing her words. When she spoke, her voice was quiet. 'She saw Sean quite recently.'

I decided not to mention the darts match on the night of the murder. 'How recently?'

'About a month ago. Christ, Imogen, d'you think I ought to tell the police?'

'No,' I said, 'I wouldn't bother. They're not interested. What happened the last time you saw Sean?'

She settled back in her chair. 'Well,' she said, comfortably, 'he'd become a bit of a nuisance.' She smiled. Her tone had changed. Camilla always said that she loved to gossip. I decided she wasn't trying to hide anything. She'd become relaxed with the opportunity of a story to tell. She lit another cigarette. 'He used to go round at night and pound on the door. Josh called the police once. Sean Docherty. That was his name. Kilburn Irish. Tattoos and everything. He was besotted of course, and that type doesn't like getting thrown over. Woman is property and all that. He was a joke really, except he stopped being funny.' She leaned forwards, confidentially. 'I was in the pub with Camilla, our usual place. Docklands. He must have followed us, because he appeared at the bar, as large as life, miles away from Camberwell. I said to Camilla, that man's followed us.'

'No,' I interrupted, 'he works there, on the Island.'

She seemed not to hear. 'He just sort of stood there, at the bar. Glowering.' She stubbed out he cigarette, violently, as if affronted by the memory. 'It was unnerving. Camilla went over but he wouldn't join us and he didn't leave. He just stared. Vicious-looking face, eyes too close together. Dead sexy, of course.' She narrowed her eyes and blew smoke at the ceiling. 'A lovely little bum.'

I thought of Sean's chest and the way his shirt buttons gaped showing gold hair. He had a dangerous body. I tried to push this vision from my mind. 'What happened?'

'He kept on staring. We were talking about Peter, or at least I was. He couldn't hear us, or at least I hope he couldn't, because I was telling her that we were all sick of seeing Peter mooning about. I told her she ought to marry him.'

'Sean was on his own?'

'Yes. At the bar.' She shuffled in her seat and pulled her cycling shorts as if trying to cover her thighs. 'Where was I? Oh, yes. Well, she just giggled. She never talked about Peter seriously. She just laughed about how boring and upper class he is and how his old dad used to be like Bertie Wooster. You know how she used to go on.'

I nodded. 'Yes,' I said, 'I do know.'

'But let's face it, Imogen, she could have done worse.' There was a brief silence. 'She did do worse.' Penny shifted, uneasy now, in her chair and chewed some skin at the side of a nail.

I said nothing.

'Maybe,' she continued, 'maybe if she'd taken Peter seriously, none of this would have happened. She'd have been safe, instead of racketing around on her own, in the dark. I told her lots of times. You should marry Peter, I kept saying.'

Our eyes met. 'Peter's OK,' I said.

Her voice shook slightly. 'OK? I should say so. He's got pots of money. He was crazy about her. He was absolutely perfect.'

I remembered saying something similar to Camilla the night she was killed. Penny and I both said it, but neither of us believed it. Whatever Camilla had wanted, whatever in the world she'd been looking for, Peter wasn't it.

Penny drank some more wine. The bottle was nearly finished. I stared at it, hoping, at the last minute, to be offered some.

She was starting to sound upset. She didn't notice my gaze. 'Apart from everything else, Imogen, what about her debts? Why be in debt? Marry him, I said to her. Marry the cash. Get real. Get yourself a life.'

I remembered the Visa statement I'd found in Camilla's room. 'Was she really in debt?'

'Oh, yes. That's why she'd rung me. That's why we'd met, that last time. She was asking me to get her some work. She really needed the money. She said she didn't want to ask Peter for a loan.' She shook her head. 'Too proud, I suppose.'

'Did you fix her up?'

'I was working on it. You know what she was like,

tons of charisma, but unreliable. Word gets around. And she wasn't getting any younger . . .'

'She used to say someone was spreading rumours, getting her blacklisted . . .'

'I know. She said that to me.'

'D'you think it was true?'

'I'm not sure. She wasn't normally paranoid. But I've heard one or two negative comments about her recently. They must have started somewhere.' She poured the last of the wine.

'What happened with Sean?'

She jumped. Wine splashed her bare knees. I wondered again if the thought of Sean made her afraid.

'He followed us into the car park. She went over to him and he grabbed her arm.'

'Grabbed? You mean violently?'

She hesitated. 'No. Not violently. He was . . . sort of . . . insistent.' She thought for a moment. Her voice became definite. 'But I still think he's the violent type. He'd be capable of violence.'

'What happened then?'

'She got in my car. He was still standing there as we drove away. She said she didn't want any more lectures so I didn't pursue it.'

'Did she seem scared?'

'No, she didn't. I think she thought she could handle it. D'you think I ought to tell all this to the police?'

I didn't reply.

'She took risks, but she was that type of person. She could look after herself, or at least I thought . . .' She was sounding really agitated. It crossed my mind that it was the first time I'd seen Penny show feelings other than boredom or cynicism. The worried lines on her brow

I cycled through the traffic, towards the river, enjoying the weak sun on my face. The muscles in my thighs ached and I wondered if the benefit of exercise outweighed the danger of exhaust fumes in my lungs.

I didn't know what to expect. I'd never used the Internet. I'd never seen a cybercafé. I had an odd, funny vision of monitors blinking in a *fin-de-siècle* coffee house. In my mind I heard sophisticated chatter, glimpsed the white cuff of a waiter, saw information passing restlessly over flickering screens.

I crossed Blackfriars Bridge and my enthusiasm, which hadn't been great, started to fade. I recalled the articles I'd read in the press about cyberperverts, use-net porn lines, digital corruption. The publicity around the Web seemed to suggest a hotbed of vice.

I remembered Al's description of her transvestite boyfriend. On other occasions she'd mentioned threesomes, videos, telephone chat lines with desperate-sounding men. She told these stories with the same giggle, the typical dismissive shrug. Everything interested her and nothing bothered her. For some bizarre reason, she'd also propositioned me. Maybe.

I suddenly thought she might be into virtual sex. I wasn't sure what this was, but the idea made me jam on my brakes, skidding to a halt in the gutter.

I wondered whether or not to continue. I imagined Al, decadent and knowing, with computer images that were unclear but depraved. I knew I couldn't handle this. I decided to approach the café gingerly, and peek through the window.

Within minutes I'd arrived at the place. Inside, it was small and looked no more sinister than a bunch of dull students working in a library. I couldn't see Al. I hesitated in the street. I knew that if I went in I would be unsure of what to do or say. I felt self-conscious when a boy looked up and smiled at me through the glass. I got on the bicycle. My legs were so tired, I went home very slowly.

That evening, still uneasy and bored, I decided to go to work and write up some of Penny's evidence in Camilla's file.

On the way it got dark and started raining. The temperature dropped. Traffic threw up dirty rainwater as I negotiated jams and lane changes. My wet trousers stuck to my legs. I was very cold. I passed a fish and chip shop but forced myself not to stop. My stomach rumbled painfully. I decided to get a takeaway in Stockwell on the way back.

I turned down Blackfriars Road and slowed at a junction. Without a signal, the car ahead of me veered in, hooting. I was forced to dismount. A young girl emerged from a doorway and stood under a street light. She was wearing a flared plastic raincoat and fishnet stockings. Her hair was long, dark and damp and her lips were orange. She tottered towards the car on thin heels and bent down to speak to the driver. As she climbed into the back seat I could see the bare flesh above her stockings and the edge of lacy briefs. She wasn't wearing a skirt. The car moved forwards slowly in the traffic. I passed it on the inside. The girl sat back and examined her face in a powder compact while a second man, beside her, undid the tie belt of her coat.

As I turned a corner, I glimpsed two people trudging down the road. It was the Electricity Couple, and they'd obviously tried to get into the Centre, despite the fact they'd been told we were closed for Christmas. I felt irritated by their persistence then remembered their situation. I knew I'd be just as desperate if I were them.

I propped up the bike outside the office. I was surprised to see a dim light inside. It was a torch. There was someone in the building who had no right to be there. My heart started beating strongly. I tried to see through the window. There was another flicker, then darkness. I looked up and down the street but it was deserted. A few snowflakes brushed my cheeks. I unlocked the front door, deliberately slow and noisy. Inside, I turned on the lights. There was a crash from the toilets. Cautiously, I moved towards the Ladies and pushed the door. I opened each cubicle gently, with the toe of my shoe. There was nobody there.

I went next door to the Gents. Again, I eased open the door. I felt a cold draught. The window was ajar and banging. I knew that this was the noise I'd heard. I opened the cubicle, but it was empty. On the window sill I could see a footprint. Someone had come in or gone out this way.

I closed the window and went back into the lobby and then down the corridor towards the main office. Pressing more switches, I set all the lights ablaze. I glanced into the waiting room.

The office door was open. Its Yale lock had been forced. I took a deep breath and went in. The burglar had gone. I'd heard him making his exit, through the toilet window, as I arrived.

The place was a mess. Files were strewn around and drawers tipped out. Several of my cases had been disturbed. I couldn't find Camilla's file at first. It was on the floor. All the clues had been tipped out and the sheets with my notes had been ripped into pieces. I noticed the petty cash was undisturbed, and contained over twenty pounds. A jam jar holding our coffee money was on the floor, but unopened. Nothing seemed to be missing. The intruder had been after something other than money.

Carefully, I Sellotaped Camilla's case notes back together. This was the only file to be attacked in this way. It was as if the intruder was trying to warn me off. I decided to keep her file with me at all times. I didn't bother tidying up. I wanted to leave.

The telephone rang. It sounded oddly loud in the empty building. I didn't lift the receiver, but let the answering machine pick up the call. I listened to a long crackly silence through the loudspeaker, and a rasping cough. Heavy breathing started and more coughing. I wondered if it was a wrong number.

'Leave it alone, Imogen!' The voice came in suddenly, violently, making me start. The line went dead. I went over to the machine and pressed rewind. My hand was shaking. I wondered if the caller knew I was in the building. My mouth was dry and I leaned against the desk for support. I forced myself to play the tape over. The machine indicated there were two messages. The first was from Penny, saying that she wanted some help making a programme. She sounded cheerful and ingratiating. The project was called 'Londoners' and she needed to be put in touch with 'poor people', in order to interview them. Her message was followed by the silence, the breathing and coughing. The aggressive voice startled me once again. I didn't recognize the caller. He sounded rough, uneducated. He was possibly drunk. He had a

Scottish accent, probably Clydeside. His few words were not only harsh but threatening.

I dialled 1471. The operator gave me the number of the last caller. I pressed button three and listened to the ringing tone. I was afraid. I wasn't sure what to say to him. The phone rang and rang. Eventually it was answered. It was a woman's voice. 'This is Veronique,' she said huskily. Her words were meant to be inviting.

'Someone just rang me from that number.'

Her voice changed. 'So? It's a bleeding callbox.'

'Where?'

The line went dead.

I placed the palm of one hand on my beating heart. A few weird things had happened recently, but I couldn't dismiss this. It wasn't just normal London aggravation. It was personal. I felt sick. There was a bottle of milk next to the coffee which Al had forgotten to throw away. I tried to drink some but it was a little stale and made me choke. I erased the tape, turned off the lights, locked up and went back into the street.

Outside, it was snowing heavily, but the flakes were melting as they hit the ground. I watched them swirl madly under the light from a street lamp. My bike was overturned. As I picked it up, I noticed that something was wrong. The brake and gear cables were loose. I bent down to examine them thinking they had been wrenched free, but saw they'd been cut.

I looked around. There was no one in sight but I was scared. I knew I would have a difficult ride ahead of me with the bike in this condition. I set off home, the briefcase containing Camilla's file slung around my neck. I shivered uncontrollably, half blind in the wet snow.

I stayed in bed most of the next day. I didn't really sleep but I had a strange daydream about buying a house in the country, with Camilla. We drove up to it in a Range Rover, which skidded slightly on tightly packed snow. I unlocked the front door and went upstairs. The bedroom window opened onto a balcony. Beyond was a semicircle of white, high mountains. A lake lay below, one half of it grey and cold. It was divided by a low dam. On the other side, amazingly, the water was turquoise, steaming and full of swimmers. 'It's thermal springs,' said Camilla, behind me.

When I got up, I discovered the flat was freezing. I stared at the boiler, my face full of hate. I thumped it with my fist. Its pilot light had blown out and I had no matches.

There was nothing to eat in the fridge. There was only bread, turning green in its plastic wrapper. I sat in an armchair and stared at the cracks in the ceiling. I made a few notes in Camilla's file, bringing it up to date. This didn't take long.

I decided my newly painted mango walls made me feel queasy rather than cheerful. The man in the flat upstairs started tuning his electric guitar.

Making a sudden decision, I shoved some things in a rucksack. I put the file in Camilla's briefcase. I plugged my reading lamp into its timeswitch, to deter burglars, and set my alarm. 'Bye, Imogen,' I said aloud closing the front door. My voice sounded strange and I bit my lower lip. I shouldered the rucksack and hugged the briefcase to my chest. As I entered the Tube station at the Oval I realized I'd forgotten my make-up and my suede jacket. I paused for a moment, but decided not to go back.

It was nearly eight o'clock when I approached King's Cross. I noticed a mother huddled in a doorway holding a baby. An old man shambled around, his rags flapping in the wind. The street was lined with young teenagers, anxious to sell their bodies. Whatever they were making, I decided, it wasn't worth it.

Inside the station, people with luggage either arrived or departed for Christmas. I bought two magazines and managed to bring forward my reservation. I accepted a seat in the smoking compartment. Walking the length of the train, I thought I saw Sean sitting in first class, but a second glance proved I was mistaken.

I dozed in the fug. I didn't feel like reading and pushed the magazines to one side. After a while, someone borrowed them. I wondered about buying some sandwiches but I wasn't hungry. My thoughts kept returning to Camilla and the time when we'd sung the 'Internationale' through the late-night streets of Kensington. The tune beat in my brain over the rhythmic noise of the wheels. The words changed. The final line became 'Cam-ill-a Hard-ing, she is dead, she is dead, she is dead'.

I remembered Camilla visiting me, at my flat, just before Easter. I hadn't eaten for days. I had the flu. She perched on my bed and tipped out her handbag, handing me a bottle. 'Painkillers,' she said, 'prescription ones, extra strong. They're Josh's. I raided the bathroom cabinet.'

'Thanks,' I said, wearily. My legs and arms were aching and I felt sick. My head was pounding.

Camilla never got the flu. She said she'd never even had a cold. 'What's the matter? It can't be all bad. Think

167

about it. A few days off work on full pay, and you even lose a bit of weight. What could be nicer? Be positive.'

'You don't know what it's like, do you?' I tried to sit up and reached for a glass of water.

She frowned. 'I don't believe in flu. My mother hadn't the time. And then at school . . . Castor oil and cold showers. Flu's all in the mind.' She didn't stay long. She said I was being too boring and left for a party.

I sat on the train, heading dead north, her voice repeating in my head. I even remembered the sound of the clasp, closing her bag, and the rustle of her dress as she got up to leave.

Chapter Eighteen

It was after midnight when the train crossed the Tyne. I looked at the city lights climbing up from the quayside and the bridges and churches and remembered my dad telling me it was the best view in the world.

Newcastle was different. Arriving at London stations late at night I always felt that all the passengers had someone to meet them, except me. Here, I didn't mind being alone. I knew exactly where I was going.

I left the city on the night bus. I got off and walked the streets of my childhood. I cut through low blocks of flats. It was late, but looking up I saw our light was on.

My family was rehoused when I was a student. I'd never thought of their new flat as home, but it was still reassuring and familiar. My mam kept talking about buying it off the council. Dad wouldn't agree. He was unimpressed with the modern world. As I climbed the steps, I remembered telling Camilla that my dad gave me a social conscience. She laughed and said hers gave her a pony.

I walked into the living room. The TV was on very loud. Mam glanced up from her knitting, smiled and said, 'Look what the cat's dragged in.' Dad didn't move.

'Hi, Dad,' I said.

'Have you taken your shoes off?' asked Mam.

I went into the kitchen and made tea. I handed Dad a cup and gestured at the television. 'Can you switch this off?'

He shook his head. 'It's a video,' he told me, 'it's going back tomorrow.'

'You're up late,' I said.

On the screen, a woman was screaming. Mam counted stitches. 'I'd go to bed,' she agreed, 'but he doesn't like me going first.'

'Have you heard about my friend Camilla?' I was almost shouting above the noise.

Mam gestured towards the kitchen, and we went in there, closing the door. I told her what had happened.

She'd never met Camilla. 'Was she the one that was on the telly?'

I nodded.

'What a shame. Your brother knew her.'

I frowned, surprised.

'He seemed quite smitten.'

'First I've heard of it.'

'You want to be careful. I don't know what you're doing down there when you've got a good home here.' She pursed her lips. She was looking older. She gestured towards the living room. 'He's deaf you know, your dad. Sinuses. The noise of that telly's driving everyone around the bend.' She reached up, holding her knitting against my back, measuring. 'You're looking a bit thin.'

I tried to smile.

She sighed. 'You should come home, where it's decent. Find yourself a nice feller.' She sighed deeply. 'What a shame. Your friend was a bonny lass. There was a picture of her once in the *TV Times*.'

I wished I hadn't told Mam about the murder. She'd

got on to her favourite subject, which was to do with me 'settling down'.

'I think I'll turn in, Mam,' I said, hastily, 'I'm knackered.'

'You know where your room is.'

I closed my door. With a tired sigh, I sat on the bed. My room was like a cupboard. Everything had been carefully moved from the old house to the new flat, even though I would never return. It was crammed with my childhood possessions, all dusted and neat. A group of glass animals sat on the dressing table. Along the window sill a collection of dolls in national costume had faded in the sun and condensation. I stared at them for a moment. They no longer had anything to do with me. Outside, an overpass carried cars towards the coast. I drew the thin curtains, knowing that the lights and noise would go on all night.

I undressed and got into bed without washing. The sheets were fresh and soft in anticipation of my Christmas visit. I touched my old teddy bear, then put it on the floor. I leaned over to the bedside cabinet, taking out a book and a pile of birthday cards. Most of these had pictures of animals in bright, old-fashioned colours. They were from relatives who'd used my real name, Susan.

Mam came in and handed me a hot-water bottle. 'Sleep tight, pet,' she said.

I opened the book. Inside I'd written my name and address in round letters joined together by little loops. Underneath, I'd added 'England, Great Britain, The Commonwealth, The World, The Solar System, The Universe'. The childish certainty of this made me smile. The book was *Black Beauty* and had a horse on its cover. I fell asleep after reading a page.

The noise from the water tank behind my bed woke me about six. Dad sang loudly as he shaved. He flushed the toilet more than once. There was a smell of frying sausages and the news came on the radio in the kitchen. Dad yelled at my brother, 'Get up, you lazy bugger!' The door slammed as he left for work. It was all normal. Outside, the traffic roared.

They had decided to let me sleep in. This meant Mam was worried about me living in London with a murderer on the prowl. I dozed a little, thinking about Sean. Eventually, I got up and rummaged in my rucksack. My packing had been haphazard and I'd brought clean underwear but little else. My clothes were creased and stale but I had no choice but to wear them again. I glanced in the mirror and was shocked by my appearance. My face was pale and shiny. Even my new haircut seemed ragged and lifeless. I thought I might go shopping.

When I went into the kitchen Mam immediately forked eggs and sausages onto a plate and handed it to me. 'Our Jimmy finished off all the bacon. Will you pop to Costcutter when you're ready? I'm working today.'

I remembered her remarks about my brother and Camilla. The front door slammed a second time. 'Is he avoiding me, or what?'

Outside, it was sunny and the sky was cloudless and blue. I stood on the balcony and looked around. The estate was better than I remembered. The trees, which had struggled so hard at first against the wind and the vandals, had grown tall. I gazed over a ripple of branches, still shedding the last of their golden leaves, and spoke to a group of neighbours who'd come out to gossip. I told them it had snowed, in London, but I could tell this was meaningless to them, as if I'd mentioned Moscow or Prague. In the distance, cranes lined the riverside, the coast road curved away east and a flock of seagulls reeled in, their white wings beating.

At the metro station I stared at the map like a tourist. A woman came over and explained the route. I remembered this courtesy was normal, here. I sat next to an old man on the train and he chatted to me as if he'd known me all his life. As I responded, I could hear my Geordie accent getting stronger. The carriage was clean and the stations looked like airports. It felt calming, after London. I slipped through the landscapes and streetscapes of my past.

I bought some Christmas presents in Fenwicks and some make-up for myself. Walking down Northumberland Street, I was jostled by the seasonal crowds and deafened by vendors and buskers. I stopped beside one who mouthed wordlessly. He had a sign which read 'The World's Only Silent Carol Singer'. I gave him fifty pence.

I was oddly relaxed. It occurred to me that I was walking differently. I'd lost the focus and tension, necessary for London. Despite the pre-Christmas rush, I ambled along, glancing in windows.

I couldn't think what to buy. The shops seemed full of sequinned party frocks with nylon ruffles. Attracted to some Newcastle United strips, I felt the urge to try one on. The thought that it could only be a joke, back in

London, stopped me. This was just a visit. I bought Peter Beardley's autobiography instead.

In the end I decided on a white T-shirt, some black chinos and a cropped lambswool sweater with a crew neck. These seemed predictable but I knew they couldn't be improved upon.

I went for a sandwich in an Italian café and watched a video of Juventus beating AC Milan. I kept looking in my carrier bags because I felt pleased. Camilla often complimented me on my street style. 'Elegance is refusal,' she said, quoting from *Vogue*.

We'd once gone shopping together in Kensington High Street. In a tiny, expensive boutique she'd pulled out a fragile fitted suit in pale-blue silk I chose from the man's rails. I found a linen shirt and a soft unstructured jacket. We undressed together in front of a big mirror. Camilla was thin. The bones of her hips and shoulders jutted. She wore a camisole top instead of a bra. Next to her, my generous curves were like the prow of a ship. Without clothes, our roles were reversed. I looked more womanly, she more boyish.

'You've got a great body,' she said, enviously.

'You wouldn't want to look like this,' I reminded her.

We tried on the outfits and the image disintegrated. I became assertive, even butch, ready to tough out some deal. She was instantly a frail blossom, drifting across the lawn of some summer garden party.

I finished my sandwich and went to the covered market to do Mam's shopping. I dodged men with stained aprons carrying newly skinned pigs and tried to avoid slipping on the greasy floor. The people, the stalls, the smell of blood and roasting coffee beans made me nostalgic and excited. I searched for the pets stall but now it sold only animal accessories and sacks of dried food. I remembered standing there as a child, longing for puppies, caged birds, tortoises.

Before returning, I walked down to the river. The north wind smelled of snow and the sun glinted off the water's surface in a way that was almost impossible to bear. I stood dwarfed beneath the arch of the Tyne Bridge, holding a clutch of plastic carrier bags. I took deep, cold breaths.

The next day, alone in the flat, I sat, resting my cheek in my hand, underneath a calendar picture of Princess Margaret in an evening gown and tiara. I made tea and opened a packet of Ginger Snaps. The place felt safe but too small. My legs hardly fitted under the kitchen table. I thought about my tiny room with its narrow, short bed, its predictable view. I felt too big for the flat, the estate, the city.

My mother still wanted to take care of me, but she had no idea who I really was. I considered the way the pattern of Newcastle's streets was as familiar as my own face in the mirror. I knew the rise and fall of the hills and in which direction lay the sea. These things were reassuring, but at the very same moment I sensed this I recognized it as a shallow, fake emotion.

I still hadn't seen my brother, Jimmy. He'd not been home last night. I noticed some letters at the side of the sink. They were addressed to him and one of them had a London postmark. Mam had commented when I arrived that he knew Camilla. I remembered introducing them once, a few months before, when Jimmy had been staying with me in Stockwell. I picked up my mug of tea and went into his room.

My brother had been a welder at the shipyards but went to art school after he was made redundant. He was in his final year. My father called him the only college boy in the family, as if I'd never been to university. Some of his canvases were propped against the wall. The top one was a naked woman, sitting with her head in her hands. The room was very neat. There was a smell of stale smoke and the stuff he used to clean his brushes. I turned over some drawings on the desk and then glanced at his noticeboard. Alongside the football fixtures and the opening times of the sports centre was a coloured photo torn from a magazine. I went to have a closer look. It was Camilla, her hair piled up, wearing a strapless silver dress. Above was the caption *Glamour!* Her smile seemed to mock me.

My hands started to shake. I suddenly realized there was no point in hiding away, taking a holiday, when there was an important job to do. Quickly and methodically I turned out Jimmy's chest of drawers. There was nothing of interest, so I went through his pockets. Then I flicked through his portfolios. At the back of one I discovered two studio photos of Camilla and some sketches based on them.

In a shoebox at the back of his wardrobe I found a box of letters. I tidied up carefully, then took them into my own room. I pulled Camilla's file from my rucksack in case I needed to make any notes.

Sitting on the floor with my back pressed against the door I read them. There was some correspondence from the art college and several letters from a London gallery with the same style envelope as the new one on the kitchen table. I examined them carefully. They were about an exhibition which was to feature some of Jimmy's work. I knew nothing about this, believing that I was the only member of the family with connections in London.

Reading through the arrangements, I found a reference to Camilla. One paragraph began, 'As Camilla will have told you . . .' The letter was from a woman called Fiona Harding, and it was clear that she was a relative and that Camilla had made the necessary introductions. Another letter from Fiona was hand written, from an address in Crouch End and talked about cocktails and 'people you should meet'. This was dated December 3rd. I copied down her home and gallery addresses and put them in the file.

At the front of the shoebox I found a letter from Camilla. The writing was unmistakable; a large spiky italic, in black ink. My fingers fumbled as I took it out of its envelope. It was written on thick paper, and as I unfolded it some pressed rose petals fell out. The dead smell tainted the air. There was no date and the postmark was smudged.

Dear Jimmy
Sorry not to have been in touch. Thanks for the roses. Here is one of them for you, and here is a tiny little bit of the money you lent me. Of course I know you're on a grant.

You're so sweet, but don't ring me again at the flat. I'll ring you!! I might be up in Newcastle soon. I loved your parents' place. I'll get a Super Apex. No, this is not a false promise! Don't come down to London, my life is too complicated. Fiona has everything in hand, by the way, and she'll be writing to you. Haven't said anything to Sister Susan, have you?

Must go. I miss my big Pooh bear, lots of kisses.

                                        Camilla.

My heart was thumping in an uncomfortable way. I put the letter in Camilla's file, and returned the envelope, with its rose petals, to the box. I put this where I'd found it and had a final look round, but nothing appeared disturbed.

Back in the kitchen I gulped down the dregs of my tea, even though they were cold. I held on to the edge of the table then forced myself to make a few notes about my discoveries.

I thought about Camilla lying on the bed in Jimmy's room having sex with him in this empty flat while my parents were at work. I remembered both Josh and Penny mentioning a Geordie painter as one of her conquests. I imagined Camilla sitting at Mam's kitchen table, laughing. I heard them calling each other pet names. I felt sick. She might have gone into my room and seen my dolls in national costume. The worst thing of all was that she'd been to Tyneside and never told me. It seemed beyond belief.

Chapter Nineteen

I knew the best way to deal with my emotions was to ignore them and do some work. I decided to use my time profitably and try to see St John, Camilla's brother. As long as I was in Newcastle, I might as well progress the case.

I looked in the file and found Camilla's list. I studied it again. There were a few jottings of things to do, two addresses and the number of her brother's direct line. It was one fifteen. I knew the university would be officially closed, but I thought he might be in his office.

The phone was picked up on the first ring. 'St John Harding speaking.' His tone was clipped and precise.

'This is Susan, I mean Imogen Webb. Can I come and see you?'

There was a pause. 'Are you a student?'

I realized he had no idea who I was. 'No,' I said, mysteriously, 'I'm more of a research fellow. What building are you in?'

I put on my new clothes and some lipstick and borrowed Jimmy's hair gel. I felt more like my old self crossing the campus and then striding down the long windowless corridors of St John Harding's department. Because I was working, I felt I had a goal. I was in control.

So close to Christmas there was nobody in the

university, and most of the doors were shut. They were all particularly narrow, as if designed for thin people. St John's was open so I walked in. There was no one inside. It was a small room and looked out over an empty car park where plastic bags were blowing around. I watched the sun disappear and raindrops hit the glass. Turning back to the room, I was shocked by a picture confronting me on the wall. I knew it was Jimmy's work. It fitted in with stuff he'd been doing a year before. There was a red circle in the middle with buildings and some disjointed words which seemed to say 'my sweetheart is a Catherine wheel'.

'Ms Webb,' said a voice, 'thank you for coming.' St John shut the door abruptly. He was wearing corduroys and a cable-knit cardigan over a checked shirt. He grinned, showing his good teeth, but as he looked up at me, his smile withered. 'Sit down,' he added, gesturing towards a chair. I stayed standing. 'Haven't we met somewhere before?'

He started talking about his field of study. I knew he recognized me from the funeral, but he was either too polite or too professional to be diverted. He addressed me as a prospective research assistant. 'Experience of QuarkXPress would be useful,' he continued. He sounded as pompous as ever.

'I haven't come about a job,' I said, interrupting. There was a pause and his eyebrows raised. I pointed to the picture on the wall. 'That's my brother's.'

He glanced away, then back again and his hand strayed towards the phone.

'Jimmy Webb,' I said. I realized I wasn't making sense. 'He's my brother.'

St John looked a little relieved. 'Oh, I see. Or rather,

I don't see at all. What can I do for you, Miss Webb?' He cleared his throat. 'Is it about the exhibition? He really should speak to Fiona, my wife . . .'

I remembered the letters in Jimmy's room. 'Is Fiona Harding your wife?'

'Of course!' He was getting impatient. 'Look, what is this? I'm very busy. I've got to make the London train in two hours.'

'It's about Camilla,' I said and sat down.

He stared at me. Rain lashed the window. I noticed that the room was bare except for some papers, two computers and the picture. I looked at the telephone cable which was carefully gathered together inside an elastic band, to stop it trailing.

'You were at the funeral,' he said eventually.

I met his eyes and smiled.

'Aren't you a solicitor?' St John stood up. He walked towards the door as if about to leave, then turned towards me. 'I think you'd better go, Miss Webb.'

'I was her friend,' I said, 'her best friend.'

'I don't think I want to talk to you.' He reached towards the door.

I leaned back and raised one foot and put it on his desk. I knew I looked relaxed, even rude.

At that moment, Josh came into my mind. He'd told me that Camilla had an affair with St John's boss. 'Fine,' I said, 'I'll talk to your head of department. He knew her better than most. I'll see what light he can shed on things.' I smiled again, then gestured, palms upward. 'I've already rung him.' I made as if to stand up. 'At home.'

St John gasped, audibly. 'Why are you bothering me like this? What d'you want, for Heaven's sake?' I noticed that a flush of red had swept upwards from his neck, covering his face. He moved round behind the desk and pretended to shuffle some papers in a drawer.

I was used to interviewing people and knew when to stay quiet. The mention of his boss unnerved him. I waited a minute. 'She was up here in Newcastle.' My voice was calm but insistent. 'I know more than you think.' I improvised. 'You felt compromised, didn't you?'

He sat on the corner of the desk. His hands shook a little and he eased them under his thighs. 'Of course I did.' His words were low and somewhat muffled. 'I don't want you raising any of this with Professor Grant. I don't want any more embarrassment.'

'Was it embarrassing? He's a grown-up. So was she. Was it so unusual?'

'She did it to get at me. She threatened to tell him . . . certain things . . . private matters, she won his confidence.'

'Private matters?' I gazed at him hard. 'Did you give her money? Did you buy her off?' As I said this, I realized I was expecting Camilla to have behaved badly.

Our eyes met for what seemed like several seconds. He seemed to nod, but then to my surprise he darted towards the door and disappeared. I sat for a while, then looked out and along the corridor. He was nowhere to be seen.

I searched through the papers in his desk. I wondered if Camilla had manipulated her brother, maybe even blackmailed him, through this Professor Grant.

I had no idea what I was looking for, and found a few buff folders containing minutes of meetings. There were departmental memos and claim forms for expenses. Underneath there was a foolscap envelope with italic writing on the front. I folded this and put it in my pocket.

Back in the corridor, I found the Ladies and went in to drink some water from the tap. It was warm and tasted of chlorine. I fixed my lipstick in the mirror and smiled. On my way out of the building I passed a wider door which had Professor Grant's name on it. I opened it and peeped inside. A man was sitting staring out the window. I coughed. 'Sorry,' I said.

He swung round. I was startled by his appearance and withdrew. He was in a wheelchair and there was a hearing aid behind his right ear. He had wiry grey hair and thick bifocals. He was a very old man.

Before returning to the flat, I wandered over to St James' Park. The new football stands dominated the skyline like a modern cathedral. The old entrances on the Gallowgate end had completely disappeared. I decided to try to get a seat for the game. I walked round, dwarfed by the scale of the new buildings, feeling both irritated and proud of the changes. At last we were a club to be reckoned with, I thought to myself. I looked around, hoping to catch a glimpse of Kenny Dalglish.

I opened the envelope I'd taken from St John's office. The writing on the front was definitely Camilla's but it was empty. I threw it away. I thought about how I'd always believed we were intimate, sharing all our secrets. She'd never mentioned Professor Grant. She'd never spoken of my brother. She'd blackmailed St John. I realized Camilla was not the person I'd believed her to be. I wondered what else I might uncover, investigating her case.

I couldn't get a ticket. The match was season ticket

holders only. 'Is this the brave new world of soccer?' I asked, pointlessly. 'I've supported this bloody club all my life.'

I was told to come back and queue for cup match tickets later in the week. 'I'll be in London,' I said.

Back at the flat I decided to search everywhere. I opened all the drawers and cupboards in the sideboard and in the kitchen. I went through my parents' bedroom and even looked in the airing cupboard. I didn't really know what I was after, but the activity was calming. Hard work on the case was the only thing that made sense.

I found a sheaf of references I'd once photocopied for Mam. She needed them for her cleaning jobs. These gave me an idea. I took two and put them in Camilla's file, then hid it, inside the briefcase, under my bed.

I ran myself a deep bath. The water was as hot as I could bear it. I tried to concentrate on the blue and yellow fishes on the wallpaper and the way that after every third fish there was a shell. It was no use. I was tense. The false moment of security that I'd enjoyed so briefly, earlier, failed to return. My joints felt stiff, despite the heat, and I was cold inside.

It was dark and the window half disappeared in the steam. I reached out and pulled the cords that switched on the fluorescent tube and the electric wall fire. My body looked big, almost bloated under the water. Sweat broke out on my upper lip and my head began to ache. I floated my toy boat and made little waves with my hands and knees.

*

When Jimmy came in I was watching TV, lying on the settee under a travel rug. I stared at the screen where a festive cook was stuffing tiny birds with foreign fruit.

'Hi there, bonny lass,' he called out from the hall.

I bit my lip but didn't answer.

I heard him open the fridge. He came into the room holding a can of beer. 'Is there anything to eat?'

I didn't look at him but sat up and took a deep breath. 'What am I? A bloody servant?'

There was a pause. 'Where's Mam?'

'Not cooking,' I told him.

He sat down, sighed and opened the can. My brother was six foot and handsome except for his nose which broke in a boxing match when he was twelve. He was still under thirty. I looked at him. His hair was close cropped and the sleeves of his plaid shirt were rolled up so I could see the bottom of his tattoos. The art school must have had some effect, because he was wearing leather-plaited wristbands and trousers with lots of zips. He looked more like an art student trying to be a welder than the other way around.

'What's this shite?' he asked, gesturing at the TV. 'It's making me hungry.'

I pushed the travel rug away, half onto the floor. 'So you knew Camilla.' There was a silence. 'Did you know she's dead?'

He took a pull on his can. 'I phoned Josh,' he replied.

I watched the screen for a minute. 'I didn't realize you knew Josh.' My voice was icy.

'He was away, auditioning.' Jimmy swallowed some beer and burped. 'I got that queer bugger, whatsisname.'

'Gay,' I said automatically. 'Pip and Josh are gay.'

'They take the piss out of my accent.' He sat up and

leant forwards, his hands between his knees. 'London gits.'

'There's a letter for you in the kitchen. From your gallery friend in Bond Street.'

'Oh, yeah? Right. Thanks.'

'I didn't know that you had friends in London.'

'I've got friends everywhere, me. I'm a friendly bloke.'

My fingers clutched the edge of the blanket and squeezed it. I cleared my throat. 'Make some tea, will you?' I pushed the rug onto the floor.

He disappeared and came back with a steaming mug and another can. 'Cheers,' he said.

I stared at the TV. It showed the news. A multiracial group of children, somewhere abroad, was singing carols beneath an enormous tree.

Jimmy whistled the tune for a few bars. It was 'O Come, All Ye Faithful'. 'D'you remember that time you sang, at the central station? You were on *Look North*!' He swigged some more beer.

I didn't reply.

'Carol-singing with the Guides on the telly?' He was trying to get the conversation onto normal subjects. 'There was a close-up of your gob open. I saw your fillings.'

I kept my eyes off his face. 'I didn't know you knew Camilla.'

'You introduced us.'

'I didn't know you were having a relationship with her.'

'Well, I stayed with her, once or twice.'

I turned and faced him. 'You mean you went down to London and didn't even bother to come and see me?'

He looked at the floor.

'Did it start that night? When I introduced you in the pub?'

He nodded.

'I never even saw you talk to her. I definitely didn't see you go off with her.' I paused, trying to remember more about the occasion, and suddenly had a vision of his arms around Camilla, her head on his shoulder. 'You deceived me!' I sounded overdramatic. I didn't want him to see tears. I blinked and pretended to rub my eyes.

Jimmy came over and wrapped his arms around me. 'Hey, let's not fight.'

I froze, wanting to shrug him off. His cheek grazed mine, harshly. I made my hands into fists.

He sat back on his haunches, rebuffed. 'I would have told you.' He sounded upset. 'It was no secret as far as I was concerned. But I'd promised her. I promised not to tell you.'

I knew that Camilla had no secrets. She told me everything. I looked down at my white knuckles. 'Have you been interviewed by the police?'

His eyes were wet now. My tears had gone. I pointed to a box of tissues beside the television. He took one and blew his nose.

'The police?'

'Were there letters from you in her room?'

He sat back again, his hands clasped in front of him. He was puzzled. His voice shook a little. 'There might have been. I doubt if she kept them.' He swallowed hard. 'I was nothing to her. The police are after this Whistler bloke, aren't they?'

I stood up. I tried to sound composed. 'The Whistler

didn't do it,' I said. I looked down at him. 'She was killed
by someone she knew.'

I went into my room and got into bed. Mam knocked at
my door later and told me the meal was ready, but I
didn't want to sit with Jimmy. I got my plate and took it
into my room. The food cooled, uneaten. Later, because
I was on my own, I allowed myself to cry. I felt
betrayed. I was lonely. The absence of Camilla cut me
like a sharp blade. After a while, I fell asleep and dreamed
about the Whistler. I saw him standing in the dark, smelly
doorway of an abandoned cinema, repeatedly tearing at
the cuff of his jacket with his teeth. He looked like no
one I knew, except perhaps the devil in my Sunday school
book, in the cabinet next to my bed. He had wiry ginger
hair and dirty hands. In the dream, I was holding my
Walkman. It made a whistling noise but I was unable to
switch it off.

Camilla rode past. She was on her bicycle; the same
one I had taken to London. She was moving in slow
motion and her hair and chiffon skirt billowed in a
sunbeam. Her pale satin feet pedalled, lazily. I wanted
to call out to her, tell her of the danger, but my throat
was tight and dry. Camilla turned and looked briefly at
the cinema doorway, not seeing. She had a small, dazed
smile and I wondered if she was stoned.

Chapter Twenty

On Christmas Eve my dad's brother and his family came round to the flat. We had two crates of Brown Ale but I didn't feel like drinking. I never drank in Newcastle. My family would have been shocked to know how much money I put over bars in London.

I'd spent some time washing and styling my hair. I'd found a stash of old make-up in one of my drawers and I'd experimented with teenage eyeshadow, pearly lipstick and a peculiar brown nail polish. The results were rather dramatic.

My dad played his Elvis Presley records. Every time the door banged I looked around for Jimmy. My mam and Auntie Flo sat on hard chairs near the kitchen, waiting to bring in the sausage rolls and mince pies. They were talking in low voices about my cousin Maureen, who'd been adopted, and who'd had to get married. 'He never used to raise his hands to her,' said Mam, 'it's the drink.'

'She drinks the same as him, pint for pint.'

'It's him that's got her on those nerve pills.' She pointed to her head. 'She doesn't know whether she's coming or going.'

I felt sorry for Maureen, but stopped myself from asking for details. We hadn't seen each other for years.

Dad started miming to 'Heartbreak Hotel'. He was

using the TV remote as a microphone and he kept pushing his straggly hair back into a quiff. On the balcony outside carol singers were knocking on the window.

My cousin Alec struggled up from the settee and walked towards me. 'Howway, Susie,' he said, 'how about a dance?'

His arms encircled me and pressed me against his soft belly. His head was up to my shoulder. Dad cheered as if witnessing an act of seduction. I tried to steer us away from the mistletoe, which wasn't easy in such a tiny room.

The music speeded up and Alec released me, only to grab my hand and start jiving. Despite his weight he was a good dancer. He spun me round so fast I thought I might be sick. My mam and Auntie Flo joined in, moving stiffly, like puppets and my dad went down on one knee, still holding his microphone.

The next track was a slow number. I backed out of the room, pointing towards the toilet. Jimmy was in the kitchen, eating the remains of some royal icing out of a mixing bowl from the sink.

'There's some food in the oven,' I said. 'You could take it through. I think Mam's forgotten about it.' I raised my voice above the thump of the record player. The walls of the flat were vibrating.

'It's all happening in there, is it?'

'He's invited the whole tribe.' The front door opened and both sets of grandparents arrived.

I started opening bottles. I was tired of swapping pleasantries with Jimmy. We'd avoided real communication since the previous evening. 'We have to talk,' I said.

He disappeared into the living room with a tray of

sausage rolls. There was a break in the music but then Bing Crosby started singing 'The Little Drummer Boy'. Dad joined in on the bongo drums that had come from Rhodesia when I was a baby. I peered in. The room was cloudy with smoke. My uncle was handing round the beer. Alec came and joined me in the doorway. More people arrived and pushed past us.

'Go on, our Susan,' shouted my dad, 'dance with the lad!'

Alec was trying to think of something to say. Eventually he said, 'Still in London?'

'Same old thing,' I replied.

'I was down there meself, back in August. In lodgings. I should've looked you up.'

'What did you think of it?'

'London? Not much. Rotten beer, too many darkies.' He put one hand on my arm. 'Have you got a feller?'

'Yes,' I lied. 'He's a plasterer. His name's Sean.' I slipped out of his grip and went back into the kitchen, closing the door.

Jimmy came in. 'I think you've scored there,' he said.

'Shut up.'

'He's always fancied you, our Alec. He used to try and see your knickers when you were up the slide in the park.' Jimmy poured himself a beer.

'Look, we have to talk.'

He threw back his head and finished the beer in one gulp. 'OK, let's go to the boozer.'

We slipped out unnoticed, and the noise of the party followed us down the stairwell. Outside, there was a thin layer of snow which had frozen over. The pavements were slippery and glittered under the street lights. I glanced up at the flats and it seemed as if blue light shone from a hundred TV screens. Above, the sky was absolutely clear. As I watched, a tiny silver dot moved through the navy blue.

'Is that a shooting star?' I asked.

Jimmy stood at my side. 'Nah,' he said, 'it's a satellite.'

We walked in silence to the pub. I matched his long strides. Jimmy was always described as a big man, but I was three inches taller. When he stopped to light a cigarette under his jacket, I slowed and almost fell over on the ice. Nearby, a Salvation Army band was playing carols. We walked past the first two pubs on the main road.

'Where're we going?'

'Somewhere where there's no music.'

We went into a dingy pub, straight through the public bar where there was a TV and no spare seats. We entered a drab little lounge which was completely empty. Jimmy bent down and switched on an electric fire. The fake coals glowed orange and flickered. He disappeared next door to get some drinks. The ashtray on the table was full and there was a stale smell. I moved nearer the fire and felt my feet stick to the carpet.

Jimmy put two pints of lager on the table. 'The old feller was on form tonight.'

'You know Dad,' I agreed, 'he loves an audience.'

'He'll be mortal, before the night's out.'

'Mortal drunk,' I repeated. I remembered saying this to Camilla, the night she was killed.

'That Alec's getting fat.'

'We're all getting older. Mam's as stringy as a stick.'

'What d'you want to say to me, our Susan?' There was a change in his voice. He sounded defensive.

'Why didn't you tell me about you and Camilla? Why didn't you tell me about Fiona Harding and the exhibition?' I picked up my pint but then put it down again without drinking.

There was a silence. 'I don't tell anyone my business.'

'You didn't tell me you were close to Camilla. You didn't tell me her brother had your work hanging on the wall of his office. You didn't mention Bond Street galleries.' I could hear my voice getting out of control. 'All this was going on behind my back!'

His head was bent forward, but he looked up and his eyes met mine. 'So, all right, I didn't tell you. Have you ever wondered why she didn't tell you? Why she insisted I didn't tell you?'

'Of course I have, but she's not around to ask, is she?' I tried to swallow some beer. 'So I'm asking you.'

There was another long silence. I wanted to say more, but I stopped myself. I could hear a comedian on the TV next door, and laughter. The electric fire smelled of burning dust and its flames made a steady whirring noise.

Jimmy drained his glass and went out again, returning with two more pints. He sat down heavily. 'Look, Susan, she didn't want to tell you. She made me promise. That's the truth.' He paused. 'I don't know why.'

I stared at him and tried to drink some beer, but my throat felt tight.

'It's not as if you and me see each other all that often. I was down in London a few times, but I stayed with her, not with you. Or with Fiona. I sometimes stayed with Fiona.'

'You mean you were giving her one as well?' My heart was beating very fast. When he worked in the yards, my brother's girlfriends had been chicken packers and trainee hairdressers. I knew his lifestyle had changed, but this was beyond all reason.

'They were both great. They liked me. There was no harm done. All right, so I didn't come to see you. It didn't seem that important.'

I thought I might be sick. I felt my face redden. My hands started to shake. I tried hard to keep my voice steady. 'Oh, so it wasn't important. My best friend is screwing the pants off my only brother, I'm just down the road, sitting on my own, chewing my nails and you don't even come round and see me.'

'Don't blame me for your naff social life.'

I was almost crying. My voice was loud. 'Don't you know how close we were? Camilla and me? Can't you see how upset I am?'

He leaned back, staring at the ceiling and blew two smoke rings.

I took a deep breath and got my words under control. 'I didn't know you knew these sort of people ... Fiona, St John ... Josh ..' I sounded pathetic, even pleading.

He leaned back even further, tilting his chair, then he came forward with a thump, his face close to mine. 'That's your fucking problem, isn't it?'

I moved backwards, afraid of his furious face.

'That's what this is really all about.' He spread his big hands out flat on the table. His eyes didn't leave mine. 'You're jealous.'

I tried to swallow again. 'Jealous?' My voice was small.

'You can't stand the bloody competition. You want to be the only one in the family who's made it. The only one who's got away from here.' He gestured around the room. 'This dump, this sodding town.'

'That's not true, I—'

'Yes it is!' he interrupted, shouting. 'You think you're the only person in the family who can string two words together and mix with our social betters. Well, I can do it too. I'll see who I like, screw who I like, sell my fucking paintings to who I like! It's none of your business. OK? If I want to go to London, I'll go to London. I don't need your bloody permission. Right?'

I stood up. My mouth was very dry and I was concentrating on holding back my tears. 'And where were you the night she was killed?'

His bright, angry eyes met mine again, then seemed to go dull. He looked down and fiddled around trying to get a cigarette out of his packet. His voice dropped almost to a whisper. 'I was playing darts at the Scrogg.'

I took a few steps towards the door, then turned back to him. 'I'll check,' I said. 'You bastard. I'll go round there tomorrow and check you out.'

I went outside and watched flakes of snow whirling under the lights of the pub. Two children, too young to be out so late, were trying to make snowballs from the thin layers which had gathered on the window ledges. As I walked away in the direction of the flat, some lumps of hard snow hit me in the back. I tried to think of other occasions when I'd had disagreements with Jimmy. He'd never answered back before, always accepting my point of view. He'd changed a lot recently. He'd become more confident. I kicked an empty beer can in the road, and lost my balance, slipping down onto my knees.

I could hear my dad's record player as I climbed back up the steps. The front door was open and the passage was full of people. They were all relatives but I didn't want to talk to them.

I thought I could hide in my bedroom but Alec was asleep on my bed. He had tinsel round his neck and his trousers were undone. I went into the living room. The overhead light was out and the Christmas tree cast a red glow in the smoke. I could see the dim shapes of people and there was a lot of laughter. I sat on the window sill next to the tree. I found a half-empty glass of lemonade and drank it.

I thought about Josh, at home in his flat, without Camilla. I tried to picture him with Pip, serving a perfectly designed Christmas meal, pouring vintage wine. His elegant hands moved with precision. Perhaps there was an empty space at the table, with a bare plate, a clean crystal glass and a folded napkin.

My back was damp from condensation on the window. Shouting began in the hall and people moved towards the doorway. I looked over their heads. The police had arrived. My uncle was squaring up to one of them and swearing. People held him back. My dad pushed through and someone turned off the music. I heard Dad apologize. He moved forward as if to shake the policeman by the hand, but the gesture was ignored. I thought how weak he looked. I remembered the confident way Camilla dealt with authority. I wanted to see her again.

After a while I lay down on the floor. My cheek pressed on the television wires and my knees were curled up. I remember closing my eyes but I don't think I went to sleep. Much later, when nearly everyone had gone, I stretched out on the settee.

I woke up stiff and uncomfortable. I made my dad some breakfast and he left for the early shift. He still worked at the shipyard, but it had closed down and now he was a security assistant, guarding the empty site. He sat in a Portakabin and occasionally wandered round with a truncheon and a walkie-talkie. He said he missed his friends, especially at Christmas.

Mam appeared in her dressing gown and started clearing up. It was seven o'clock.

'I hope that Alec's not still in my room,' I said.

'Don't be daft,' replied Mam. 'You better start washing these glasses.'

We filled a bin liner with torn decorations and leftover food. She piled crates with empties to go back to the pub. I hoovered the living room. Later, I took Jimmy a cup of tea. 'Here,' I said. 'Are you staying in?'

He was lying on his bed in his underpants, reading *Viz*. A cigarette smouldered in an ashtray at his side.

I forced myself to smile. The flat was too small and Christmas Day too long to ignore each other.

'Fancy a spin down the coast?' he asked. 'Get me a clean shirt.'

Outside, he opened the door of a van advertising Lightning Pizzas.

I looked at the drawing of a sizzling boxful, a flash of lightning and a phone number. 'What the hell's this?'

He shrugged and we climbed in. It smelled of garlic.

'I'm working a few nights on delivery. Cash in hand. Use of the van.'

'What about your grant?' I paused. 'What about the commissions?'

He frowned and switched on a tape. It was Blur and he sang along to a few bars. Then he said, 'I lent her the money, didn't I? I'm skint, me.' There was another pause. 'I lent her all my fucking money. Never got it back.'

The music was loud and uninterrupted while I took this in. 'Camilla?' I said at last. My voice was a whisper.

We headed east and a powdery layer of snow covered the playing fields and grass verges. The sun broke through and they turned dazzling white. As we passed some waste land, a pony on a long string ran alongside the road, following us. I noticed that a lot of people had sprayed fake frost in their windows and put fairy lights around their doors.

When we got to Tynemouth the wide sky was cloudless and blue, and the Long Sands were empty apart from a man in the distance throwing a stick for his dog. The sea was grey and flat. We went down the steps onto the beach to get out of the wind. The hut that sold tea was closed, and we walked towards the harder sand. The air smelled clean and cold.

Jimmy started singing 'The Little Drummer Boy', but he only knew one line, so I joined in. We sang loudly but our voices were carried away in the open space. The sea rolled to and fro. Jimmy unzipped his leather jacket and pulled me towards him. We leaned together. I held his waist, under the jacket, and he felt warm and solid. I thought about Camilla as we sang the song again. I had a plan of action. I wanted to go back to London.

Chapter Twenty-One

On Boxing Day I was doing the family's ironing when the phone rang.

'It's for you,' Jimmy said, wandering past in his underwear, picking up his newly pressed jeans. He was eating a turkey sandwich.

I raised my eyebrows. I never got phone calls in Newcastle. For some reason, I thought it might be Sean. 'Hello,' I said, crossly.

A familiar voice answered. 'Are you surviving, Imogen?' It was Al.

I was surprised. 'How did you get my number?'

'I've tried nearly all the Webbs in the book.'

'What d'you want?'

There was a pause. Her voice became lazy, disaffected. 'I thought we might meet up. I'm just nearby, you know.' She sighed. 'I'm bored.'

I remembered her parents lived in Northumberland. I glanced around. The television was on loud. Dad was back off shift, watching *My Fair Lady*. Mam had gone to play bingo at the community centre. Jimmy was just about to start delivering pizzas. The pile of unfinished ironing was high. 'OK,' I said, resigned. 'Where?'

*

I got a metro, then a train to Hexham. It was raining heavily as we rattled through the empty countryside. I wasn't looking forward to seeing Al, but the outing would help pass the time. I wanted, more than anything, to get back to London, do some more work on Camilla's case and enact my plan. I intended leaving the following day.

Al met me at the station. She looked different in a long skirt and a blazer. Her hair was pulled back in an elastic band. Parental pressure, I thought. I tried to smile.

'I've had a nipple pierced,' she said.

Standing in the quiet country station, this sounded ridiculous.

'Where? Here?'

'Yeah. There's a tattoo place in Hexham. Don't tell my mother.'

She led me into the car park and unlocked a Toyota Espace. I was surprised by its size, its brand-new smell. In London, she always claimed to hate cars. We climbed in. Expertly, she manoeuvred it into the road.

'Did it hurt?' I asked.

She looked puzzled.

'The nipple.'

'Yeah. In a sexy sort of way.'

I coughed. 'Awful weather,' I offered in response.

We drove down narrow lanes, edged by hedgerows and old stone walls. I wasn't sure what to expect. Al's parents had money. She'd been to private schools and her voice rang with the controlled tones of many elocution lessons. I remembered my surprise at the size of the Hardings' country home. I decided to be prepared for anything.

*

After a long drive, peering through the beating wind-
screen wipers, we turned into a village. We passed
cottages, a post office, an ancient church and climbed a
hill. At the top was a wide cul-de-sac of houses. They
were all new, but built in a style that suggested age.
They had Tudor façades and mullioned bay windows.
Each had identical patches of earth in front, which would
become gardens. 'Here we are,' said Al, impassively,
pulling up. She hurried inside, out of the rain.

She took her jacket and shoes off in the hall, so I did
the same. She started climbing the stairs. I turned and a
woman waved from the kitchen. She had long, loose hair
and wore a miniskirt. She was filling a water jug. I hesitated, then followed Al up to the first floor. I expected to
be taken into an upstairs living room, but she entered
her bedroom.

'I didn't know you had a sister,' I commented.

'That's my mother.' She picked up a small camera and
pointed it at me. It flashed rapidly, several times.

I held my hand up to my face. 'Stop it!'

The camera flashed again. She laughed and tossed
it to one side.

I looked around. The walls were covered in posters
of horses. Along a shelf was a row of silver trophies.
There were horse ornaments and a printed horse on the
duvet cover. I remembered my own collection of dolls in
national costume, but this seemed different. My room
in my parents' flat was a museum. Al's obsession
appeared current as well as juvenile. My eyes strayed
over the custom-built teenage furniture, the Boyzone calendar. 'What are we going to do up here?' I asked. 'Read
comics?' I was annoyed. 'I want to go downstairs.'

Al sat on the bed. 'Come here,' she suggested.

I went over and perched on the edge.

'Look,' she said. She lifted her sweater, revealing her chest. She wasn't wearing a bra. Each nipple was erect and one sported a silver ring. It looked sore. She put on her little-girl voice. 'What d'you think?'

I stared at her round, delicate breasts, then looked away. I was embarrassed. I stood up and went back to the door. An aroma of coffee wafted up the stairs. I turned to Al and she dropped her sweater. The expression on her face was one I couldn't read. 'I'm going down,' I said.

In the kitchen, Al's mother smiled brightly. I was self-conscious without my shoes, but didn't feel I could go back and put them on.

'My, you are tall,' she said, and then appeared startled as I drew closer. I knew she was surprised by my age. She tried to cover up her discomfort. 'I'm Karen, by the way. Would you like a coffee?'

I perched on a high stool and watched her organize cups and spoons. She opened a packet of biscuits. She was wearing too much jewellery, and she had a deep, fake tan, but the way she squared her shoulders, the way she snapped open the cellophane with strong fingers was familiar. She had long hair and she was a little heavy for her height. She was over forty years old, but despite this she was not unlike me.

We went into the lounge. It was tidy, with repro-duction furniture and framed prints on the walls, each with its own little brass light. The carpet was plain and thick. An artificial Christmas tree stood on the sideboard. I sank into a new-looking armchair and gazed at the rain through plate-glass patio doors.

Karen poured out three cups of coffee. She chatted about the weather and her holiday in Tenerife in November. I was reassured by her broad Tyneside accent. Al didn't appear, but upstairs a radio started playing pop music. She was sulking. I told Karen we'd had the whole family over on Christmas Eve.

'I'm from Byker,' she said, empathically. 'Newcastle born and bred. We moved out this way before Allegra was born. Her father's got his own business.' She paused. 'We split up two years ago.' She told me about her divorce settlement, her two new cars, her fitted bedroom furniture. She was both open and boastful.

We finished the coffee and she made some more. She asked me about the Advice Centre. I lied and said Al was a real asset. I felt relaxed with her because she was so pleasant.

'To be honest,' she confided, 'I didn't want Allegra to go into . . .' she hesitated, 'that line of work.'

'Really?'

She sniffed. 'She was groomed for the stage. Ballet lessons, singing and drama lessons, speech training. Years of it. Cost a bloody fortune.'

I thought I heard Al in the hall, but it was an ancient golden retriever. It came in and lay down in front of the fake coal fire.

'She could have tried for RADA. She could have been a model. She won Miss Pears 1981.'

I tried to look concerned. My cup and saucer were balanced on my knee. I drained the cup and put it on the glass-topped coffee table.

'I took her round all the agencies. She did a lot of catalogue work as a child. She was beautiful. She got a

modelling contract in London, you know. That's why she
went down there.' She blew her nose on a tissue.

I checked to see if she was crying, but she wasn't.

'She wouldn't stick at it. She got in with the wrong
crowd. Now it's the environment this, the environment
that. I'm sick of hearing about it. Bugger the environment. That's what I say.' She picked up Al's cold, undrunk
coffee and took it into the kitchen. 'Allegra!' she shouted
very loudly. 'You can bloody well get yourself down here!'

Karen came back into the living room and sat on
the floor near my feet. She beckoned me towards her,
as if to tell a secret. I leaned forwards. She smelled of
roses.

'I used to model,' she said very quietly, 'when Allegra
was a child. For Binns department store. Every season
there'd be a show for account holders. I walked up and
down, and around the tables, wearing their new stock.
Coats and suchlike. They had a lot of well-off customers.
I loved it. It was fun.'

'It was sad,' said Al from the doorway. She was eating
a lump of Christmas cake. 'You looked like a freak.'

I continued chatting to Karen. Al came and sat with us, on
the settee, looking bored. Her mother got out photograph
albums and showed me pictures of their previous houses,
holidays abroad and Al in her ballet dresses and riding
in gymkhanas. She pointed to a small pair of ballet shoes,
cast in brass, on the mantelpiece.

After a while Karen disappeared to unload the dishwasher and to make lunch. Al leaned forwards and sighed,
deeply. 'Take no notice of her,' she said quietly. 'She's a
toss-pot.'

I was about to protest.

'She didn't tell you I got chucked out of school, did she?'

I shook my head.

'She's full of shit.'

'You were expelled from school?'

She nodded and smiled.

'What for?'

'Bullying.' She picked up a plastic box and opened it. She started typing. I realized she had a laptop computer. She glanced over at me. 'I was pretty angry most of the time. Back then. Before I came to London. Before I met you.'

There was a silence. Her fingers tapped rapidly. 'There's something I want to show you,' she said. She came over and sat on the arm of my chair.

I turned the pages of a photograph album.

'Look!' she insisted.

I was expecting pornography, or at the very least, pierced body parts. I glanced at the screen. I was relieved to see words, not pictures. 'What is it?'

'Well,' she said. 'You know that Sean Docherty?'

My heart jumped in my chest.

'You know you thought he might have done Camilla?'

I put the album on the floor. I turned around and looked into her face. My mouth went suddenly dry. 'How the hell did you know that?'

'It was obvious.'

I tried to swallow. I wondered if she'd seen or read Camilla's case file.

'I know you, Imogen. I know what you think, how your mind works.' She scratched her head and spoke slowly. 'It's obvious.' She gave me a hard look. 'So. What's

gone and happened? You introduce him to her. She shags
him a few times. He likes it. He really likes it. She gets
bored. He's boring. She dumps him.' She blinked and
smiled, shrugging her shoulders. 'Then? He's pissed off
rotten. Everything's normal with her. Yeah? OK?'

I nodded.

'But she ends up dead.' She paused. 'You worry. You
introduced them.'

I took a deep breath. 'Right, Al. What've you got?'

She smiled, conspiratorially. 'I've done some research. His sister Mary came in about their housing
problem. I asked her where he works. It's just a simple
hacking job.' She pointed to the screen. 'This is the work-
sheet and pay records of the building firm. Sean's
employers.'

I grabbed the laptop. The information was as clear as
day. Sean had worked overtime from eleven fifteen on
the night of the murder and clocked off at six thirty the
following morning. Figures and other details indicated
where he'd worked, the names of his colleagues and
when they'd stopped for a tea break. His alibi was con-
firmed.

'D'you want a printout?'

My voice was quiet. 'No, it's all right.'

'You see. It wasn't your fault. Don't blame yourself.'
She switched off the computer and folded it away. 'You
can sleep at night. It's cool. Everything's OK.'

'Thanks, Al.'

'Anytime.' She stood up and grinned.

'I'm doing it for Camilla,' I offered. My voice was low.
I felt I had to explain. 'You know. Checking things out.
Making sure.'

She looked me in the eye. Her gaze was penetrating. 'Yeah. Well, I did it for you.'

After lunch, Karen drove me to the station. I liked her. I felt comfortable with her and gossiped, amiably. It occurred to me that I liked her better than Al. I told her about my brother's redundancy, his painting and our trip to Tynemouth the day before. Her presence chased thoughts of the murder from my mind. As she parked at the station I felt a rush of warmth towards her. I wanted her to be my friend. 'You must come down to London,' I said impulsively. 'Come and stay. I've got a sofa bed.'

For a minute she didn't reply. She released the door to let me out. She was frowning. 'London?' She spoke the word with distaste. 'Why would I go down there? I spend all my time trying to get Allegra to come home.'

I felt rebuffed. She gave me a puzzled, offended look, as if I'd said something improper. I jumped out and hurried away. She didn't say goodbye. I heard the drone of the engine as she drove away.

Chapter Twenty-Two

It was a relief, finally, to get on the train, back to London. I'd a plan based on something Camilla told me, during our last night in the pub. I thought I'd be able to relax on the journey, but I couldn't. I was edgy. The newspaper of the man opposite was written in French. I concentrated and followed the news items in a vague kind of way, but they were very dull. I wished I'd bought a magazine at the station.

My new clothes were crumpled and there was the smell of my family's breakfast in my hair. My hands were shaking and my vision was peculiar and spotted with bright lights. As we sped through Gateshead and hit open country the straight lines of the train's windows and the sides of the track seemed to tilt strangely to the left. For the first time in ages I was suffering from alcohol withdrawal, and it wasn't pleasant. Just after we got past Durham I went to the bar and bought three cans of Carlsberg.

Camilla's file was safely inside the briefcase and it was firmly between my feet on the floor. I stashed my rucksack above my head. I remembered my mother's job references and thought about how I was going to use them. Her line of work kept her thin but didn't make her fit. She cleaned the houses of women in Jesmond, the posh end of town. One of them had twelve cats. Like me, my mother was allergic to cat hair. She hadn't had a rise in over three years and was well below union rates. I threatened to ring her employers but she told me to mind my own business.

After a while I took out Camilla's file. I read through it again, then started a fresh page and added St John Harding to the catalogue of suspects. Camilla had compromised him at work in a way that seemed to involve his boss. I wrote: *Money???*

I leaned back in my seat, squinting at the clean sheets of paper. I looked at the empty page under Josh's name. I was still unable to think of much to say. He had no reason to harm Camilla. I wrote, *Ambitious. Snobbish. Pushes himself hard.* I added that I might have seen him in his car, driving past Camilla at the Elephant and Castle on the night of the murder.

The notes on my brother made me uneasy, but I told myself I was only doing my job. Jimmy had a motive. He'd been exploited and jilted and he might or might not have had the opportunity. The letter Camilla had written to him was in the file.

Finally, I brought up to date my evidence on Sean. I wrote down details acquired by Al. I drew a red line under his notes then forced myself to return everything to the briefcase.

The beer eventually made me dozy. After a while it became pleasant on the train. It seemed reassuring to be speeding along, not fixed in one place. I wondered about staying there for ever, watching the landscape constantly change in an unthreatening kind of way, eating over-priced sandwiches and swigging from cans. For a few minutes it seemed like an attractive option.

I fell asleep and dreamed again of Camilla. She was on a marble table but looked nothing like herself. Her chest and yards of filmy drapery were covered in blood. A voice announced, 'She's been dead for more than two weeks.'

When I opened my eyes, I was somewhere in that featureless suburb that surrounds London like a dirty glove. A vision of the Elephant and Castle formed in my mind. I grasped the briefcase in both hands and set my shoulders in an aggressive slouch. 'London Paranoia,' I said to the man opposite, as we moved to leave the train. He raised his hands in a French kind of way. I knew the only antidote to London was to stay busy.

I got a Tube from King's Cross, then a bus. Some of my fear returned and I was aware that I kept looking over my shoulder. I tried to suppress this as I headed south. I opened the briefcase and the file and looked again at Camilla's list. This was proving to be helpful. I'd already used it to get St John's direct line. Now I was on my way to Dulwich. She'd told me that Peter had just sacked his cleaner and one item on the list which I'd taken from her parents house said 'Cleaning' and an address. This was probably the organization Peter patronized. It might be open.

The agency turned out to be called Spit 'n' Polish. The lights were on. I left my rucksack behind the street door. It was up some steep stairs above a Chinese takeaway and was one small room. On the door were the words IN A STATE? WE'RE OPEN LATE. UNTIL EIGHT. AREN'T WE GREAT? As I pushed open the door I removed the stud from my nose and put it in my pocket.

A black woman with heavy make-up and a ropelike ponytail was sitting behind a desk, buffing her nails. She made me feel big and crumpled. I seemed to fill the room. I told her I wanted a job. My Geordie accent had become very pronounced and I made an effort to modify it. I needed to be understood. She yawned, handing me a form. I gave a false address in Herne Hill and handed over my mothers' references as a cleaner.

'Been in London long?' she asked.

'Just arrived,' I said. I told her I wanted light work in the Dulwich area and mentioned the street where Peter lived.

She tapped on a keyboard, gazing at the screen, frowning and shaking her head. Her scalp was wet-looking, with gel. After a minute she stopped, turned to a filing cabinet and pulled out a folder. She flicked through. 'One pub, one domestic. The pub pays better, but my girls don't fancy the Rottweiler. How are you with dogs?'

'What's the domestic?'

'Desperate, I think,' she smiled. 'Only three hours a week, that's the problem. Hardly worth the taxi fares, for most girls.' She read out Peter's address.

'That's perfect,' I said.

She gave me a funny look.

'It's straight through on the bus.'

'Hmn.' She read through a page of typed notes. 'Fussy client. He doesn't make much mess, except when his girlfriend's staying. Wants his ironing done. Four eighty an hour.'

'I'll take it,' I said.

She picked up the phone. 'He's given me the number of his mobile.' She smiled. 'Probably got no shirts ironed.'

The phone was answered immediately. I tried to hear Peter's clipped tones.

'Yes, sir. Yes, brilliant references . . . no, not too young.' She looked over at me and winked, saying, 'You have to be very careful, sweetheart. Antiques.'

I nodded.

'She says she's used to valuables . . . OK, sir?' She gave me the thumbs up. 'You want her tomorrow?' She looked at her calendar.

I nodded again.

'Yes, we're holding your keys. Cheers.' She dropped the phone with an air of achievement, opened a drawer and rummaged amongst sets of keys. 'I'll have to check one of these references.'

'That's fine by me.' I couldn't believe my luck.

She picked up the phone again. It rang for a long time. 'We have a Mrs Webb in our office . . . you gave her a reference . . .' There was a long pause while she talked to my mother's ex-employer. She turned to me. 'You're in, sweetheart.' She yawned again, handed me the keys and scribbled Peter's address and burglar-alarm code on another Spit 'n' Polish form. She went to a cupboard and pulled out a laundered overall. 'This is "large",' she said. She shook it, glanced at me and frowned. She produced another. 'Outsize,' she decided. Her voice was pitying. I took it and hurried off, in case she changed her mind. My feet clomped down the uncarpeted stairs.

'Pop in on Friday for your wages,' she called.

Chapter Twenty-Three

There've been a lot of cleaners in my family. My mother used to say cleaning was in our blood. My grandmother spent her teenage years in service. She met her husband, my grandfather, when he was an errand boy, carrying groceries on the front of his bicycle. My grandmother had an attic room and got up each day at a quarter to five. She worked for a doctor. When she was an old woman she used to say that she would have liked to have been a doctor, or maybe a midwife, or a nurse. Instead she carried coal and scrubbed out the scullery.

My cousin Maureen cleaned at the airport. My Auntie Flo cleaned at Burger King before she got a job cleaning buses. My mother always did domestic work and claimed to enjoy it, apart from the house with all the cats. She insisted that her favourite smell in the whole world was Domestos.

I worked as a cleaner during one of the long vacations when I was a student. I put an advert in a newsagent and two ladies rang me up. One turned out to be old and snooty and got me to carry in the tea things when she had afternoon visitors. The other was young and had several small children. She lived in a big house that was being renovated, and it was in such a mess it never looked any better, even after I'd finished. There was rough plaster and bare floorboards, and for a while they had no bathroom and had to use the toilet next door. I told her it was like Walker in the sixties, but actually it was worse. I think she felt guilty about having a cleaner. She was incapable of instructing me and tried to pretend that we were friends.

I never enjoyed the work. My hands came out in a rash and hoovering made my back ache. I told my mother that due to a genetic blip cleaning wasn't in my blood. I was pleased to discover that it was useful, in the end. As I set out for Peter's house, late the following afternoon, wearing the Spit 'n' Polish overall under my jacket, I felt confident in my role.

I'd spent the morning buying new cables and brakes for the bicycle and in the first half of the afternoon I fixed it properly. This took longer than I expected, but it was easier to ride than before. I cycled over to Peter's and hid it behind a bush in his front garden. His keys were clearly labelled and the alarm easily switched off. I found the utility room in the basement and collected everything I needed. Starting at the top of the house, I prepared to begin dusting, polishing, hoovering and searching.

It was getting dark outside. The sky was pink streaked with navy blue. It was four o'clock. Peter was never home before seven, usually later. Within minutes of arriving, I wished I'd come earlier. I'd underestimated how long it would take to do all the work and make a thorough search. I decided to do what I could, and if necessary come back a second time.

One attic room contained boxes of files and books, some of which seemed to date back to Peter's days as a student. Others were old business records. One box contained Conservative Party minutes and memoranda. There were old tennis racquets, canvas chairs, a sun lamp which looked broken. None of it was interesting. I didn't bother cleaning. The second attic room was tidy and contained only a bed, a chair and a washstand. I wiped over the surfaces and went down to the first floor.

There were two bathrooms, one en-suite to Peter's bedroom. Here I discovered Camilla's make-up in the cabinet and an unopened bottle of her perfume. It was Chanel's Coco. I disentangled hair from the shower plug and decided that some of it was hers. I opened her scent and sprayed some on my wrists and neck. I decided to keep the bottle. I was disturbed by the image of her murderer, copying the Whistler and pouring her perfume over her body. On the other hand, the smell reminded me of her. I liked it. It seemed important to keep the bottle for ever, sniffing it occasionally, taking pleasure in it, using it to bring Camilla into my mind.

I cleaned both bathrooms thoroughly, watered the plants, picked up dirty clothes and made a pile ready to take downstairs. Peter used expensive English cologne and his shaving brush was badger hair with a brass handle and stand. There was a print on the wall of a red-haired woman, bathing.

In his room, I studied a framed photograph of Camilla. She looked sulky and young. The bed was unmade and Camilla's nightdress was still under the pillow. I stripped it, found clean sheets, remade it and added everything, including the nightdress, to the laundry. Methodically, I searched through the cupboards and drawers. There were contraceptive pills, a rail of beautiful suits, an old teddy bear in the wardrobe. I pulled out a white shirt and held it up to my chest. It was hand sewn and not too small. I decided to keep it, as well as a gay pornographic magazine hidden under a pile of sweaters. I also pocketed a small bundle of photographs which were at the back of a drawer. A silk scarf of Camilla's was draped on a chair and I tied it round my neck.

I rubbed the mirrors and glass ornaments with my duster and swept the stripped-pine floor. I sprayed polish on the mahogany furniture and the brass bedstead and brought up a shine. Next door, I cleaned the big, silent drawing room but didn't find anything. A glass of brandy helped me to keep going. I took off my shoes, climbed on a chair and dusted the paintings, trying to remember which one was the fake.

At five forty-five I carried the laundry down to the basement and put it in the washing machine. Back in Peter's study, I knew I hadn't time to be thorough. I went through all the papers in the desk and the filing cabinet. There were a lot of bills, neatly organized, insurance policies and bank statements. I found references to stocks and shares. There were documents related to Peter's publishing house. I started filling a large empty envelope with anything of interest, including postcards, personal letters, a few bank statements and a stray copy of the *Tatler*, which might have been Camilla's. Without completing the task, I dusted and tidied and went back downstairs. I put everything I had taken into Camilla's briefcase which was with my jacket, on the hallstand. Time was running out. Peter needed some shirts ironed. I went down to the basement and found the basket of clean washing.

Draping the ironed shirts on hangers, I returned them to his wardrobe. It was a quarter to seven. I decided to give myself ten more minutes, then I knew I had to leave. I quickly washed the kitchen quarry tiles with a mop and put bleach in the sink. A framed picture, covered by the long fronds of a hanging fern, was a drawing of Camilla, done by my brother. I was wiping down the worktops when the front door banged. I moved towards the back basement door, but then I remembered Camilla's brief-case and everything I'd taken, upstairs with my jacket, in the hall. Listening, I stood on the bottom stairs. I tied Camilla's silk scarf around my head like a turban. I tucked all my hair inside so that none of it showed.

His footsteps went up to the first floor and he clat-tered the toilet seat. Still holding the dishcloth, I ran up to the hall. I glanced in the mirror. There was a smear of dirt across one cheek and I was unusually red-faced. Without make-up and with my hair concealed, I looked nothing like myself.

The toilet flushed. He was coming down the stairs. I couldn't get out in time. I knelt down to disguise my height and pretended to be wiping the skirting board. I said a quick prayer.

'Hello, there,' Peter said. 'How have you got on?'

I looked up and met his eye. I exaggerated my accent. 'I haven't managed to do it all. I'm sorry. I haven't done the stairs or the rooms on the ground floor.'

'Don't worry,' he said, smiling. He stood leaning against the wall. He looked boyish and charming in the shadows. 'You'll get used to it. And it hasn't been done for a while. It'll be easier next time. Did you find everything?'

'Yes, thanks. There's washing still doing in the ma-chine and mind the kitchen floor's wet.'

'Jolly good,' he replied. He didn't recognize me. He

didn't expect to recognize someone in an overall. 'You can go now.'

I didn't want to give myself away by standing up. Carefully, I folded my dishcloth. 'Thanks.'

He turned to go back upstairs. 'It's a frosty night,' he said. 'Take care.' He disappeared.

I cycled home. The streets of Stockwell were deserted. I called into the off-licence for some wine and then waited in a queue for an Indian takeaway. Beyond the pool of its brightly lit window everything was in darkness. In the distance, a police siren wailed. I hung the carrier bags over my handlebars, then got back on the bike. As I pedalled along my body felt leaden and heavy from the cleaning but I was elated. I'd got away with it. I'd searched Peter's house like a real private eye. I was so relieved I forgot to check if I was being followed.

As soon as I turned the corner to my road I knew something was wrong. There was a light on in my flat. My door was open. I put my bags down on the pavement and hesitated. I walked round the corner and rang the bell to the upstairs flat. There was music playing so I knew someone was in. There was no response. I rang again. It wasn't unusual for the man upstairs not to answer his door. Like me, he had a siege mentality.

Across the street an argument started behind closed curtains. There was a sound of breaking glass and shouting. 'That's right,' a woman screamed, 'try and kill your old mother!'

I had no choice but to go into my flat alone. My heart pounded and I was suddenly damp with sweat. I pushed the door wide and stepped into the hall. I dragged in the bicycle, dumping my jacket, the wine, the takeaway and the briefcase. In the kitchen the drawers were all tipped out and there was a peculiar smell. A bottle of vinegar was spilled on the floor, mixed with sugar and Persil. I picked up a vegetable knife, and holding it in front of me I moved across the hall. The living room was brightly lit and disorganized but there was no one there. Still clutching the knife, I checked the bedroom and the bathroom. The flat was empty but every cupboard was ransacked, every drawer dragged out and emptied. My bed was stripped and the mattress overturned. I examined the burglar alarm and discovered it ripped from the wall, the wires cut.

The locks on the front door had been dragged from the splintered frame. I leaned the bike against it, to hold it closed. I turned on the heating. I couldn't find the corkscrew so I struggled and opened the bottle of wine I'd bought with the end of a fork. My glasses were all smashed so I glugged it down from my souvenir United mug, which was not normally used for drinking. I sat on the floor of the living room, shaking. My television, video, radio and hi-fi were all still there. I went into the kitchen. My microwave was on top of the fridge. In the bedroom, my camera had been pulled from a drawer. It lay on the rumpled sheets. I checked my jewellery box. My earrings had been tipped out, but even the gold ones, even my grandmother's diamond ring hadn't been stolen. With a start I saw some writing on my mirror. Someone had picked up my lipstick and used it to write the words DON'T MESS WITH ME CUNT.

I remembered my previous burglary. It had been efficient and barely disruptive. My video and CD player were taken, but nothing else, and afterwards the security firm I hired completed their work and told me not to worry. I went back to the wrecked alarm and dialled the emergency number printed on its cover. Forcing myself not to cry, I also rang the police.

A uniformed constable came round after an hour.

'It's not an ordinary burglary.' I was almost shouting. He picked his way through the debris. 'It's all to do with my friend being killed.'

'We see them like this all the time,' he replied. He was taller than me and looked about eighteen.

'He hasn't taken the video,' I insisted, 'or the telly, or my camera.'

'No transport,' he said mildly, looking down at me.

I realized I was still wearing my overall. 'He hasn't touched my jewellery.'

'They can only carry so much.'

I stood silent for a moment. 'You don't understand,' I said quietly. 'He hasn't taken anything.'

He leaned against the mantelpiece and his radio crackled eerily. He smiled and shrugged. 'Kids,' he said. 'All they want is a few quid to buy drugs. They'll have gone straight out to score.'

'You don't understand. This isn't what you think.'

He raised his eyebrows and looked at the empty wine bottle. 'I've got all the details,' he murmured. He made as if to leave, glancing into the bedroom. 'Don't clean that mirror. CID will want to check that.'

I caught hold of his arm as he stood outside the front door. 'I'm being victimized,' I said. 'Followed. He's after the file.'

He looked very sympathetic, gently freeing his arm. 'Would you like me to send a WPC round? A lady police officer?'

I sighed. 'It's OK,' I said.

'Get someone to come and stay with you,' he advised, disappearing into the night.

About eleven o'clock, the man from the security firm arrived. He was very small and dark, with a Greek accent. With amazing speed he replaced the damaged doorframe and reinstated the locks. He checked all the windows. 'There's nothing I can do about that alarm tonight,' he said, 'there'll be someone round in the morning.'

I found a lager six-pack and opened a can. I stood head and shoulders above him. 'Would you like a drink?' I offered.

He shook his head. 'I'm on duty all night.'

'I've got window locks, bolts, an alarm. No one takes any notice of alarms. They sound normal, around here, like traffic. What am I supposed to do?'

It was meant to be a rhetorical question but he answered me, deadpan. 'Get a steel door,' he replied, 'metal window grilles.' He started to pack away his tools. 'You're my sixth tonight,' he added.

'What area d'you cover?'

'Lambeth, Stockwell, Brixton. It's all go.' The clash between his idioms and his accent was comic, but I was too upset to be amused.

'Me, I've moved away,' he continued. 'I live in Berkshire.' He buttoned up his jacket.

I didn't want him to go. 'Do burglars often make a mess? I've got mess but nothing missing.'

'Some do. Some don't. Some make urine on the carpet. Or worse. Some write on walls. Others are tidy operators and just take the CD.'

'Mine didn't take the CD. Is that strange?'

'Pretty strange. Maybe he was disturbed by a

neighbour.' He looked up at me quizzically. 'Maybe a pervy sex thing.' He stepped out into the darkness. 'Take my advice, darling. Get a friend to come and stay tonight.'

I tried to tidy up. I threw away my Indian take-away. I knew the police wouldn't bother to take fingerprints. I got some bleach and tissues and rubbed the message off the mirror.

All I could think was that despite my precautions anyone could get into my flat, any time they wanted to. It wasn't difficult at all.

I made up my bed with clean sheets and climbed in. I listened for someone trying the windows. It was only the rain. Once or twice I got up to check if certain items had gone. A few old folders from work, ones I'd been meaning to return, had disappeared from under my bed. They were closed cases and of no value to anyone. This seemed significant. The tape was missing out of my answering machine. My leather jacket was still hanging on a hook in the hall. I couldn't sleep. The bed felt hard and I was restless. There was aromatherapy oil in the bathroom and I sprinkled some on my pillow. This didn't work. I listened to my radio. In the end I swallowed two Temazepam and spent the night in a daze, seeing a squadron of policemen and joiners break down the walls with pickaxes before marching rhythmically round and round my bedroom.

The next morning the CID didn't show but a different man from the security firm arrived. He was Scottish, with ginger hair. He fixed my alarm.

'I want a steel door and metal grilles,' I told him.

He fished a phone out of his overalls and telephoned his office.

'When will they be fitted?' I imagined several sleepless nights waiting for my order to be processed.

'I'll measure up,' he offered.

'When can I have them?'

He looked at his watch and whistled to himself for a moment. 'Twelve thirty this afternoon.'

Al phoned. 'I'm back in London,' she said brightly.

I told her what had happened.

'Wow!' she said in her fake hippy accent. 'What a bummer!' She offered to come round and help. She started telling me about a time when her laptop was stolen at a festival.

'Please don't,' I said weakly, interrupting, then putting down the phone.

Later, I waylaid my guitar-playing upstairs neighbour but he said he hadn't heard anything. 'I'm pissed off,' I told him.

He went to the nearest takeaway and came back with sandwiches. 'Ground-floor flats are the worst,' he said knowledgeably. 'You should move.'

'I've just decorated,' I said. It sounded lame.

'I don't know anything,' he offered. He knew that I knew about the used video recorders and CD players which moved mysteriously up and down his stairs.

'I know you don't. This was a personal thing. Not a normal job.'

'You don't shit in your own nest,' he agreed. 'But I'll try to find out. I'll ask around.'

*

I spent the day clearing up. Two more security men arrived on time and fixed a steel plate to my door. They took out the wooden frame and replaced it with metal. The new bolts were twelve inches long. I was struck by the firm's efficiency. They were fast, neat and expensive. Compared to the police, they were really on the ball.

I phoned my bank manager and told him I needed an overdraft. 'I'm buying a car,' I lied.

I swept and hoovered the floors and cleared up the tomato ketchup, the honey and the vinegar. The sheets and clothing which had been handled by the intruder I put in the washing machine. My framed autograph of Les Ferdinand was broken, so I removed the shards of glass and put it carefully back on the mantelpiece. I tried to keep moving because activity stopped me thinking. Eventually, there was no more to do. My upstairs neighbour called and said he'd found out nothing. He looked puzzled. 'Nobody round here,' he said with confidence.

There was a lot of hammering and banging. The workmen were still in my flat. I raised my voice. 'I know.'

He winked. 'Come up if you need anything.'

I didn't smile. 'You never answer your door.'

I sat on the settee finishing off the lager as the grilles went up. They were the non-ornamental models and the effect was like a medieval jail. The rooms darkened and it was impossible to see the street. I drew the curtains and decided to leave them that way. I tried very hard to look calm. 'No one can touch you now,' said one of the workmen as I signed the cheque.

Chapter Twenty-Four

I decided to go into work on the thirtieth. The Advice
Centre was still closed for the holidays, so I knew I'd be
alone. I cycled up Blackfriars Road, my wheels crunching
through frozen puddles. I discovered Al had been in and
tidied up. When I sat at my desk, I felt I was back on
Camilla's case. It had been too long. I decided that my
desk, my end of the office, had to be the HQ for this case
alone. Nothing else mattered.

The light was flashing on the answering machine. I
remembered the mysterious threat that had been left
before Christmas. Nervously, I listened to a string of pleas
from desperate people whose benefit was cut, whose
Christmas presents were stolen, whose roofs were leaking
from melting snow. The female half of the Electricity
Couple, who'd been in several times before Christmas,
had left six halting, inarticulate messages. Another client,
who was known to me, phoned because her daughter
went to stay with her dad and ended up in care. There
were two calls from Penny. She was still asking for help
in finding interviewees for her programme *Londoners*. I
made some notes, but there was little I could do during
the holidays.

At the end of the tape there was the voice I was
dreading. At first I heard a cough, then silence. There

was a television in the background. It sounded like the
National Lottery Draw. Finally he spoke. 'If you don't lay
off and stop poking around . . .' and the tape ran out. My
heart was jumping in my chest but I ignored it. I played
the message over. It was the same voice and the same
Scottish accent as last time. Again, I thought I might
take the tape to the police, but I knew they wouldn't be
interested. Putting it back in the machine, I rewound it
and wiped it clean. I dialled 1471 and was given a number
in Camberwell. I checked the file and my suspicion was
correct. The last person to ring the office had been the
tiresome woman without electricity. There'd been no
tape left to record yet another one of her pleas.

I tried to light the Calor gas fire, but the ignition was
faulty. I shut the door and switched on my desk lamp.
My breath condensed in the cold air. The street outside
was deserted and wet with a heavy rain which was
thawing and dispersing the ice. I hugged my jacket
around my chest and breathed on my hands. They were
shaking. I tried not to shiver. There seemed to be nothing
to do but press on. I opened the file and examined the
new evidence I'd taken from Peter's house. The bank
statements revealed nothing I didn't know. Peter had a
lot of money and spent it in a predictable way. There
were no payments into Camilla's account although one
standing order was for her disposable contact lenses. I
studied statements from Selfridges and Harrods. Some
of the amounts were clearly for Camilla's clothes and
cosmetics. Other receipts showed money spent on Peter's
handmade shoes, his club expenses, his garage bill, his
account with a florist.

I looked through the postcards and letters but nothing
seemed relevant. The photos were more interesting.

There were snaps of Camilla and Peter with other people, taken at Kew. One of them may have been St John Harding. They all looked very young. Their clothes seemed old-fashioned. I remembered Camilla telling me that she'd known Peter nearly all her life.

Other photos showed Peter as a student. He looked moody and poetic with too-long hair and a second-hand overcoat. One of them was taken in the summer and a group of young men lounged on a lawn with college buildings in the background. They had bare feet and they were all smoking. Two of them were reading books. On the back was scribbled 'Finals '82'. I looked at the students again. At their side was a big old tree. Peter was leaning back to back with someone who looked familiar. I squinted at the face, then held it under the light. It was Josh. He had more hair and was a little fatter but those aquiline features were unmistakable. I was surprised. I didn't know that Peter and Josh had been at university together. I'd assumed their acquaintance was shorter, and that they'd got to know each other in London, through Camilla.

I opened the *Tatler* I'd found in Peter's study. I flicked through it, listlessly. As I replaced it in the briefcase, a slip of paper fell out. It was the typed draft of a letter from Peter to Camilla with handwritten alterations and crossings out. It was dated the day she was killed.

'Darling,' it read, 'I'm sorry about what I said the other night.' Then there was something heavily scored out and then the word 'Sean'. The next paragraph said, 'I love you so much and I just can't stand it. Why won't you marry me?' The following bit was crossed out, then, 'hurt me like this? I'll do anything, just ask – sell the house, give up the business, leave London, anything. People can change. I can try. I could make you love me more if you gave me the chance. Why can't you forgive me? It was all so long ago. I know we can put all that tiresome business behind us, it's all in the past. I was a different person then. There's no reason for us not to marry. I want you so.'

There was no second sheet although the letter wasn't finished. I felt guilty reading it. Peter was so buttoned up, it seemed indecent, prying into his emotions. I couldn't imagine why he might be asking for forgiveness. As far as I knew, his loyalty and reliability had never been questioned.

I opened Camilla's file. Peter had been in love with Camilla and she treated him badly, but he refused to give up. She stayed at his house frequently, but only when it suited her. She was fairly free with his money, although only in small amounts. The letter suggested she had perhaps given a reason, from the past, why she didn't want to marry him. I considered this for a moment and decided it was probably just some excuse she was offering to avoid a wedding. They had quarrelled on the Wednesday night before she died and he had been trying to make it up, as usual. I'd discovered that Camilla and Peter had known each other for a long time, but this was no secret. The only really new and slightly surprising thing was that Peter and Josh were old friends. I made a note of this in the file, under both Peter and Josh's names, and slipped the photo and the letter between plastic covers.

I flicked through the pornographic magazine. It was full of pictures of naked men. I couldn't imagine Peter looking at it with anything other than distaste. I put it back in the briefcase.

In the file, I turned to the page headed JIMMY WEBB. I

read through the notes I'd made on the train. My brother's deception was outlined in short, angry sentences. I added to the page that Peter had one of Jimmy's drawings framed in his kitchen. After a minute with Directory Enquiries, I dialled a Newcastle number.

'Hello,' I said, 'is that the Scrogg public house?'

In my notes, my brother's alibi was a darts game. I assumed a strong Geordie accent and pretended to be from another team. I asked about fixtures and results. The team had played, not only on the night of Camilla's death, but also the following lunchtime. I thought of Jimmy seeing Camilla's face on the TV screen in the pub. The news was announced about three in the afternoon.

'Was Jimmy Webb playing on those days?'

'We've never played without Jimmy.'

'Are you sure?'

'Of course, man. He's our star player.'

'What time did the game finish?'

There was a pause.

'Was he there until closing time?'

'After then. We were celebrating. That's the night we won the league.' There was a hesitation. 'Who did you say you were?'

I hung up and wrote all this down. It was clear Jimmy hadn't killed Camilla. The rail service was fast, but it wasn't that fast. He couldn't have been in the pub that evening until after eleven and still have got to London in the time. He'd been in Newcastle, and this put him in the clear. I drew a red line under his notes.

The day had never got light and what little brightness there was ebbed away. I leaned back in the chair and watched my reflection in the window. The outside world disappeared in the gloom. Under my eyes there were wide grey circles and my haircut had entirely lost its sharp edges. I smoothed it down at the sides. I studied myself in the window, sitting at my desk, my hand under the lamp, holding a pen. For the moment I looked as if I knew what I was doing. This thought was calming. I crossed the room and opened Al's drawer. In the back was a tobacco tin and a packet of Rizlas. There was a small square of foil. I rolled a joint and sat down in her chair to smoke it. Staring at the cracks in the ceiling, I tried hard to smile.

I remembered sitting in a pub in Brixton with Camilla. We were already stoned and we started drinking Bacardi. We were with three black guys but they were talking quietly amongst themselves. Every so often one of them nodded, politely, and bought us more drinks. After a while two of them moved over to play pool.

'This is my friend Earl,' Camilla said, gesturing to the third.

'Hi, Earl,' I murmured, 'how's it going?'

'It going,' he said, sighing.

Camilla wandered over to the pool table. She put some money down. She wanted to play the winner of the game that was in progress. Earl grinned. 'Man, no do,' he warned.

After a while, she picked up a cue and chalked it.

'Oh, no.' Earl's smile was wide.

'Don't mock her,' I warned him.

She tapped a few balls lightly. Her opponent laughed and nudged his friend. Camilla knotted her hair at the back of her neck and frowned. The game got going.

Earl passed me a joint. He was leaning on the padded

bench, his legs splayed. We both watched Camilla pot ball after ball.

'Hey,' he said.

I expected him to be surprised. I blew smoke at the ceiling. She finished the game and put down her cue. She walked up to the bar and bought drinks for us all.

'I told you,' I said.

'Mock?' Earl spread both hands on the table, palms down. He shook his head slowly. 'Her never, ever loses. Her wins. I's not mocking she. Never. No.'

After a while I went back to Camilla's file. I thumbed through it again, trying to set priorities. I wondered how many other suspects there might be. Making out a page for her brother's boss, Professor Grant, I couldn't think of much to say about him. She might have flattered, offended or threatened many people. Any one of them could have a motive.

It was freezing in the office. My jacket wasn't warm enough and I blew on my hands again. There was little I could do, but I felt I wanted to make progress. I telephoned Fiona Harding at her gallery, and got an answering machine. I consulted Directory Enquiries, then rang St John's number in Finsbury Park.

A woman with a Spanish accent answered.

'Mrs Harding?' I was glad it wasn't St John.

She sounded flustered. 'No please, I am maid.'

'Can I speak to Fiona Harding?'

There was a long pause and a lot of distant laughter, as if they were entertaining. I remembered St John's noticeable lack of grief.

'Hello, there,' said a breathless voice. She sounded as if she had just run upstairs.

I decided to be direct. 'I'm a friend of Camilla's,' I said bluntly. 'Can I come and see you?'

She said nothing. Her breath was wheezy and laboured.

'You weren't at the funeral,' I persisted. 'I'd very much like to talk to you. Can I come on the second?' I knew from long experience that people are more inclined to back down on the phone. 'I can come in the morning.'

When she spoke she was defensive. 'The funeral? I rarely go out of London.' Her breath caught in her chest again, as if to prove the point.

'I'd like to talk to you.' I was friendly. 'I'd like to see you on your own.' My voice was slightly pleading.

'Are you from the press?'

I took a chance. 'No.' I paused. 'No. I'm Jimmy Webb's sister.'

There was another silence. 'Is Jimmy in London?' She sounded intrigued. Her voice had an odd intonation. I wondered if she was South African.

'No,' I said, 'he's not. But I'm in London. I'll come on the second. In the morning. Will you be alone?'

'Oh, all right,' she said finally. She was baffled.

Chapter Twenty-Five

I stayed in bed until late the next day. When I got up, I turned on the heating and the radio and ate some oven chips. After a while, I remembered it was New Year's Eve. I went back to bed with a bottle of vodka. I lay contemplating the pattern on the duvet cover. It was yellow and covered with orange marigolds. I decided no one had ever seen it, except perhaps Camilla, when she visited me, that time I was ill with flu. I had a single bed. No one had ever slept in it, beside me. I had no reason to spend money on nice bedlinen.

I sang along to some old pop songs on the radio, then tried to read Camilla's *Tatler*. I dozed a little. When the phone sounded, I couldn't be bothered to answer it. Eventually, because it rang rang rang, I got out of bed.

It was Al. 'Hello, Imogen,' she said cheerfully, 'we're going to a party tonight. It's on a boat.' I heard her suck on her roll-up. 'You know. Like, the river. I'm worried that you're on your own.' She sounded sorry for me.

'I'm pretty busy,' I lied, 'with one thing and another.' I hung up.

I checked the television schedules and went back to bed. I turned off the radio and switched to a comedy film on my portable TV. It was Robin Williams but I didn't pay much attention. I tried to remember last New Year's Eve, and the one before. All I could picture was Camilla dancing, her hair wild, wearing a tiny silver minidress.

I thought about her involvement with men in the months before her death. There had been four that I knew of – Jimmy, Sean, Peter and Professor Grant. It occurred to me that she might have taken advantage of them all.

I cast my mind back. She didn't always do this. She schemed and partied through lots of affairs, for reasons of bravado, vanity, experience. She enjoyed herself. She was in control. She got what she wanted and who she wanted, but there'd been a lightheartedness, a sense of fun.

Some of her past lovers came to mind. There'd been an Athenian shipping heir, a postmodernist sculptor, the headmaster of a public school. She avoided pop stars and actors in case their egos eclipsed hers. She dated a BBC cameraman, a trainee hairdresser, the owner of a super-market chain. I tried to think of times when she was unhappy.

I remembered a week when she was working in Fulham, on a TV commercial. It showed Camilla spooning up a last mouthful of cereal, leaving the table, throwing off her wrap and entering the bedroom. Shot from behind, she was naked and slim. Eat this for break-fast, it suggested, and you could look like her, be her, have her.

'Do they realize,' I said, when I met her in the pub after her second day, 'you've never eaten breakfast in your life?'

'It tastes like pony shit,' she agreed.

'What's wrong with your hair?' I asked. It seemed lank.

'It's gel. They kept putting more and more on. I'm supposed to look like I just had a shower.'

We were in Chelsea. It was a hot, airless night. As it got darker the pub became very crowded and karaoke started in the room next door. Camilla said she hadn't eaten.

'D'you want a bar meal?'

She nodded. 'I'm starving,' she admitted.

The air was dense with smoke. Outside, I thought I heard thunder. Camilla seemed depressed. She'd bought a Babycham and she pushed the cherry around the glass with the end of a fingernail. 'I'm in love,' she said, unexpectedly. She started talking about the brand manager. He'd been briefing her on the merits of his breakfast cereal. 'He's gorgeous,' she insisted.

'Oh, God,' I moaned. 'What about Peter? What about that architect? The one with the sports car?'

'No,' she argued. 'This is the one for me. He's Welsh. He's got a divine accent. He used to play rugby.'

I tried to be light. 'Does he sing in a male voice choir?'

'Probably.' She stayed serious. 'His name's Gwyn. He's from Aberystwyth. He doesn't like me.' She refused to cheer up.

I spoke encouragingly. 'What's the matter? Have you tried getting him drunk?'

'He's got a wife called Bronwen.' She started crying, a little too noisily. People on nearby tables turned around and stared. I rummaged in her big model's bag and found some tissues. She dabbed her eyes but then cried without restraint.

'Have you told him how you feel?' I was helpless. I wanted her to stop.

'He said . . .' She sobbed some more. 'He said . . . he

likes being married.' She reached for my hand but I felt inhibited. I moved back a little.

After a couple of minutes she scrubbed at her cheeks with the tissues. She got out a mirror, foundation, lipstick and eyeliner and effortlessly redid her face. Two middle-aged women next to us nudged each other.

'Forget him,' I advised. 'What's so great about him, anyway?'

She didn't smile. She seemed chastened. She fished in her bag for a bottle of prescription pills and took two. At that moment, the bar meals arrived. They were dumped, hot and greasy, in front of us.

Camilla stood up, grabbing her bag. 'I'm not eating that,' she said quickly. Her voice was scathing. She pulled a brush from her bag and started nervously pulling it through her hair. She was suddenly panicky. 'If I get any fatter, no one will want me.'

Before I could stop her she'd left the pub. I followed her out into the street but she'd disappeared. Thunder rumbled then crashed overhead. Rain cascaded down and the black road steamed.

A week went by and then we arranged to meet again. It was the end of the assignment. I waited in the same pub. It was a Saturday afternoon and the day was cloudless, hot and bright. I sat near the door, which was propped open with a chair. London sunlight streamed in, pale and sparkling with dust. The jukebox played quietly. The pub was almost empty apart from a few tourists and cab drivers, lounging at the bar. There was a rattle of dominoes and a smell of cigars. I sipped my pint. It tasted smooth and sweet. Outside, I could see pigeons pecking for crumbs and there was a haze over the traffic.

Camilla arrived smiling. She was wearing a pink strapless sundress and held a carrier from Harvey Nichols. I bought her a gin and tonic.

'It's hot,' she said, cheerfully.

I took off my denim jacket and blew down my T-shirt.

'Are they heavy?' She laughed. 'What size are you, anyway? Forty-six double-D?'

'Shut up, will you?'

She giggled and tied her hair in its customary knot at the back of her head. Her shoulder blades jutted.

'Just because yours are like flea bites,' I joked.

Some workmen walked past, still in their overalls. They offered to buy us drinks but we just smiled and shook our heads. We were happy and too warm and the pub was nice. I decided not to mention the Welshman.

After about half an hour two men appeared in the doorway, carrying briefcases. They dragged chairs up to our table. Camilla laughed and introduced me. 'This is Imogen,' she said, 'she's a hot-shot solicitor.'

I shook my head, smiling. 'She always says that,' I apologized.

They were both wearing ties with their shirtsleeves rolled up. I glanced from one to the other. They were lean, handsome and well mannered. They had expensive haircuts. 'This is Gwyn,' said Camilla, leaning towards him with her cigarette. He lit it and stroked her cheek.

'We thought we'd all go for a meal, later,' said his friend. I looked at him, hopefully. He winked at me. 'Gwyn knows a great new Italian place, up in Camden Town.'

Towards midnight, when I'd almost finished the vodka, Al called again. Her mobile phone hummed and distorted.

'I forgot to tell you the address.' She giggled. 'I mean where the boat is, you know, sort of tied up.'

I could hear the sound of the party in the background.

'There's some people here. There's an actor, who used to share his flat with your friend Camilla. There's a very interesting woman called Penny. She wants to make a TV programme about—'

'I'm not coming,' I interrupted. 'I've had a better offer.'

Lying in bed, after midnight, I tried not to think about Al, at a party with Camilla's friends. Instead, I listened to roaming bands of revellers. It was impossible to sleep and I pulled the covers over my head. A group of men stood outside my window, trying but failing to sing 'Auld Lang Syne'. They were unsure of the words and kept repeating the same two lines over and over again. I felt angry with them for not knowing the song. I kept willing them to remember. I said to them, under my breath, 'If you can't even get that right, then what hope is there?'

I awoke late the next morning, the telephone ringing again. For a split second, irrationally, I thought it might be the mystery caller.

'Hi, Imogen, it's Al. Happy New Year.'

My head was throbbing and I had a raging thirst. I realized I must have finished the vodka. 'What, again?' For a moment I thought the party must be still going on. I was confused. I looked at my watch. It was twelve fifteen.

'I've been trying to get you all morning. Since eight o'clock. Where've you been? Have you heard the news?' She sounded excited. 'They've got someone. They've got the Whistler!' She said a man was helping the police with their inquiries. 'That's not all,' she continued. 'He was holed up just near us. Round the corner from the office. Isn't that spooky? You know those empty houses? The ones that are boarded up? He's some kind of tramp!'

I crashed the phone down and threw on some clothes. I swallowed a pint of water and some aspirin. I grabbed the briefcase and my keys, took the bike outside and hastily locked the flat. It was raining and very cold. With the briefcase slung across my chest I cycled past the office, across the square and cut through the flats. Beyond, outside a row of derelict houses, within yards of the river, two policemen chatted and huddled inside their overcoats. A television crew were loading themselves into a Ford Transit. Three sightseers wandered up and down. A gust of wind lashed us with freezing rain. The Transit drove away.

I stopped for a moment, dismayed. The police didn't look friendly. Counting along the row, I calculated that the guarded house was number twelve. I went round the back, into the lane. There was nobody there. I propped the bicycle against the wall of number twelve and climbed onto its seat. It wobbled and I pulled myself up with my arms. There was a sharp pain in my hand. Too late, I noticed the broken glass cemented into the top of the wall. I dropped down into the yard, the briefcase dragging against my neck. For a second I held my breath, but there were no police. Blood ran down my fingers and dripped at my feet.

The boards on the door and the windows were solid, but the rear brickwork had been broken away. Someone had made a hole in the crumbling masonry. The yard was strewn with rubble. I bent and peered through the hole, into the building. At the front, the door had been opened properly. It gave a glimmer of light into the hallway. I crawled in, with difficulty, pushing the brief-case ahead, easing myself forwards. The person who'd used this means of entrance and exit had been much smaller than me.

There was a smell of the river and urine. The air was musty and unused. I sat on my haunches, in the dark, wondering if there was anyone else inside. My hand continued to pour with blood. I could see the policemen through the open front door and heard their muttering voices. I wished I had a torch.

I went into the kitchen. As my eyes became accustomed to the darkness, I noticed a candle in a saucer and a lighter. They were on a table. With difficulty, I lit the small flame and held it aloft. There was an unopened box of candles, a packet of bread and an empty tin of peaches. Apart from a few strewn papers on the floor and bits of refuse the room was empty. I wrapped my injured hand in a sheet of newspaper. Cautiously, guarding the candle, I went into the hall. The back of a policeman, through the open door, was very near. The floor creaked. I turned and saw that the staircase had been boarded up and there was no access to the upper storey. There was a door down to a basement. I lifted my candle and peered down the steps. The flame flickered. River water flooded the cellar. There was a scampering sound and then the squeak of rats.

I went into the living room. If I was caught, I decided to pretend to be a journalist. I remembered Camilla's motto. 'Never explain. Never apologize.' I looked around. The room was bare, almost clean. There was no furniture. A sleeping bag lay next to a dead fire in the grate. In the corner was a pile of newspapers which looked new. They were *The Big Issue.*

I picked up the sleeping bag. Underneath was a pair of jeans, a shirt and an empty cigarette packet. There was nothing else. Someone had made a pathetic home here. I felt disappointed. This wasn't Camilla's murderer. I crawled back outside and climbed on top of an old cooker to scale the wall. The bike was still there. My injured hand was a tight fist and my jeans were covered in blood. The briefcase still dangled, safely, around my neck. I bent my head into the wet, driving sleet and headed for home.

It was a relief to get back to my flat, I turned on the television, waiting for the news. Because of the holiday scheduling, I had to wait for an old Steve McQueen movie to finish, then a rerun of *The Snowman.* My hand was bandaged and throbbing. I'd thrown my bloodstained clothes in the bedroom. After a hot bath, I was wearing my dressing gown. I lay on the settee, a towel around my head, my feet warm in my cerise fluffy slippers. My hangover had been driven away by the pain in my hand. Opening a bottle of wine, I had a sensation of being safe. It was cosy inside, with the heating full on and the curtains hiding the grilles. The wine freed my feelings in a temporary kind of way. When Aled Jones sang 'Something in the Air' I burst into tears. Later, I changed channels and watched *Morecambe and Wise.*

The news item, when it appeared, was disappointing. There was a brief flash of the outside of the derelict house, with the two policemen. This was followed by a press conference. Reporters were baying for details, but

the statement was brief and the chief inspector wouldn't
be drawn further. For once, he was almost monosyllabic.
He said a man known as James Kerr was helping with
inquiries.

It was clear that the roving TV crew had done their
best, but all they'd discovered was that he was a schizo-
phrenic and a former patient at the Maudsley. There was
a still shot of the front of the hospital, but no statement
from a psychiatrist. James Kerr had been sleeping rough
for a year, after discharge into the community. He was
twenty-three and had no known family. Other rootless
young people in the area, squinting suspiciously at the
camera, had no information. They said he kept himself
to himself. They said he sold *The Big Issue*. He sometimes
went to the Salvation Army hostel and had a shower.
They thought he might be from Lancashire, but they
weren't sure.

I knew him. He was like all the other homeless people
who called into the Advice Centre, most working days of
my life. He was a man with no past and no future. He
was either desperate or resigned, but neither would make
any difference. He was a loser; flotsam on the London
tide. He had nothing to do with Camilla, and because of
this he didn't interest me at all.

There was a knock at the door. I pulled myself upright
and sat still, frozen with surprise. Apart from Camilla,
I never had visitors. There was another, harder knock.
'Imogen!' someone shouted.

I thought it was my upstairs neighbour. I was pleased.
'Hang on,' I yelled in the hall. I ran my fingers through
my hair. It was still wet. I drew back my long bolts. The

heavy door swung inwards. Two serious faces stared into mine. It was Josh and Pip.

'Come in,' I said, flustered, trying to smooth the sides of my hair.

It was their first visit. For a mad moment I wondered if I could talk to them in the hall. Pip carefully wiped his feet. Josh walked past me and turned into the living room. I followed him. In an instant, I saw the room through his eyes. I didn't notice the stepladders, the dust sheets or the paint pots, not yet cleared away. Instead, I saw the football memorabilia, the patterned nylon carpet, the giant teddy bear, the plastic chainstore lampshades. It wasn't deliberate enough to be fashionable kitsch. It was working class. Josh glanced around, his long nose raised.

'It's very hot in here,' said Pip behind me.

'Sit down,' I offered. I took Pip's coat. Josh was wearing a leather jacket with a great number of zips. He kept it on.

They sat together, on the settee. Pip perched forwards in a worried way, his knees together. Josh lay back, trying to be languid, crossing his legs. He wasn't as relaxed as he pretended. Nervously, he dusted his thighs. I went into the kitchen. My armpits were wet and I turned down the heating. I opened the fridge and was relieved to find a bottle of wine. I hoped it was enough. The off-licence had closed. My hands shook a little. I hadn't yet replaced my broken wineglasses. I washed two cups and got myself a can of beer.

'This is a cosy little flat,' said Pip. 'How long have you been here?'

Josh sipped his wine, studied it, grimaced, then put it aside.

I moved a heap of old newspapers and other debris from the armchair and sat down. I was conscious of my braless bosoms moving under my dressing gown. 'Oh,' I said, 'a while.' I gestured around. 'I'm decorating.'

'Have you finished,' Josh drawled, 'or are you just about to start?'

There was a silence. I pressed a button on my CD player. The room was immediately filled with jolly Irish fiddle players and penny whistles. They sounded ridiculous. I switched it off again. 'So they've arrested somebody,' I offered.

Surprisingly, they didn't respond to this. 'Have you hurt your hand?' asked Pip. He sounded even more tentative than usual. He put his full cup of wine on the floor, on top of a stained box that had once held takeaway pizza. He took a pack of Nicorettes out of his pocket and popped one in his mouth. 'Sorry to intrude. We want to ask you something.' He blinked behind his spectacles. His little face looked pleading and his hands knotted, then unknotted in his lap.

I drummed my fingers for an instant. I leaned sideways, trying to look normal. I was conscious of my lack of make-up, my stupid slippers. Upstairs, my neighbour played a single loud chord on his electric guitar.

'It's kind of embarrassing,' said Pip. He chewed his gum.

I tried to smile. There was another silence.

Josh spoke, his voice unnaturally forceful. 'Camilla had something of mine.' He sat very still, his face impassive, a tiny tremor flickering in his cheek. He adjusted his tone. 'She stole it. I think she took it to Berkshire. To her parents' house.' His lips straightened into a thin line. He sipped his wine again, frowned and put it on the floor. His tone became accusing. 'You were sneaking around her room in Berkshire.'

I tipped back my head and swallowed some beer.

He touched the side of his nose with a long index finger. 'I know.'

'How?'

'You've been poking around, Imogen. Asking questions. Do you have my property?'

I took another swig from my can and held down a burp. The electric guitar upstairs played the opening riffs of 'Don't Look Back in Anger'. It was almost deafening. After a moment it stopped.

'No,' I said, 'I don't have anything of yours.'

Pip shifted uncomfortably and coughed.

Josh answered quickly. 'Do you have a magazine? It has compromising pictures in it. Of me.' His cold eyes rested on my face.

I tried to meet his gaze but looked away. My hand was throbbing like a heartbeat. I held it tightly, willing away the pain. I remembered the gay porno mag I'd lifted from Peter's house. I'd barely glanced through it. 'I didn't search Camilla's room,' I insisted. 'I certainly haven't got a magazine of yours.' I sounded indignant. 'Why should I have it?'

Because,' said Josh, his voice like ice shards, 'you're a nosy bloody parker.' He gave me a hard stare.

I tried, unsuccessfully, to shrug. The beer was making me feel sick. 'Maybe she threw it away. How d'you know she—'

He interrupted. 'Threw it away?' his tone was level, his words slow and resonant. 'No, she certainly didn't do that.'

Pip chimed in. 'She intended using it . . .' His voice trailed off. 'For reasons of her own.'

I picked up my beer can and crunched it in my good hand.

'She was intending to blackmail me.' Josh's words hung for a moment, all around us.

I threw the can down. I sat forward in my chair. 'Hang on,' I said quickly, my anger finally rising. I knew Camilla had been fond of Josh. It was an absurd idea. 'She wouldn't do that. What are you suggesting?' As I said these words, I remembered St John. I thought for a second. 'Is that what you're accusing me of? A plan to blackmail you?'

Josh pursed his lips and looked at the ceiling.

'No, no,' said Pip hurriedly, 'we're worried, that's all.'

'I've never seen it,' I said abruptly. 'I don't want to see it. I don't have it.'

They both stood up at once. Josh looked down at me. 'Well then,' he muttered, 'if you haven't got it, we're wasting our time.'

'We better be going,' agreed Pip. He smiled at me, his little mouth wincing.

We all went into the hall. Pip unhooked his coat and put it on. I slid back the heavy bolts and opened the door. There was a blast of cold air. Josh hesitated a moment. He was about to speak, then stopped.

Pip stepped outside, then Josh. They didn't hesitate or smile.

'Goodbye,' I said.

They walked away together, Pip turning briefly in a nervous gesture of farewell.

'Happy New Year,' I whispered.

I immediately went into the bedroom and opened the briefcase. I knelt on the floor at the side of the bed and turned the pages of the magazine. Nude men posed, their penises swollen. Some were alone, some were active in pairs. There were five photographs of Josh. He was very young. He looked almost innocent amongst the lurid colours, the thongs, the studs, the paraphernalia of gay lust. His sneer, back in those days, was less convincing. He was too young then for an attempt at thin-lipped arrogance. In these crude pages he was only practising for what he had become.

I took out Camilla's file. I tried to accept that she'd been about to blackmail Josh. Although she'd joked about his ambitions and laughed at his vanity I'd always thought she'd seen him as her friend.

I leafed through to Josh's sheet and scribbled down that he believed he was about to be blackmailed. This meant he had a motive to harm Camilla. He was an important suspect now, along with Peter, St John and maybe even Pip.

I forced myself to imagine Josh strangling Camilla. The image wouldn't stick. All I could bring to mind was them sitting together in his bare white beautifully designed flat, reading style magazines, sipping gin, gossiping, listening to Classic FM.

Chapter Twenty-Six

In the morning I got up early, swallowed three aspirin and turned on the television. The newsreader said that the police had released, without charge, the homeless man who had been helping them with their inquiries. A tired-looking detective said they'd been acting on 'information' but this particular line of inquiry had come to a close. There were shots of the derelict house, but the cameras had been unable to track down the hapless suspect. He'd melted away, penniless and browbeaten, into London's mean streets.

I showered, then changed the dressing on my hand. The cut was very deep. I wondered if it needed stitches. I threw the bloodstained bandage away and covered it with a more discreet plaster. I found some clean grey jeans, a white T-shirt and a heavyweight black rollneck. I wasn't hungry but I ate a bowl of Frosties. I looked at the A–Z and decided it was too far to cycle to Finsbury Park. Wearing my leather jacket and a little woollen hat, I set off for the Oval. It was cold but sunny with a blue sky. Traffic inched along, filling the air with fumes. I shoved my hands in my pockets and joined the stream of commuters on their way to the station. I felt safe with lots of people around.

The Tube was packed. The doors could barely close.

People clutched bags and umbrellas to their chests. Those lucky enough to sit down held newspapers to their faces. Perfumes and aftershaves mingled together, but nobody smiled or spoke. An Italian-looking student, holding a physics textbook, pushed past me and for an instant, slid his hand inside my jacket, deliberately moving it upwards, to cup the underside of my right breast. There was nothing I could do.

Fiona Harding lived in a part of London with high trees and proper front gardens. Everything seemed calm and suburban. Her house was a large double-fronted semi, with a new Audi in the drive. A woman in an overall answered the door. I recognized her Spanish voice from the telephone. She showed me into a wide hall and I sat on a church pew. A big vase of chrysanthemums scented the air. I picked up a copy of *Elle Decoration* and flicked through it. After a while, the woman reappeared with a cup of pale, milkless tea. A grandfather clock chimed. It was only nine thirty. I sipped the tea, then wandered around, glancing into rooms. Beyond the hall, the style was contemporary, clean edged, spare. I saw a modern dining table, with pale, elegant chairs. At the end of a corridor, I passed a kitchen where the maid unloaded a dishwasher. She glanced at me, impassively. I entered a wide, bright conservatory. Creepers were trained up the glass. Two canaries chirped in a cage. A table was laid for breakfast. I took off my jacket, draping it over a chair. I sat down, hot in my sweater. I worked out that Camilla had been dead for more than twenty days. I remembered the article I'd read about serious crime being solved quickly. If I was to break her case within a month, before the trail turned cold, I needed to make real progress.

At ten o'clock I heard a voice, followed by a laugh. Camilla's sister-in-law was downstairs and on the phone. After a minute she appeared in the doorway. She grinned and held up her hand in greeting, as if we were old friends. She was wearing a short towelling robe and her hair was tied back and wet. She was enormously fat. She filled the entrance. I stood up. She was a foot shorter than me, but twice as wide. She came into the room and I heard her laboured, wheezy breath. Her ankles were very swollen. She struggled noisily into a narrow, woven chair. 'Sit down, Imogen,' she said, pleasantly. 'I phoned Jimmy last night. We talked about you.' Her voice was teasing.

I tried not to stare at her. There was a bank of geraniums behind, still in flower. They were the same colour as her robe. The sun streamed in. I took off my sweater. Sitting near her, in a white T-shirt and jeans, I felt thin. The maid appeared with coffee and toast. 'Help yourself,' Fiona said. Her accent was clearly South African. She smiled again and untied her hair, shaking it across her shoulders and down her back. Her chair creaked in protest. From across the low table, I saw her stomach, the wide folds of her neck. Her hair fell in damp auburn waves. I looked at her face. Her features were small and even. Inside this fat person was a beautiful woman. I tried to imagine Jimmy kissing her.

'I like your house,' I said politely.

'Yes,' she agreed, 'the conservatory was St John's idea. I practically live in here.' She pulled a comb through her hair. She was very relaxed. She poured two cups of coffee and handed me one. She smeared jam generously on a slice of toast and spooned sugar into her mug.

'I'm sorry to barge in—' I began.

'No, no, no,' she interrupted, 'don't apologize. I need the company. Jimmy's always arriving at short notice. I don't see enough people.' She began her breakfast. 'St John's never here. I hardly get out.' She munched through her toast and then started a second piece. 'We bought the gallery last year. He said I needed an interest.' I watched her eating, greedily. She looked at me. Her gaze was quizzical. 'D'you paint?'

'I'm a rights adviser,' I said. I began to explain my job, but she wasn't listening. I realized she was the kind of person who was friendly and open, but uninterested. She wanted someone to listen to her.

'I've come to see you,' I said assertively, 'about Camilla.'

She looked away. She stirred her coffee, slowly. 'Camilla,' she repeated, quietly. She turned towards me. 'They've let him go! What do the police think they're playing at?'

'He didn't do it,' I said quickly. 'They would have held him otherwise.' I drank a mouthful of coffee, slopping some into my saucer.

Her eyebrows shot up, then down.

'It's not as if he had friends and relatives banging on the door of his cell, shouting about his civil liberties. He was a down and out. They would have hung onto him indefinitely if they'd thought he'd done it.' I rubbed my forehead. I was still too hot. I moved my chair into the shade of a tall plant.

She pursed her lips. 'Did you say you're a solicitor?' She looked disdainful.

'No,' I said. 'I was Camilla's best friend.'

She buttered more toast. She picked up the coffee pot. 'A top-up?'

Her chair groaned. She blotted her mouth with a napkin. She sighed. 'Camilla and I were also best of pals.'

It occurred to me that I'd never even heard Camilla mention Fiona. She hardly ever referred to her brother.

There was a silence. 'We'd lost touch a little, since she moved south of the river.' She added quickly, 'But we were the best of pals.'

I watched her eat. Camilla had always lived in South London since leaving college, fourteen years ago. 'Had they fallen out, Camilla and St John?' I asked. I noticed that her nails were bitten right down.

'Yes,' she replied, 'but that was Camilla's fault. She could be such a parasite.' She sighed heavily. 'Money, money, money,' she added.

'Camilla borrowed money from St John?'

'Constantly.'

'I thought she had an allowance from her father?'

'Mr Harding was a Lloyd's Name. He lost all his money. Camilla didn't get a penny from him. Not in ages.' She picked up a tiny bell. As it tinkled, the maid reappeared. 'More toast,' Fiona ordered.

I took a deep breath. 'Why did they fall out?' I kept expecting her to clam up, to tell me to mind my own business.

'She borrowed. She never paid back. St John felt obligated to her. She was his sister, after all. But then it got worse.'

'Worse?'

'She began an affair with his boss.'

My heart quickened. 'Professor Grant?'

She nodded.

'But he's an old man!'

'He's very famous.' She shrugged. 'Rich. He was besotted. His wife found out. She's a Catholic, very devout. It was bad. There was a scandal, unpleasantness but he wouldn't give her up. The Vice-Chancellor got involved. Alan Grant declared publicly that he wanted to marry her. Silly old goat. St John was humiliated. It was a bloody mess.'

I remembered Josh mentioning this affair, and how, not really believing it, I'd used it as a weapon against St John. It still seemed so unlikely. 'What happened?'

'She asked St John for four thousand pounds. To clear off. To get out of Alan Grant's bed.'

I remembered the Visa statement. 'Last summer?'

She nodded. 'That's what it cost us to pay her off.' Her little mouth pouted. She began eating again. 'St John said she was vain,' she added, 'that she liked enslaving men. She wanted to stand in the spotlight. I always thought she did it for the money.'

The hum of the Hoover started within the house. The phone rang, the Hoover stopped, the phone was answered. Fiona laid back in her chair, as if exhausted. There was sweat on her neck.

I rubbed my own damp brow. My armpits were wet. It was hard to believe it was January. The conservatory felt like the glasshouse at Kew.

'I wouldn't have met St John, without Camilla,' she continued. 'She introduced us.'

I smiled encouragingly.

'We had the same specialist in Harley Street. It was three years ago.'

'Really?'

'We were both there for the slimming pills. You can't get them on the NHS any more. They're very expensive.' She grasped both arms of her chair and tried to get up. Her breath was noisy and laboured.

'It must have been a shock,' I said, 'the murder. Were you and your husband in London that weekend?'

'No,' she said, managing to get to her feet. 'There was a faculty dinner. Mrs Grant was attending. St John wanted us both there. He sent a car down. We were both in Newcastle.'

'When did you hear?'

'On the Saturday morning, first thing. We drove straight back here. St John phoned Mrs Grant. She broke the news to her husband.'

We moved towards the hall. She stopped beside a framed photograph. It was Take That in a promotional still from a video. Her finger rested on a dancer at the back. She was a willowy redhead, wearing tight white leggings and a matching bra top. 'That's me,' she said proudly.

'Never!' I spluttered, changing the word into a cough.

The front door was open and I stepped outside. The photo on the wall had been the last straw. My composure was gone. 'Thanks for the coffee,' I managed to say.

'Come again,' she smiled. 'Tell your brother to come and see me. He's been neglecting me.' There was a desperate look in her eye. 'It's so dull here, on my own.'

Chapter Twenty-Seven

Al phoned the next day to invite me to another party. She was very persistent.

'It's at my place,' she said. 'Raymond, my house-mate, arranged it when he thought they'd caught the Whistler. You know? They arrested that homeless guy?' She paused, inhaling on a cigarette. 'Raymond's invited a few people from his course.' She added, by way of explanation, 'He's a feminist.'

'They've let that suspect go,' I murmured. 'He was just some derelict.'

'Yeah, right. But we thought we'd go ahead anyhow. OK?'

I didn't say anything.

'It's fancy dress.' She hesitated again. 'Well, if you like. Or not.'

I was suddenly sorry for her. It was getting boring, snubbing Al all the time. 'OK,' I said, graciously. 'I'll come.'

The address was in Bermondsey, off Jamaica Road. I held my *A–Z* under a street lamp, trying to read the tiny print. In my other hand was a carrier bag, containing a six-pack of Stella Artois. I was wearing my normal clothes – jeans and a leather jacket.

I knew that Al shared a house with three men, who she referred to as The Boys. She'd told me tales of them all falling asleep together, sharing the bathtub and watching late-night TV under a king-sized duvet. These stories made me uneasy, even though she insisted that they were all just good friends.

I went into a pub and drank two pints of bitter to give myself courage. Then, without any difficulty, I found Al's street. I was expecting a rundown place with a rubbish-strewn garden, possibly boarded-up windows, deliberately untidy, like her clothes. Instead, I walked down an elegant, whitewashed terrace of tiny dwellings, each with its bijou brass door furniture and newly painted railings. The windows were neat with blinds and shutters and each house had a name. Al's was called Tupelo.

I entered a cream-painted hallway with a wood-block floor. Beyond, in the kitchen, there were voices. I found five or six young men. I was too early. They smiled at me, politely, then resumed their conversation. I opened a can of Stella and stood in a corner. There were a few beers and wine bottles on the table, plenty of soft drinks, but no food. I looked around. The kitchen units were expensive and there was a ceramic sink. It was dirty, but it had French taps. Washing-up was piled high. The white-tiled floor was grubby. It occurred to me that the place was rented and the tenants weren't looking after it properly.

The young men weren't in fancy dress. They wore baggy shirts, trousers and trainers. Their hair hung in their eyes. One had a long thin plait and was eating from a carton of Pot Noodle. I realized they were students. They sipped from cans of cider and tried to sound cool, but this was difficult because they were discussing essay deadlines.

'Where's Al?' I interrupted.

One of them pointed upstairs. I put a second can of lager in my pocket and moved away. In the dark living room, three people were watching television. A woman came out to join me. 'Freda!' she said, 'I'm going to fix your car.'

I looked down at her. She was stout and had a pink Mohican haircut. I shook my head.

'Your car. You left a message? Cooling system and cylinder head gasket?'

'I haven't got a car.'

She looked offended. I thought I'd seen her some-where before, maybe on *The Word*.

'I'm sorry,' I said pointlessly, climbing the stairs.

I stood on the tiny landing. The pale carpet was stained. Screwed to each door was a nameplate. They said MUM AND DAD, BARTHOLOMEW and SASKIA. I pushed open the door of Mum and Dad's room. Al was sitting at her computer. She turned and smiled.

I glanced around. The room was bare and neat. Above the bed were a row of photographs, taped to the wall. They were all of me. She'd taken them at her mother's house, when I'd visited, just after Christmas. She saw me look at them but appeared unruffled.

'How did you find this place?' I asked, awkwardly.

'Young couple,' she shrugged, 'two kids. He lost his job in the City. They're living with her parents in Godalming. We've got a two-year lease.' She switched off her machine and stood up. 'I didn't think you'd come.'

'It's nice here,' I said.

Al was wearing a pink floaty chiffon dress, short, low

cut, with tiny straps. Her arms and shoulders were bare but she wore black fishnet tights and ballet shoes. Her hair was pinned up and resembled a damaged bird's nest.

I said, 'I thought it was fancy dress.'

'It is,' she said. 'I'm Tinkerbell.' She twirled around on her toes. She looked very young. 'Who are you?'

I thought for a second. 'James Dean.'

She smiled.

I thought how pretty she looked in her costume. 'Let's go down,' I said.

'Oh, right,' she agreed. 'I've got some good grass somewhere.'

I went back to the kitchen. The rooms were full now and there was a crush. I worked my way through the lager. The woman with the Mohican, still mistaking me for Freda, talked again of the car. She said she was cheap, but not too cheap. 'I won't rip you off,' she promised. I noticed that her nails were black with oil.

After a while, I knew I was drunk. I pushed through to the living room. The television was still on but was drowned by loud music. I leaned against the wall, feeling disconnected but not unhappy.

There was a carpet in the room, no furniture and a strong smell of marijuana. A few people stared at the screen. Others were dancing. One man was dressed as a fireman, another as a construction worker. They collided for a few seconds and performed a synchronized tango. A Mexican bandit with a bare chest pulled Al to her feet. She began dancing and a space cleared for her in the middle of the floor. Everybody clapped and gestured to her, as if wanting to be her partner. The light from the

TV screen caught her bare shoulders, her wisp of a dress. I was reminded of someone. My heart beat in an uncomfortable way. Her heart-shaped face, her long, slender limbs, her hair escaping its knot – I'd seen all this a hundred times before. She was both wild and controlling. High on the music, the grass and the attention, she was exactly like Camilla.

Much later, I half lay on the stairs. My head was spinning. A teenage boy talked about astrology. He said his chart was so watery, he was carried through life on a fluid, swirling wave. He said he was anchorless.

I nodded sympathetically. He was very good-looking.

'Are you Raymond's mother?' he asked.

At one fifteen, the police arrived. 'Stay cool,' announced the Pisces boy. 'It's not the law. It's just fancy dress.'

The music was pounding. The policemen stood in the hall, both stern and bemused. I felt nervous.

'There's some cowboys in the kitchen,' the boy told them, drunkenly.

Their radios crackled. They were bulky in their uniforms.

Al appeared. She had two red circles, high on each cheek, and the crack between her breasts glinted with perspiration. She was a little breathless. The noise from the CD player suddenly became deafening. She gestured into the living room and the volume dropped. It was a relief. Somewhere, a phone was ringing.

'I'm sorry,' Al smiled. The fingers of one hand rested on an officer's sleeve. 'We'll keep it down.'

I saw their eyes travel over her. They looked at each other then back at her body. They grinned. They were both young and a little sheepish.

259

'Come in,' she said, gesturing towards the kitchen.

They followed her.

'We've got Appletise, you know. Kaliber. We've got Highland Spring. Don't go yet. Stay for a bit.'

I turned to the Pisces boy. He leaned against the wall, his eyes half closed.

I nudged him. 'I used to know somebody,' I said. I poked him harder. 'I used to know a woman who was just like her.'

Chapter Twenty-Eight

The next day was Wednesday. My Christmas holiday was officially over. I went into the office and immediately played back the answering machine. The mystery caller hadn't rung. There were two messages and two notes from the Electricity Couple as well as another plea from Penny, asking me to get in touch.

Leafing through Camilla's file again and again, I felt cold and depressed. I'd been busy, since my Newcastle break, but I wasn't getting anywhere. All I was doing was uncovering facts about her life that had been unknown to me. This was distressing but the information wasn't helping me solve the case.

I decided to use my telephone skills again. I dialled the number of Newcastle University. It rang for a long time. I suspected there would be a skeleton staff operating until the beginning of term. Eventually, I was put through to St John's department. I was in luck. A woman answered. 'This is Professor Grant's secretary,' she said. She sounded very keen.

'University catering.' I spoke gruffly. 'That faculty dinner, before Christmas. You've not sent me the ND 1567.'

'I'm sorry,' she said uncertainly, 'I'm quite new here . . .'

I adopted my most bullying tone. 'The guest list! Was Professor Grant dining? What about St John Harding?'

'Oh, yes,' she said quickly, 'they were on the top table.'

'I've got enough to do,' I insisted, 'without worrying about waitresses and their flaming time sheets. When did it finish?'

She paused. 'Well, Professor and Mrs Grant took me home in their car. It must have been eleven fifteen.'

'And what about Dr Harding. Was he here until the bitter end?'

'Oh yes, definitely. He was entertaining the Vice-Chancellor, he was here—'

I put down the phone. However much I might want to draw in Camilla's secret financial and sexual liaisons, there was no way either her brother or her ex-lover had been in London on the night of her death.

When I saw Al coming along the street, I decided to leave. I wheeled the bike outside. 'I'm going,' I said. 'I'm taking extra holiday.' I knew the first advice session was going to be busy, but for once I didn't care. Camilla's case was the only thing on my mind.

That afternoon, back at home, I lay on the settee again in my dressing gown, drinking wine. My feet in their fluffy slippers dangled over the arm. The room was over-heated, as usual, and the curtains were still closed over the metal grilles. I'd turned off the television and the CD player blared with the uncompromising lyrics of Alanis Morissette. I wasn't really listening.

The phone rang. It was Al. I had a sudden vision of her dancing, at the party and in that instant, strangely, I confused her with Camilla. My heartbeat quickened, as if I was excited. I took a deep breath.

She was ringing from the office. She said the Electricity Couple had been in yet again, and that Penny had been in touch. She asked my opinion on two new cases she'd tried to deal with by herself.

As she chattered, her voice both childish and knowing, I regained my composure. I focused on her questions and told her the best way to proceed. She seemed grateful for my advice and unresentful of my abrupt departure. We talked again about the Whistler suspect being released. I didn't tell her I'd visited his squat.

'I've found out something that might help you,' she said tentatively. 'You help me, so often. It shouldn't be all one way.'

I took a swallow from my glass. 'Oh, yeah?'

'It's about Peter. Camilla's friend. The one who lives in Dulwich.'

I was surprised, so I said nothing.

She hesitated. 'He's got a security system that videos everyone who goes in and out of his house. It also logs the times.'

I felt nervous. I thought she was going to say something about me being at the house, disguised as a cleaner. The idea of a video was scary. I wondered if Peter made a habit of watching it. 'So what?'

'All that information is digitally transmitted back to the security firm.'

I paused. My heart was beating fast again. 'Well?'

'Look. I can tell you something definite. The householder, I mean Peter, entered his house on the evening of the murder . . .'

I gasped.

She sounded pleased with herself. 'He went in at twenty-three fifty-seven and didn't come out again until nine forty-six a.m. on the tenth. It's certain. The system was activated the entire time. He was in all night.'

'How d'you know?'

She started to explain.

Her computer jargon was above my head.

'It's illegal,' she admitted, sounding a little ashamed.

'So he's got an alibi?'

'Yes.'

I was silent, but my heart was thumping in my chest. Peter was in the clear. 'How did you know I was . . .'

She paused. 'It's your case, Imogen. It's what you're doing. I've guessed all along what you've been up to.' She sounded sympathetic. 'It's the least I can do. We're supposed to work jointly on outstanding cases.'

'Thanks, Al.' I felt grateful, but I was unable to think of anything else to say.

'Anyway,' she continued, sounding happy, 'I'm also ringing about the march.' She gave me details about a protest march, the next day, along the Walworth streets where the Whistler prowled. 'Women only. It's called Reclaim The Night.'

It was the first I'd heard of it. I remembered similar events, years before, when I was still a student. In those days, women were angry about violence all of the time. 'I'll see you there,' I promised.

I went into the kitchen and opened another bottle of wine. I picked up my giant teddy bear and sat him in an armchair. I settled down in front of *Rocky III* with a big bag of vinegar-flavoured crisps. Later, I drank a four-pack of Carlsberg, reading and rereading Camilla's file. Peter was innocent. I considered his frustration, his doomed attempts to take possession of Camilla. She'd been blatantly unfaithful to him, but whenever I tried to picture him in a jealous rage it was impossible. He was decorous, cool, urbane. For Peter, murder was simply too messy and too vulgar an option. Although I'd treated him as a suspect, I'd never been convinced.

I pictured Camilla in a poorly lit underpass, drunk and a little unsteady with her big white model's bag. Her face was hard and wary. Suddenly a dark shape overpowered her, taking her by surprise. I tried to give this vision an identity, but failed. All I could imagine was a tall figure with dark clothes and a blank disc where his features should be. He picked up her bag and put it over his shoulder.

I looked through the suspects I'd ruled out of my enquiries. Professor Grant and St John Harding were definitely cleared. Along with Fiona, they were in Newcastle on the night of the murder. Pip was in Dymchurch, unless he'd managed to slip away and back without being noticed. This seemed unlikely without a car, and I knew he hadn't borrowed Josh's Scirocco that night. Sean was working. Peter was at home. My brother Jimmy had been playing darts in Newcastle.

I read through Josh's notes and thought again about his claims. He said Camilla was 'about' to blackmail him. Even allowing for her parasitic relationship with her brother, I still didn't believe this. Josh was worried about his homosexuality. He thought it might mess up his career. I was sure this lay behind his accusations.

I remembered a time when a well-known tabloid

journalist turned up at one of Peter's parties. Josh had taken Pip aside and insisted that he go home. He'd removed his earrings and bangles. He'd adopted a deep, macho voice and chatted to the journalist, laying on the charm. He'd introduced Camilla as 'the woman who shares my life'. We'd all laughed about it afterwards. I was sure his suspicions about blackmail and the pornographic magazine were unfounded. It was just his own paranoia.

Camilla wasn't perfect. I'd discovered she'd exploited a number of people, but she'd been Josh's friend. She'd only ever wished him well. I couldn't accept that she'd ever done anything bad enough to provoke him to violence, to make him into a murderer. I didn't really believe Josh was a suspect.

I was left with a blank page, an unnamed, unknown assailant. It seemed the only door open to me was to discover more acquaintances who might have wished Camilla harm. I tried to think of circles she'd mixed in which were unfamiliar to me. I decided to ring Sean.

I picked up the phone and fixed a date. I arranged to meet him the next evening, in a pub in Peckham. I decided I'd become indifferent to him, since our last meeting. In contrast, he sounded chirpy and flirtatious at the prospect.

Chapter Twenty-Nine

The following day, I went swimming. It was raining so I pulled on an old parka and my woolly hat. I cycled down to Brixton. Inside the lobby of the baths, the familiar smell reminded me of the days when I was younger and fitter and used to swim regularly.

The receptionist glanced at me. 'Excuse me, sir, are you an old-age pensioner?'

I pulled off my hat angrily, throwing down some coins.

'Oops!' she giggled. 'Sorry!' She turned to her colleague and they both collapsed, laughing.

I changed, plunged into the water and ploughed along furiously, scattering everyone in my path. I swam forty lengths. Afterwards I was so tired I had to push the bike home.

In the evening it had stopped raining and I decided to risk wearing my suede jacket. I caught a bus to the Elephant and Castle because there was nowhere to leave the bike and I wasn't sure of the route of the march. I joined a group of Reclaim the Night protesters in the shopping precinct. It was cold and windy, with a clear, dark sky. By six fifteen there were far more women than I expected. By six thirty there were about two thousand. Some held placards with photos of the women who had been killed in Walworth in the last few months. I was reminded again that the victims were all young, white and blond, all pretty. Other banners read WOMEN ARE ANGRY and THESE STREETS BELONG TO ALL OF US.

There was an excited atmosphere and laughter, but we all stood together in an orderly way. The crowd parted to let through two black women in overalls. There was a cheer as they raised their thumbs. The police looked worried. A sergeant radioed for reinforcements.

Bundles of long poles were unloaded from a van. I noticed their ends were wrapped in rags. As the march moved off, they were handed around and set alight. They burst into flame and were carried aloft, flaring in the breeze.

Mounted police arrived and a squad of Panda cars. We walked slowly, five abreast, circling the roundabouts. I felt slightly embarrassed at first, and uneasy. The demonstration was old-fashioned, even pointless. It seemed to be referring back to a time when politics were clearer and ideals shared. Somehow, in a contemporary setting, it had no meaning.

Waitresses in an Italian café waved enthusiastically. The torches shone brightly. There was a smell of burning oil. The leaders started singing and everyone joined in. They sang 'I Will Survive' and 'We Shall Overcome'. We tramped slowly along. No one pushed or jostled or broke ranks. I began to be glad I'd come. It was less like a march than a proper funeral profession. It felt more real than the religious ceremony in Berkshire.

We entered the dingy backstreets which separated the shops and offices from the estate. I was cold. As each of the murder sites were reached, a group of young girls stepped out from the lines, laying flowers and placing small flickering candles in glass jars. Some women were crying and my grief for Camilla welled up. We passed under railway arches and bridges.

'What about the other two?' my neighbour asked a steward in a black armband.

I felt relieved that we weren't going underground.

'The police limited the route,' she replied, 'don't worry. The others have already got their posies and lights.'

We all linked arms. A chant started and spread through the procession. 'Reclaim The Night!' we called out, rhythmically. 'Women Reclaim The Night!'

'I wonder if he can hear us,' the woman next to me said.

We circled back towards the tall buildings and traffic of the Elephant and Castle. In the wider spaces approaching the shopping centre our voices rose more thinly and the procession broke up into groups. I looked for Al but the crowd was too dense. I decided not to stay for the speeches.

My bus stop was through an underpass. I felt a wave of fear, but suppressed it, running down the steps. There were pools of urine at the bottom, and it was suddenly quiet, with only the weak boom of cars passing overhead. None of the women from the march had ventured below ground. Football slogans were daubed on the walls and names like Rambo and Dek were painted in Day-Glo colours. Many of the lights were broken and there was a strange, stale draught, like in the Tube. I concentrated on my route. I turned a corner and straightaway saw the candles. The spot where someone had died was heaped with flowers. I prayed it wasn't Camilla. I didn't want to stop. My heart was pounding. As I hurried past, I saw a photograph of the dead woman. She had a round, smooth face and her hair was permed. Someone had written 'God Bless You, Laura'. I could smell roses and the warm aroma of burning wax.

At the bottom of the staircase ahead, three youths were lounging together. As I drew alongside, I saw them passing and sniffing a can of lighter fuel. I remembered seeing them, or a similar group, above ground, the night Camilla was killed. They were very young, but threatening. I hurried by, taking the steps two at a time. One of them called out, 'You'll be next.' They laughed.

Chapter Thirty

The wind became blustery and blew me up Rye Lane. I felt dishevelled. Arriving at the pub about half an hour early, I went into the Ladies and combed some water through my hair, trying to coax it back into its style. I put on some deep red lipstick. Looking at myself critically in the mirror, I seemed pale, but my skin was clear. I'd lost weight. My cheeks were slightly hollow and my eyes dark-ringed. I took off my suede jacket and tucked my black angora sweater inside my jeans.

The pub was almost empty. There was no sign of Sean. I bought a pint and sat down. A young black man approached me. He was wearing a heavy gold neck chain. 'Last w-watering hole before the d-desert,' he said as he slid into the seat next to me. He was tall and graceful as a dancer. I noticed his silver silk shirt, his perfume, which smelled of lemons. He held a free newspaper, folded onto 'situations vacant'.

'You know, honey,' he said, running a finger down a column, 'them j-j-jobs is no good to me. The m-man, he say get a job.' He smiled, showing two gold teeth. He saw me look at them. He pointed to the stud in my nose. 'But m-me, I like to shine.'

We chatted for a while. His name was Winston, but he said everybody called him Zig.

'As in Ziggy Stardust?' I suggested.

He was uncomprehending. 'As in Z-Zog,' he explained. 'Zog as in W-Wog.' He spun a coin on the tabletop. 'This is my last pound, my f-friend.'

'I'll buy you a drink,' I offered.

The pub was filling up. A group of men stood at the bar and others began a darts game. I was the only woman in the room. Sean was late. After two pints, I decided I wasn't worried. Zig took out a tin of tobacco and rolled several cigarettes, as thin as matchsticks. He lit up and offered me one. I shook my head and he returned the rest to the tin. I noticed that his skin was so black it was almost blue.

Eventually Sean arrived. He walked straight over. 'Hi, babe,' he said. For a moment I wondered if he'd forgotten my name.

Zig grinned sheepishly and melted away. Sean was staring at the group of men. The barman came over with a whisky. 'That's on the house,' he said, mysteriously.

Sean swallowed the drink. 'Won't be a minute,' he muttered. He joined the men at the bar. He was wearing Cuban-heeled boots and leather trousers. I noticed his narrow hips and his hair, gathered in a short ponytail. His shoulders seemed wider than ever in a faded blue shirt. I realized I hadn't thought about him in a sexual way since I got back from Newcastle. I was startled anew by his looks.

I leaned back in my seat and finished my beer. Sean's denim jacket was folded over the brass rail below the bar, as though he intended staying there. He slapped the backs of two men and shook some hands. A fat wad of notes was passed over and he swiftly counted it before thrusting it inside the pocket of his jacket.

I felt like going home. Eventually, he bought two pints and came back to join me. He tossed his jacket on a seat. 'You've lost weight,' he said. He was looking at my breasts. 'Your face is thinner.'

'You smell awful,' I replied. 'What's that aftershave? Eau de Peckham?' It was the same scent he had worn at Camilla's funeral.

'That's not aftershave.' He sniffed down the neck of his shirt. 'That's virility.' He picked up my hand and brushed his lips against it. 'Long time, no see.' He sat down. 'How was Christmas? New Year?'

'You know. Hanging out,' I shrugged, 'getting pissed.' I fiddled with a beer mat. I felt embarrassed. 'I've never been here before.' I looked around. It was an uncomfortable pub with hard chairs and plastic tabletops. The walls and ceiling were covered in holiday postcards, many of them curling and very old, featuring saucy cartoons or photos of women on beaches, wearing only bikini bottoms. A row of games machines blinked and beeped along one wall.

Sean's friends at the bar let out a gale of laughter. They wore casual but expensive clothes and loafers with white socks. They all had thick bodies, some as a result of body-building, others from too much beer. 'Is this a criminal hang-out?' I asked. I gulped down half of my beer. 'Christ. It's just like the telly. What is this place? The set of *Minder*?'

Sean laughed. 'You're full of shit.'

'I thought you liked me.'

He leaned over and kissed my ear. 'I do like you. I like clever birds. Especially if they've got big tits.'

I remember drinking several more pints. Sean paid for them all, because he didn't want me to go to the bar.

I didn't argue. I found a copy of the *Sun* on a window sill and noticed an announcement of the Reclaim The Night rally. There was a photograph of the organizers. 'Dykes on the March,' it said. 'Lesbians to Invade Whistler's Patch'.

'I was there.' I turned the page. Someone had drawn a moustache and beard on the pin-up.

'You shouldn't go out on your own.'

'There were two thousand of us.' I was too lightheaded to tell him he'd just summed up the reason for having the rally. I started doing the crossword. 'I worked in a canteen once,' I told him, 'when I was a student. In the holidays. The canteen workers all did the *Sun* crossword, every day. I kept coming out with the right answers. They didn't like it.'

'You should have kept your mouth shut.'

I felt my eyes fill with tears. I realized I was drunk. 'I knew I was different, then. I'd left everyone behind, from my old life. There was no turning back.'

Sean raised his eyebrows. 'No turning back? I've never managed to move forwards.'

'How many people know you've got a degree?'

'You. Mary. My old mum.'

'I used to think that you and Camilla were the same.' I slurred my words slightly. 'You looked the same as each other. But I was wrong. The truth is, you're the same as me.'

A pair of women came into the bar. They were over forty but wore tiny hotpants and black sheer tights. One of them held a shoe in her hand. The stiletto heel had come off. They both had manes of hair, styled and sprayed stiff.

'Look at those old dogs,' said Sean. 'They're always in here. They come in to warm up.'

'Are they on the game?' All evening, I'd sounded innocent.

'Who'd be that desperate?' wondered Sean.

As he spoke, the two women turned towards me. They had painted faces and dead eyes. I studied Sean. Despite his words, I could see neither contempt nor hatred. He looked at the prostitutes with pity and a kind of puzzlement. There was no anger. I wondered why I'd ever thought he was a murderer. He was just an ordinary bloke. I sighed and lay back in my seat. I tried to remember why I'd rung him. I had no reason to be in the pub.

Several drinks later, we left. The cold air outside hit me like a shock wave. Sean guided me by the arm. I felt dizzy and unclear. 'Where are we going?' I kept repeating. Another group of his friends stood outside a big van. 'She's had a skinful,' one of them said. They were all wearing overalls. Sean helped me into the back of the vehicle. Two men joined us and others climbed into the front. I sat on a tarpaulin and Sean leaned against me, his arm around my shoulders. The van started, lurching backwards. Some of the beer I'd just swallowed came back up into my mouth. There was a screech of tyres. I wondered where we were heading.

Talk was of the building site. These were Sean's work-mates, going home off shift. We rattled along. I joined in a discussion about the premiership and insisted that Newcastle United were in with a chance. I impressed them with my knowledge of players' form. There was friendly banter about goal averages. Suddenly, the van stopped. The back doors were flung open and bright floodlights shone in my eyes. For a mad moment I thought we were at a football match. Sean pulled my arm and I was standing in the courtyard outside his flat. The van drove off at high speed, with its back doors banging open.

I felt abandoned. 'Aren't they all coming?' I asked, stupidly.

'What do we want them for?' Sean caught hold of my hand.

I stumbled slightly. 'Are these bloody lights on all night?'

Sean's living room was tidy and well furnished with a leather three-piece suite and an off-white carpet that had been stained, near the door, with blackcurrant juice. He drew the curtains and turned on the gas fire.

'Where's Mary?'

'She went back to Kerry. Back to our sister. This estate got right up her nose.' He sighed. 'Her old man's in Parkhurst.' He plumped up a cushion on the settee. 'Sit down.' He disappeared.

There were horse brasses all around the imitation-stone fireplace. A video recorder clicked and whirred under a huge TV. On the walls were framed prints of opera-goers and elegant ladies in big hats. My head was spinning. The embossed wallpaper was painted-over white and the curtains were fake velvet. I tried to make them stay still. I concentrated on a full ashtray on the hearth, willing it not to move.

Sean returned with a bottle of brandy and two glasses. He turned on the television.

I was still wearing my jacket. I wondered if taxis were prepared to come to this address and if not, how I was going to get home. 'Did you do this place up yourself,' I asked, 'or was it the council?'

'I did the heavy work. Mary did the finishing touches.' He sighed. 'I feel bad. This estate really got her down.'

I closed my eyes briefly, leaning back on the shiny leather. My hair slipped across one eye. I drank some brandy. The shock of it, hitting my throat, woke me up. Sean took off his shirt. He was wearing a string vest and a St Christopher medallion on a gold chain. He had tattoos on his shoulders and he was very brown.

'Have you been on a sunbed?'

'You're full of shit,' he said again, smiling.

I looked at the definition of his muscles and a shadow of hair on his chest. I remembered desiring him. 'D'you do weights?'

He knelt on the floor in front of me. He took hold of my suede jacket and prised it off. 'I do bags of plaster and cement.'

As he spoke, I realized he'd just cleaned his teeth. There was a smell of peppermint above the lingering warmth of his cologne. He lifted my jumper and stroked my bra, cupping my breasts in his hands. I swallowed more brandy. It hit my stomach like a flame. I felt my nipples go hard. He leaned over and turned the sound off the TV. I watched his back. A rock band came on the screen then an advert for a sleek grey car. There were scenes of deserts and dizzy mountain roads.

'Were you in love with her?' I whispered.

There was a silence. He sighed. He didn't reply. He

turned to me again and knelt in front of me. He took my arms and gently moved me down the settee. He took the glass from my hand. He laid his head on my breasts, nuzzling, his face between them.

'Were you angry when she finished it?'

He raised his head. 'Not again,' he murmured.

I struggled up to a sitting position.

'Look, babe . . .'

'My name's Susan.' I pulled my jumper down. 'Susan,' I repeated. I felt I had to get this clear.

'Susan?' He smiled, then frowned. 'Of course I wasn't in love with her.' He sat back on his haunches. 'What gave you that idea?'

'Did you bang on her door in the middle of the night?'

He loosened his little ponytail, shaking his head to free the hair.

'Did you pester her?'

He drained his glass. Our eyes met. 'I lent her money.'

I retrieved my drink and swallowed it. He refilled our glasses. He held up the bottle, checking how much there was left. 'That's what I do. It's a sideline. I lend money. With interest. Eighty-five per cent.'

I remembered the wad of notes changing hands at the bar, the impression that those men were working for Sean.

'You were lovers,' I said. The words sounded ridiculous.

He smiled. 'She shagged me in repayment. Sometimes it was all she had to offer.'

I let this sink in. 'What happened that last night?'

'She still owed me. I hadn't seen her for ages. She rang me up and asked me to meet her. She said she wanted to clear it all up, once and for all. I thought she was going to pay off the debt.'

'And did she?'

He shrugged. 'She bloody disappeared. One minute we were playing darts, the next, I'd lost her.'

I remembered going with Camilla into the lounge, sitting out of sight behind the women footballers. I thought about my neat page of notes on Sean in Camilla's file.

He shrugged. 'I was used to it. I'd written it off.' He brushed my hair out of my eyes. His hand was gentle. 'I'm not the violent type, me. Other people, they put the frighteners on.'

I gasped. 'Was someone you know threatening Camilla?' My heart started beating fast. For a second I thought I'd solved the mystery. Camilla had been bullied then killed by one of Sean's debt-collecting henchmen.

'No,' he said, 'not my boys.'

I paused. 'Are you sure?'

His hand moved up inside my sweater again. 'I didn't let any of them near her. Not ever.'

Suddenly the feel of his fingers on my breasts was exciting.

'There's not that many perks,' he added, 'in this line of work. I wasn't going to share her around.'

I sipped more brandy. His words had a ring of truth. I believed him. The glass was overfull and he knocked my hand. It spilled on my jeans.

I breathed deeply, then leaned forwards and stroked his hair. It felt dry and rough. I remembered my desire and the memory of it stirred me again. I placed my hands on his shoulders and pulled him towards me. I felt the hard muscles in his back under the pattern of his vest.

'She got through a lot of money,' he added.

I brushed my lips against his. I felt him relax. He sighed and said my name, quietly. He called me Susan. He began kissing me. I felt myself slipping down the smooth surface of the settee. I tried to hold onto him but my fingers slid over the smooth leather of his trousers. I felt out of control but didn't struggle. He began kissing my neck and then lifted my jumper again and undid my bra. He kissed my breasts then sucked each of my nipples in turn, several times. It felt nice. 'You're so sexy,' he murmured, rubbing and squeezing my breasts with his hands. He pulled my jumper and my bra over my head. Our eyes met and he grinned.

I laughed. 'I used to think you liked thin women.'

'I like you,' he said, 'you're great.'

I lay back and stared upwards as he undid my belt and the button and zip of my jeans. He took off my shoes and socks. For a curious moment I felt I was in the far corner of the ceiling, staring down at both of us. I felt like a camera, watching myself act out a part in a film. Without looking, I helped him ease off my jeans and my pants. Naked, I felt strangely free, unhampered and unconcerned. With gentle hands, he lifted my legs onto the settee, so that I was lying on my back. I glanced down. There was a red mark around my waist where my belt had dug in. My breasts were heavy and droopy. There was a smear of my lipstick across one nipple, transferred from my lips to his, then back to me. My stomach was a little white mound above a forest of black hair. Instead of feeling self-conscious, or uneasy, after my period of celibacy, I saw my body through his eyes. It appeared inviting.

I looked at him. He was half turned away and I

watched him undress. His lower body was white, below the line of his trousers. I thought of him stripped at work, in the summer, unloading a lorry, sweat on his chest.

He tore open a packet and slipped a condom over his penis. He took off his socks and threw them into a corner of the room. He kneeled on the floor in front of me and began stroking my thighs. He began talking quietly, looking at my body. He said 'baby' and 'darling'. His fingers eased between my legs, so I parted them. He carefully felt inside me and then delicately applied pressure to the small folds. I closed my eyes. After a minute I felt the insistent probing of his tongue. I became wet inside and opened my legs wider.

When he climbed on top of me I breathed his smell. He felt light and agile. He slipped inside me without effort. I could hear him breathing, but I was quiet.

Around the side of his rhythmically moving chest and arm, I could see the TV. It was silently transmitting an advert for shampoo. The model turned her back, picked up and dropped her long, blond hair as if it was a silk shawl. There were tears in my eyes. I wished it was Camilla.

Chapter Thirty-One

Early in the morning, before it was light, I left Sean
sleeping and caught a bus home. My head was throbbing
and my eyes were dry and sore. I realized my contact
lenses had been in all night. I wanted to swallow some
aspirin and bathe my eyes with Optrex. More than these,
I wanted to get back on the case. I felt I'd wasted a lot of
time.

I had a shower and wrapped myself in my dressing
gown. I sat on the floor of my living room, surrounded
by all my evidence and the notes from Camilla's file. The
phone rang twice but I didn't answer it. I noted down
that Sean had a motive to threaten, even harm Camilla,
but not to kill her. He had an alibi, but I decided to keep
him in the picture. I crossed out the red line I'd previously
drawn under his notes. He might still be implicated
through the actions of his 'boys'. They made their living
through intimidation. Despite his protestations, one of
them might just have gone too far.

I examined again the photographs I'd taken from
Peter's house and the album which came from the Hardings'. Camilla had been a serious, pale child with her hair
pushed back under an Alice band. I found a teenage
picture of her riding the bike which now stood in my
hallway. There were several shots of her sitting on a

pony. Her real mother only featured near the beginning and was small, vapid, with dark eye make-up and a pillbox hat. There were some scenes from a ski lift which looked like Switzerland.

I examined Josh's magazine and compared his pictures with his face in the Oxford photo. As usual, he had his head tilted back, staring down his nose, in his normal supercilious way. He looked cold and possibly ruthless. I decided to put aside the times when I'd laughed at his wit, queued with him in bistros or felt grateful for lifts in his car. I banished the vision of him sitting with Camilla, in his flat, sipping Bacardi, listening to opera. I had no real leads. It was a long shot, but I decided to treat him as a suspect.

I got dressed and dried my hair. I found a copy of the Yellow Pages and sat on a kitchen chair, working my way through the list of theatrical agents until I found the one who represented Josh. His name was Piers de Courtney. Fortunately, he was in his office.

'It's Felicia from *Cosmo*,' I said in my best London drawl.

He hesitated for only one beat. 'Darling,' he said, 'hello!'

'I know it's a pain,' I got straight to the point, 'but it's Josh and this Camilla Harding thing. You know she used to model for us. Aeons ago. Features are pestering me about it. Moggy and Sally won't let it drop. Sweetheart, just do me a favour. Talk me through it, will you?'

'There's nothing to say.' He was quick and definite. 'They were flatmates. They were in the same pub, early evening. You know all this, surely?'

'Just go on, Piers, be a love.'

'He went to a party at Penny Mortimer's place in Vauxhall. Camilla never showed. I met him there. We drove back to his flat in Camberwell at about midnight. Camilla wasn't home. Her door was open and he peeped inside, worried about waking her. Her bed was empty. I was there until gone three. She was killed during the time we sat there. We had some really good grass. We got smashed. That's it. End of story. I went up to Manchester the next day. Josh had already auditioned. The rest is history.'

'Did you know her?'

'I was screwing her in '92.'

'Did Josh know her when he was at Oxford?'

There was a pause. He sounded puzzled. 'He didn't go to Oxford.'

'He didn't go to Oxford with Camilla's fiancé?'

'Hang on.' I heard him tapping on a keyboard. 'I've got his CV. He didn't go to university. He was a stagehand at the Oxford Playhouse. '79 to '81. His connection with the Harding woman was . . .' he paused, 'recent.'

Carefully, I replaced the receiver. I was shocked and dumbfounded. Josh had built a whole fiction around his days as an Oxford undergraduate. I remembered his strings of anecdotes about parties, poets, the debating society. Peter knew the truth, but for some reason had decided not to challenge him. Camilla had also known he was telling lies. He must have hung around the student set, holding on like a parasite, bathed in reflected glory.

I thought about my own struggles to get to university, my loss of identity, the anxiety of trying to find my way. I decided I hated Josh. He was nothing more than a lying fraud.

I made notes in the file. The most important thing was that his agent had given him an alibi. I doodled in the margin. His deception about Oxford was astonishing but didn't seem worth following up, as far as the case was concerned. Josh was an image builder and a social climber. As far as I knew, all of his personal history could be invented. His fantasies didn't interest me at all. It crossed my mind, briefly, that Piers might be lying about the small hours after the party, in order to avoid bad publicity. I noted this doubt.

I wandered around my living room, picking up ornaments, replacing them, tidying newspapers into piles. I cleared away the paint pots, brushes, stepladders and dustsheets that had been around since my decorating spree. I felt uneasy. Camilla's case was no nearer resolution than it had been in the beginning. I seemed to be getting nowhere.

Sean phoned and told me he missed me. He tried to arrange another date. I was vague and said I'd get back to him.

I sat down and scratched my head. I picked up the file and bit the top of my biro. I reminded myself again that I'd confined my enquiries to the small group of men who surrounded Camilla in the months before her death. Some of them had only come to light in the course of my investigations. There may have been further affairs or friendships which had turned sour. She might have approached other moneylenders, apart from Sean. I felt helpless and uncertain about what to do next. I decided to phone Josh and ask him who else visited the flat, who else regularly telephoned Camilla.

Pip answered. 'He's in Manchester,' he said, sounding proud. 'He's gone. He's on the set of *Coronation Street*.'

We arranged to meet later that day.

*

I cycled over to Camberwell and locked the bike to the railings, outside a pub. Pip sat in a booth near the door, half obscured by hanging Christmas decorations which had come adrift. As I approached, they swayed in the draught and he shivered visibly. He dabbed at his nose with a tissue. He was wearing a Peruvian hat with long earflaps. He studied a postcard, self-consciously, and looked up. 'It's from Josh,' he said. 'He sends me one every time he goes somewhere new.'

I glanced down. It was a picture of a wide road junction with buses and shops. 'Lovely,' I said. I bought myself a pint of Courage. Pip wanted a sherry.

He was pale. 'I've got a shocking cold,' he told me. His pointy little-boy's face looked old and the end of his nose was red and chapped. I sat down and we chatted for a while about his dole money and the implications of moving in with Josh. He was worried that a change of address might disrupt his claim. He pursed his lips and shredded his tissue.

'Don't worry,' I said pointlessly. 'Have you got any auditions coming up?'

'No,' he said, 'and I'm past caring. I feel awful. I think it's flu. I'm going to just crawl away somewhere and finish off this breakdown I'm having. I mean. I've got this far. I may as well complete the job.'

I changed the subject. 'How's Josh getting on in Manchester?'

Pip cheered up. 'Oh, brill. He's living in Myra Hindley's old house in Gorton. He's got a delightful landlady. Like Andy Capp's wife. Rollers, headscarf, that kind of thing.'

'We all wear those up north. I always get changed on

the train. Slippers in the street, rolled-down stockings. Josh'd better get himself a cloth cap.'

'Oh, he has already,' Pip enthused. 'And a whippet. He's playing accordion in a working-men's club.' He giggled but then his face dropped. 'Actually, he says its a great gay scene up there. I'm a bit worried.'

'Don't be daft. You're a married couple.'

He smiled and leaned back as if he had received a compliment. He stretched out his little legs. We sat in silence for a while, sipping our drinks in a companionable way. Until recently, we'd always been relaxed together, because we had nothing to prove. Camilla's death had changed this.

'I'm sorry about that night . . .'

I remembered the embarrassment of his visit with Josh. I didn't want to discuss it. 'Never mind that,' I said hastily. I took a swig of beer. 'I've always meant to ask you, where did you two meet?'

He munched his French bread. 'Oh, Brockwell Park. Weren't you there?'

I shook my head, playing with my food.

'It was a music festival. Paul Weller was playing and a band from West Africa. Josh's crowd were all there, sitting on the grass, looking very glam and sophisticated. I was on my own. After a while, it got crowded. Anyway, he suddenly leaned against me, back to back. We were . . .' he paused, searching for words, 'sort of propping each other up. It was a lovely sunny day. We just stayed there. I couldn't believe there was this divine man sort of resting against me. Anyway, after a while, we went off together.' He sighed at the memory. 'Peter was there. He was green, of course.'

'What?' I froze, my pint halfway to my lips.

287

'He was so jealous. I thought, if looks could kill . . .' He cut a sliver of cheese and put it in his mouth from the knife. A blob of chutney clung to his upper lip. He licked it off. 'He thought Josh should stay loyal to his memory.'

I tried not to react. I swallowed my beer and put the glass down, carefully. I spread my hands on the cold marble of the tabletop. They looked big and tired. 'They had a history? Josh and Peter?'

Pip wanted to tell me. He was excited. His ego needed a boost. 'Oh, yes. It's not common knowledge, of course. I shouldn't be saying this.' He smiled mischievously. 'But I can trust you, Imogen.' He popped a Nicorette into his mouth, and gave a disdainful smirk, clearly aimed at Peter. He was reliving his triumph. I realized he was drunk. I wondered how many sherries he'd got through before I arrived. 'It really put the cat among the pigeons,' he added, 'that day.'

I said nothing, allowing this information to sink in. Pip took off his hat, preened a little, then replaced it.

'But presumably,' I was hesitant, 'Peter was with Camilla by then?'

'Yes, well, he'd followed her around for years with that engagement ring in his pocket. It was always a stormy relationship. She was there, that day, too, for a while but she got bored and went shopping.'

'But he and Josh . . .'

He gave me a hard look. He was enjoying the fact that he knew more about all this than I did. 'In a way, for a time, he wanted them both. Camilla and Josh. They represented the two sides of him. He was jealous of Josh's new partners long after they'd split. Long after he'd decided he was straight . . .'

I was sure Josh wouldn't like it if he knew Pip was

discussing his business. I though about the photograph of him I'd found in Peter's bedroom, and the magazine. 'So they met at Oxford?'

'Yes,' he sighed. 'Student days. They were in the same college.'

I smiled to myself. 'I see.' Pip didn't know everything. Josh's deception was deep and inflexible. Even his partner didn't know all of the truth.

Pip laughed a little and swayed in his seat. I bought him another drink. 'So that's how Camilla met Josh? Through Peter?'

'Yes. But that's another interesting thing. Camilla didn't know about their affair. Not for years. Josh was sworn to silence. Peter didn't want her to know he'd been gay. She found out about a year ago.'

I wished I had a pen and paper to make notes. I felt drunk. I hoped I was going to remember all of this.

'That was her latest reason for refusing to marry him. She said she wasn't marrying a poof.' He smiled conspiratorially. 'Don't tell a soul!'

I took another gulp of beer. 'She didn't want to marry him anyway.'

Pip hummed a tune and finished his sherry. He tapped his fingers on the table. 'Maybe. It was still a big shock for her.'

'Who told her?'

'Josh.'

'Why?'

'They were having a fight. I don't know. He wanted to hurt her. He succeeded. Think about it, Imogen. Number one, she didn't like gays.'

I interrupted. 'Camilla wasn't prejudiced.'

He continued as if he hadn't heard me. 'Number two,

she saw Peter as her own property – as far as she knew he'd never wanted anyone apart from herself. She couldn't bear him having that kind of long-term intimacy with anyone else. Number three, she was humiliated. She hated not knowing. She accused them both of laughing at her.'

He got up to go to the toilet. He stumbled a little as he eased himself out of the booth. I looked around. The pub was empty. The barmaids whispered together, pretending to polish the optics. I felt sick and decided to stop drinking. I undid the button of my trousers and took some deep breaths. I got Pip yet another sherry.

He returned but his mood seemed to have changed. He was anxious again. He chewed another Nicorette.

I remembered why I'd come. I felt instinctively that he'd given me enough information but I still said, 'Who d'you think killed her?'

He frowned. 'The Whistler killed her. What are you on about?'

I shook my head.

'The police know what they're doing. They've got computers.' His voice trailed off. 'Forensic. That kind of thing.'

'Look,' I interrupted, 'we both know this. The DSS is inefficient. The council is corrupt. The NHS is a disaster. Social services are a joke. I spend my life sorting out the messes made by big organizations. I don't trust any of them. And that includes the police. OK? So Thatcher gave them a pile of money. They're no nearer to catching this murderer. They don't know their arse from their elbow.' My voice was emotional.

'All right. I hear you. So maybe they won't catch the

Whistler. Maybe they really are hopeless. That doesn't mean the Whistler didn't do it!'

My mind felt fuggy with beer. I couldn't remember what I was arguing about. 'They haven't got a clue, down at that nick.' My words were slurred.

'They must have clues,' insisted Pip. 'I bet they've got lots and lots of clues.'

I decided it was time to go. I was in no state to pursue my enquiries. I stood up and put on my jacket. 'I'll see you.'

I turned back to wave to him from the door. He'd turned the flaps of his hat upwards. They pointed to the ceiling, like rabbits' ears.

Outside, it was raining heavily. I fished in my pocket for the keys to the padlock, but there was no bicycle chained to the railings. It had been stolen. I was dismayed. Turning my collar up, I trudged down the hill towards the bus stop. I felt nervous and afraid of being followed. The damp cold air chilled my bones. It was a long walk and darkness was creeping towards the skyline. A BT van screeched past, crushing an empty cardboard box. A woman shouted abuse at her child in its pushchair, waiting to cross the road. I looked for the bike in court-yards and gardens but there was no sign of it.

Chapter Thirty-Two

I spent the weekend in a daze. Apart from a few trips to the off-licence, I didn't go out of the flat. I was beginning to enjoy its womblike security. Camilla's case dominated my thoughts, but I couldn't move things forward. My mind seemed to be stuck in a tape loop of ideas which ran in a continous but unsatisfactory circle.

On Monday morning I left for the office feeling guilty about having wasted so much energy on one single problem. My job was being neglected, clients were being short-changed, but I knew I couldn't stop now. I had to go on.

The room was warm. 'I've fixed the fire, said Al. 'I just unscrewed that little round thing and you know, sort of poked it . . .'

'Great,' I muttered.

The waiting room was full. Al and I worked steadily, talking to people, making phone calls, writing hurried notes. Not surprisingly, the Electricity Couple were in again and I heard Al trying to explain that we'd tried all the options. 'Speak to your MP,' she said.

The woman shook her head. 'We have,' she replied, 'seven times.'

At that moment Penny telephoned. She started going on again about her new series, *Londoners*. I'd heard it all before. She still wanted me to suggest people who might give an interesting interview. She thought I had nothing better to do. I felt irritated, both by her persistence and the dogged determination of the Electricity Couple, sitting beside me. I covered the phone with my hand and turned to them. 'Would you like to go on the telly,' I offered, 'talk about your situation?'

The man stared at me blankly. The woman shrugged. 'How much do they pay?'

I handed her the phone.

Later, when the session was over and everyone had gone, Al sat typing letters and bringing case files up to date. I made us both a drink and rested my head in my hand. I drank my coffee, slowly. The phone rang. Al answered it and transferred it to my extension.

The voice was familiar. 'Imogen?'

I sighed. It was Penny.

'She's perfect,' she breathed. 'Penniless, racist, embittered. Not only that. She's a Tory voter. I could put them alongside my yuppie Labour couple from Crouch End. Brilliant contrast.' She sounded excited. 'Fabulous. Thank you so much.'

'I'm pleased,' I said, ironically. 'Any time.'

'But you don't understand. The lady didn't say yes. She sounded keen but she didn't commit.' There was a pause. 'I need them badly, Imogen. I want to go and see them. Give me their address.'

'Are you paying them?'

'Enough to clear their bill. Get them reconnected.'

I hesitated. I felt guilty about my role in this. I shouldn't have dumped Penny and her demands on unsuspecting clients without an explanation. I'd been unprofessional. 'OK,' I said reluctantly. 'I'll go. It's my problem. I'll go and see them and sort it out.'

I read through Camilla's file again. I yawned and added the information about Josh and Peter's old liaison. It was surprising but it didn't seem to have much bearing on the case. Camilla would have been unhappy about it, but I didn't believe she'd been as upset as Pip suggested. If she'd been that distraught, she would have confided in me.

I tipped out the briefcase and picked up the address book I'd taken from her room in the Hardings' house. I flicked through it again. The small, cramped writing in red ink was not Camilla's hand. Then I noticed something in the back, in her italics. It was the initials *M.M.* and a London address.

I stared numbly at the little book. I had nothing to go on, no clues, no leads. I felt I was at a dead end. I was becoming convinced that Camilla's killer was a man she'd known, but that he was unknown to me. I had no way of finding him. I looked at the pages of telephone numbers. Idly, I started ringing them. I mentioned Camilla's name and asked the person on the other end how well they knew her. I repeated the process, mechanically, several times. It seemed pointless, but I couldn't think of anything more meaningful to do.

One or two people were baffled. One woman said her boss had recently passed away. However, the majority quickly put down the phone. I was puzzled. I was being polite and persuasive. There seemed to be no reason for so much rudeness. I rang another pageful of numbers.

They were all in London. I met up with hostility, silence, surprise. Everyone hung up on me. It was very strange.

I leaned back in my chair and put my feet up on the desk. I scratched my head. Al switched off her computer. 'I'm going to see my reflexologist,' she said, sounding tired. 'I'll be back in a while.'

'Put the answering machine on.' I yawned again and stretched. I studied Camilla's writing at the back of the address book. I consulted the *A–Z*. I made a quick decision and followed Al out, locking up behind me. We walked over Blackfriars Bridge. It was a cold, bright day and the river glittered. We separated at the Tube. I went in and bought a ticket to Green Park.

I walked down Curzon Street, studying my map like a tourist. I felt less nervous than usual. Away from my home patch, London was unthreatening. The sun was shining and people looked prosperous and busy. I wasn't afraid of being followed.

The mews I wanted was very hard to find. I walked through Shepherd's Market twice, seeking the help of a waiter and a traffic warden. I remembered the area was famous for prostitution, but there were no women hanging around, or kerb crawlers, like the ones I'd noticed near my office. It was clearly a discreet enterprise and well organized.

Businessmen sat together in cafés, chatting into mobile phones. Well-dressed people jumped in and out of cabs. Professional women strode purposefully around, holding leather bags. I didn't feel out of place. People gave me interested looks, as if I might be a pop singer, or an artist. The pubs had polished brass fittings around the doors. I could imagine summer umbrellas, geraniums and tables in the street.

Eventually, I found the address. It was tucked away, in a tiny square. Window boxes trailed ivy. The pavement was wide, the railings ornate. The house was very grand, with blank windows shrouded in white nylon. I climbed the steps. There was a row of bells. The top three had the names Cherie, Mandy and Lizbeth. The bottom one said only M.M. I pressed hard.

The intercom buzzed and I pushed open the door. Inside, the hall was spacious with colourful tiles. An impressive oak staircase curved away. I knocked on the door of the ground-floor flat.

After a long time there was the sound of locks turning. The door opened a tiny crack. I shoved my toe in the space. 'Hello,' I said gently, 'I'm Camilla Harding's best friend.'

The door opened a little further, to the extent of its security chain. I glimpsed a woman with a round, sallow face. She was wearing a black silk wrap, over white pyjamas. She regarded me seriously.

I smiled. 'May I come in?'

She had smooth skin and a dark shadow above her upper lip. Her black hair was plaited, tightly. As we looked at each other she raised a hand and smoothed both her eyebrows. There was a chink of gold bracelets. To my surprise, she unfastened the chain. I stepped inside and she relocked the door. She was very short and smelled faintly of garlic. I followed her into a large living room. It was sparse but elegant. She gestured towards a low divan. 'Sit down.' She had a faint accent. I thought she might be Spanish, or possibly Arab. She disappeared.

The few ornaments and the style of the room were

foreign. A pale tapestry covered one wall. Next to an armchair was a pile of books and a sheaf of notes. It was cold. The window was open behind an ornamental grille. The nylon curtains puffed inward in the breeze.

She came back with a tray. She poured me a drink in a small glass. I sipped it gratefully. It tasted of aniseed. She opened a can of Pepsi for herself and transferred it to a thin tumbler. 'I'll close the window.' She had wide hips and a tiny waist. She wore embroidered Turkish slippers with curled toes.

She sat down opposite me, in the armchair. Her fingers were heavy with rings. 'How is it you are here?'

I stretched out my legs. I felt big and masculine next to her delicate feet, her frail wrists. I unfastened Camilla's briefcase and pulled out the address book. I flicked its pages in her direction. I drained my glass. 'Is this yours?' I asked.

She nodded.

'How did Camilla get hold of it?'

She met my gaze. 'I sold it to her.'

A taxi pulled up noisily, outside. Its engine revved and the front door slammed. We listened as it drove away. I held the book up. 'What are these telephone numbers?'

She was very still. There was no emotion, no reaction in her face. She stared at me. 'What is your name?'

'I'm Imogen. I was Camilla's friend.'

'Ah, Imogen, yes. Of you she was most fond.'

I looked at the books at her feet. They were scientific textbooks. The notes alongside were written in red ink, in the same small cramped hand. There was a long silence. She stood up and I quickly pocketed the evidence. She held out her hand. I realized she wanted my glass. Politely, she refilled it and handed it back to me.

I coughed. 'How did you know Camilla?'

She sat down and leaned back in her chair. Her robe slipped a little and below her pyjamas I could see that her calves were rounded and hairless. 'Why are you here?'

'I found this address book.' My voice sounded evasive. I tried to be more assertive. 'What d'you mean, you sold it to her? Tell me and I'll go away.'

'OK, OK.' She sipped her Pepsi. 'It doesn't matter now.' She straightened up. 'Nothing matters now. The poor girl's dead.'

In another room, a telephone rang. She ignored it. 'I was a gentleman's escort,' she said. 'I retired. Now I am a student of medicine.' She gestured proudly towards the textbooks. Her eyes continued to meet mine.

There was another silence.

'I made enough money. It was time to stop.' Her gaze never faltered but her eyes were black and impenetrable.

'The address book?'

'My clients.'

'You sold it to Camilla?'

'She gave me a good price.'

My heart bumped wildly in my chest. My mouth went very dry. I drained my glass again. Despite the chill of the room, I felt a trickle of sweat between my breasts.

'You seem shocked.' She stood up, picked up the decanter and refilled my glass again.

I drained it for the third time. 'I am shocked,' I whispered. 'I am.'

The telephone rang a second time. She went out to answer it. I wiped my damp hands on the brocade of the divan. I stood up. My legs felt unsteady. The aniseed drink was making my head swim. I walked around the room, clutching the address book in my pocket. The woman returned.

'How long was she doing . . .' my voice croaked, 'this work?'

'A few months. I own this house. She rented a flat upstairs.'

'You were here when . . .'

'I was in Izmir when she died. I came back in the New Year.'

'Is it possible . . .' My voice had become hoarse. 'Is it possible that this . . . work . . . led to her death?'

Her response was immediate and definite. 'No, no, no.'

'How can you be sure?'

'She was murdered a long way away by this Whistler fellow. She only worked up here. In this nice area. No one here knew where she lived. South London. There was no connection . . .'

'She may have been followed. '

'Impossible!'

'Why is it impossible?' I felt suddenly angry. 'Are you stupid or what?' My voice was loud.

She took two steps backwards towards the door. Her face didn't change. 'That's not what happened. She died all the way down there . . .'

'It's not the bloody South Pole!'

She stared at me impassively. I realized it was point-less arguing with her. 'I'm sorry,' I said, quietly.

'Sit down.' She gestured again towards the divan. She sat opposite me, as she had before. 'Imogen, let me tell you this.' She sighed. 'What Camilla did, what I did, it wasn't so terrible. It was nothing. You do it once, twice, three times, then it's not so terrible. It becomes nothing.'

I felt tears coming to my eyes. 'I can't believe it. I just can't believe Camilla was a prostitute.'

She sighed. 'She was a very bad prostitute.'

'What d'you mean?'

She picked up her glass of Pepsi again and sipped it. She wiped her lips, delicately, and put it back on the floor. 'To be a good whore, you have to forget yourself.' She repositioned her emphasis. 'You have to forget your *self*.'

I said nothing.

'Camilla wasn't interested in service. She wasn't interested in becoming what men wanted.' She stroked both her eyebrows. 'Prostitution is an act. She didn't like acting. She was too much herself.'

'What are you saying?'

'If it makes you feel better, Imogen, although God knows why it should, her heart wasn't in it. She wanted quick money. Short term.'

'Why?'

'I've no idea.'

I stood up and refastened the briefcase. I felt disorientated. I took the address book from my pocket. 'D'you want this?'

She raised her eyebrows. 'It's very valuable.'

I offered it to her. 'Sell it again,' I said harshly.

She seemed reluctant to touch it.

I realized it might contain the name of Camilla's killer. I put it in my pocket. I walked into the hall. She followed me and unlocked the door. Neither of us spoke again. Without looking at her, I left. I hurried down the street. When the Tube station came into view, I started running.

Chapter Thirty-Three

I was awoken the next day by the noise of a van pulling up, outside. Its door slammed, there was cheerful whistling, then, surprisingly, a ring on my bell. I pulled on my dressing gown and opened the door. I was bleary-eyed and unfocused without my contact lenses. A uniformed man from Parcelforce handed me a box and I struggled, blindly, to sign for it. In an instant, he'd roared away down the street.

I carried the parcel indoors and placed it on the table. I found an old pair of spectacles and put them on. They made the kitchen tip sideways in an odd way. I got a knife from the drawer. The parcel was the size of a shoebox. I didn't recognize the writing on the packaging, so I knew it wasn't a present from home. Looking closer, I thought the postmark could be Bradford.

I slit the Sellotape and paper round the edges and opened the box. It contained a plastic bag which felt soft. I cut carefully along an edge. Immediately, there was a terrible, sickening smell. It filled the room. I stepped back, horrified. After a couple of seconds, holding one hand across my nose and mouth, I looked inside. The carrier bag contained rotten meat. It was dark red, turning black. I picked up the box, retching. The smell was overpowering. I carried it outside into the street and was about to drop it in the dustbin when I decided there might be a message. Holding my breath, I tipped the meat into the bin. There was nothing else inside the bag. I pulled apart and inspected the outer wrapping and the box. The carrier was from Asda and the box said 'Cable & Co.'. There were no clues, only my name and address scrawled untidily on the outside. Whoever had sent it wanted to remain anonymous. I put everything in the dustbin and replaced the lid. As I went back indoors, my upstairs neighbour passed by. Self-conscious about both my appearance and the terrible smell, I ignored him and quickly shut the door.

I felt ill. The air was unbreathable. I stripped off my dressing gown and stuffed it in the washing machine. Naked I sponged myself with carbolic soap and then cleaned the table and the knife with bleach.

I couldn't open the locked, barred windows, so I rummaged around for something to mask the stench. I found Camilla's perfume. It was the bottle I'd taken from Peter's bathroom cabinet. I sprayed it in the kitchen, then in the hall. I sprayed myself from head to foot, then all the other rooms in the flat. The air was heavy, sweet and dense. I carried on until the whole bottle was used up.

Later, I went to work. There was no advice session scheduled, but just being in the office helped me concentrate on the case. I opened the post, tidied up, then took the messages off the answering machine. As I expected, there was another pestering call from Penny. She wanted to know if I'd been to visit the Electricity Couple.

'Give me a bloody chance,' I said aloud. I listened to the rest in trepidation. It had been a while since the mystery caller had bothered me, but I always expected him. As if aware of my state of mind, he'd phoned. It was the same tight, nasal Scottish accent. He sounded drunk. 'Gettya present, hen? Gettya present?' There was a pause, then, 'I've told ye once, I've told ye twice . . . I've told ye thrice . . .' There was no mistaking his cold aggression. He hung up.

I dialled 1471, like I'd done before, but this wasn't helpful. Although she hadn't left a second message, the final person to call the office that morning had been Penny.

I sat down in Al's chair. My hands shook. I opened her drawer to see if she had any drugs but I could only find tobacco. I rummaged through the old cake tin that served as our first-aid kit. Al had put this together a few months previously, after a client had collapsed in the waiting room. It contained bandages, plasters, an eye patch, an empty packet of foot powder, glucose sweets, aspirin and what I'd hoped to find – prescription tranquillizers. I swallowed three.

I drank a mug of coffee, waiting for the tablets to kick in. When my heart rate slowed and a numbness began to creep over me, I made out a new page in Camilla's file. I headed it PERSON UNKNOWN and wrote down everything M.M. had told me. At the bottom I wrote *Is it possible to truly know someone?* but it looked stupid, so I crossed it out.

I leaned back in Al's comfortable chair, fiddling with the levers that adjusted its height and posture. I felt woozy, but better. Camilla's secret life seemed to have moved from its nagging, painful lodging inside my head, to a place slightly beyond the window.

I tried but failed to come up with a reason why she'd

been so desperate for money. Somewhere beyond the glass pane, I stared at an image of her, pouting. She wasn't posing for the photographers' lens. She was in front of a shadowy queue of lonely men, with fat wallets and blanked-out emotions.

My mind wandered. I remembered the days when I'd first arrived in London, before I got a proper job, and before I'd found a permanent home. I'd shared a flat in Wandsworth with an Israeli couple who used to yell and hit each other. For reasons I couldn't understand they said they wanted a baby. Outside the back gardens were filled with rubbish, picked over by feral cats. They often sat on the walls and window ledges, staring into the rooms, with a stillness and concentration which were terrifying.

At night-times I worked in a club. I served behind the bar, wearing a white shirt and waistcoat. I mixed and watered down overpriced drinks. The place was in a basement, poorly ventilated and lined with mirrors. Women danced and removed their clothes. One or two of them could be persuaded, by customers, to go outside into the back lane. This was a way of supplementing their pay. I recalled telling Camilla about this. I expected her to be shocked, but she was dismissive. She thought they were fools. 'If you're going to sell it,' she'd said, 'you may as well get a decent price.'

I thought about M.M.'s elegant flat, the silk robe, the jewellery. Hers was a different style of operation from the few pounds changing hands at the back of a strip club. Camilla had joined an élite band of specialists. She had not sold herself cheap.

It occurred to me that a lot of the money she'd borrowed must have been used to buy the address book and then fix herself up with the right accessories. She'd needed good things – blouses, shoes, perfume, underwear, possibly even sex aids. She also had to meet the rent on the flat in Mayfair. This would have been expensive. It was becoming clearer why Camilla had borrowed so much money. What wasn't explicable was her central motive – why she'd been so desperate as to choose the easy but degrading option offered to her by M.M. I tried to work out why she'd made the decision to do this kind of work.

Her modelling career was in decline. She'd been one of the highest-paid women in London, but had moved to a position where she enjoyed little money of her own. She'd often said someone was bad-mouthing her, making assignments impossible to find. She said she was sick of chasing work, tired of rejection. She'd insisted someone was trying to do her down. She'd said the same thing to Penny. I wondered if these allegations were true. They might be connected with the threats she said she'd received. On the other hand, they could be what I'd always thought – a paranoid reaction, a kind of excuse for failure.

I made myself more black coffee. I felt calm, but less sleepy than I expected. I found the number of Camilla's agent. Bambi Pellegrino was a partner in an agency in Knightsbridge. They handled most of the top models in London. I imagined her, plump behind her spacious desk, with her phones, her American hair, her tan, her big designer jewellery.

'Ms Pellegrino? Hello, it's Imogen Webb.'

There was a silence.

'Imogen. I was a friend of Camilla Harding.'

'Oh,' she said, uncertainly.

I remembered we hadn't met for some time. 'I came to your party,' I reminded her. 'The pink party.'

She didn't say anything.

'We all wore pink. All the food was pink.' I realized I was babbling. 'I came with Camilla.' I hesitated. 'I hope you don't mind. I want to ask you a few questions.'

'I'm real sorry about Camilla.' She sighed.

I picked up my pen. I jumped straight in. 'Bambi, how much work was she getting? Was her career really on the skids?'

There was a silence, a crackle on the line and then the clunk of her bangles. 'I'm sorry, honey, I don't know what you mean.'

'Was she worried about work? Was someone trying to stop her getting work? Spreading rumours?'

Bambi sighed. She sounded remorseful. Then she took a deep breath and her tone changed to her professional coldness. 'Hey, what's it to me? I haven't worked with her for maybe a year. Nearer two years. Was she my problem?'

I was shocked. 'Oh,' I muttered, 'I'm sorry, I didn't . . .'

'Try Zuckerman's,' she snapped. She gave me an address and number in Lewisham. She was about to hang up.

'Did you fall out?' I asked. 'Why did Camilla leave you?'

Bambi sighed again. Under her hard glaze, she was sorry. 'I had to let her go.'

'She used to be the best-paid model on your books.'

'Yeah, maybe. Once upon a time. But she had a diet

problem. It was getting out of hand . . . And she was what? Thirty-three, four? She wouldn't do *Woman's Journal.'*

I was puzzled. Camilla never told me she'd changed her agent. She hadn't mentioned that Bambi dropped her. I reminded myself that she'd told me little of what was happening in her life. This was just one more surprise.

I thought about her playing with her food, weighing herself, starting then leaving aerobics classes. I knew she had an eating problem, but she'd had it all her life. She refused to talk about her age. She blamed the fact that she was often 'resting' on this mysterious individual, determined to do her down.

I realized I was a bit dozy. I drained the cooling dregs of my coffee. I loosened the laces of my shoes and kicked them off. I turned down the heater. Unable to keep my eyes open, I slept for about five minutes then rang the Lewisham number. A recorded voice put me on hold. I listened to an electronic version of 'River Deep, Mountain High'. After a while there was a beep and a voice said, 'Becky Zuckerman speaking, how may I help you?'

I explained that I was a friend of Camilla. 'Can I ask you some questions?'

'Are you from the press?'

'No. A personal friend.'

'Ah, *oui. Ça va?*' Her accent was pure Hendon. I heard her blow out smoke. Another conversation started, behind her, somewhere in her room. It sounded heated.

I paused. For some reason I had an imaginary vision of a small, cramped office, cracked lino, dirty frosted glass. 'There's a few things to sort out. Have you got a minute?'

She inhaled. '*Mais oui, d'accord.*'

'How much work was Camilla getting?'

There was another pause. One of the background voices shouted, 'Over my dead body!' She sighed. '*Pas du tout.*' She started speaking quickly. Her voice had a throaty rasp. 'Don't blame me. She wouldn't do catalogue work. Older woman stuff. She said she wasn't ready.' The phone became muffled. I imagined her swivelling around in her chair. 'Shut the fuck up, will you? I'm on the bloody phone.'

I waited a second. 'Was she in debt?'

There was a snort. 'Christ, yes. She was desperate. But she wouldn't do catalogue work.'

'You couldn't help her?'

She inhaled again and coughed. 'Help her? It was *trop difficile.* I tried. I really tried. Don't blame me.'

'Was somebody bad-mouthing her? Saying she was unreliable?'

She didn't hesitate. 'I'm saying she wouldn't take what was on offer. This isn't bloody Knightsbridge. I could have got her work. At one time she was the most requested model in London.' She paused, coughed and wheezed. 'Camilla Harding? You're asking? Work I could always get. It wasn't my bleeding fault. I could sell her. Ten times over. I got her promotional stuff. Trade journals. The Motor Show. Was it my fault she was choosy?'

The argument behind her raged. Becky covered the phone again and screamed, 'Chill out, you mother-fuckers!' The room went quiet.

'Was someone bad-mouthing her?' My voice was a whisper because my throat and mouth had become so dry. 'Was anyone saying she couldn't hack it? Bulimia, whatever?'

There was no reply.

'Mrs Zuckerman?'

Her attention was elsewhere. '*Oui?*'

'Who was it?'

I heard her rummaging in a drawer. There was the puff of an asthma inhaler. The background voices had ceased.

'Who was it? Who was trying to do her down?'

She coughed again. 'No, sweetie, you're wrong. I heard her say that, lots of times, but it wasn't true. It was just something she liked to say. *Quel dommage.* She just wasn't getting the work she wanted. Not any more.'

I dropped the phone in its cradle and leaned back in my chair, squinting at the street. An old man walked past, dragging an ancient spaniel. It peed on our railings.

I made more coffee and forced myself to drink it. I was becoming more alert. I picked up my pen and noted everything down. Camilla was mistaken about someone harming her job prospects. Perhaps she'd imagined it, or invented it. Her new agent had no reason to lie. I wondered again if she'd spread this story about as a kind of excuse. She hated admitting failure. I scratched my head. The more I went on the more I discovered. I'd believed Camilla was my best friend and that I'd known her well. It was clear that I hadn't known anything about her, at all.

I stared at the noticeboard. There was a yellow Post-it note stuck on top of the calendar. It said Penny Mortimer, London Weekend TV, and a date and time. Another label showed the address of the Electricity Couple.

I felt irritated by the idea of Penny and Al meeting without me. I swivelled from side to side, staring at Al's computer and the folders on her desk. There were sticky

Post-it labels everywhere – on the monitor, the filing cabinet, the drawers. They were all reminders of things to do. I felt furious. I couldn't understand why she didn't have a Filofax, like everyone else.

I doodled in the margin of Camilla's file, contemplating her insistence that someone was trying to mess up her prospects. If it was true, if the word on the street was that she'd become unreliable, it would have damaged her chances of getting any kind of job offer – prestigious or mundane. It could have ended her career, provided a reason for her resorting to prostitution. However, if her agent was to be believed, this was just a smokescreen, used to explain away the fact that her star was in its descent.

There was still the other allegation to consider. This was the one which had got me started on the investigation in the first place. Camilla had said that someone was trying to scare her. I was still convinced there was a link between this and her murder.

It seemed possible that it was one of M.M.'s former clients, who'd turned nasty. If this was the case, Camilla was unlikely to have confided in anyone. It was also true that it would be very hard to track him down. There were nearly two hundred numbers in the address book and none of the men concerned would be willing to talk about their dealings with her.

My only hope was that the person who'd issued threats was someone she knew well, someone I could discover for myself. It was painful to admit that Camilla hadn't confided in me, but when she finally did so, that last night, I was too drunk and too tired to listen. I wondered if she'd been more open with anyone else.

I decided the only person she might have talked to

was Peter. She might have told him who was bothering her. She spent a lot of her time with him and he'd been loyal to her for years. Their relationship might not have been going anywhere, but it was intimate and to an extent, exclusive. There was complicity between them. These thoughts brought my anger and anxiety flooding back. I clenched my fists. The effects of the tranquillizers had worn off. I thought about taking some more, but decided they were useless. I felt jealous of Peter and there was a tightness in my chest.

'I hate him,' I said aloud. He'd failed to recognize me the day I'd cleaned his house. He'd been cold and distant on the night when I'd cycled over to see him. He'd thrown me out of Camilla's room after the funeral. He thought he was superior to me. Maybe, in important ways, Camilla had thought so too.

I twisted from side to side at Al's desk, kicking the drawers. At that moment, she arrived. She was in a good mood, singing to herself. Some of her dreadlocks had been wrapped tightly in coloured thread, giving her an ethnic look. She picked up some papers from her desk. 'You smell nice,' she said. 'Chanel?'

I ignored her, still occupying her chair. I telephoned Peter's publishing house. His secretary was firm. 'He's in conference for the next few days. I'll take a message.'

The calm insistence of her tones made me even more annoyed. I rang back and disguised my voice. 'This is Annabel Fawcett from Picador. It's both vital and urgent that I speak to him right now.' The response was the same.

I scribbled him a fax. It said, *Ring me right away, you poofy bastard, or I'm telephoning the Sun about your sex life.*

I waited.

'What's cooking?' asked Al.

'Shut up,' I said.

Peter phoned five minutes later. His voice was careful, measured. 'What's the matter, Imogen?'

I felt a release of emotion. 'I know all about you and Josh,' I shouted. 'D'you think the tabloids wouldn't be interested? Listen to this. How's this for a banner headline? "Baronet Boyfriend of Whistler Victim Linked to TV Star." They'd bloody love it.' I could hear my Geordie accent getting stronger and stronger. 'I just have to pick up a phone. I just have to mention why she wouldn't marry you. You think that wouldn't be news? Here we are, it's just after Christmas and the papers have nothing to print except rehashes of the Whistler story. You think they wouldn't be interested?'

There was a silence. Then Peter said, 'Imogen, whatever is wrong? Why are you yelling at me like this?'

'I want to see you, you posh git. Don't give me the runaround.'

'All right,' he said quietly, 'when?'

'Now,' I replied. 'I'm coming over.'

As I replaced the phone, it rang. It was Penny. I shouted, 'Piss off, you cow!' and banged down the receiver. I glanced over at Al. She was staring at me. I grabbed my jacket and left the office without speaking to her.

Peter worked in Bloomsbury, in a beautiful building near the British Museum. An elderly man, wearing old-fashioned military-style uniform, stood under the portico, holding open the door for me. Inside the huge hall, with its ornate plasterwork and ceiling frescos, my footsteps echoed. A security guard sat behind a desk, a row of monitors showing him different views of the interior. I asked him the way. He was expecting me. He gave me a badge to wear and pointed upstairs. I felt big and unkempt as his eyes travelled over me. He spoke into his phone as I climbed the marble staircase. At the top there was a series of heavy dark wood doors with brass nameplates. I rubbed my sweaty hands on my jeans.

Inside Peter's suite I found myself in a kind of anteroom, with low leather seats grouped around a glass-topped table. In contrast to the public space outside, it was understated and modern. I helped myself to coffee and sat down. I tipped a dish of foil-wrapped mint chocolates into my pocket. Everything in the room was beige. I leaned over to pick up one of the big, glossy house books and knocked over my coffee cup. A dark stain spread across the carpet. There was a camera pointing at me from the ceiling.

I felt hot. Not just my hands, but my whole body felt sweaty. I wondered if it was a side effect of the pills I'd taken. I wasn't well.

I didn't want to wait any longer and went through another door. This led to a bigger, second room which was empty but seemed to have been recently occupied by Peter's secretary.

At the far end was a third door. Approaching it, I read the sign DIRECTOR. To the right hung a painting. I hesitated, examining it. A man sat at a table in front of a window, his hand on a globe. There was a little gold nameplate in the ornate frame. It said the word VERMEER.

Without knocking, I walked into Peter's office. The image was curiously replicated. He sat at a desk, lit from the side, his right hand tapping a keyboard, his left fingering some papers on top of a screen. His light suit was made of silk and his position, his gesture, the sheen on his jacket were identical to those on the painting I'd just passed.

He glanced over. 'Sit down, Imogen.'

I took off my leather jacket and draped it over the back of a chair. My armpits were damp. They smelled rank and sour, mingling with Camilla's scent.

A floor-to-ceiling window looked over a narrow balcony and out into the winter trees of the square. It was getting dark.

There was an arrangement of expensive, hothouse daffodils on his desk and a large framed photograph of Camilla. Together, these made me think of the funeral. Another flower nestled in his buttonhole. His tie was loosened and his collar was undone. There were dark shadows under his eyes and his cheeks looked sunken.

'I may as well tell you immediately, I've contacted my solicitor.' His voice was gentle, even kind. He picked up a paperweight and passed it from one hand to another. Absently, he replaced it on his desk.

I saw it was a little carved figure with an enormous erect penis. 'Cut the crap,' I replied.

He turned to face me, leaned back and made a steeple with his fingers. He sighed. 'What d'you want?'

'You know I'm investigating Camilla's death?'

'So you informed me.'

'She told me that someone was intimidating her, scaring her, making threats. I want to know who it was.'

He sat upright and lifted the flower in his lapel to his nose. He raised his elegant eyebrows. He didn't speak.

For some reason I thought about making love to him, but I pushed the idea away. 'Well?' I said.

He sighed again. 'I don't know, Imogen. I don't know why you're pursuing this fantasy.'

'Just answer my questions and I'll piss off out of here.'

He sighed for a third time, regretfully. 'I don't think anyone was threatening Camilla. I've no reason to believe they were. Why would anyone want to threaten her?'

'I don't trust you.'

He paused, his eyes meeting mine. 'I do know she complained about not getting work. She said that someone was spreading rumours about her. I didn't take much notice. I told her to give up work. I suggested she stop worrying about modelling. She didn't need to work. I would have taken care of her.'

'She wanted to work!' I felt another wave of anger. He was so cool, so self-satisfied. I suddenly realized why Camilla, as desperate as she'd been, had never asked Peter for a significant sum of money. It would have been humiliating. He didn't take her job seriously. Admitting her failure to him would have given him the chance to patronize her even more.

I also saw that I was wasting my time. He noticed nothing outside his own world. He couldn't see the significance of her dwindling reputation. 'Of course she wanted work,' I repeated, 'she needed the money!'

'No she didn't.'

'Of course she did, man!'

'She didn't.'

'Why else would she work as a fucking prostitute?'

Peter froze. His hands grasped the arms of his chair. He swung round to face his desk, then back again. His throat pulsed as he struggled to swallow.

I took a deep breath. I could feel wetness between my breasts and on my brow. I rubbed my face on my sleeve. I fished in my jacket pocket and pulled out the address book. Several foil-wrapped chocolates fell to the floor. I held the book aloft. 'This,' I said loudly, 'is a list of punters. Camilla bought it from a high-class call-girl. She rented a flat and worked in her house. Why the hell was she doing that? What the fuck was going on?'

He reached out. A muscle quivered in his cheek. I gave him the book and he flicked through. There was a silence. He handed it back.

I held it up again. 'Tell me! Was it one of these sad bastards in here who was threatening her?'

He picked up the paperweight again and closed his hand around it. The little colour he'd had, drained from his face. He tried to speak but his words were trapped. He coughed. 'I don't know,' he whispered. 'This can't be true. I would have given her anything . . .'

'Of course it's true. I can give you the address. I spoke to the woman yesterday. There's no doubt about it.'

He replaced the paperweight again. 'Why are you telling me this?'

'I need your help.'

He leaned forward slightly, his head in one hand. He said nothing.

I wondered if he was ill. I waited. 'Well?'

His eyes met mine again. His lower lip trembled. 'I can't help you.' His voice sounded croaky, finished. 'I don't know anything.'

I stood up and put on my jacket, pocketing the book. 'Well,' I said, 'I'll be going, then.' I moved towards the door.

'You didn't have to tell me,' he murmured.

My feet were noisy on the marble stairs. Out in the street my whole body felt damp and dirty. I decided to go home and soak myself in a hot bath. The more I thought about this the more I was looking forward to it, but as I pushed open my heavy front door I was engulfed in the sweet, cloying smell of rottenness and perfume. The place stank of death.

Chapter Thirty-Four

The next morning I lay in bed, staring at the crack in the ceiling that looked like a map of India. The phone rang several times. I'd replaced the tape in the answering machine, so I let it pick up the calls. Later, after I'd eaten a bowl of Frosties and opened a few bills, I played it through and discovered five messages. One was from Pip, asking me to call, another was Sean suggesting a date and the rest were from Al. She sounded breathless and keen. She was phoning from her mobile and said she needed to speak to me urgently. I didn't ring anyone back.

I remembered my guilt about the Electricity Couple and how I'd dumped Penny's demands on them. I quickly dressed and took a minicab to the tenements where Camilla had once lived.

I looked at the windows. Most flats were managed by a housing association and let to pensioners. A few, like Josh's, were gentrified and privately owned. I wasn't sure into which category the Electricity Couple fitted. I pulled out a piece of paper from my pocket, where I'd scribbled their address. I discovered they were on the ground floor, in a flat immediately below the one Josh shared with Camilla. I'd noticed the place before, on previous visits. It was different from the others. The window was shrouded in dirty net. The front door had been kicked in, then patched up with hardboard. The place hadn't been painted for decades. It had a desolate, empty look. There was no bell. I knocked with my fist.

Immediately, a large dog flew towards the inside of the front door and crashed against it, barking wildly. I took two steps back. There was a lot of shouting and a long delay whilst the dog was pulled away. I waited. A girl walked past. 'Are you a health visitor?' she asked, pointing at Camilla's briefcase.

I shook my head.

'You don't want to be going in there, then.'

I glanced up at Josh's flat. The blinds were drawn, as if no one was home. I remembered he was in Manchester.

The door in front of me opened a crack. 'I'm from the Advice Centre.'

The woman let me in. I glanced into a bedroom, where someone snored and turned under a pile of dirty blankets. There was an unpleasant smell. We entered the living room. The curtains were closed and the light was very dim. It was cold. 'I thought Al got you a Calor gas heater?'

'It's stopped working.'

'They run out. You have to get the canister refilled.'

The woman shrugged and dropped heavily into an armchair. I looked around. I moved a pile of newspapers and correspondence from the other chair and sat down. 'Has Al made any progress with the electricity board?'

As my eyes became accustomed to the gloom I realized that the room was full of junk. Magazines and mail-order catalogues were stacked against the walls. Empty jam jars and milk bottles were lined up on the mantelpiece. There were boxes and cartons, overflowing

ANDREA BADENOCH

with what looked like old clothes. A narrow passageway was left to each chair and the table. Otherwise, there was nowhere to move. The dog barked in the back yard.

The woman sighed. She was still wrapped in her anorak. Her face hung in grey folds, lipstick escaping into the wrinkles around her mouth. She wasn't wearing her teeth.

I remembered why I'd come. I told her what Penny was offering and gave her the phone number. She didn't seem very interested. I told her it would be easy money. 'She wants both of you,' I explained, 'you have to go as a couple.'

She nodded and placed the card with the number on top of a pile of papers on the hearth, beside the dead electric fire.

I had no reason to put her under pressure. There was nothing more I could do. The stale air was making me feel ill. 'You must know Josh,' I said, trying to sound pleasant, standing up, ready to leave. 'He lives upstairs, immediately above you.'

'I should say so,' she replied. Her voice was dull. 'I'm his auntie.'

I sat down again. My mouth went very dry. I struggled to speak. 'His auntie?' I wondered if this was a figure of speech, meaning 'old neighbour'.

'His mum – Dot – well, she's my sister. Lives up East, in Whitechapel. Terrible legs, she has. Never gets this far.'

'You mean Josh is your nephew?' My voice was incredulous, almost squeaky. I realized I was staring, open-mouthed. I coughed into my hand.

The woman leant towards me and picked up a small, flat tin from the floor by her feet. 'My dad, that's Josh's grandad – he's dead and gone now, God bless 'im – well,

320

he owned these two flats. Upstairs and downstairs. He never sold 'em.' She sounded proud. 'He left this one to me and the one upstairs to Josh's mum. She didn't want to move over here, like we did, so she let Josh have it.' She opened the tin and pinched something between her finger and thumb, pushing it up each nostril. She breathed in and sneezed. 'Filthy habit,' she apologized. She sneezed again. 'High and mighty now, ain't he? Not that we aren't all proud.' She gestured towards the blank TV screen. 'Me? I can't watch him. Not without electric.'

It crossed my mind that Josh could easily have paid her bill. I wondered why he hadn't.

'Mind you. I never see Mr High and Mighty. I never see Dot.' She pointed upwards. 'But that girl upstairs. The one that was killed. She came to see me. She visited all of us.'

'All of you?'

'Me and my old man, here. My sister Dot. Frank, her husband. Josh's brother, Gerard.'

'Why?'

'Search me.'

'Where did you say they live?'

'Off Commercial Road. That's where we're from. All of us.'

There was a harsh shout from the bedroom. The woman picked up an empty jam jar and moved towards the hallway. The dog barked again and flung itself against the back door. 'See yourself out,' she said.

Back in the courtyard, I sat on the bottom flight of the steps leading up to Josh's flat. I opened the briefcase. A pair of hopeful pigeons circled my feet. I went to the back of the file and carefully smoothed out the piece of paper I'd taken from Camilla's bedroom in Berkshire. It was her list, that had proved useful in the past. My memory was correct. The second address scribbled there, under Peter's cleaning agency, corresponded to the area described by Josh's Aunt, in the East End. There was also a name. It was Gerard.

I walked out of the courtyard and stood at the Green for a while, waiting to hail a cab. A row of drunks sat on a bench, handing a bottle to and fro. They were silent and depressed, huddled in their thin jackets. Litter blew down the pavement, in small eddies. A plastic carrier bag was whisked aloft, and hovered like a white bird on a current of air above the road. One of the drunks gestured to it and then turned to me. 'That's fucking amazing,' he offered.

I told the cab driver to take me to Commercial Road. I sat in the back listening to him give his opinions on European monetary union. I paid him off, and on foot turned down a side street. The wind had become persistent and cold, with a smatter of rain. Bengali women, carrying shopping bags, trudged along, their brightly coloured clothes battened down by heavy overcoats. I crossed a wide bomb-site, strewn with refuse. Children played amongst the bulging bin liners, the abandoned mattresses, the burnt-out cars.

I shifted the strap of the briefcase from one shoulder to another. I coughed. In my mind, I was rehearsing alternative excuses I could offer Josh's family, for my visit. I decided to pretend to be a journalist, writing up his life story.

The air smelled of smouldering rubber. A poster on

a hoarding advertised Caribbean rum. 'Welcome to Paradise,' it proclaimed.

Meadowgate Mansions were a series of ancient tenements. Most of them were boarded up, and some blocks seemed on the verge of demolition, with gaping holes in their roofs. Some flats had been set alight and sooty stains covered their façades. Other rows were inhabited and had scraps of curtain in their windows, or they were squatted, with defiant posters plastered on their doors.

I stopped to get my bearings. I consulted my *A–Z*. A gloomy looking Asian man sat on a step. I asked him the way and he pointed up the street. A young woman peeked out at me, briefly, from behind a blind, then withdrew. A pack of dogs raced past, turned a corner, then entered an alley. I climbed the hill. Two cars were parked, without wheels and propped up on bricks; a white teenager, his head shaved to baldness, leaned against one, drinking from a can of Lilt.

I found the close I wanted. I climbed a staircase which reeked of cats. I was about to knock on the door of Josh's family home when it gave under my touch. The locks were broken. 'Hello!' I called out. There was the blare of a TV. I stepped into the hall. A chest freezer partially blocked the way. It was empty and unused. 'Hello!' I called again.

I went into the living room. A man sat on an unmade bed, holding a piece of toast, his eyes fixed on the television screen. He had a strange pudding-basin haircut.

'Hi,' I said, 'the door was open, so . . !'

He turned to me and smiled. He had squinting narrow eyes and a dribble of saliva escaped from the corner of his mouth. His face and body were wide.

'Are you Gerard? Are you Josh's brother?'

He nodded in a deliberate, babyish way. 'Gerard.' He gestured with his thumb towards his chest. He turned back to the TV.

I stood for a moment, watching a chat-show host encourage members of an audience to talk about sex. I looked around. The room was empty apart from the TV, which was coin operated, and the dishevelled bed. The floorboards were bare. There were no curtains. There were marks on the walls where furniture had recently stood. I had seen this before. The room had been stripped by bailiffs. I touched a radiator. It was cold. I sat down on the bed next to Gerard. We both watched a woman in a leotard demonstrate exercises. Gerard shuffled his feet and raised his arms up and down slightly, in time to the music, Noisily, he finished his toast.

'Where are your mum and dad?'

'In the pub.'

'Shall I make you a cup of tea?'

He nodded again.

In the kitchen there was a cooker and a sink. Screw holes in the walls showed where the units had been removed. I held the cups under the cold tap, then decided to wash them in hot water from the kettle.

'I'm a friend of your brother,' I said, handing him the drink I'd made. 'My name's Imogen.'

He blew into his cup. He spoke slowly. 'Have you come from the day centre?'

'No,' I said, 'I'm a friend of Josh.'

He turned to me quizzically and stared for a moment. Then he fumbled in his trouser pocket. He pulled out a folded photograph, holding it away from me, as if I might take it from him. He opened it up. It was a creased portrait of Camilla. 'Friend of Josh,' he said. He smiled at the publicity photo then carefully replaced it.

'Did she give you that?'

He moved away from me, defensively. 'Mine,' he said.

'Don't worry. You can keep it. Did she come to see you? Did she give you that?'

'Yes.' He focused on the television again. 'Mine,' he repeated.

Back outside, the chances of finding a cab seemed slim. I walked to Aldgate East, the briefcase slung over my shoulder, thinking about Josh. His reinvention of himself was the greatest role he'd ever play. To the world, he was upper class, slightly bohemian. He was privileged, travelled, educated, sophisticated. His conversation was peppered with references to wealthy relatives, public school, the family Bentley. He'd set out to create an image of the spoilt boy made good, the rich kid with street cred and talent. Playing this part, he was totally convincing. His actual feckless family was beyond anyone's imagination.

I wondered why Camilla had visited them. I remembered Josh's accusations of blackmail. I felt agitated and upset. I was nervous in the Tube station. A peculiar man with long, tangled hair walked up and down, coming much too close to me. For a crazy moment, I imagined him pushing me under a train. I moved away from the track and stood with my back against the wall. He veered even closer and I could smell sourness and alcohol. I got into the busiest carriage and sat next to an old lady.

The train stopped, without explanation, just past Liverpool Street. I took out the file and made some notes.

On the page headed JOSH I wrote about Camilla visiting the Electricity Couple and the flat in Whitechapel. Then I chewed the top of my pen and printed carefully: *Did Camilla Threaten to Expose Josh? Porno Pictures? Background in East End?* It occurred to me that if this was true it could have driven him to extremes, maybe even to murder.

Back at my flat, there was an envelope, stuck with Post-it notes to my front door. Inside was a letter from Al. She wanted me to get in touch immediately. I ignored this and also wiped my answering machine of several messages without bothering to listen to them. I wasn't interested in any crisis that might have erupted at work. Solving Camilla's case was my only priority.

I rang Euston and booked a seat on a train to Manchester. I phoned Pip to get details of Josh's whereabouts, but discovered that he'd left his bedsit. The forwarding address was Josh's flat. I smiled to myself. He'd finally decided to move in.

I tried the Camberwell number three times but Pip was out. All I heard was Josh's camp public school voice leaving precise, pedantic instructions about contacting his agent.

Later my phone rang and rang. I didn't want to speak to Al, or Sean. I didn't want to hear their messages. In the end, I unplugged it. 'Just bugger off,' I said and put it at the bottom of my dirty laundry basket.

The next morning, I phoned Pip again from the Manchester train. He answered, this time, but the line was terrible. I was abrupt. 'It's Imogen. Give me his address.'

There was a long pause with the echo of a hundred ghostly electronic voices, pingponging from north to south.

'Imogen?'

'I need his address, OK?'

He hesitated. 'Imogen, did you get my message? I'm really worried about the other day. I was pissed.'

'Just give me his address.'

Frightened, he blurted out the details.

I jotted them down. 'Thanks,' I muttered, about to hang up.

'I was terribly indiscreet. I should never have told you all that stuff about Josh and Peter. You must promise not to tell Josh . . .'

A loudspeaker, announcing the opening of the buffet, drowned out his words. I replaced the phone.

I was thinking very clearly. Pretending to be from *Attitude*, I phoned Josh's agent, Piers de Courtney. I spoke to an assistant and got details of the Manchester schedule.

In the toilet I was surprised by how untidy I looked. I'd overslept and left home in a rush. I wetted my hair, combing it back behind my ears. It needed cutting. Not for the first time, I decided that short hair was a lot of work. I found some lipstick at the bottom of Camilla's briefcase and darkened my mouth.

I went to the buffet and bought a few cans of lager. A small child, further down the carriage, stared at me with a fixed gaze. I pulled a face and she burst into tears.

Chapter Thirty-Five

I sat down and opened a can. As each swift mile took me closer to Josh, my thoughts began racing. Camilla's visits to his family were puzzling. It was difficult to imagine how they might have been well intentioned. She was never interfering or altruistic. Her interest in other people was limited and almost entirely self-centred. She wouldn't have been curious. The possibility of blackmail kept returning to my mind.

I felt uneasy. It was hard to understand why she would treat a friend in this way. I thought about her discovery of Josh's old liaison with Peter, but it didn't seem worthy of this kind of revenge. As usual, all I was left with was her need for money.

Her new agent, Mrs Zuckerman, had told me she could still get Camilla assignments. I understood that these weren't the kind of high-profile work she might have wanted, but they had to be better than sex with total strangers in a borrowed room. I decided there could be only two reasons why Camilla resorted to whoring. She either believed, for some reason, that her job prospects were entirely drying up, or she wanted to earn a lot more money than catalogue work could bring in.

I drank my beer. Staring out of the window at fields and trees I thought about how my best friend was a woman I'd hardly known. I'd been captivated by her glamour and her confidence but I'd never understood anything about her family, her love affairs, her career and, most significantly of all, her finances. A sense of desolation swept over me. I wanted to cry. Trying to make sense of it all, I searched my memory for an occasion when Camilla had disappointed me.

I lay back in my seat and closed my eyes. I remembered a time when we were students. Camilla was lounging on my bed, reading Shakespeare. It was late and I was trying to finish an essay. We were drinking port, smuggled from her stepmother's sideboard on a recent visit home. She'd started experimenting with small black cigars and the room was full of pungent smoke.

There was a timid tap on the door.

'If that's bloody Barbara,' muttered Camilla, 'I don't want to know.'

Barbara came in, clutching a bottle of whisky. I tried to smile. I rummaged in a drawer for another paper cup. I noticed she'd been crying. She looked a little unsteady.

'What's the matter?' I asked. I liked Barbara. She was kind and a little dim and totally out of her depth. Camilla called her The Gnat.

Barbara sat down on the floor. Her beaky nose was red and shiny. She blew it, noisily. Her skin was inflamed and pitted with acne. She smoothed her old-fashioned tweed skirt over her calves. 'I'm so ugly,' she said, 'nobody will ever want to kiss me.'

Camilla snorted and lit another cigar.

'Don't be silly,' I murmured, pouring us all some whisky. I felt uncomfortable. I was somehow unable to offer sympathy, with Camilla in the room.

'No one's ever wanted to kiss me,' she confided.

I thought about the sweaty embraces of engineering students in the union bar, their probing tongues. 'Go to the union bar,' I said, but then I added more loudly, 'You're not missing much.'

'I'm ugly,' she repeated.

I realized she was very drunk. I glanced at the bottle. It was almost empty.

Camilla raised her book in front of her face and pretended to stifle a loud yawn. There was a silence. Embarrassed, I looked at the floor. Barbara leant forwards, her head between her knees. I prayed she wasn't going to be sick. 'Shut up,' I mouthed at Camilla. 'She's mortal.'

Camilla laughed silently, the book in front of her face. Her shoulders shook. Barbara raised her head and saw Camilla's mirth. Her face was wet with tears. 'I hate you,' she said.

Camilla threw the book aside and grinned. She stood up and peeled off her sweater. Her jeans and vest were skin tight. She pulled an elastic band off her ponytail and shook her head. Her hair was glossy and very long. She plucked my Chinese jacket from the back of my chair and put it on. 'I'm off next door,' she said. She was referring to the men's hall. 'I fancy a fuck!' She tossed the bottle of port towards me and I caught it. 'You can mop up here.' The door banged behind her.

Barbara carried on crying. I was angry with Camilla. I might have been able to save the situation without her contribution. Tentatively, I leaned towards Barbara and tried to put my arm around her shoulders. She shook me off, got up and stumbled from the room.

*

The train sped through a green valley which was smeared on one slope with snow. I stared absently at an abandoned farmhouse. I opened Camilla's file and turned to Josh's page. I read through my notes and drank more beer. After a while I felt dozy. I slept for a while. When I got off the train in Manchester, it was raining. I walked into the centre of town. It was too early to try to find Josh – I'd been told he was filming all day. I wandered around and passed the plate-glass window of an expensive hairdresser. I went in and asked for a haircut.

It took me a few minutes to get used to their accent. The music was loud and insistent. I was glad of my leather jacket, my nose stud, the aggressive lipstick. 'I'm from London,' I thought to myself.

I emerged an hour later with sharper hair. I went into a chemist and bought foundation and a grey eyeliner. I chose a new shirt from a men's boutique. In a ladies room, I completed my makeover. My face once more became interesting and stark. I took off my T-shirt and put it in the bin. The new one was crisp and had a button-down collar. It looked good.

I remembered the last time I'd smartened up my act. It had been in Newcastle. I wondered why I did this, as soon as I was out of London. Lingering in front of the mirror, I remembered I was only a month from my thirty-sixth birthday. Forty was no longer that far away. Camilla was the same age. She must have been thinking about this, all of the time.

I turned this way and that. I'd lost some weight and there were lines on my forehead and eyelids that I'd never noticed before. Despite this, I looked better than I'd done in a while. 'You've got ten years,' I told my reflection. 'After that, it's polyester cardigans and big roomy slacks.'

I found a taxi. The driver nodded when I mentioned the area where Josh had lodgings. The inside of the cab was full of red-and-white pennants. We chatted about the Premier League. When we arrived he turned off the meter and pursued the conversation. He was friendly in a Northern way. His ability to recall score lines and technical manoeuvres from the recent past was even better than my own. We were impressed by each other. I paid him but he refused a tip. 'It's your lot or ours,' he asserted. 'Forget Arsenal. Forget sodding Liverpool. They're history.'

I walked along for a minute, feeling jaunty. Then I remembered why I'd come. I stopped and glanced around. Josh had located himself in an area where he could remain in role. It was just like Coronation Street, with rows of brick terraces, their front doors straight onto the pavements and back alleys between, with strings of soaking washing. A gang of tiny boys kicked a ruined tennis ball.

His landlady turned out to be nothing like the Florrie Capp caricature supplied by Pip. She had carefully tousled jet-black hair and pearly violet eyeshadow. I followed her inside. Her breasts were small under a red sequinned sweater. She wore leggings and fluffy mules with heels. Her voice was warm. She told me to wait and disappeared to make tea.

The lounge was full of chairs. There was a huge TV screen and vases of plastic flowers. The air was heavy with aerosol lavender. This was the residents' area. I could hear the family squabbling in the back kitchen. I stood at the window watching the rain. The narrow strip of visible sky was dark grey. The houses opposite looked blank and the street was now deserted. The landlady brought tea and disappeared. I drank it down and it was strong and refreshing. From the back of the house I could smell bacon frying. A radio started playing pop music. After a while the door opened and a middle-aged man came in. He was wearing a jacket and tie and carried a suitcase. He looked up at me, startled.

'I'm a visitor,' I reassured him.

He went out and then returned without his case, wearing an overwashed sweater instead of his jacket. He grinned nervously and turned on the television. He sat down on the settee. I saw a shiny bald patch on the top of his head. 'Rotten day,' he said. He had a West Country accent.

'Are you staying here?' I asked, pointlessly.

He nodded. 'I'm a travelling salesman.' He kept his eyes on the screen.

'What d'you sell?'

'Condom dispensers.' He coughed, apologetically.

There was a silence apart from the tail end of *Home and Away*. I remembered Pip's comments on the area. I gestured outside. It was dark. 'Is this the street where Myra Hindley lived?'

'Who?'

'Myra Hindley.'

'I'm only here three nights a month. I've never met the locals.'

I gave up. I sat on the arm of a chair and flicked through *Reader's Digest*. The salesman watched *Granada Tonight*.

The front door banged and Josh came in. He hid his surprise behind a smile. 'Hello, luv,' he said. 'You're a long way from home.'

As I expected, he was still playing his soap-opera part. He was wearing a green waxed jacket, old trousers, a cheap open-necked shirt without a tie. He talked with a local twang. His hair was longer and untidy and his jewellery had gone. Instead of being a camp London actor he was like any Joe Soap you might meet at the bus stop.

'Can we go to your room?' I asked, following him into the hall.

'If you can't be good, be careful,' called out the man from the settee.

We went upstairs in silence. Josh's room was almost filled by a double bed covered in a cerise satin spread. The wallpaper was wreathed in roses and there was a curious smell, like mothballs. I sat on a dressing-table stool next to a framed photo of Pip and a bottle of Christian Dior Fahrenheit. He perched on the bed, by the door. The room was cold. I was still holding the dregs of my tea and tried to warm my hands. Josh leaned forwards and turned on a radiator.

'I went to see your brother,' I said.

For a second, I saw his face twitch, as he registered shock. In the instant it took him to look away, then back, his expression went blank. He spoke in his normal, actorish voice. He became his London self. 'You're a nosy bitch. Has anyone ever told you that?' He straightened his body and raised his chin in the supercilious way he'd perfected.

'He's living in a flat with no furniture.' I put my mug

down, with a clunk. My palms had become sweaty. I breathed evenly. I repeated twice, in my head, 'I'm not afraid of you, you bastard.' I met his gaze.

'This game you're playing. What makes you think you'll win?' His eyes were hard, like wet pebbles.

'Your brother's front door won't close. It's broken. There's no food.'

A muscle in his eyelid flickered. He pursed his lips.

I took a deep breath. 'Have you been ringing me at work? Leaving nasty messages?'

There was a long silence. I decided not to break it. Footsteps clattered on the vinyl-covered landing. Voices went downstairs and the front door slammed. Josh's eyes narrowed. His mouth became a cruel line. He started speaking in the Scottish accent that had frightened me on the office answering machine. 'Leave it alone, Imogen. I've told ye once, I've told ye twice . . .'

'Stop!' I shivered, then tried to hold my body still. My heart was pounding. I was suddenly back in London, in an empty room, with a murderer on the prowl. I looked at Josh's long, intertwined fingers and imagined them around my neck. He was smiling in an odd way. I was scared. I measured the distance between myself and the door. He stretched a leg out, blocking the way. I remembered there were plenty of other people in the house. Suddenly I felt a wave of anger towards him and this replaced the fear. I struggled to keep my voice level. 'It had to be you, didn't it? You sod. It had to be you, pretending to be someone else.' My words dropped to a menacing whisper. 'Why?'

'Poking around, making a nuisance of yourself, asking questions.'

I realized that my enquiries had been driving him

crazy. All the time, he'd been afraid I'd find out his secrets. Our eyes met. I held his gaze, defiantly.

His accent became cockney, rough. He was suddenly an East End boy. 'You're a pain in the arse.' He regarded me with loathing. He sniggered and then said, 'Don't mess with me, cunt.'

I remembered these words written on my bedroom mirror, when I was burgled. I remembered the mess, my fear, the workmen fitting grilles. 'You broke into my flat. You sent me that parcel!' I was so angry, I clenched my fists. I wanted to hit him.

He nodded. The strange smile returned to his face. 'To stop you doing it. To scare you into stopping.' He still spoke in the cockney accent of his childhood. 'I hoped you'd think it was the Whistler.' He laughed. 'If you thought he was after you, then maybe you'd drop everything. All of it. The whole damn thing.'

I sat staring at him. I could hardly believe it. He'd been so paranoid about me uncovering his deceptions and his past he'd gone as far as violating my home. I wondered what else he was hiding. He was at that moment my only suspect. I hated him. My voice was icy. 'I've been investigating Camilla, not you. I'm not interested in you.'

His eyes were expressionless.

'You'd have done anything to scare me.' I thought about the food spilled on my kitchen floor, my smashed autograph in its frame, the stinking box that came through the post. I was furious. 'You're fucking mad. You're a madman.'

In a quick movement his hands unlocked. I flinched, but he held open his palms in a gesture of honesty. 'It's me who's afraid of you. Of what you might do to me.'

I sat up straight, my shoulders broad. I raised a fist. 'Yeah? Good. You bastard. You just carry on being afraid. You fucking coward.' Just then, I knew if it came to a struggle I was stronger. I felt very powerful. My eyes travelled over him. I saw him in a new way. His lean, patrician face became narrow and shifty. His long limbs that had been so elegant now revealed an undernourished childhood. His snobbish, superior air was nothing more than a pathetic sham. He was working class. He was the same as me. No. He was worse than me.

I leaned towards him. My voice was harsh, Northern. 'You're a Meadowgate wide boy. You're East End rubbish. You don't fool anyone.'

He winced as if I'd struck him. He moved backwards on the bed, drawing away the leg that had blocked my path to the door.

I raised a finger and pointed at his face. 'It always shows. In the end. You're shit.' I forced a laugh. 'Did you think you could fool me? It takes one to know one.'

He was very white. His lower lip trembled. He slid open the drawer of the bedside cabinet, put his hand inside and produced a gun. It was small and grey. He laid it on the bedspread next to his thigh.

I swallowed hard. 'What're you going to do? Shoot me?'

I set my face into an emotionless mask. I stared at the gun, then at his pretend clothes, and decided it was fake, like the rest of him. I could hear his watch ticking. He fingered the bottom of his anorak. He spoke again in his cockney accent. 'What did you say to my mum and dad?'

I shrugged.

'What do you want? Money?'

'I keep telling people. I've told you. I want to know who killed Camilla.' Acid rose in my chest. I forced it down. 'I've got to know.'

'But that's not all you want, is it? There's more, isn't there, Imogen?'

The radiator gurgled and expanded. The air was slightly warmer. I tried to sound less aggressive, more resigned. 'No, there's not more. You don't interest me. I don't give a bugger about you, or your stupid career. Why should I care about your pathetic family? Your boring bloody sex life? What makes you think you're so interesting? I'm not out to expose you. I want to know who killed Camilla. That's the only reason I'm here.' I paused. 'It was you, wasn't it?'

He turned. 'Me?' His mouth opened then closed. He was astonished. 'Kill her? Me?' His tone was indignant, shocked. 'Of course I didn't.'

I hesitated. 'No?' There was something in his voice which made me believe him.

His eyes met mine. 'No,' he said firmly. As if dismissing the idea, he picked up the gun and put it back. There was a tap on the door. He closed the drawer hurriedly. His landlady stepped in with a tray. She plonked it on the bedside cabinet. There was more tea, with china cups and sandwiches. She smiled at me and felt the radiator. 'It'll warm up,' she said, 'in a few ticks.' She closed the door gently behind her.

I stood up, walked over and sat on the floor, next to Josh, with my back to the radiator. I felt its heat through my jacket. I hugged my knees. 'OK,' I said.

He straightened up, poured the tea and put the plate of sandwiches on the floor. I ate one. 'I've come about Camilla,' I repeated. I sounded mild.

'I didn't kill her. I had no idea you thought I . . .'

'What was I supposed to think? You've tried to scare me off . . .'

There was a silence.

'I didn't kill her. I didn't. Can we get that straight?'

I believed him. I shrugged. 'OK. Go on.'

'She made my life hell. Sure. But Christ, Imogen. I'm not a murderer.'

I sipped my tea, my eyes still on his face.

He sniffed. 'She said my brother was a cretin.'

'Was she blackmailing you?'

'She called my mum a slag.'

I waited. I ate another sandwich.

He took a deep breath. 'Yes, she was blackmailing me. First of all, about my sexuality.'

'But everyone knows . . .'

He interrupted. 'I'm not exactly a closet gay, but I'm not "out". It's not talked about. I wouldn't have got this part' – he gestured towards his clothes – 'this part I'm in now, if it was common currency.' He paused. 'It's easy to forget that outside the circles we move in . . .' He smiled. 'I mean outside the circles we've invaded . . . queerness is still an issue. But believe me, Imogen, it's an issue. In the wider world. She threatened to go to the papers. They would have picked it up, printed it, screwed me. I'd be nowhere.'

'She wanted money?'

'Money and revenge. First of all. Then more money. She was pissed off about Peter, to begin with. About not knowing.'

I nodded.

'Then she found the magazine. In my room at the flat. She upped the ante. It got worse. She went to the floor below to complain about the dog crapping on the stairs. She met my aunt. Won her confidence.'

'So she had even more ammunition . . .' My voice was neutral. I wanted to keep him talking.

'She went to Whitechapel. After that, she asked for ten thousand. I was trying to raise it. Mortgage the flat. Then when I was in the running for this latest part, she upped it to fifteen.'

I drank some tea. I said in a measured way, 'Sounds like you've got a motive.' I studied his face. I no longer believed this.

He held his head in one hand. His eyes had become hurt, baffled. 'I didn't kill her. I'm not that bad . . . OK, I did other things. I know she told you. Don't pretend you haven't been investigating me. I know you're planning to take me to court.'

I hesitated. I'd lost his drift. 'What d'you mean?'

'She told you everything I did to her.'

'No.'

He gave me a hard look. 'She did.'

'Look Josh. I don't know what you're on about. You level with me. I'll level with you. Then I'll go away. I've told you. I'm not interested in you. I'm not planning anything. I want to know who killed her, that's all.'

His voice came out in a rush. 'She said she was going to tell you. She said she was going to ask your advice. She said you know all about the law. Slander, libel, whatever. It's your job, isn't it? You're a lawyer. She said you'd take me to court. She said she had witnesses prepared to reveal my. . . what is it? Defamation. She tied me in knots. I thought you were both gunning for me. You and your libel case. The law of the land. Judges, juries.'

I was confused. 'So what was it you'd done?'

'You mean you don't know?'

I shook my head.

He took a deep breath.

'Tell me.'

'Look. I put the word out that she was unreliable. I know people. Advertising. PR. I spread it around that she was bulimic, unstable. Every time she was in the running for something, I put the knife in, slagged her off. She couldn't get work.' He sighed. 'It's a jungle, modelling. Rumour is ruin. I threatened to do more. I told her, "Sweetheart, two can play at this game." I left notes for her. On her pillow. In the fridge. Messages on the answering machine. I said, "Guess who I rang today, baby . . . Guess who's got the dirt on you now." ' He paused. 'It served her right.'

I remembered Camilla's words that final night. She'd said someone was threatening her, leaving scary messages. I realized now that this allegation was exactly the same as her insistence about being blacklisted as a model. She'd been talking about the same thing. 'But you still paid her?'

'Yeah. A fortune. And I'm not a rich man. It was a war. She'd win one battle. I'd start another. I'd defeat her. She'd plan another offensive. It was crazy.'

'She wasn't getting work as a result.'

'She bled me dry.'

I leaned back, my head against the radiator. I closed my eyes. 'I thought you were the perfect flatmates. I used to imagine you, sitting in that white room, sipping gin and tonics, listening to Mozart. Good friends.'

'I was desperate. We got locked into this thing.' He paused. 'It was like a bad marriage. We both kept upping the stakes. It was madness.'

I sighed.

'I'm sorry. I'm sorry, Imogen. About messing up your flat. All that. She said she'd told you what I was doing to her. She said you'd sort me out. Prosecute me.'

'She did tell me. But I didn't understand.'

'I thought you knew. When you started asking questions, I thought once you had all the details, you'd take me to court. Do me for character assassination, whatever it's called. She said you'd prepare a case. Take it to the DPP. I was crazy. Desperate. I thought there'd be a scandal. It would all come out, in court. It always does. Her blackmail, all the reasons for her blackmail. All my secrets. Plastered all over the papers.'

I let this sink in. I could hardly believe his naivety. I sighed. 'Josh, I'm not a lawyer. I'm an advice worker. I'm not in that league.' I almost laughed. 'Not only that, I didn't even know in time. She said something, that last night, about being threatened, but I didn't understand. I never knew what you did to her. I've only just found out what she did to you.' I paused. 'So who killed her?'

He raised his shoulders in a gesture of ignorance.

'Why did she blackmail you? Why did she start all this?'

He poured himself more tea and spooned sugar into the cup. 'She wanted money. She wanted to get her face done.'

'What?' I put my cup on the floor. I spilled a little tea and rubbed the carpet. I was incredulous. 'What did you say?'

'That's what it was all for. All of it. She wanted to be young again. She wanted to turn back the clock. She'd already had a tummy tuck. She'd had her bum lifted. I paid five thousand for those. She'd disappear for a week, ten days. You thought she was in Berkshire. She was in a clinic in North London.'

The room suddenly tilted, in an odd way. The sandwiches I'd eaten felt like they'd lodged in my chest.

Josh's words flowed over me. 'She was obsessed. Don't underestimate how obsessed. She wanted to get her boobs made firmer. Three thousand. She wanted something done to her thighs. Fifteen hundred. When it came to her face, she wanted the big one. She showed me the brochure. Have you any idea how much *that* costs?'

I shook my head.

'Thousands. Many thousands. God knows who else she hit up for cash. The only people she never pestered were you and Peter.'

'Why?'

'Some sort of pride. But believe me, all she really cared about was not getting old. She went to a beauty salon two, three times a week. The last time she asked me for fifteen thousand, but then . . .'

'She was murdered.'

He held his head in both his hands. 'Yes.'

'Not by you.'

'Not by me.' He opened the drawer of the bedside cabinet again. I stiffened, watching his hands. He rummaged around, then pulled out a pack of cigarettes. Placing one between his lips, he struck a match. The air smelled burnt, then fragrant. 'She wanted to be young again. She was losing her beauty, so she tried to fix it. That's all there is, Imogen. As far as she's concerned, that's the story.' He cut the air with his hands in a gesture of closure. '*Finito.*'

I stood up. 'I'm not a lawyer. I'm not taking you to court, right?'

'Right.'

'Was that gun real?'

'No.'

'I'm going now.'

'OK.' He held out his hand, looking sincere. Without hesitating, he'd taken on another role. He couldn't help it. He was now playing at being my friend.

I shook his hand, formally. 'Who are you anyway?'

'God knows,' he smiled. 'Who the hell are you?'

Chapter Thirty-Six

I took a bus back into Manchester city centre and went into a pub. It was quiz night and the turmoil of my thoughts was interrupted by attempts to recall trivial facts. I searched my mind for the answer to 'who or what produces sepia?'

After three pints, drunk quickly, leaning against the bar, I left for Piccadilly. I'd missed the last train. There wasn't another until five in the morning.

I found the buffet and stayed until it closed. The beer helped me push Camilla from my mind, so I bought a six-pack carry-out. I wasn't sure what to do. I'd booked on to the early train and it didn't seem worth paying for a hotel room for such a short time. I decided to sit it out in the station.

Loitering was obviously not encouraged. The waiting room was locked and the Ladies had no chairs. I wandered up and down, looking through grilles into small shops which were closed. A few people hurried past. Trains came and went. I felt both bored and tired. A policeman approached me. 'What're you doing?'

I'd had enough for one day. 'What d'you think I'm doing.'

'You can't stop here.' He was unfriendly. He thought I was soliciting.

'This is a station,' I said. I produced my ticket and waved it. 'I'm a passenger. I'm entitled to wait for my train.'

He examined my ticket and strode off, muttering into a walkie-talkie.

Eventually I sat on the ground, drinking my beer. I was approached by two men wanting sex, a young boy anxious to score and a woman from a hostel service for the homeless. Somehow, I managed to sleep, the briefcase between my feet, my hands folded defiantly over my chest, protecting my credit cards.

On the train I brought the file up to date again. Things were clearer but I was no nearer a resolution. I tried to remain objective, writing down what Josh had told me. The nagging thought that he might have been lying occasionally surfaced in my brain and I wondered if he really had killed Camilla after all. She had given him a motive. I played and replayed his words and gestures. His rejection of my accusation had been quick and straight. I'd believed him. However, he was such a good actor nothing could be certain.

I flicked through M.M.'s address book. This could contain the name of Camilla's murderer. For a moment, I considered masquerading as a call-girl and trying to meet all of the named men under false pretences. I realized I was losing heart. There were too many for this to be realistic. It would take months and it would be dangerous and unpleasant. Apart from anything else, none of them had any reason to agree to talk to me about Camilla. It was a job for the police. With a sigh, I decided to hand over the address book to the authorities. I wondered if they would release details to the press about

Camilla's flirtation with prostitution. It occurred to me that I no longer cared.

I leaned back in my seat. We passed through the suburbs of a small town. People were beginning their day. I saw a milk float and a postman. I imagined sleeping children and mothers preparing breakfasts. Everything seemed ordinary and safe. I reflected on the giddy chaos of my own recent life and wanted very much to get back to normal.

I tried not to examine my feelings towards Camilla, but, confused and insistent, I was aware of love, disgust, pity and anger all jostling together in my mind.

I arrived back in London and bought a plate of bacon, egg and fried bread in a small café off the Euston Road. I had no appetite. I struggled to eat, drinking two cups of strong, dark tea. I felt tired, hung over and depressed. I took M.M.'s address book from the briefcase and turned it over in my hands. I intended to take it to the police station in Borough Road. First, I decided to go to the Advice Centre and help Al with the session, until it ended at lunchtime. Having a definite plan for the morning made me feel more in control.

I arrived at the office shortly before opening time. I found a notice Sellotaped to the door. It said 'back soon-ishly'.

The wall clock clicked onto ten. I glanced at the calendar. It was Friday the 13th of January. Camilla had been dead for just over a month.

The Electricity Couple came in and pulled up chairs. 'We're still in the dark,' the woman announced.

I flicked through their file. I could hear the waiting room filling up and Al's voice in the corridor.

I felt very weary and lay back in my chair, reading through their notes. I sighed. Their disconnection case seemed hopeless. We'd gone through all the normal channels and there was nothing we could do to help them. 'Did you go on the telly?' I asked. 'Did you get paid?'

'Yeah,' she replied. 'Spent the money, though.' She shrugged. 'None left.'

I rummaged in a drawer for a pen. I entered the details in their file about the TV programme. I wished I'd asked Penny to pay their bill direct. 'There's nothing more we can do.' My voice was flat, discouraging.

The woman seemed to sink lower in her chair. She thought for a minute. 'They still haven't caught him,' she said.

I glanced at her, eyebrows raised.

'The Old Bill. They haven't caught the Whistler. Him that did for your friend.'

'No,' I agreed. I stared at her husband. He appeared to be asleep.

'She was a lovely looking girl, that one. She lived upstairs . . . with my nephew.' She was playing for time, trying to engage my attention. She was reluctant to leave.

I didn't want to talk about Camilla. 'We really have exhausted every possibility . . .'

'She was a good girl, too. Smashing manners. I said only the other day . . .'

Abruptly I stood up. 'I'm afraid you'll have to go. Other people are waiting.'

She met my eye. Her mouth hung open in a stupid way. 'We nearly saw it happen,' she said, suddenly.

'I'm sorry?'

'That murder. We nearly saw it happen.'

I sat down again. I let her words sink in.

'We were in the incident room. The police told us not to talk to the press or nobody.' Her tone was self-important. Realizing she'd regained my attention, she smiled. She picked up a Sainsbury's carrier bag from the floor and pulled out a packet of ready-made sandwiches. She placed one on the knee of her husband then bit into the second one. Mayonnaise ran down her chin. She wiped it with the back of her hand. 'We might have to go to court. If they get him.'

I sat very still. I was conscious of the sound of my own heartbeat. I watched her finish her sandwich.

She burped, gently. 'We saw you all that night at the Elephant and Castle.'

'Who?'

'You.' She paused for effect. 'And your pretty friend what was killed. And that other girl who works here.'

'Al?' My mouth was suddenly very dry. I stood up, poured some cold water from the kettle into a mug and drank it. I sat down again. 'She was there, too?'

She nodded.

'Go on.'

'We were there, that night, me and him, at the bus stop.' She sighed. 'We'd waited ages. It was freezing cold.'

'I was there.' My voice was a whisper. I remembered seeing them, surrounded by bags of shopping.

'That's what I said. You was all there. You went off towards the Tube. The other one, she was on a corner, trying to hail a cab. She was talking on her portable phone. And the dead one, well, you know what she done. She went down the underpass.' She grimaced. 'More fool her.' She nudged her husband. He opened his eyes, stared at the sandwich on his knee, then picked it up, as if uncertain what to do with it.

'She went down the steps. I said to him, "Look out, there's that girl from the flat upstairs." She was carrying that big white bag she always had. "She's got the right idea," I said to him, "that one. She's going for a number sixty-three." We followed her down.' She turned to her husband. 'Didn't we?'

He looked at her then placed the sandwich on the desk. She picked it up and began munching.

I placed my trembling hands underneath my thighs. 'What happened?'

'The police said we was to tell nobody.'

I stared at her. Her eyes were unblinking.

'You went down the steps. Then what?'

She ate in silence for a moment. 'We couldn't see her. She'd turned a corner.'

I struggled to speak. 'What did you do?'

'We lost her. We must've gone the wrong way. I wanted to get out. I didn't like it. We weren't sure. We walked around a bit. For quite a while. It's a maze down there. She must've gone down a different passageway.' The woman rubbed her mouth with the back of her sleeve.

There was a silence. The fax started whirring. I looked from one to the other. They were both as impassive as ever.

'We got out of there,' she continued, almost proudly. 'Back to the bus stop.'

'What then?'

'The bus came. We went home.'

'Did you hear anything? See anything?'

She shook her head.

'When did you tell the police?'

'The next day.'

'Have you discussed this with Al?'

She looked puzzled.

'The other woman who works here.'

She shrugged. 'She never asked us. Nobody's asked us. Anyway, we were told to say nothing. Keep mum.'

'Have you told anyone else about this, apart from the police?'

'Only you.'

I stood up. My knees felt weak. 'I've got to go out,' I muttered. I moved towards the door.

'Hang on,' the woman shouted indignantly. 'What about us? What about our electricity?'

I left them sitting there. The office door banged behind me. Al stood in the entrance of the waiting room. She was holding a sheaf of case files.

'Get rid of this lot,' I said hoarsely. 'Now. Close the bloody Centre. We need to talk.'

I walked down the road, passing the place where Camilla and I had met, that final night. I turned down a side street and went into an unknown pub. It was very gloomy. No daylight penetrated the old coloured windows and the lights were turned off. I blinked. A group of uniformed postal workers stood at the bar. As my eyes adjusted, I saw a rank of games machines around the walls, winking and glinting. Christmas decorations had been roughly torn down and several tattered ends moved in a draught from the stairs. The lino on the floor was worn through into holes and there was a smell of stale beer and smoke from the night before. I stood at the bar, holding its edge, steadying myself. I thought about Al. I knew she would try every pub in the area, anxious to find me.

A woman who'd been emptying ashtrays came over to serve me. She didn't speak. She had bruises on her lower arms. I ordered a pint and noticed two framed photographs behind her. One was the Queen Mother and the other was Margaret Thatcher. They were both about fifteen years out of date. They were draped in a grimy Union Jack.

The postal workers guffawed and swore. I sat down in a booth and picked up my drink but my hand was shaking and I spilled a little. I swallowed a mouthful and it hit my stomach like a cold flame. I drew patterns in the foam on the pitted mahogany of the tabletop. The door opened and closed. A long-haired man with a dog on a string came in to buy cigars. A small child with a red skin rash ran through, then up the pub stairs, shouting, 'Dad, Dad!'

Al appeared and sat down opposite me. 'I'm here,' she said.

I felt relieved. She'd managed to find me. I sighed and rubbed my face. The jukebox started playing a song by a band called Everything But The Girl. I tapped the rhythm with a pound coin on the stained wallpaper below the window frame. I looked at my watch. It was only ten forty-five.

'I'm here,' said Al again.

I swallowed hard. 'They saw you,' I said. 'The Electricity Couple. They saw you that night. At the Elephant and Castle.'

Al made a steeple of her fingers and sniffed.

'You must have been interviewed by the police.'

'Sure.' She shrugged.

'What did you tell them?'

Al rested her head in one hand and stared at me. As usual, the look on her face made her seem about twelve years old. 'I told them I was there, but saw nothing. I said I didn't see where she went. I got a taxi home. They checked it out with the driver.' She bit her lip. 'They weren't very interested.'

'What were you doing? I never saw you there.'

She pursed her lips, disapproving. 'Of course you didn't. You were pissed.' The condemnation in her voice made me suddenly ashamed. 'You were both completely mortal.'

I remembered using this expression myself, with Camilla. It was one of the last things I said to her. I drank some of my beer. I was conscious of Al watching me. Her expression, behind her girlish face, was one of pity. Pity and a kind of knowingness. I felt I'd lost control. For some reason, Al seemed different. She was older and somehow superior. I was conscious of seeing her in a new way. She'd moved to a place beyond me, somewhere I couldn't reach. I felt that she knew and understood far more than me – about that night, about the murder, about every damned thing. I was used to telling her what to do and think, as if she was a child, but now I realized she'd always thought and done exactly as she liked. I had no influence over her. I'd probably never had any influence over her, except in my own mind. I felt powerless. I tried again. 'You never mentioned this to me. That you were there. Something happened, didn't it? You know something. What was it? Tell me what happened.'

There was a long silence and she continued to look at me. I couldn't hold her gaze. Eventually, she spoke, very slowly. 'I was always intending to tell you, Imogen. When you were ready. When we were both ready. I thought it might be easier,' she paused, 'when we'd got . . . you know . . . kind of closer.'

I remembered all her friendly overtures, her persistence, my suspicions that she fancied me. This had always made me feel dominant. I knew now that it was an illusion. She was a law unto herself. I tried to sound insistent. She knew something important. 'Tell me, Al. Tell me now.'

She took a deep breath and leaned back in her seat. Her eyes met mine, then looked away. 'I didn't like her.'

I wasn't expecting this. My face was rigid and I could feel sweat trickling down under my clothes. 'So?'

'I knew her from my modelling days. You know I did a bit of modelling when I was younger?'

I nodded.

'She was always a bitch. A classic bitch.'

I wiped my hands on my knees, steadied them a little, then finished my drink.

'I couldn't stand her, actually.'

'Go on.'

'She owed me money. I lent her all the funds from the Sumatran Tiger Appeal. Seven hundred. She said she'd pay me back double. She cheated me. She was a liar. She never did.'

'She owed everyone money.'

'This wasn't my own money.' For a moment she sounded petulant, but her face was hard. I could see now that behind her girlishness, there was ice.

I wondered why I had ever patronized her. She wasn't a child. I remembered Camilla had done the same. I felt afraid.

She picked up one of her ratty pigtails and examined it. 'Anyway. I was sick of her monopolizing you. Ringing you up. She'd ring up and you'd drop everything. Leave me behind. Go running after her. It used to make me so mad. She wasn't worth it, Imogen. She was a cow. You must know that by now. You're so wonderful. You deserve a better friend. A proper friend.'

I rubbed my shirt under my arms and between my breasts. My body was wet with perspiration. For a second, a vision of Camilla drifted through my consciousness, beckoning me like a seductress in an advert.

'You did it to me again that day. You went chasing after her. You were meant to be going for a drink after work with me.' Her lower lip trembled, childishly, but seeing her now, in this different way, I felt she was doing this for effect. 'You shouldn't have left me like that. On my own. You promised.'

I couldn't remember this. Thinking back, all I could see was Camilla sitting in the pub, lounging elegantly, waiting for me.

'She rang the office, wanting something, as usual. Some favour. You were off like a shot.' Her voice was plaintive. I looked at her eyes but there were no tears. They glittered with resentment. 'I went to the pub. To join you. You didn't even notice. You'd forgotten all about me.'

I thought back to the people in the pub. She was right. I hadn't seen her there. 'Tell me what happened.'

She opened her tobacco tin and rolled a thin cigarette. Despite everything, she was quite calm and self-possessed, even self-righteous. In contrast, I was conscious of my own body shaking, as if I was ill.

'I stayed in the pub.' She shrugged. 'I don't know

why I bothered. I left just before you. Later on, at the Elephant, I tried to get a taxi. You'd gone home on the Tube. I decided to cross through the underpasses, to the south side. I suddenly saw her down there, ahead of me. I wasn't expecting to see her. It wasn't planned or anything. But she must have seen me coming. She was waiting halfway up the steps on the other side. She was drunk. Very drunk. It made her almost . . . sort of . . . friendly.'

'And?'

'She was staggering. She put her arm round me. It seemed a good opportunity so I asked her again for the Tiger money. She just laughed at me. I pushed her away. I told her she was disgusting. Then I said she should leave you alone. That you were too good for her. She thought that was really funny, too.'

She fished inside the pocket of her army greatcoat and pulled out an embroidered silk purse. Inside were two small photographs. One was of me. It was a passport photo, cut from an ID card, I'd once needed at a conference. She must have retrieved it from the waste bin at the office. The other was a school photo of a teenage girl in uniform.

'It happened before,' she said. Her voice was unemotional. 'At school. I wanted to be her friend.' She pushed the photo towards me, tapping it with her finger. 'Someone else was in the way.'

'Yes?'

'Another selfish, attention-seeking bitch like Camilla.' She took the photo from me and stared at it. 'Monopolized her. Left me out. Made fun of me.'

'What did you do?'

'What could I do? I waited for her in an alley behind

the playing field. I hit her a few times. I used a brick.' She smiled. 'Her mother got hysterical and complained and I was thrown out of school.' She examined both the photos again then put them away.

'Al, what are you telling me? What happened that night?'

'I was angry. There was a . . . a kind of a fight. I pushed Camilla a second time. Not hard. Not really hard, or anything. But she fell down the steps. She was drunk. Her head hit the tiles at the bottom with a kind of crack.' Al raised her face and looked at me. Her expression was unreadable. 'It wasn't the same as the other time. It was an accident.'

I said nothing. Behind the bar, there was a clink of glasses in the sink. The postal workers left, noisily, banging the door. There was a lump in my throat. I tried to swallow. 'You didn't go for help?'

'I could hear voices. Those people, you know, that couple, from the Centre. They were wandering around, lost, arguing about the signs. I thought they were coming.'

'If it was an accident you'd have got help. Called for help. Got an ambulance.'

She raised her eyes to the ceiling, then stared at me. 'Yes.'

'But you didn't!'

'No.'

She didn't sound guilty. Her voice was matter-of-fact. 'I thought she was dead. I was shocked and everything, but I just kept thinking, this serves you right, you bitch. You've had this coming for a long time and you can't have Imogen's friendship now. It was like a film. Then I remembered the Whistler. He would have strangled her with her scarf, so I pulled it tight, very tight around

357

ANDREA BADENOCH

her neck, for what seemed like ages. I took my time.
Then I found perfume in her bag and sprayed her with
it. I dragged her away from the steps into a darker place
where the lights don't work. I took her bag. That's what
the Whistler does. It was surprisingly . . . easy. That's
what I remember.' She paused to think. 'It was too easy.
You'd think something like that would be hard, impossible
even, but it wasn't. It was weird, but it wasn't. Not at all.'

'And the police?'

'They never suspected me. They saw what they
wanted to see. Heard what they wanted to hear. They
talked to me, but I was just an ordinary girl on her way
home from the pub. Like you.'

We sat for a while in silence. The jukebox played the
same Annie Lennox song that I remembered from that
fatal night. I couldn't tell what Al was thinking. She
hummed along to the music for a moment then stopped.

'Al.' I hesitated. 'This is . . . a *terrible* thing.' My voice
sounded strange, not at all insistent. It was quiet,
subdued, like somebody else.

'No,' she said. 'No, it's not.' She was decisive, definite.
'It only seems that way at first. You can get used to it.
You can accept it.' She paused. 'Actually, when you think
about it, her death was inevitable. Not only that, it was
completely and absolutely necessary. She was so . . .
worthless.' She gently placed her fingers across the back
of my hand. They felt soft and cool. 'I did it for you,
Imogen,' she said. 'For us.' She considered these words,
then she added as an afterthought, 'For everyone.'

I felt incapable of argument. Weak tears filled my
eyes. Al had done this appalling thing for me. I couldn't

358

be angry. She'd done it for my sake. For my sake. This meant I was to blame. She'd said Camilla was worthless. So it must have been Camilla's fault, too. I couldn't think straight. I tried to imagine myself getting up, walking briskly to Borough Road and reporting Al's crime to the police. I attempted to picture my old self banging on the desk, harassing the officer, insisting on being heard, being both clear and coherent, making a statement. That's what I would have done, only a few weeks, a few days before. This image of myself formed in my mind but then straightaway dissolved. To do all this, I needed to be angry, only I wasn't angry. Not any more. I closed my eyes. I felt unable to move. I had a peculiar sense of my assertive, troublemaking self melting away leaving me with nothing. I felt passive, tired, disillusioned. 'I'm all washed up,' I murmured.

Al stirred, stood, went to the bar, bought me another drink and then gently picked up both my hands. She wrapped them around the glass. She rummaged in her bag and found a chocolate bar. She pushed this towards me. I looked at her fingers, covered in rings. She smelled of jasmine. My tears fell and splashed on the tabletop. I couldn't hide them. 'I'm sorry,' I said, automatically.

'It's OK,' she said. 'Just let go.'

Andrea Badenoch

Driven

Andrea Badenoch's new novel, *Driven*, is now
available in hardback from Macmillan.
Chapter One follows here.

Chapter One

Much later, when it was all over, after she'd been away on holiday and come back again, Jaz told everyone that she'd celebrated her twenty-first birthday at the best hotel in London. She said it with a smile and a shrug, but it was true. Her party was held in a luxury hotel, but not in the glowing dining room or the sumptuous lounge. It took place in a tiny scullery off the side of the kitchen. She crouched on the floor there, almost hidden by an industrial dishwasher and a trolley of stacked plates. Trace and Harm were the guests and they sat alongside and toasted her birthday with champagne, sipped from antique crystal glasses. Jaz joined in with chilled tomato juice, the colour of blood. She never drank alcohol. This was still one of the many rules which she used to run her life.

'These little gobfuls are nice,' said Harm, scooping up exquisite hors d'oeuvres from a polished platter and stuffing them into her mouth.

'I'll find some more,' offered Trace vaguely. 'There's loads of them, somewhere.' Trace was helping out at the hotel, off the record, no questions asked, cash in hand. What this meant was that every weekend and sometimes during the week, she took charge of the dishwasher, the crockery trolleys and sink-loads of precious metal and glassware that required 'hand rinsing'.

She stood up, wearing her regulation overall and hairnet. She went into the kitchen with confidence, smiling, mingling with foreign chefs, their stressed sous-chefs and calm, overtrained waiters in red cummerbunds. They all ignored her. She pushed another trolley of dirty dishes towards the scullery, this time bringing a half empty bowl of salmon mousse, more hors d'oeuvres and a paper carton, containing olives. Jaz and Harm dug into the glass bowl with silver spoons. 'These black things are weird,' said Trace, handing around the olives, 'but you get used to them. Better than the snails.'

Jaz was happy. This, she decided, was one of the best birthday celebrations she'd ever had. She was glad Trace had organized this, pleased she had such good, reliable friends. She pursed her lips thoughtfully, sipped her drink, remembered another good party when she was eleven. Blow had come back to the farm that morning in an open-topped Armstrong Siddeley. The chrome was crazed and pitted and the hide seats were mildewed but he pulled up outside the door hooting the horn and giving a mock gentleman's wave. Jasmine and her sisters were excited. They climbed all over the bonnet. 'I've just bought this from a duchess.' He grinned. 'Go and borrow your ma's finery. We're all going for a drive.'

Jasmine, her mother and her two little sisters searched through the big old bedroom wardrobe for hippy Indian cotton, lace, feathers, velvet and fur. They found leather boots and costume jewellery. They tried on hats. Blow squeezed into an old dinner suit. The family drove to Middlesbrough in his new old car where they turned heads and stopped traffic. They had tea in Burger King and Blow said they should eat as much as they liked, because it wasn't every day that someone special was eleven.

Jaz chewed on an olive and refilled her friends' glasses with champagne. Around the corner from their scullery, the kitchen was now busy. Even the waiters were running and raising their voices, but in their own special, private party corner, it seemed peaceful, wrapped in its cloudy, damp, dishwasher air. Harm burped quietly and announced that she'd had enough to eat. She eased her back away from a hot water pipe, sighed and stood up. 'S'pose I better go outside,' she suggested, 'for a ciggie?'

'Yes,' agreed Trace. 'This is a smoke-free zone.' She laughed. 'You could go and sit in the lounge.' She cleared their dishes from the floor, stacked some expertly in her sink, packed the rest in her dishwasher, closed it and switched it on. The jets roared.

'It's been nice,' said Jaz. 'Thanks.' She stood a little stiffly as Trace bent down and kissed her cheek.

'It's OK,' said Trace, stepping back and wiping her damp brow with the back of her hand. 'It's not every day your mate turns twenty-one.'

'What about that champagne?' asked Jaz.

Trace smiled. 'Come with me.' The three friends walked through the jostling kitchen. Harm ducked the flailing meat cleaver in the raised hand of an assistant's assistant. Instructions were shouted in French. There was sizzling and a flash of flame and Jaz closed her eyes for a second as two live lobsters were dropped into a steaming cauldron. 'Come on,' insisted Trace, catching both her friends by the arm, but not one of the kitchen staff bothered them.

They went down a corridor which led to the back of

the reception desk. Computer monitors winked, white on green. Above, on the marble counter, enormous vases of lilies were mixed with white roses. Only one uniformed receptionist was on duty and she was talking on the telephone. She giggled and swivelled from side to side on her high stool. Beyond her stretched the wide, glittering lobby lit by a dazzle of chandeliers. A group of guests in dinner suits talked and smoked. Two small children ran from the staircase towards the open door of a lift. Outside, a row of taxis idled. 'Wait here,' Trace said.

Harm and Jaz stood in the shadows. Trace slipped unnoticed in front of a computer and tapped for a moment on its keyboard. The receptionist didn't turn round but laughed again down the phone. 'You dirty beast!' she exclaimed.

Jaz turned to Harm. 'I didn't know Trace understood computers,' she murmured. 'She can't even read.'

Harm smiled. 'She understands what she needs to understand,' she replied. 'Never underestimate Trace.'

Their friend returned. 'You better go now,' she said.

'What've you done there?' asked Harm, pointing to the monitor.

'Taken care of the champagne,' Trace whispered. She smoothed her overall over her thin hips. 'I've just put it on Dustin Hoffman's room service account.'

Jaz and Harm stepped out, laughing, into the warm night. Harm lit a cigarette. Her mobile phone rang and she took it out of her bag. She exchanged a few words. Jaz knew it was Wesley, her current pimp. He had a client waiting for her in Belgravia.

Harm sighed. 'Time to earn a crust. I'll be going.' Her

words were slurred and soft. 'See you later, alligator.' She grinned. 'Happy Birthday.' She blew out a stream of smoke. Steadying herself against a lamp-post, she bent down and kissed the top of Jaz's head, then wandered away into the darkness. Jaz listened to her stilettos clicking for a moment above the hum of distant traffic.

She looked up at the BT tower and noticed that behind it, the moon was as full as an eye. The streets were empty, comfortable and strange. She passed several doorways where street people had bedded down under cardboard for the night. A ragged man came into view, then lurched past, pulling a tiny handcart. She switched on her Walkman, adjusted her headphones then set off at a steady jog in the direction of Tottenham Court Road. She imagined that she was one of the few people left on earth. The city is mine, she thought. She was happy.

Jaz lived in south London. For the last six months she'd been staying with Fat Andy, a friendly car thief, sharing his council flat in the badlands near Peckham Rye. She'd reminded him about her birthday, two nights before. They were in bed and she'd caressed his big stomach in a way she knew he liked. He was drinking Tia Maria from a plastic tumbler and reading *What Car?* magazine.

'You thought about my present?' she'd asked.

'What d'you want?'

'You know,' she murmured. She moved her hand downwards, gently. 'You know what I want.' She licked around his mouth, delicately, then her tongue probed inside his lips.

He tossed aside his magazine, put his drink down and

rolled heavily onto his back. 'Don't tell me.' He sighed. 'I know.'

'I know you know.' She climbed on top of his bulk and pulled on the child's nightdress, which was covered in pictures of Minnie Mouse. He'd bought it for her and it was the one he most liked her to wear.

Her body was small and thin, like a young girl's. 'I want to drive your car. You know I do. All around London. I want to drive it like I'm going to drive you.'

Andy rolled her pink nipples in his fingers, groaning slightly. Jaz was almost as flat-chested as a ten-year-old. 'Like what?' he asked, 'you sexy little baby.'

'Like crazy,' she laughed.

He kneaded her bony hips for a moment then raised his head. She knew the routine. She turned, leaned forwards and slipped a nipple between his lips. He sucked it greedily then fell back on the pillow. He always said the same things. 'Little baby, do it to me. Do it nice.'

'OK?' she said, as she guided him between her legs.

He shuddered and sighed. 'Nice. That's nice.'

Her hands pressing on his shoulders, she moved her hips quickly up and down. 'On my birthday?' she insisted. 'The Lotus Cortina? Is that a deal?'

Jaz jumped off a bus and ran lightly towards the estate. Her good mood was evaporating. Fat Andy hadn't come home last night and she'd waited on her own most of the day. She knew he might not keep his promise, but the thought of driving his car for the first time had kept her in a state of excitement for hours. Eventually, she'd admitted to herself that he wasn't coming. Her anticipation turned to anger. She'd tried his mobile for the tenth time but it was still switched off.

When Jaz had left the flat to meet Trace and Harm at the Savoy, she'd been furious with Andy. Now she was no longer emotional, just resigned. It's time to move on, she thought, running across the concrete courtyard. This wasn't the first time she'd decided to leave him, but she felt a stronger resolve than usual. She'd had enough.

I'm sick of living with a man I hardly know, she told herself. I'm sick of this feeling that I don't really understand him. Jaz felt close to only part of him. He wanted her to pretend to be much younger than she really was, and this had become a tiring game. He was secretive and evasive about many things. He'd forgotten her birthday.

Jaz felt a sense of relief at the prospect of change. Maybe he's back, she thought. If he's back, I'll drive the Lotus Cortina, but afterwards, I'll leave him anyway.

She pictured the shiny car, ermine white with its green flash and polished chrome, and the image led her to thoughts about Blow. He too had been big and fat with great old cars, and he too was unreliable. For some reason, she suddenly felt a pang of regret about leaving home and Blow and her sisters. This was followed by another feeling she couldn't name. What do I want? she thought. She decided at that moment to quit London and return to Teesside. Having a plan made it easier to dispel unwanted emotions and regrets. It gave her a sense of purpose. Only for a visit, she thought. I'll just stay for a while. See how they're getting on. Blow would let her drive his car, she was sure. He'd let her do anything she liked. He'd let her drive all his cars.

She remembered how in the months before she'd left,

he'd come into her bed a few times, late at night after her mother was asleep. He made the springs creak. He'd liked exactly the same things that Fat Andy liked. She'd been thirteen years old. She'd sat on top of him in the moonlight and she had worn a little girl's nightdress. He said he loved her. She never told tales. She never told anyone. Because of this, she knew he'd never deny her anything.

Slightly breathless from running, but not tired, Jaz entered the flats through the underground car park. It was twelve thirty. The Lotus Cortina was parked, gleaming and sleek on its low suspension, in Fat Andy's bay. He was back. A few teenagers stood around, sharing a joint, but Jaz knew they wouldn't touch the car. Fat Andy was known and respected on the estate.

Inside the building there was a sour odour and the strip lights were harshly bright. Jaz waited for the lift then decided it wasn't working. She started on the stairs, two at a time. From the doors she could hear televisions and arguments and a baby crying. The sourness was replaced by the smell of frying onions. Her trainers tapped quickly and evenly as she maintained a rhythm. She glanced at her watch. She was three seconds within her normal time. On the twelfth floor she stopped to catch her breath. A Vietnamese man passed her on his way down. He smelled of garlic and carried an extra large bottle of gin. He did not meet her eye. Jaz continued her rapid ascent. On the sixteenth floor, breathless, she began to unlock Fat Andy's door, but it swung open against the pressure of her hand.

It was oddly quiet in the flat. She'd been expecting

television or loud music or the jangle of Fat Andy's banjo. There were no lights on. 'Andy?' she called, pressing the switch in the hall. The small table by the door was overturned and the telephone was on the floor. Jaz picked them up and restacked the directories. 'Andy?'

She turned on the kitchen light and glanced inside. Her heavy breathing steadied but she was tense and wary. She went into the living room. The computer monitor was on and it cast an eerie glow. She walked over, pressed a key and examined the words that came up on the screen. It was an e-mail. 'Vinnys NOT a happy man', she read. 'Vinny says he wants his proparty back STRATE away. He wants his disk. Allrite? Allrite you Peckham git?'

Something bad had happened here. Jaz felt her pulse quicken again, but with the ugly, irregular flutter of uncertainty and fear. She looked around. The room was a mess. The sofa was on its side and a chair was broken in pieces. CDs and computer disks were scattered. Cups, plates and playing cards were strewn across the floor. Glasses were broken. A framed photo of Andy and his previous girlfriend, Princess, was smashed on the hearth. There was a smell of whisky and Jaz saw a bottle had been flung against a wall, streaking it brown. Andy's banjo was lying face down in the debris. She swallowed hard. This wasn't a burglary. Nothing was missing and no one on the estate would ever bother Fat Andy.

She went into the bedroom. It was in complete darkness. Jaz paused, aware that her brow was sweaty but not because she'd been running. Her whole body was suddenly clammy with a sense of dread. Something very bad had happened. This is scary, she thought to herself. This is very scary. Her fingers felt for the string that turned on the light. She couldn't find it. There was a strange smell and a chilly, nameless kind of quiet that was unnatural and new to the room. At last her groping fingers located the cord and the bed was suddenly illuminated. 'Andy?' she whispered.

He lay on his back, his boots dangling, toes pointing inwards. One hand was above his head, the other below his throat. Blood had oozed through his fingers and coagulated. It covered, thickly and glutinously, his neck, chest, waist, arm and half the bed. It had run down and made a large, sticky-looking pool which hadn't entirely sunk into the carpet. Jaz stared. She had seen blood before but never so much. It smelled strongly, salty, like fresh meat. She felt the urge to scream and cry out but held a hand over the bottom half of her face. The cold stillness of the room and the blood that had stopped flowing meant one real, definite thing. Fat Andy was dead. She went over and touched his raised hand. It was ice cold. It didn't feel like human flesh. His face was ghastly white, his eyes half closed, his mouth slightly open as if in surprise. His cheeks were like sunken, grey dough. Jaz couldn't move. She examined with her eyes the gash in his neck which reminded her, at that moment, of a woman's sexual parts. 'Andy?' she said.